Dancing Daisies

Sara Pyszka

ISBN-13: 9780615910604
ISBN: 0615910602
Library of Congress Control Number: 2013920514
Sara Pyszka, Wexford, PA

Dancing Daisies
Sara Pyszka
JUST BE
Book 1

Just Be
Book I

For more information about Sara Pyszka:
www.sarapyszka.com

Dear Reader,

Thank you very much for taking the time to read my debut novel, *Dancing Daisies*. For those of you who know me, I am honored you want to see my work. For those of you who don't know me, I am honored you took a chance on a first-time author. *Dancing Daisies* has been my baby, especially over the last few years, and I am thrilled to be sharing it with the world.

Like Brynn, I have cerebral palsy. I am in a wheelchair and use a communication device to talk with. I do not have the use of my hands. Although all of the events in this book are fictional, most of Brynn's feelings about her disability are my feelings about my disability. Or, at least they were my feelings when I was seventeen . . . .

So many people see the disability first. Some people can't even get past the disability. I wrote this book in hopes of showing people that I am so much more than my disability. I have likes. I have dislikes. I make mistakes. I fall in love. When you are done with this novel, I can only hope you will have a different perception about people with disabilities.

Dancing Daisies would not be where it is today without the help of my unofficial developmental editor, Nicole Frail. She was absolutely amazing to work with, and I truly hope I will be able to work with her on future novels. Many thanks to all of my beta readers for telling me what worked and what didn't. A huge thanks to my friend Brenda who made me realize writing for yourself and writing for other people are two separate things. Another thanks to my dear friend Christian who let me bounce thousands of ideas off him, even though the young adult genre is far from his specialty. Thank you to Lucas Richman, who I collaborated with on the lyrics that are in this book. And, of course, a big thank you to my parents and brother, who always support me in whatever I do.

This is the first novel in what I hope to be a promising series, where you will watch Brynn go through all the twists and turns of becoming an adult. I hope you fall in love with the characters as much as I have, and I hope this is the start of a long lasting relationship with you.

Sincerely,
Sara Pyszka

Chapter One

The second to the last bell of the year sounded throughout all the classrooms, indicating summer vacation was just forty minutes away. After I handed in my literature book filled with short stories, I took my regular spot in the front row. I had nothing else to do except wait for a summer I so desperately wanted to start. Unlike my classmates, who were having friendly last-day-of-school conversations about how they were going to miss each other and making plans to hang out on their first official night of summer, I stared at the clock above the board and counted down the minutes until I wouldn't have to see anyone from school for three whole months.

Thirty-nine . . .

"I bet you can't wait to go to camp this summer," Mrs. B said, turning from her usual seat at my side.

I absentmindedly nodded my response. Mrs. B was in her late forties and was a typical—and literal—soccer mom with three kids. I always liked Mrs. B; she was the best aide I had had so far. She let me ramble about what was going on in my life without judging me as a ridiculous, obsessive, teenage girl like some of my other aides had. However, she was one of the reasons that made me different from my classmates. And, in my opinion, she was one of the reasons most of the kids in my graduating class wouldn't talk to me.

Unfortunately, I had to have Mrs. B with me from the moment the bus dropped me off at school in the morning until the bus came back for me in the afternoon. I needed Mrs. B by my side, though, because I didn't have any control of my hands. I wasn't in a car accident where I was paralyzed or anything; I had a physical disability called cerebral palsy—or CP. Basically, when my mom was in labor with me, my oxygen supply was cut off for a minute or two. Doctors didn't really know why or how it happened, but as a result of a lack of oxygen during that time, the part of my brain that is supposed to be in charge of my motor control was damaged. In other words, I could move my arms and legs a bit, but the only part of my body that I could control 100 percent was my head. I couldn't walk and I used a computer to talk, but my head was totally in my control—as was my mind.

I usually didn't care having Mrs. B with me, since I needed help writing down my answers, handling my books, and eating at lunch, but the school district wouldn't even let me travel through the hallways without her, which scared away the other students. The fact that she was about thirty or so years older than me also pretty much killed my social life. My mom may as well have come to my classes with me and held my hand as we passed through the halls.

Thirty-four minutes . . .

"My daughter went to a soccer camp last year," Mrs. B continued, "and she just absolutely loved it."

I faced Mrs. B and tried to look as interested as I could. She listened to me whine about all my drama over the past school year; I could humor her for a few minutes.

"She made friends that she still talks to a whole year afterward. I know you will, too."

I smiled. I hoped I would. That was really why I wanted to go to camp this year instead of sitting at home all summer with my parents. I desperately needed some new friends, considering my only two friends broke my heart earlier in the school year. These days, the only people I was having conversations with were all over the age of forty. I figured camp would be a better place to make friends my age, especially since the counselor who would act as my aide was only a couple years older than me.

Thirty-one minutes . . .

"Hey, since we aren't doing anything in here, and you know how much the drivers like to get a head start before the mad end-of-the-day rush, do you want to go out to the bus now?"

I mockingly rolled my eyes.

"Come on, it's the last day, and they're old. It would make their day if you came out to the bus early. And besides, you hate this place anyway, right? Why would you want to stay another minute when you have a school bus that is more than willing to leave early?"

Because it was just not normal to have a bus driver to want you—actually ask you repeatedly throughout the year—to leave your class twenty minutes early just so he could get out of the parking lot before the crowd of kids came, I thought. *Not to mention it was a super cool mini bus . . . . AKA, the short bus . . .*

I could see where the bus driver and his bus aide were coming from, being that I was the only one on the bus who didn't come out early on a regular basis, but I wasn't like everybody else on the bus. It wasn't like I was in a life skills class all day, like the others. I was cognitively able to do everything every other student in the school could, and my last class was English, which just happened to be my favorite subject.

Today was different, though. The writing prompts I looked forward to weren't happening. I looked around me at the chattering students, the empty desks, and my teacher, who was reading a book quietly. Realizing there was no point in staying, I agreed to leave school thirty minutes before I was supposed to. Mrs. B was right about one thing: I hated this place. Why shouldn't I jump at the opportunity to leave?

Not bothering to tell my English teacher goodbye, Mrs. B and I slipped out the door. Just a few feet down the hall, another teacher's aide stopped Mrs. B to wish her luck with her daughter's soccer team. I decided to leave the adults to talk to each other and I just kept going. I figured with only having twenty-eight minutes left of the year, nobody was going to stop me for not having my aide with me. On a normal day, however, I would surely receive some sort of lecture about driving away from Mrs. B. And I'm sure she'd hear about it, too. The school district absolutely did not want me to be alone—ever. It was like they thought I was going to have a heart attack and drop dead at any given moment, but . . . I only had one more year of high school left. Thank God!

A few kids seemed to have the same idea of leaving class early and were already in the hall cleaning out their lockers. I made my way to the front of the building and was forced to wait for Mrs. B to finish her conversation. Staring out the two double doors at the sun pouring down on the parking lot and not being able to go bask in the early summer afternoon was absolutely tortuous. Even though my high school was considered "wheelchair accessible" with its one elevator, it didn't have automatic doors. Luckily (or unfortunately, depending on your viewpoint), all the junior classes were downstairs, so I didn't have to hassle with the elevator, which frequently got stuck between the first and second floors. But the doors? I should have probably sued for wrongful imprisonment.

The sound of giggling made me turn my head. Three girls were heading outside, their identical blonde ponytails swinging as they walked down the hall in some of the shortest shorts I'd ever seen. (Seriously, I didn't know how they managed to miss getting sent to the principal's office that morning.) Now, being that about 90 percent of people judged me within ten seconds of seeing me, I strove for not meeting stereotypes. I always received outstanding grades on tests (so people wouldn't think I was intellectually disabled) and I absolutely refused to wear sweatpants, like many disabled people do. These girls, however, reinforced every stereotype that existed about their kind—cheerleaders. They were skinny as toothpicks, cliquey, airheaded, and they acted like guys who didn't play some type of varsity sport were from Mars. It actually made me kind of sad that they so obviously lived up to the stereotypes that ultimately defined them.

Amy, the girl in front of the group, turned around and opened the door using her back. She caught my eye for a split second and I quickly hit the on/off switch to my wheelchair, which was on the armrest of my chair. I was sure she saw me coming toward her. She sat right next to me all year in World History, and although she never said a word to me, I figured, or at least I hoped, she would hold the door for me. Just as I neared the door, and just as quickly as Amy glanced my way, she was outside and the door was shut in my face. The three cheerleaders were officially on summer vacation. I reminded myself I would be, too. Any minute now . . .

Most people would probably feel bad for me or any person in a wheelchair in a situation like this; they probably think that all disabled people wish they could get up out of their wheelchairs, skip out the door, and live happily ever after. This wasn't the case for me at all, though. The fact that I wasn't able to open the door myself honestly didn't even cross my mind right then. The fact that Amy *saw* me driving to the door and *chose* not to hold it for me drove me absolutely insane. Why couldn't she have waited ten seconds and held the door? Would it have destroyed her reputation to help me get outside, or did she think because I didn't have Mrs. B with me, she would be letting me escape school grounds or something?

Another thing people usually assumed was that kids in wheelchairs were stared at, laughed at, made fun of, and whatever else the cool kids in movies do to outcasts. This wasn't the case for me, either. What really happened to someone who "didn't fit in," or at least someone like me anyway, was incidents like what just happened with Amy and the door. People acted like I was invisible. Girls I had known since first grade wouldn't look me in the eye. Guys who heard I thought they were cute would make sure they stayed fifty feet away from me. Even teachers would ask Mrs. B for my homework instead of asking me. On one hand, some people simply didn't realize that I *could* hear them, *could* understand them, and actually *was* capable of responding to them using a computer attached to my chair called a TechnoTalk. On the other hand, some people did know that I could talk with them, but there appeared to be some unspoken theory that I would absolutely bite their heads off if they came in contact with me.

As I slowly drove away from the door, I heard my name, which reminded me that not everyone shared these assumptions and feelings. Some people actually weren't afraid to talk to me. The familiar voice I heard did not comfort me, though; instead, it made my stomach clench. I closed my eyes as I spun around. Why couldn't she have walked out of the building without saying anything to me? I wouldn't have been pissed this time for not being noticed.

I opened my eyes and tried to make the situation less awkward than it was by putting on a half-smile, only to have my body flinch. Not only was Meg walking toward me, wearing an outfit she probably spent a week picking out for the last day of school, but Dave was following close behind her, decked out in his typical button-up and cargo shorts. Six weeks ago, this scene made me the happiest girl in the world. They had been the only ones at school who treated me like a normal seventeen-year-old. We went to the movies. We went to the mall. I talked to Meg about how I was madly in love with Dave. I talked to Dave, secretly wishing he would just lean over and kiss me. But now I just wished I could cut myself out of the picture and forget they even existed.

"Do you want me to let you outside?" Meg asked in the tone I knew so well.

Before I could answer, Meg was holding the door and motioning to Dave to get the other one. She knew I wanted to go outside—she probably saw what Amy did—and I knew she liked the fact that she could "rescue" me. I could just hear it in her voice when she asked me, and I could see it in her smile when she opened the door. Now, before the whole . . . event . . . a few weeks ago, in my mind, we always had fun together. She always told me everything, I always told her everything, and I thought we were best friends. I was in no position to compromise friendship. I really was grateful for what we had shared. There was just always *something* about Meg, though, that even my mom picked up on.

When we were alone, Meg would act normal. She would really listen to whatever I had to say about Dave that day, she would ask me for advice with whatever guy she liked that month, and she would help me if I needed something like a door opened as if it wasn't a big deal. When we were around other people, though, it was a completely different story. Looking back on it now, I didn't know why I never ended it before *that* day. When Meg and I were around other people, Meg always had to have one up on me. When I dyed my hair a shade lighter so it would be a honeycomb blonde, Meg full-out bleached hers. When we went out to dinner for my mom's fortieth birthday, I wore a really cute sundress. Meg went and found her outfit at a boutique in the mall, even though she didn't really have the money to be shopping at a place like that. Her need to show-off became even worse around Dave, making me look like an infant she was baby-sitting. Whenever I would be telling him a story about something Meg and I did, she would interrupt me, finish the story herself, and point out how she had to "save the day" again. It was like she wanted him and anybody else around to give her a gold star for being my friend.

At that instant, with Meg and Dave holding the doors for me, I desperately wanted to turn around and go in the opposite direction. That was what I should have done to show Meg I didn't need her, to leave Dave standing there confused, to have them feel like what they were doing for me was so insignificant that I didn't need to thank them or apologize for not taking advantage of it. Instead, something between fear and embarrassment took over me, and I quickly went out of the two doors, my body crashing into the thick blanket of heat.

Passing Dave on my way out, I caught a scent of the cologne he had been wearing since seventh grade. I used to think it was the best smell on the face of this earth. Of all the memories it could have triggered, the scent took my brain back two years. My parents were out to dinner and it was one of the few times Dave and I were at my house without Meg. We agreed to pop in a movie and I decided I was going to take my chances. I told Dave I really needed to get out of my wheelchair because "my back was killing me," but really I just wanted to be in his arms for a second. To my surprise, my little scam worked to my advantage—and then some. Not only did Dave help me get on my bed, but suddenly he was lying beside me and placing his head on my chest. We didn't do anything more than lay there and watch the movie, but being that I was fifteen at the time, I thought I died and went to heaven. I mean, the boy I was in love with was basically cuddling with me. We laid there in perfect silence—until we heard the garage door open.

That day made me sure of one thing: We were meant to be together. He wouldn't have acted the way he did if he didn't like me, too. I was positive someday that dinners, movie dates, and planning around my parents' nights out would be a regular thing for us. I knew someday I would be able to call him my boyfriend. I just wanted him to make the first move. Because I needed so much help from so many people on a regular basis, I normally held my opinions and feelings back. After all, people often went out of their way to help me. It just didn't seem right, to me, to ask more of most people. It was best to just go with the flow, which meant waiting for him to ask me out. Little did I know . . .

Needing to get away from his scent—one that I wouldn't allow to get me high anymore—I quickly drove away from Meg and Dave, who were still holding the doors open for me. It wasn't until I was about a foot away from running into a cement wall that I realized I was going in the opposite direction from everyone else. Coming back to reality, I twirled around, hoping nobody noticed. Nope. Not my kind of day. As I made my way back to the front entrance, my two ex-best friends stood there, staring at me.

"You okay there?" Meg smirked.

I quickly nodded, avoiding looking her in the eye.

"Kay, we're going to go, then. Bye, Brynn."

"Have a good summer, Brynn," Dave sheepishly said as they turned and headed towards the parking lot. I didn't say anything in return; I hadn't wanted to speak to them to begin with, so why bother wishing the two of them a good summer?

Idiot. Why did I always have to be a total idiot and completely embarrass myself in awkward situations? In fact, why did I let that situation happen in the first place? I could have just driven away when Meg asked me if I wanted to go outside; I should have just driven away. I should have showed them. I hadn't told them how much they hurt me, so they probably thought it was okay to still push me around. Well, Dave never really pushed me around, and he didn't really talk to me since *that* day, but Meg was still Show-Off Meg. Why did I give into their little mind games?

What happened between the three of us? What did they do that was so repulsive that I could no longer stand to be in the same room with them? Simply put: They betrayed me.

I first realized something was different when we were at my house a few weeks before the end of the school year, watching a movie. The lights were low, the movie was loud, and my parents were once again out for the night. Dave had tucked the couch pillows tightly around me and then took the seat between Meg and me. Ever since our . . . moment . . . two years earlier, I had been looking forward to every movie night with Dave, secretly hoping that maybe it would happen again. And, maybe, if it did happen again, he would tell me how he felt about me, I would tell him how I felt about him, and then we'd live happily ever after.

However, the opportunity never presented itself, because it was hard to hang out with Dave *without* Meg. Meg and I had spent plenty of time alone, but it'd recently occurred to me that every time I tried to make plans with only Dave, he would some-how end up inviting Meg—or she'd invite herself.

Halfway through the movie, I caught myself absentmindedly staring at Dave—at the light scruff on his cheeks and chin, at the slight curve to his nose, at the black watch he wore around his wrist. I was so caught up in my feelings for him that I almost missed Meg casually sliding her fingers up and down his fore-arm. *What?* My eyes followed her left hand up and down his arm until it finally rested beside his right hand. The confusion I'd been feeling bubbled into anger when I watched their pinkies intertwine.

Their pinkies parted shortly after, and Dave excused him-self to grab us some drinks. Sitting on the couch with Meg, my mind felt hazy. She made a comment about the movie and I just stared at her. It was like my face was paralyzed. She didn't seem to notice, or at least she pretended not to, anyway. I was dying! I knew there was a slight chance that I could be overreacting; after all, Meg knew how I felt about Dave and she had never expressed any interest in him before. And Dave had recently been talking about hanging out with Nina, a girl he'd be working with at the community pool this summer. So, in a way, the dynamic of "Meg and Dave" didn't make sense. So maybe what I had witnessed didn't mean anything?

When Dave returned, he handed Meg a bottle of water and then helped me take a sip from mine. Even though the room was dark, only illuminated by the light from the TV, I was able to look him straight in the eyes. *Do you like me? Or do you secretly have a thing for my best friend?* He smiled at me when I finished my drink and then took his seat at my side. The next chance I got, I'd ask him how he felt about me. Then, if he didn't want to date me, I'd deal with it. But at least I'd know I tried.

The following Monday, I got off the bus and met Mrs. B with a plan in mind. I'd get Dave alone—even if it meant having Mrs. B with me—and ask him if he wanted to do something later that week. *Just the two of us,* I'd stress. Once we made a plan, I'd practice what I wanted to say to him and the minute we were alone, I'd let him know everything and ask him what was going on with him and Meg. I just had to know.

Later that day, the four of us—Meg, Dave, Mrs. B, and me—met in the hallway and walked to the cafeteria. When we reached the lunchroom doors, Meg and Dave stopped to talk to Nina. Although I should've kept going, I slowed my chair and waited for them to finish their conversation. Mrs. B went on ahead of us; I knew that when we went inside, I would find her at our usual table with my lunch. She wasn't supposed to leave me alone, but sometimes she was cool and understood that I needed to be with my friends without the presence of an adult.

"Joey and I had so much fun with you guys on Saturday night!" Nina was saying. My ears perked up. Saturday night? Meg had told me she went to the mall with her sister Saturday night.

"We had a great time, too," Meg said with a smile and slipped her arm around Dave's waist. "I'd wanted to go mini golfing since spring, but Dave kept saying it'd be lame if we went alone."

"Well, you know Joey. He can make pretty much anything into an 'extreme' sport," Nina giggled, making air quotes with her fingers when she said the word. "Life definitely hasn't been boring since we've been dating. Do you guys want to go out again this weekend? Maybe we can see a movie or go for pizza?"

"Sure!" Meg responded, hugging Dave closer to her. He put his arm around her then and returned the hug.

"Great! I'll tell Joey. I'm so happy you guys are together. You make such a cute couple. I always knew there was something between you two."

Bam! There it was. My heart all but stopped and I felt a cold sweat begin on my forehead.

With a quick, perky wave, Nina turned to enter the cafeteria and happened to catch my eye. "Oh, hey, Brynn! I didn't even realize you were there," she said as she walked through the open doors and disappeared into the crowd.

At the sound of my name, Meg immediately dropped her hold on Dave, and the two of them quickly spun around. We looked at each other, but none of us spoke. My tiny little world froze right there. The busy hallway suddenly became a blur. I finally looked away, fighting the urge to cry with all of my might. I sat there trembling and focusing on breathing. Dave, who I was infatuated with since the sixth grade, who I thought about every minute of the day, who I wanted to be my first kiss, was dating Meg, the girl who claimed to be my best friend.

What I'd suspected a few days earlier was true. Everything I had feared, but told myself not to focus on, was true. Imagined instances of Dave and me locking fingers, kissing, laughing, and holding each other close shattered into pieces. I'd been so sure we were headed down that path. And now . . .

Meg knew that the love of my life was never going to love me and she never told me. All the reassurances Meg gave me that Dave might want to date me were lies. All those signs where I thought Dave was starting to like me were in my head. All this information was thrown at me in a matter of seconds. I couldn't handle being there anymore. I hit the on/off switch on my wheelchair and sped into the cafeteria, nearly knocking a student over and startling another one so much that she dropped her books.

Dave wouldn't make real eye contact with me after that day; I didn't even get an apology from him. I had one conversation with Meg before I started to actively avoid her. Even though I

thought an apology from both of them was so obviously necessary to keep either friendship alive, neither of them made an
effort to give one. All Meg said when we spoke about it was that
they didn't tell me because they were afraid to hurt my feelings.

I still had trouble wrapping my brain around it. The day I had
that last, final conversation with Meg was the day that I realized
that our friendship had been a joke, because nobody who was
truly a friend would do that to someone. I was angrier with Meg
than I was with Dave, mostly because she *knew* how I felt about
him. Dave, on the other hand, probably thought we were just
friends. I'd never told him how I felt, and we weren't dating, so
he had all the right in the world to date anyone he wanted—even
Meg. But Meg . . . There was no forgiving her. We could never
be friends again. I wouldn't throw a temper tantrum every time I
saw her, as I just proved when she opened the doors for me, but
there was nothing between us anymore. And there never would
be again. She might think she was still my best friend—especially
since I'd never really told her how hurt I was or how much I now
despised her—but I knew the truth.

As I watched Meg and Dave disappear among the buses, I
tried to forget what just happened. Even though I was outside
now and could be on my way home in just a few minutes, I felt as
if someone came along, popped my balloon of summer excitement, and just kept walking like it was no big deal. I tried to
think about camp (that has been the only thing that cheered
me up lately) and reminded myself that summer vacation would
mean that I wouldn't be forced to see Meg and Dave for three
whole months. Just as I started to make my way to my bus, Mrs. B
came back behind me.

"Sorry about that, Brynn." She adjusted her shoulder bag,
"Mrs. Costa's son is playing on a travel soccer team, too, and she
wanted to know about Shannon's team's registration process. I
see someone was actually nice enough to help you get outside."

I shot her my annoyed look.

"What? Was it someone you don't like? It wasn't Meg or Dave, was it?"

I gave her the same annoyed look.

"I'm sorry, Brynn. I suppose junior year just had to give you one last going away present. Just think: You don't have to set foot in this place until September. C'mon, let's get you to your bus so you can go home."

I was still annoyed, but I was relieved to just get out of there. Summer was here. And I was determined to make it one I'd never forget.

Chapter Two

"Today's the day!" My mom ripped the covers off of me. "Now, wake up!"

I slowly opened my eyes, unsure of what was happening. The room was still a little dark, which meant it was way too early to even consider waking up.

"There we go. You know, I have been trying to wake you up for the past five minutes, and I was starting to think you might be in a coma. I really hope they wake you guys up with a loud blow horn, or your counselor is going to get annoyed with you real quick."

I slowly turned my head and squinted at her. What was she going on about? Oh, right. Camp.

"Good morning!" Mom said in mocking enthusiasm. "I'm so glad you finally decided to wake up. What would you like to wear today?"

A groan escaped my throat that sounded more like a growl.

"You're going to camp today. You have absolutely nothing to be growling about." She busied herself, moving about my room, as I laid there and watched the familiar scene playing before me. This was our morning routine. "Now, what do you want to wear? You want to wear jean shorts?"

I managed to nod. I wasn't awake enough to care what shorts I wore. My mom pulled my legs so they were hanging off of the bed. She slipped my shorts on one leg at a time and buttoned them. Knowing that I didn't care what socks I wore, she picked out light pink ones and made sure they didn't come up higher than my ankles. Tube socks were just not cool in my book. A few minutes later, she was tying the laces on my favorite blue Converse sneakers and we were moving along, even though all I wanted was more sleep.

"Ready to get in your chair?"

I wasn't entirely ready—I was exhausted. I'd had a difficult time falling asleep the night before. It reminded me of the first day of school, nerves and all. Only this time, at camp, if something upset me, I was stuck in the woods with it for two weeks. This thought occurred to me a few minutes after I got in bed and stuck with me for quite some time.

Even though I was anxious, I was still mostly excited. And now that I was more awake, I could feel the energy building up inside me. I glanced down at my bed and wondered what the camp beds would be like. I figured they wouldn't be as comfy, but I wondered if they'd all look the same, wooden frame and all. I knew there'd be bunk beds, and I also knew I'd take the bottom bunk due to the probability of falling and cracking my skull attempting to get up on top.

My mom pulled my arms to sit me up. I forced my still heavy eyes to stay open. I leaned my upper body over my mom's shoulder. She scooped up my left leg and I was en route to my wheelchair. If people unfamiliar with A Day in the Life of Brynn Evason had been watching, they would probably think my mom was doing some wrestling move on me that might have qualified as child abuse, but this was what we did every morning. I landed in my wheelchair with an awkward thud. I was awake now.

My mom strapped my feet into my footrests and buckled my seatbelt. Once I decided on a shirt to wear, she'd strap my arms into my armbands. I motioned with my eyes toward my closet, where the shirt I wanted to wear had been hung.

"You probably want a tank top, because you want to look cute, don't you?"

My mom knew me well. Whenever I would go anywhere and I knew that I would be meeting a bunch of new people, especially people my age, I went with a tank top. Even when it was really cold outside, I'd choose a tank top to wear under a sweater. That just was what most of the girls wore.

"Do you want a certain color?"

I shrugged.

"How about turquoise?"

I nodded.

My mom took the tank top off the hanger and reached for my underwear drawer. "Let me guess. You still want your regular bra even though this tank top has a built in one, because you want to make your boobs look bigger."

I started to nod, but looked away, smiling in embarrassment. She was on to my trick. I wondered when she had figured me out. Maybe she knew me *too* well.

"You know, most moms would not approve of this," she said, rifling through my drawer and choosing a cute bra with polka dots. "I only do this because I know you would be doing it anyway if you didn't need my help getting dressed."

I blew my mom a kiss to thank her for understanding and respecting the fact that I was a typical teenage girl and liked to do what typical teenage girls did. I hoped the counselor who would be helping me get dressed every morning would understand that she wasn't just helping me get dressed—she was also helping me look cute.

My mom came back over to me with the bra, tank top, and deodorant. She bent me over and pulled the wrinkled t-shirt I had slept in over my head. Sitting me back up, she held up each of my arms and did a few quick strokes of deodorant. She slipped both bra straps on my shoulders and leaned me forward to clasp it. Even though extra-small tank tops fit me perfectly, my mom always had trouble putting them on me; they didn't have enough flexibility to put my arms through once it was over my head. When the shirt was successfully on, my arms went right in my armbands. I now had control of my chair.

"Do you want to attempt to do something else with your hair? I will try my hardest, but I'm not promising anything."

I sympathetically shook my head.

"Okay. I'm sorry. Maybe your counselor will be good with hair."

I purposely gave her my puzzling look, trying to ask her if she really thought the counselor would be able to do more with my hair than she was capable of.

"What? You do want me to try to do something else with it?"

I shook my head and looked up at my hair, keeping my questioning look. When I didn't have my TechnoTalk, communicating was like playing a game of twenty questions combined with using my best acting skills. Some people thought that this game was very frustrating for me, but it wasn't a big deal at all. It just was what I had to do sometimes to get my point across.

My mom continued to try to guess what I was saying. "You just want a regular ponytail like you wear every day?"

I simply nodded. It was easier. Without my computer, there was no way she was going to get that I was asking her about my counselor's assumed hairdressing abilities and not about my specific hairstyle that morning.

"Yeah, I figured that is what you were going to do if you weren't going to do anything special."

I chuckled to myself as I turned my wheelchair on and went in front of the mirror. My mom took out the ponytail that was already in and started to untangle the mess. I had dyed my hair again the night before camp so it still had a faint smell of ammonia. Once it was all brushed out, I officially decided I liked it. It was just a shade lighter than honeycomb, but didn't look as though I dumped an entire bottle of bleach on my head. My mom scooped all of it up and put it into a high ponytail so it wouldn't be in the way of my headrest.

"Maybe you will get a little tan while you're at camp. Some color would do you good."

I pretended to be offended by that statement.

"Brynn." My mom placed her arm against my shoulder. "Look at me and look at you. Except for our hair now being the same color, we don't even look like we're from the same family. I'm not saying you look horrible; I just think if you got a little tan, you would be even cuter. That's all."

Okay, maybe my skin was a tad bit pasty, but at least I didn't look like Edward from *Twilight*.

"Hey, I'm going to take a shower before we pack. Go out in the kitchen and Dad will feed you breakfast."

My mom walked out of my bathroom and I followed her. My dad was sitting in the living room, reading the newspaper.

"Good morning, Brynnie!" He looked over his glasses at me. "Do you want me to make you breakfast?"

I smiled as if to say, "That would be great!"

"What do you want? Those French toast things you like?"

I nodded as he put down the newspaper and his glasses. We went into the kitchen together and I pulled up to my regular spot at the counter. I found it easier to have whoever was helping me eat standing up as opposed to sitting down, so I very rarely sat at the table. My dad pulled the French toast sticks out of the freezer and I told him I wanted six. He then asked me how long to heat them (he couldn't remember for the life of him it was only a minute) and popped them in the microwave.

He presented me with choices of water and apple juice to drink and I went with the juice. He poured some in a green Tupperware cup similar to what toddlers typically use to drink. Part of how I took a drink required me to actually bite down on the cup, so paper cups and glasses just didn't work for me.

The microwave beeped and my dad brought my breakfast over. He grabbed the syrup from the pantry and quickly drizzled some on. He put the first bite to my mouth and I shook my head.

Realizing that I wanted a drink first, he put the fork down. With one hand, he held a paper towel to my chin, and with his other hand he held the cup to my lips. I bit down on the plastic, tilted my head back just a smidge, and drank my juice in three quick gulps.

My dad put the piece of the French toast in my mouth and pulled the fork out. I mashed it around, tasting the sweet syrup.

"Are you excited to go to camp?"

I swallowed and smiled.

"I was never interested in going into the woods and sleeping in a little rickety cabin." He gave me another bite. "But I'm happy you are. I know you're mainly going to make friends."

I nodded and started on the second French toast stick.

"Would you keep in touch with them over the Facebook?"

I chuckled at the unnecessary "the" and nodded again.

"What would you do without the internet? You probably wouldn't be going to this camp today."

My dad was right. I came across Camp Lakewood online. It was about a month after I found out Dave was dating Meg and I had finally accepted that our friendships were over. My mom told me that I needed to get out of the funk I was in and that I should look for places we could go that summer. My parents were willing to take me on a vacation to any location I wanted. In the midst of searching for the perfect summer vacation spot, I came across the Camp Lakewood website. After reading about what a typical day was like and looking at the pictures from the previous year, I decided this was where I wanted to go to get away.

Camp Lakewood wasn't a camp for little kids. The camp was well-established and welcomed returning campers and new campers in every session, every year. I'd be one of the older campers in my session—ages fourteen to seventeen—but the photos and testimonials on the website assured me that I would not be the only person entering her senior year of high school.

At first, I thought that was a little weird. I mean, most people go to camp when they're in middle school, right? However, the more research I did, the more I realized that there were plenty of camps across the eastern United States that accepted campers my age. Some camps had training programs for campers fifteen and older who wanted to become counselors in future years. From the website, I could tell that Camp Lakewood did offer that opportunity in earlier summer sessions, but I decided that I just wanted to go to camp to have fun, get my mind off everything with my ex-friends, and just enjoy the last summer I'd have without the stress of college on my mind. I didn't mind being a regular camper without the responsibilities of making sure others were behaving, safe, and entertained. In fact, I was really looking forward to relaxing, breathing fresh air, and making new friends.

Luckily, Camp Lakewood also wasn't a camp designed only for kids with disabilities, either. At first, my mom was afraid they wouldn't take kids like me and tried to get me to think about going to another camp that was specifically for people with disabilities. I was afraid that kind of camp would have more kids who were like the students on my bus with cognitive disabilities and that I would be stuck in front of a TV watching *Winnie the Pooh* every day. Once I realized that the camp allowed young adults, I had my mom call Camp Lakewood and, although they never had someone like me come to camp before, they were more than willing to work with my mom and me so I would be able to go. The fact that they were so accommodating and excited to have me already made me feel welcome.

They agreed to assign me a counselor who would be with me all day, kind of like how Mrs. B was with me at school. I was never crazy about having someone attached to my hip 24/7, at school or at camp, but this was the only way I was going to be able to go. My mom was also sure that because this counselor was a summer camp counselor (and not an older adult who was working for a school district), she was going to be way more fun to be with than my aide.

I finished the last of my French toast sticks and had one more cup of juice, realizing this was going to be my last meal at home for two weeks. Somehow that thought made me the tiniest bit sad. I really wanted to go to camp and had been waiting for this day for three whole months, but I was going to miss my mom and dad. The longest I had been away from them was when they went to Niagara Falls for a weekend and I stayed with my aunt. I was going away for two weeks . . . across the state . . . without anyone I knew. What was I thinking?

After my dad put my dishes in the dishwasher, we headed back to my bedroom so I could go to the bathroom. Meg (and, I'd imagine, every other girl our age) could never understand how I was perfectly okay with my dad helping me pee, but this was normal to me. My dad had been helping me with stuff like this ever since I was a baby, and I didn't know any differently.

I had a lift to help me get on and off of the toilet. It was basically like one of those things to move refrigerators, but only for humans. The lift was wheeled up in front of me, my arms and legs were strapped in, and I was wheeled to the toilet and back. It was pretty easy to use. Once I was back in my wheelchair, my dad hooked up my communication device. I was officially ready to go for the day.

My dad took the lift for the toilet to the van while I went over to my computer. Through Bluetooth technology, my TechnoTalk acted like a remote control to my desktop. If I wanted the mouse to go up, I would just hit the up button. If I wanted to type something, I would use my keyboard screen that was meant for the computer. It was kind of hard to explain, but it worked.

I woke my desktop up and opened a browser. Facebook was set as my homepage and I slowly moved the mouse to the box that always cared to know what was on my mind. I clicked on it and the question disappeared, leaving a cursor that was patiently waiting for my answer. In capital letters, I typed out CAMP FOR TWO WEEKS! CAN'T WAIT TO GET THERE! I moved the mouse to the blue button that said SHARE. I clicked on it and, just like that, my message was broadcasted to my forty-seven friends.

Just as I was about to send my mouse up to the right-hand corner to close the internet, I noticed the little red flag indicating I had a friend request. When I saw who it was, my jaw dropped open in amazement. It was Amy, the cheerleader from my History class who never said a word to me. I stared at the screen in complete puzzlement. If she was too cool to have a conversation with me when I was sitting right next to her all year, and much too cool to open the door for me on the last day of school, why the hell did she want to be friends on Facebook? What made her think I would accept her?

I stopped the mouse on the decline button and for a second I hesitated. She must have had a reason for requesting me. And what if I did accept her? She would be able to see my profile and she would learn some pretty personal things about me, which kind of made me uncomfortable. But . . . if I accepted her, maybe she would see that I was more like her than she thought. I decided to take a chance and moved the mouse to the opposite button. Click. Amy was now my Facebook friend.

"Okay, Missy," my mom walked into the room behind me. "Are you ready to get packing? We have to get to camp a little earlier so I can show your counselor how to do everything."

I closed the internet, shut my computer down, and spun around. My mom flung our big red suitcase on my bed.

"So, I think you should take all your socks and all your underwear. You're going to be there for two weeks, and you can never have enough."

I chuckled as she opened the dresser drawer, scooped everything up, and threw it in the suitcase.

"I will organize everything later. Do you want your bathing suit?"

I hesitated.

"I could tell them how to help you swim."

I shrugged and nodded.

"Do you want your one piece or two piece?"

I smiled and motioned to my answer.

"Of course. Why did I even ask?"

My hot pink bikini went in along with sheets, towels, body wash, shampoo, conditioner, my toothbrush, toothpaste, wheelchair charger, TechnoTalk charger, extra armbands, hairbrush, hair bands, deodorant, shorts, one pair of jeans, and an extra pair of shoes. Looking at the small mountain that had formed in the suitcase, I didn't know how we were going to fit everything *and* be able to close it. We were just about to pick out what tops I wanted to take when my dad walked in.

"Telephone for Brynn." He handed the cordless phone to my mom.

"Thanks. Can you take the shower chair out to the van?" My mom put the phone on speaker. "Hello, Brynn is right here."

My dad quietly wheeled the blue chair out of my room.

"Hi, Brynn! This is Nunna. I just want to tell you to have a wonderful time at camp."

"Yeaaaahhh," I said without my TechnoTalk.

"I know you have been looking forward to this. I just want you to make sure the counselors are able to help you. If at any time you don't feel like they can, just have them call your mom."

I looked at my mom, unsure of what to say. I knew my grandma and other relatives weren't crazy about me going away without my family, but I didn't know they were actually *worried* about it.

"She will," my mom jumped in. "We're going early so I can teach the counselor how to do everything, and I'm going to stay until Brynn and her counselor both feel comfortable."

"Good. Just make sure Brynn knows she can come home if she doesn't feel comfortable."

I stared at the phone. *Really?* What did she think I was going to do? Let myself starve to death if they didn't know how to feed me? Pee in my chair for two weeks if they couldn't figure out the bathroom? Sexy. Incredibly sexy.

"She knows." My mom played it cool, but shook her head. "But we better get going now. We're leaving in a few minutes."

"Alright. I love you, Brynn. Have a good time, and I will see you when you get back."

I just nodded for my mom to answer for me.

"She loves you, too. See you later."

"Bye, now."

As soon as my mom hung up the phone, I immediately hit my head switch to start typing. I flipped to my keyboard screen and my TechnoTalk scrolled through the letters. My mom waited patiently as I built my sentence by tapping the switch with my head, even though she probably knew what I was going to say. Two minutes had gone by when I finally hit the SPEAK button.

"Was that really necessary?" my computer's monotone voice asked.

"Brynn, they just are being protective of you. Overprotective? Maybe a little. But, in two weeks when you get back, you have my permission to brag to everyone about how you just had the greatest time. That is . . . if you survive. There may be bears in those woods."

We both smiled.

"Come on, you have to tell me what shirts you want to take because we gotta go."

My mom went over to the closet and I told her I wanted all tank tops. She ended up convincing me to take a few baby tees and a hoodie. After I had everything that I wanted from my closet, my mom took on the task of fitting it all into my suitcase, which she completed in less than five minutes. She grabbed my two pillows and plopped them on top.

"Okay. Are we forgetting anything else?"

I motioned to my dresser.

My mom looked in that direction. "Something in your dresser?"

I tilted my head up.

"Something on top of your—oh, I should've known." She grabbed my iPod and earphones. "You probably want to listen to this in the car."

I grinned. Listening to Abbie Bonza's songs on the way to camp would definitely get me pumped up. She was my favorite artist; I loved everything she sang—especially since she wrote the lyrics and the music herself.

"Gotcha, gotcha. Anything else? Do you want to take your monkey?"

I hesitated for a second.

"I'm sure the other kids sleep with stuffed animals and probably won't think you're acting like you're five years old."

What the hell. I gave in. My mom shoved my monkey in the backpack that was attached to the back of my chair. If nobody else had a stuffed animal, I just could leave him in there. And besides, I really didn't like to sleep without him anyway.

"Okay. I think we are ready to head out. Brynn! This is it!"

I squealed.

"I know! I'm so excited for you. Let's get moving."

I turned my wheelchair on and said goodbye to my bedroom for twelve days. The next time I came back to it, I may have had the experience of a lifetime (which I hoped was the case), or I could come back into it not wanting to spend another night away from my bed. I didn't know what I had gotten myself into, but a surge of excitement came over me as I realized I would soon find out.

Once settled in the van, my mom put my iPod next to my leg, closed the door, and climbed into the passenger seat. My dad came out of the house and threw my suitcase in the back. When he slid into the driver's seat, he tried to say something to me, but my mom told him I couldn't hear. He started the ignition and we were off to Camp Lakewood.

As we turned the corner, I let myself relax and simply listen to my music. I didn't just *like* music, nor did I love it. Music was absolutely essential to my life. When I listened to any type of music that I liked, it was like I escaped to a different world. In this fantasy world of mine, I didn't have a disability. Not that I wasn't okay with having cerebral palsy; I never thought being able to walk or talk would miraculously make everything better. But in my mind, when I was listening to music, I liked to imagine myself up on a stage singing and dancing around . . . and playing the guitar, just like Abbie.

Four songs had passed by the time we were on the highway. I never pictured myself actually being one of today's more popular artists; I just wanted to be a singer and play the guitar. In the front row, like always, were Meg and Dave, but my attention was more on Dave. Just as I started to sing, his blue eyes met mine and we were connected for the rest of the song.

I would be the first to admit it: The world inside of my mind was 100 percent cheesy and 100 percent unrealistic. I knew I was never going to be able to walk, or talk, or sing, or play the guitar. I knew now that I was never going to have a magical chick flick moment with Dave. This world was just where I went to if I wanted to just . . . *be.*

About an hour and a half into the trip (and after I imagined myself impressing Dave in every way possible with each song), I started to notice fewer and fewer buildings. I jumped out of my fantasy world and looked out the window. It wasn't long before the only things I saw were trees; this was a beautiful part of Pennsylvania I'd never seen before. I could feel my anticipation build and I couldn't help but smile. This was it. This was my chance to make some new friends. This was my chance to prove I could be somewhere—and survive—without my parents.

My mom caught my attention and pointed out the windshield to the wooden sign hanging up ahead. It read CAMP LAKEWOOD. Ready or not, my adventure was about to begin.

Chapter Three

The van crunched the gravel as we pulled into the parking lot. I was here. For most of the last semester of my junior year, I had been counting down the days and trying to survive. Every one of those days had been absolute torture, but school was out now. It was summer, and Pittsburgh was far behind me. I was finally here!

My dad turned the key and pressed the button for the wheel-chair ramp to automatically unfold and lower to the ground. As my mom stepped out to take the tie-downs off my chair and put my iPod away, I tried not to look as if I was five years old and eager to journey into the wonderful world of Disney. Despite my best efforts, I couldn't shake the excitement—or the enormous, cheesy grin on my face.

"I know, you're excited," my mom said and took the last heavy-duty hook off my chair. "But you have to concentrate so you don't drive yourself off the side of the ramp and end up at the hospital before you even meet your counselor."

I took a deep breath and managed to drive successfully off the ramp without tipping over and killing myself. We moved toward what we assumed was the check-in table. At that moment, a girl in a blue Camp Lakewood polo shirt looked up, smiled wide at us, and started walking our way.

"You must be Brynn!" she said. I assumed she was in her early twenties. Her blonde hair was pulled back in a loose ponytail.

She reached out to shake my parents' hands as my mom introduced us.

"This would be Brynn," my mom answered for me, "and I'm Sherry, and this is Paul."

"Hi! I'm Christine! I'm going to be your counselor, Brynn. Welcome to Camp Lakewood. They have been telling me a lot about you, and I'm thrilled to finally meet you!"

I'd only known Christine for five seconds and I already liked her. She spoke to me—not to my mom, even though my mom was speaking for me, and not to my dad. This wouldn't be like school at all. I knew it.

"She's so excited to be here," my mom said. "She usually talks with that device in front of her. It's called a TechnoTalk, and she can't see the screen very well outside, so that's why I'm talking for her."

"Oh," Christine's brow furrowed. "Is there anything we can do to help her see the screen better?"

"Not really. Shade helps a little. But she can shake her head yes or no to anything you ask her. You guys are probably going to be outside a lot, huh?"

I frowned. The thought hadn't ever occurred to me. *How stupid was I?*

My mom read my mind. "Well, you should have thought of that, Missy," she said with a smile. "I told you that you might not be able to do everything here since this is more for able-bodied kids. And isn't that what you do at camp? You go outside. And become one with nature. And whatever else you camp people do. It's a little too late now to worry about that."

Christine chuckled. "It's all good. I'm sure we will make it work."

"I know you will. I have complete faith in you two. And Brynn, you're here now. You're here to stay. There's no turning back now."

I gave her an unsure smile. She was right, but I was beginning to realize this process was going to involve more than my parents simply dropping me off and saying "Have a good time!"

"I'm not worried," Christine said and shrugged. "Everything will be cool. Do you want to check in so we can head to the cabin?"

"Yes," my mom replied. "Should Paul start unloading her things from the van?"

"Sure, we are going to be in the cabin straight ahead with a few other girls, but most of them aren't here yet," Christine pointed at the nearest cabin.

My dad nodded and went back to the van for all my stuff as Christine led us to the check-in table. A counselor sat behind the table, also wearing the blue Camp Lakewood shirt, and shuffling a bunch of papers.

As I looked around, I realized that the cabins were much larger than I thought they would be. The trees were also taller, and the air, I'd noticed, was the freshest I'd ever inhaled. The online photographs and descriptions of Camp Lakewood didn't do it justice. This place was beautiful. I couldn't wait to see the lake! Although I still wasn't sure if I'd actually go *in* it . . .

"Brynn, this is Evelyn, the other counselor in our cabin," Christine said. "Evelyn, this is Brynn."

"What's up, Brynn?" Evelyn waved. She had dreadlocks down to her shoulders. "We're super excited to have you at camp this year."

"I can't thank you enough for letting her come to this session even though it's more for kids who have been here before," my mom started. "She debated for a while about going to a camp that was more for people with disabilities, but after attending a local program that was for disabled people. She was afraid she wouldn't fit in. There aren't too many kids like Brynn. I always tell people she's like a brain inside of bowl of Jell-O. Her body doesn't work, but she's cognitively all there."

"No problem," Evelyn said, waving a hand like it wasn't a big deal. "I think this session could use someone new. You and your mom just need to answer a few questions, and then you can go check out the cabin. . . . Do you take any medicine?"

I shook my head. Evelyn checked something off on a neon green card that had my name on it.

"Do you have any allergies we should know about?"

I shook my head again.

"No meds and no allergies? Rock on. Who should we call if there's an emergency and what's his or her number?"

"Me. I'm Sherry." My mom rattled off the house number, her work number, and her cell phone number.

"Okay," Evelyn finished writing everything down. "I think that's it. Brynn, I'll see you a little later back at the cabin. Christine will show you around."

"Nice to meet you," my mom said as we both turned around.

We fell into step beside Christine, who named the cabins, buildings, and people as we strolled. It was clear that she'd worked at Camp Lakewood before. And it was also obvious that she felt at home here. I hoped I would, too. I hadn't driven off of the path or accidentally ran into any stationary objects. I was off to a good start.

We passed a building that Christine said was the dining hall, and, to my surprise, it was also where all the bathrooms were. *Interesting*, I thought. I didn't realize there was a strong possibility I would be peeing in a completely different place from where I would be sleeping. Luckily, I usually didn't have to go in the middle of the night.

Christine led us to the cabin. My cabin. The fact that I wouldn't be sharing this cabin with my mom, my dad, my grandma, or anyone from my hell hole of a high school made me smile. This was *my* adventure, and I had my very own cabin (along with cabin mates, of course) to prove it. I made a mental note to ask someone to take a picture of me in my cabin—and one with my cabin mates and me, eventually—to show off when I got home.

"This is going to be our home for the next two weeks, Brynn!" Christine faced my mom and me. "Luckily, Camp Lakewood has a few cabins that are ground level, so we don't have to worry about steps. What do ya think?"

I squealed.

"That means she's excited," my mom translated. "Can we go in?"

"Yep."

Christine held the screen door open and my mom and I went inside. The lights overhead were dim and made a slight humming noise. The cabin was rectangular and it had an old, musty smell to it. Three pairs of bunk beds were positioned on each side of the large room, leaving an open space in the middle. Other than the beds and little wooden nightstands, there wasn't really anything else in the cabin, which made me guess that we weren't going to be in it too much.

"Brynn, I was thinking you and I could take one of the back bunks, if that's okay with you."

I nodded.

"Okay, cool. So now that we're inside and we have some time to ourselves, what do I need to know?"

My mom went through the entire spiel with Christine; it was something she was used to saying and I was used to hearing. Every time someone new learned how to help me, I got to listen to my mom talk about my armbands and how I had more control over my arms if they were strapped down. Then she'd warn Christine that without the bands, I may accidentally punch her once or twice, but my mom swore—and I nodded in sincere agreement—that it would be a complete mistake and that if it ever happened, Christine shouldn't take it personally.

If Christine wanted to run away screaming in terror, her face certainly didn't show it. In fact, she looked interested. She asked questions—good questions!—and even laughed at my mom's lame jokes. While they talked, I imagined what my cabin mates would look like. And then, although I would never admit it, I found myself wondering what the guys in the cabins down the path looked like. As my mom had planned, we arrived pretty early, so there weren't too many people to watch or meet when Christine was showing us around. I hoped the girls were all cool and didn't want to be friends with me just to get gold stars . . . . And, if nothing else, I hoped the guys were hot.

"So," my mom was saying as I tuned back in. "She has enough control in her arm to hit the on/off switch for the chair. Because she has good control of her head and neck, she can drive her wheelchair. She would never have enough coordination to drive her chair with a joystick using her hand, so the wheelchair company custom made her headrest, putting three switches in all of the pads. When she leans her head back, her chair moves forward."

My mom looked at me and I rolled my eyes, but demonstrated moving forward so Christine could see how it all worked.

"If she hits the left pad, she turns to the left; same with the right."

I turned in a clockwise circle and then I went counterclockwise. It was my mom's turn to roll *her* eyes.

"Because they were out of room on her headrest, and because she has a little control of her legs when they are strapped down, they put her reverse switch in her right knee pad."

I moved forward and backward and grinned at Christine. The show was almost over. She still seemed like this didn't even faze her. The entire process sounded way more complicated to some people than it actually was. Then again, I had been driving a power wheelchair since I was six years old, so I really didn't have to think about it anymore.

"Sorry, I know this might be a lot to take in, but you're going to be with her for the next two weeks, and I want you to know everything, and be comfortable with everything," my mom said.

"No problem. I need to know everything," Christine agreed. "Now, how does the computer work?"

I motioned to my mom to help me with the explanation. Christine and my mom stood on either side of me.

"As I've mentioned and as you've seen, although Brynn can't walk or talk, she can comprehend and she can communicate. The TechnoTalk helps her do that."

My mom pointed to the other blue switch (which kind of looked like a hockey puck) that was attached to the left pad of my headrest. "She does it with her head. This is her main screen, the keyboard screen. There are four rows of buttons. The device automatically scans through these four rows, and whenever it gets to the row she wants, she hits the switch by her head. Then the device will scan button by button, and again when it gets to whatever she wants, she just hits her switch. The first row is all word prediction buttons. They work like some cell phones work. If she presses a T, all T words come up. If she then presses the H, all words that start with TH come up."

Christine nodded and continued to watch my screen.

"The last three rows are obviously letters, numbers, and punctuation. Her TechnoTalk doesn't speak each word while she's writing. Whenever she wants to say what she has typed, she just hits the SPEAK button. She also has a screen with general phrases and a screen of her favorite movies and her favorite music."

"Wow. That's so awesome," Christine said. Her interest and her enthusiasm were genuine; she wasn't being overly cheery or fake and she hadn't once spoken to me like a toddler. Things were looking good—real good.

"I take it you have never worked with somebody with a disability before?"

Christine hesitated. "Not exactly . . . So, Brynn, please forgive me if I screw up."

"She will," my mom reassured her. "Brynn is very patient, especially with new people. Can I ask you what made you want to work with Brynn?"

Christine shrugged. It reminded me of Evelyn's wave. *No big deal,* her body language said. "They just told us about Brynn and that she needed a little more help, and I was the first one who said I would like to."

"Good." My mom's smile slowly stretched across her face." I think you two will work very well together. It's really not hard to help her once you know what you're doing."

Just then, my dad walked in with my suitcase.

"What took you so long?" my mom joked.

"Got to talking to some people out in the parking lot," he explained. "Brynn, I really think you're going to like this place. The people here are very nice, and they all are excited to have you."

I smiled.

"Where do you want me to put this?"

Christine pointed to the bed in the right corner. "There should be okay."

My dad flung my suitcase on what was now my bed. "I'll be back with the lift and the shower chair."

"Actually, don't bring it here," my mom started. "They don't have a bathroom in the cabin. Take it to the dining hall."

"Jeez, no bathroom in the cabin? You really do rough it here, don't you?" My dad winked at me.

Christine grinned. "Welcome to camp!"

While my dad was getting my other stuff, my mom unzipped my suitcase to get the sheets out. As they were making my bed, my mom continued to give Christine an accelerated course of "Helping Brynn 101." She explained how to put my TechnoTalk on, how to shower me, how to help me eat, how to lift me, how to charge my chair and TechnoTalk, and about fifty other things.

After Christine said she felt comfortable enough, we moved on to the bathroom.

"Alright," my mom said a few minutes later, the course now complete. We left the bathroom and moved into the dining hall. A few people were around, but I was suddenly too nervous to pay much attention to them.

"Do you have any more questions?" my mom asked Christine.

My stomach suddenly twisted. I knew this was it.

"No, I think we're good to go. Anything else you want me to know, Brynn?"

I frowned and hit my talking switch to begin scrolling. "Are ... you ..." I typed out word by word, "okay ... with ... helping ... me ... with ... everything?" It wasn't until I hit SPEAK that my TechnoTalk asked my question.

"Oh, of course! It's not a big deal at all, really. I just want you to be able to have fun at camp, and I'm willing to do whatever I can to help you. You don't have to worry about me." Christine put her hand on my shoulder and gave it a reassuring squeeze.

"See?" Mom asked. "She's okay. You need to relax." She turned to Christine. "Brynn worries a lot that she is being a pain."

"Nah, I can tell right now that you definitely aren't going to be a pain," she said again as we stepped outside and into the sun.

I felt my lips begin to quiver as the conversation came to an end. I was happy that Christine was so willing to help me, but I was slowly realizing that I would miss my parents. I'd been so eager to spend some time without them, but now . . .

"Hey, no crying," my mom instructed. "You were the one who wanted to come."

"Yeah," my dad added, "but if you really need us to come visit, just give us a call."

I nodded.

My mom bent down to hug me. "I love you and I'm so proud of you. You are going to have a blast! And remember, when you get home, you have every right to rub it in everyone's face that *you* went to camp, and *you* had the best time. I will even help you call Meg and Dave, if you want."

I fought back tears and forced a smile. Hopefully, talking to Meg or Dave would be the *last* thing I'd want to do when I got home from camp.

My dad kissed my forehead. "I love you, Brynnie! Have fun!"

"Okay," my mom sighed, again turning to my counselor. "Are you sure you're good?"

Christine chuckled. "Yes, we're good."

"Okay, see ya, love ya, bye!"

Christine waved as they turned around. I watched as my family got into the van and drove away . . . without me. I looked up at Christine.

"It's okay. Most first-time campers cry when their parents leave."

I gave her a questioning smile as a tear ran down my cheek.

Christine smiled back at me. "Yeah, really. Even some of the sixteen- and seventeen-year-olds."

The van drove farther away from me as a million new thoughts rushed into my head. What were my mom and dad going to do without me? Were they planning to go out tonight because I was gone? Was my mom excited she wasn't going to have to get me up for the next twelve mornings? Was my dad happy he was getting a break from helping me in the bathroom? Were they upset that I chose to go to camp instead of going on a vacation with them? What was I going to do if I didn't like it here?

Suddenly, I found myself considering a totally new set of questions. What was Christine thinking? Did she really feel comfortable? What if she just said she did and really didn't? What were the other campers going to be like? Would they understand that I talked with my TechnoTalk? What if they didn't? Would they just pretend that I was invisible like everyone at school? What if someone tried to talk to me when I was outside and Christine wasn't around to explain that I couldn't see my screen?

I forced myself to take a deep breath. I needed to calm down. The answers to these questions weren't just going to fall from the sky. What was the point of getting myself worked up about it now? I needed to take it one day—one hour, one minute—at a time.

Christine wiped the last of my tears away without using a tissue. The fact that she did it with her bare hands was comforting. It was something a best friend would do, although my history with "best friends" was anything but rainbows and butterflies. Still, maybe Christine really was cool with helping me. Maybe I was just overanalyzing everything.

"Why don't we go back to the cabin?" Christine suggested. "I'm really excited to get to know you, and the other campers will be coming shortly. I'm sure you want to talk to them, as well."

I slowly nodded as I turned my wheelchair on and followed Christine into what would be my home for the next twelve days.

Chapter Four

"Is this the first time you have been away without your parents?" Christine asked, sitting down on my bunk.

I nodded and turned my chair off.

"That's cool. What made you want to come to camp this year?"

I thought for a second. How was I going to answer that? Was I going to tell her the reason I came to Camp Lakewood was that I had my heart ripped out by my two best friends and was about to fall into a very real state of depression? I didn't want her to feel sorry for me, though. I didn't come here for a pity party; I just wanted to get away from the possibility of running into the happy couple all summer.

Before I could explain my decision, a tall girl with bright pink hair entered the cabin and put her suitcase on the floor near the door.

"Hey!" she said, mostly to Christine.

"Hey, Randi! How's it going? It's nice to see you!" Christine jumped up from the bed and gave her a quick hug.

"Good. What cabin are you in?"

"This one!"

Randi frowned. "Aw, shit. Your voice? Again?"

Christine faked an evil laugh. "Every morning!" she grinned. Then she motioned to me. "Hey, this is Brynn. She's in our cabin, too."

"Hi, Brynn! I'm warning you now. Christine likes to wake us up every morning by singing . . . and she's horrible!"

"Wait a minute! What kind of welcome is this? I haven't seen you since last summer. How do you know I didn't take voice lessons this year?"

"Because I know you," Randi replied with a grin. I could tell that she spoke the truth; I figured Christine and Randi must've been sharing camp sessions for a few years.

Christine rolled her eyes and shook her head, signaling to me that she clearly didn't think her singing was *that* bad. She turned back to Randi, who had grabbed her suitcase and placed it on a bed at the front of the cabin.

"I like the new hair," Christine told her. "Very different from the black and blue stripes from last year. Brynn, I think your mom said you just dyed your hair last night again for camp. Do you ever do anything crazy, or do you just stick to blonde?"

Since the question demanded more than a yes/no answer, I hit the switch near my head and started to type. As I hit my head switch to start typing my answer, I realized how nervous I was. I wanted to get my answer out right away so Randi wouldn't think I was ignoring them. Then I realized how lame I probably looked beating my head against the switch as fast as I could. This was ridiculous. I was at camp. I should have expected campers and counselors would talk to me. It was what I came here for. Why was I being like this?

A few minutes later, I hit SPEAK to say what I had typed. "Stick to shades of blonde."

"That's cool. I like it!"

". . . Thanks," I responded as Randi took a seat next to her on the bed.

"Brynn uses this computer to talk to us," Christine explained. "But she can't really see it outside because of the glare from the sun, so if you're ever outside and she doesn't answer your questions, that's why."

I smiled and nodded. This was one of the things I was most anxious about and Christine was taking care of it right off the bat. She was awesome.

"Oh, cool. I'll try to remember that," Randi said.

"Thanks," I said again, this time to Randi. She didn't even seem to notice my manic typing episode.

"So, Randi, are you still with Jonah?" Christine asked.

"Yep."

"Are you serious? That's amazing! You started dating my first year."

Randi shrugged. "I'm just nice enough to put up with his crap for this long."

"Oh, is that it? Is he coming?"

"Unless he changed his mind between this morning and now."

Just then, the door to the cabin opened again and a girl and her father walked in with a large suitcase. Christine went over and introduced herself. To my surprise, Randi stayed put.

"So, how do you like camp so far? I know you just got here, but Christine must've given you the tour, right?"

I was actually caught off guard. Randi asked me a question. She wanted to talk to me. The last person my age who I had a conversation with was Meg, and that was months ago. My body tensed up a little. I hoped again it wasn't obvious I was nervous. Even though it took me about a minute to get the three little words out, it felt more like an hour. "I . . . like . . . it." SPEAK.

"Cool. How old are you?"

I started hitting my switch again. Luckily, I had that answer already programmed in so I didn't have to make her wait that long. I flipped to my About Me screen. I went straight over to the button labeled AGE.

SPEAK. "I'm seventeen."

"Oh, cool. I'll be seventeen next week!"

I smiled at her.

We were suddenly interrupted when a girl screamed her name and ran up to her. She wore a green sundress and a crap-load of makeup. Her light brown, highlighted hair was parted to the side and she didn't look like she was coming to camp for two weeks. And she definitely didn't look like she would be friends with a very pink-haired girl.

"Raaaaaaaaaaaaaaaaaaandi!" she squealed as she threw her arms around the other girl.

Randi just stood there with her arms straight down at her side, looking like she didn't know what was going on. "Hi?"

The girl pulled back and tucked her hair behind her ear. "I missed you."

"You just saw me last week."

"I know. I missed you anyway."

Randi rolled her eyes. "Brynn, this is my ever-so-obnoxious best friend, Carly."

"Oh, hey, Brynn! What's up?" Carly asked

I smiled at her, hit my talking switch, and flipped to my keyboard screen. Carly looked confused.

"Brynn talks with that computer thing. It's cool," Randi told her.

"Oh."

After a two minute pause in which Carly uncomfortably struck up a conversation about how she was just so bored on the ride there, I hit SPEAK. "Not much. How are you?"

"That's so amazing! How does it work?"

Ugh! Not to be rude or anything, but I hated when people told me my TechnoTalk was amazing, especially when I was trying to have a regular conversation with them. In my mind, I wasn't really conscious of the computer that was in front of me, except for, of course, when people didn't know I talked with it and I found myself typing quickly, racing through the letters, numbers, and phrases on my screen as fast as I could. If I had something to say, I just typed it without really thinking about it.

It was just my voice. I don't tell them the way they talk is amazing. Then again, I could understand where they all were coming from. They probably had never met someone who used a communication device before. But still, I liked the normal conversation I had been having with Randi much better than the one I was going to have with Carly.

I went back to my About Me screen and selected the TECHNOTALK button.

SPEAK. "This is my TechnoTalk. I talk with it using the switch by my head. I spell out what I want to say."

"That's so amazing," Carly said again.

I half smiled and nodded. My question went unanswered.

"I need to go make my bed. Randi, come with me!"

"You wanna come over with us?" Randi motioned to the front of the cabin. "We don't bite, I promise."

I laughed as I turned my chair on. Even though I didn't know how I felt about Carly yet, I could tell I was really going to get along with Randi. And I was pretty sure she wasn't talking to me for the same reasons Meg did. Then again, I didn't realize at first that Meg had no intentions of actually being my friend.

You can't think about Meg. You are at camp now. This is why you came; to not sit at home, think about her or Dave, and make yourself go into an all-out freak out session! Just go hang out with them, and everything will probably be okay.

I drove over to where Randi and Carly shared a bunk. They started to pull their bedding out of their bags.

"So," Randi grabbed a green sheet, "why did you come here?"

There was that question again. I decided that, realistically, it would take me an hour to type out the real answer. I opted for the two-minute one. SPEAK. "To get away."

"Join the club. I think that's why everybody comes here."

"Randi!" Carly exclaimed, holding up a bright pink dress. "What do you think? I got it yesterday. Isn't it so adorable?"

"Why do you get dressed up for camp? I will never understand this. It's *camp*."

"Beeeeecauuuse! I have to look cute!"

Randi tilted her head in mock confusion. "You really think people, especially people here, are gonna care if you wear a regular comfy tank top and shorts instead of one of your girly look-at-me-I'm-so-cute dresses? Look at me and Brynn! She's not all dressed up and neither am I. We're just wearing regular tank tops and regular pairs of shorts."

"I don't know!" Carly looked frazzled for a second. "Gabe might care!"

"Seriously? You seriously just said that?"

"Hey! Shut up! You already have a boyfriend, so you don't need to worry what you look like."

Randi put a hand on her hip. "Do you really think I would care if I didn't have a boyfriend? Brynn. Tell me something. Did you bring any dresses to camp?"

I thought for a second and then shook my head.

"How about makeup?"

Even though I put on a little this morning, I immediately shook my head. When we were unpacking with Christine, I realized I forgot to tell my mom to put my makeup bag in my suitcase.

"See?" Randi turned back to Carly "Why can't you be more like Brynn? She's smart."

My smile faded away. I wasn't going to tell them that I specifically picked out each outfit I packed so that I could be like any other girl.

Before Carly could come back with a comment, Christine walked towards us. "Hey, Brynn, I see you met someone else."

I nodded and grinned.

"That's cool. Well, it's time for the first night cookout-slash-bonfire, so why don't we all head down to the amphitheater?"

Randi put her suitcase under her bed and stood up. "Do you wanna sit with us at the cookout?"

My face probably looked as if she just asked me to marry her. It had been so long since anybody had asked to do something with me other than physically help me, so I didn't know how to react at first. I slowly nodded and felt my cheeks getting red.

"Are you sure? Because . . . it just seemed like you didn't want to?"

I laughed, shook my head, and then nodded. *Smooth. Real smooth.*

Randi paused. "Alright then. I'm just gonna take that as yes unless you specify otherwise."

I nodded for a final time, hoping to redeem myself.

"I think that's a definite yes this time," Christine confirmed.

I smiled.

"Kay. I'm hungry. Let's go eat."

By this time, all the beds were made and suitcases were spread everywhere, but nobody was left in the cabin. I turned my chair on and led the way out the door, pausing once we were outside when I realized I wasn't quite sure where we were going. Christine took the lead.

"So, Carly," Christine began, "I already caught up with Randi. How was your year?"

"It was good! I missed you!"

"Missed you, too. Who's the new guy this week?"

"Oh my God, you know Gabe?"

"Gabe . . . from last year? Buzzed head? Big muscles?"

Carly jumped up and down. "Yes! He Facebooked me!"

"And?"

"We have been talking!"

"And?"

"I like him!"

"Way to be not obvious," Randi murmured.

"Really?" Christine pretended to be surprised. "You like him? Could never have guessed."

"Shut up, you guys!" Carly whined, but I could tell she loved the attention.

Christine chuckled. "Is he coming?"

"Yes! He's gonna meet me at the cookout. Do I look okay?"

"No," Randi said as bluntly as she could. "You look like shit."

"Randi!" Christine exclaimed.

A laugh came out of me before I could stop it.

"Brynn! You guys are so mean! Car, don't listen to them. You look gorgeous," Christine assured her.

"Thank you, Christine! At least someone is honest with me."

After walking for what felt like a mile, we finally got to the amphitheater. It was basically stadium seating, only with wooden benches. We all decided to sit at the top since, obviously, stairs were not my friends. The sight of the bonfire down in front made me smile. This was ridiculously cheesy, but bonfires on TV or in movies always gave me a sense of togetherness . . . like people bonded at bonfires. I laughed to myself. No wonder I didn't have any friends. I was so lame, a bunch of ninety year old men would think I needed a social life.

"I'm going to go get us some food," Christine said. "Brynn, what will it be? Do you like hamburgers?"

I shook my head.

"Hotdogs?"

I nodded.

"Do you want anything on it?"

Head shake.

"Kay. Want anything else? Baked beans? Watermelon? Macaroni salad?"

Head shake.

"No? Boy, your mom was right. You are picky. You want two hotdogs?"

Head nod.

"Okay. What do you want to drink? We have water and camp juice. I don't suggest camp juice. It's basically sugar water with blue food coloring."

Head nod.

"Water?"

Head nod.

"Alright. Will you be cool by yourself if we all go up?"

Head nod.

"Rock on. Hey, girls. Come get your food!"

Carly and Randi followed Christine over to the food table and jumped in the back of the line. I was left to simply people watch. I noticed that there were only about sixty total campers; so many new faces and stories. I looked forward to becoming close with a few of them. I knew it wasn't realistic to expect to leave here with sixty new best friends, but maybe a handful of close friends and a number of acquaintances would help me get back on my feet and feel . . . normal . . . again. I looked forward to meeting the other girls in my cabin at some point that evening. I hoped we'd all get along as well as Randi and I seemed to be so far.

I noticed that many of the counselors were talking to campers like they were long-lost siblings. A kid in front was talking to three blonde girls, looking like he wanted to impress them. Who was Gabe? Who was Jonah? Who would I be friends with? Who was wondering who the girl in the chair was?

"Yo!" Randi was back in less than five minutes and had startled me. "You okay there? You looked like you were in a daze."

I nodded. She sat back down with her plate on her lap. She just had baked beans and watermelon. Vegetarian? Or just not hungry? A moment later, Carly followed. And then Christine.

"I got you a chocolate chip cookie, too. I figured if you don't want it, I'll eat it."

I chuckled.

"I have to be on your right side to feed you, right?"

I shook my head.

"Left?"

I nodded.

Christine took a seat on the bench beside me. "I'm sorry, Brynn. I promise we will get the hang of this."

I nodded to say everything was all good.

"Now, this should be interesting. Let's see how much I can suck at feeding you."

Nervously, I opened my mouth. I wasn't really nervous about Christine. I was used to having new aides at school help me. I just didn't particularly like eating in front of people I didn't know very well because I knew it could be gross at times. Fortunately, Christine was pretty much blocking the girls' views.

She put the cup and a napkin to my mouth, just like my mom showed her. I took a big gulp and managed to get only a few drops on my shirt. Success! She then held out the hotdog. I leaned forward, took a bite, leaned back, pushed it to the side of my mouth, chewed, and swallowed.

"Hey! Not bad! Want another bite?"

Christine held out the hotdog and I repeated the process two more times while she ate her hamburger with her other hand. Multitasking. Nice. I was halfway done with my hotdog when a guy in a green sleeveless shirt approached us. He held an old water bottle filled with what seemed to be red juice.

"Hey, baby!" He sat down next to Randi and kissed her.

"Hi," Randi greeted him. "I want you to meet my new friend, Brynn. Brynn, this is my pain-in-the-ass boyfriend, Jonah."

I swallowed my last bite of my first hotdog and smiled.

"Okay," Jonah said. "So, anyway. You didn't call me back. I wanted you to come out and meet me."

He totally ignored me.

Carly and Christine stared at him. I was used to people doing stuff like that, so it didn't really bother me. Well, maybe it did. But I wasn't about to freak out on somebody I just met. After all, his girlfriend thought we were becoming friends. Actually, we were friends. That was what she just said, wasn't it? She would probably never talk to me again if I told him off.

Before Christine could interject, Randi smacked his arm. "What the hell kind of greeting was that?" Then she turned to me. "I'm sorry; my boyfriend can be a real ass sometimes. Don't be offended by anything he says or does. He doesn't know how to think."

I forgivingly nodded.

Before there could be an awkward moment of silence, an older gentleman went in front of the fire and waited for everyone to quiet down. He wore a dark green Camp Lakewood polo with khaki pants. A walkie-talkie was attached to his belt. The chatter quickly died down and he began to speak as everybody filled their stomachs.

"Hello! Welcome to camp! My name is Jim Thomas. People call me JT for short. I'm the new director of this camp. I'm so glad that I am able to be here with you this summer. It is my understanding that some of you have been coming here for years, while others are new—just like me. I'm so glad Camp Lakewood continues to give you the opportunity to be able to come out here, take it easy, and form new friendships."

A few people cheered, but most clapped politely. JT was brand new, and he called the shots now. They were all watching him carefully, wondering what way the captain would steer his new ship.

"Because some of you all are probably pros at this by now, and I assume all of you have a bit of common sense, I take it you know the ropes—or at least have an idea of them. If you have a problem at camp, you come to me. If you break one of the three rules we have, I come to you. Those rules are: no sex, drugs, or alcohol; have respect for one another; and listen to your counselor. Please don't do anything stupid. Think before you act."

He paused, his eyes roaming up and down the rows of teens to enforce his point, and then started again.

"Now, because I am new, I want to try something that might be a little different for you guys. I want to have the theme of this camp be DAISY. It stands for Discovering and Accepting Individuality in Society and Yourself. In my experience with teenagers, they don't have enough appreciation for people's uniqueness. Throughout the two weeks you are at camp, you will be participating in team missions, cabin discussions, and individual activities, all to help you with DAISY. Hopefully when you leave camp, you will have a new respect for people you consider to be different, weird, freaks, whatever."

I could feel the confusion in the crowd.

"I know this seems kind of odd to be reinforcing at your age—after all, these are all things you should know by now, right? And truth be told, this is really something I developed for the younger campers in the later summer sessions; however, I don't see why touching on these subjects can't occur in this session, too. It never hurts to try to understand your neighbors a bit more and everyone likes to be and feel respected . . ."

He drifted off, aware that a few of the campers were rolling their eyes and a few were groaning obnoxiously (obviously testing their new director), growing more and more disinterested.

"Alright, I'll come down off my soapbox. Enough about that—for now. As you may know, at the end of camp we put on a talent show. You will be doing one act with the group I assign you and you can do one with your friends or whoever you'd like to team up with. Your parents and people outside of camp will be here watching, so you better make the acts good. Now, as I understand, there are two groups you can join to help get ready for the show. They are Stage Stuff and People Prep. There will be counselors coming around to ask you what you want to do. Once you are signed up for a group, you can head back to your cabins. And that is it for me. Have fun, be good, and see you later!"

JT went off to the side as we all cheered and clapped. A moment later, he turned around and walked back in front. Everybody went quiet again.

"I'm sorry, I forgot to mention: When the counselors come around to ask you what group you want to be in, they are going to give you a little daisy. On it, I want you to write down a goal you would like to achieve while you are at camp this year. You are then going to hang it somewhere in your cabin where you will see every day. If you don't have a goal, that's okay. You can take a day or two to think about it. Got it? Good. Go for it!"

JT went off to the side—for good this time. I started on my cookie as I pondered what my goal was going to be. Why did I come to camp? To make friends for one thing, but that was a lame goal, and it seemed like I was already accomplishing that. Maybe. What else could it be? I took another bite of my cookie when a male counselor walked up to us with a clipboard. He wore a nametag that read MIKE.

"Daisies! Daisies! Get your daisies! Who wants daisies? I have daisies!"

"You're so gay," Jonah said.

"Hey! Watch it! I do not think that statement is DAISY appropriate."

"Your mom isn't DAISY appropriate."

"You're starting early this year, I see," the counselor said, his tone flat and unimpressed.

Christine sighed. "You have no idea."

Mike handed a paper daisy to Carly, Randi, and Jonah and then gave a pen to Carly so she could pass it around when she was done. He tried to give me my daisy. I looked at Christine.

"I'll take Brynn's," she said and reached out to Mike.

"What's up, Brynn?" Mike asked as he handed Christine my daisy.

I smiled.

"Do you know if you wanna do People Prep or Stage Stuff?"

Unsure of what to do (or what I could do, for that matter), I turned to Christine.

"Do you like to paint?" she asked.

I held back a laugh and shook my head. Was she serious?

"Do you want to figure out a way to paint?"

She was serious. I thought for a second. That could be fun. Sure. Why not? I nodded.

"Stage Stuff it is then."

Mike signed everyone up for a talent show group and moved on to campers sitting a few rows away from us. Randi and Carly said they "owned" People Prep last year and that it was too much fun to not do it again. Because he said Stage Stuff needed his amazing artistic ability, Jonah would be joining me. Great. I took another bite of my cookie just as Carly jumped up and ran to a guy as he approached our group.

"Tommy! You're here!" She threw her arms around him. "Hi! I missed you!"

He patted her back in return. "Hey, Carly."

"What's up, my man?" Jonah high-fived him. "Where's Jenn? Is she coming?"

Tommy paused and shoved his hands in his pockets. "I don't know."

"Uh oh. Did you guys split?"

"Yeah. We kinda sorta did."

"Oh," Carly sat back down. "She didn't tell us that."

Tommy looked confused. "Don't you guys talk?"

"Of course we do, and she didn't say anything about it. Actually, she was really looking forward to seeing you."

"Awkward monkey!" Randi shouted.

Jonah turned to her. "Isn't it awkward turtle?"

"Yes, but I like monkeys better," Randi said, matter-of-factly. She turned to me and made yet another introduction on my behalf. "Brynn, this is Tommy. Tommy, Brynn."

"Hi, Brynn." His brown eyes met mine—something that happened very rarely with people, and even more rarely with guys.

I swallowed the last of my cookie and hoped that I didn't have chocolate running down my face. I smiled at him, and this time hoped that I didn't have chocolate stuck in my teeth. Tommy was cute. He wore a plain black T-shirt and khaki pants. Unlike Jonah, who had blonde spiky hair, Tommy's black hair was wavy and on its way to becoming a fro. And unlike Jonah, who looked like the gym was his favorite place to be, Tommy was thin, but not the emo-skinny-jeans type thin.

"Brynn talks with the computer in front of her," Christine explained, "but she can't see the screen when she's outside."

"I see," he simply said, peering down at my computer screen briefly.

"Hey," Randi whispered, "here comes Jenn."

"Shit. Crap. I really have to—"

"I have wanted to do this for weeks now," said a voice I didn't recognize. A tiny girl wearing basically the same outfit as me came into my view and put her arms around Tommy.

The whole time she hugged him, Tommy looked as if he didn't have the slightest clue as to what was happening to him. She finally let go and he slowly stepped away from her.

Jenn tucked a strand of blonde hair behind her ear. "So, how is everybody?"

"Good," everyone replied, trying to ignore the awkwardness Jenn brought to the table. It was hard to hide, though. Confusion was obvious in everyone's tone. We all watched as Jenn reached for Tommy's hand. Not only did he pull back, but he slowly turned around and walked away without saying another word.

"Jenn . . ." Randi said slowly, as though she didn't know if she was talking to a sane person. "Do you want to tell us what's going on?"

Jenn crossed her arms and huffed. "I don't know what the hell his problem is. I don't get why he's acting like this."

"Why didn't you tell us he wanted to break up?"

"Because I really don't think he does. I think he just needs some time."

Carly sighed. "Guys suck."

"I know, right!" Jenn agreed. Then she quickly added, "Except for you, Jonah. Why can't they all be like you?"

"Maybe because I'm awesome?"

Randi rolled her eyes and Jenn took a seat next to Carly. "You are awesome," she told Jonah. She pointed to the bottle in his lap. "Hey, can I have a sip of that?"

Jonah handed her his bottle of red juice. She took a big swig and gave it back to him.

"So, how is everyone doing?" she asked, nonchalantly.

Chapter Five

*A*fter the group finished their conversation with Jenn about her breakup with Tommy and had determined that she really was okay (though possibly in denial . . . or maybe a bit mental), Christine and Randi decided that I needed an official tour of Camp Lakewood. Christine had already shown me around with my mom earlier that day, but this tour would be different—Randi promised to show me all the cool spots where everyone hung out when we weren't doing camp activities. Carly didn't want to come because she was going to hunt down her camp crush of the year, which was apparently something she'd done every summer since she was twelve. Even though Randi practically begged Jonah to come along, too, he said he had to see more of his "peeps." I felt bad for Randi, but I couldn't help but feel relieved that he wasn't coming. I didn't want to judge him from our first interaction, but I already had a feeling we were *not* going to get along.

We started with the dining hall, which Christine had already showed me. Nothing too special there; we would eat, we would talk, we would complete our activities there if it happened to be raining. We moved on to the pool, which mysteriously turned the green color of the Wicked Witch the year before, Randi informed me. I detected a hint of pride in her tone and wondered if she had something to do with the prank or if she knew who did. I made a mental note to ask her later when Christine wasn't around. We then saw what they told me was the basketball court, but honestly? The area just looked like whoever built the camp wanted to get rid of the left over cement in a random spot in the woods. If I played basketball, I would've been highly disappointed. We ended the tour at Camp Lakewood's namesake: the lake.

"You know, this lake has magical powers," Randi began.

I stopped myself from laughing. Not only did it seem like a very un-Randi thing to say, but the lake looked anything *but* magical. It wasn't that big, and it had some type of mossy fungi thing growing around the edges. Although it wasn't as green as I imagined the pool had become last year, it looked like its crystal clear–water days were long gone. It also had a dock that I was certain had a weight limit of one person, otherwise the whole thing would probably collapse.

Christine seemed to pick up on my skepticism. "Randi's right. The lake is magical. Campers take one or two trips down to the edge of the water with the person they like, and all of a sudden, they are an 'official' couple. There must be something in the water."

I gave her an I'll-take-your-word-for-it nod. If only I'd known about this six months ago . . .

"Speaking of liking people," Randi turned to me. "Do you have a boyfriend?"

I probably would if fricking Meg didn't steal him away from me!

Suppressing a frown, I shook my head. *On second thought, no, I probably wouldn't have a boyfriend . . . if they pretty much looked at me like everyone else did at my school. Invisible.*

Despite thinking about Meg and Dave, I found myself wanting to hug Randi. Did I have a boyfriend? That was the first time someone my age asked me that question. Actually, that was the first time anyone asked me that question. Did everyone just assume that nobody would want to be with me, or were they so distracted by my chair and TechnoTalk that they didn't think to ask me regular girl questions?

"Do you have a girlfriend?"

"Randi!" Christine exclaimed.

"Hey, ya never know," Randi said with a shrug and a smile.

I chuckled and shook my head again. Who knew I would be asked both of those questions for the first time within the same five-second period?

"Why don't we head back to the cabin?" Christine suggested. "I'm sure you have a lot to say with not being able to talk for the last hour. Although, it's starting to get dark. Can you see your screen now?"

I nodded.

"Oh, okay. Well, do you want to go back to the cabin?"

I shrugged.

"Whatever you two want to do is cool with me. We could stay down here and soak up the lake's magical powers."

"Ah, let's save the magic for when we really need it. I say we are going back to the cabin," Randi said, making the decision for the three of us. The more time I spent with her, the more I liked her. She seemed like a really strong, funny, cool, independent girl—the type of girl I hadn't seen nearly enough of in all of high school. If my mom was here, she would probably even get her to help me dye my hair.

As we made our way up the hill, Jenn and another girl were coming down. They saw Randi and picked up their speed.

"Hey," Jenn scooped up her hair off of her neck, "did Tom say anything about me when you were talking to him?"

"Just that you broke up," Randi replied, obviously not wanting to be pulled into the drama.

"Anything else?"

"Not really. What did he say to you when he told you he wanted to break up?"

"He told me he wanted to, but I was like 'Can't we wait and talk it out at camp?' I just tried to go up to him again, but he keeps walking away. I don't know what to do."

"When did he tell you that he wanted to?" Randi inquired.

"Like two months ago."

"Why didn't you tell us?"

"Because . . ." Jenn let her hair go. "I don't know. But, I think we're gonna go back to our cabin. You can come if you want." The invitation was clearly only to Randi; Jenn had barely noticed my presence—or Christine's, for that matter—during the conversation.

"Okay. Just hang in there. Give him time. I'm going to my cabin with Brynn," she said. "I introduced you two after we finished eating, right?" she asked.

I smiled and nodded.

Jenn nodded at me, simply to acknowledge my presence, and looked back at Randi. "Have fun. I can't wait for the night hike. Can we do it any earlier . . . and can we not invite Tom?"

"Maaaaybe," Randi slyly replied.

Jenn smirked. "See ya."

We parted, each small group heading in our opposite directions.

"Looks like the drama has already begun," Christine whispered.

Randi sighed. "It's going to be one hell of a summer."

The cabin was just how we left it; empty, with suitcases sprawled everywhere. Randi and Christine sat on my bunk again and I pulled up in front of them. For a moment, I wished this was how it was going to be for the rest of camp; it wasn't that I thought I wouldn't like any of the other campers (well, Carly and Jonah were questionable). It just already felt like I bonded with Randi and Christine and I didn't want to throw anyone new into the mix who might ruin that.

"So, how was your year, Randi?" Christine asked. "How did you do in school?"

"Eh, it was okay, I guess. Let's just say I can move on to the twelfth grade."

"Moving on to the twelfth grade is definitely a good thing."

"Yeah. What about you, Brynn? How do you like school?"

I automatically squinted my face up the way I did when I didn't like something. My mom always found it funny I could do this, but yet I didn't have enough coordination to point my finger at something.

"That good?" Randi asked.

"Is it just because it's school?" Christine asked.

Not exactly. I did pretty well in school. Actually, I made it a point to do pretty well in school, being that just about everyone thought I had a cognitive disability. Getting A's or B's in almost every class was a helpful fact whenever this would come up.

I hit my talking switch to start typing.

"Can we watch what you're doing? Randi hasn't seen how it works, and I just like to watch because I think it's cool."

I nodded. They stood and went behind me. Christine repeated my mom's explanation.

"People . . . my . . . age . . ." I typed word by word, "don't . . . really . . . talk . . . to . . . me . . . so . . . for . . . me . . . school . . . is . . . kinda . . . like—"

"A hell hole?" Randi finished my sentence.

I nodded a big nod. *Exactly!*

"Yeah, I know what you mean. I don't really talk to anyone from my school, either, because most of my friends are here. It kinda sucks," Randi admitted.

I kept typing.

"And . . . I . . . have . . . to . . . have . . . my . . . aide . . . with . . . me . . . all . . . day . . . every . . . day. I . . . think . . . that . . . is . . . why . . . people . . . don't . . . talk . . . to . . . me. I . . . hate . . . being . . . around . . . an . . . adult . . . all . . . day. How . . . can . . . I . . . expect . . . other . . . people . . . to . . . want . . . to?"

They were still standing behind me reading my screen, so I didn't have to hit SPEAK.

"Hey," Christine sat back down on the bed, "you two are at camp now, so it's all good. And Brynn, I'm sure the kids here will talk to you. Randi is already talking to you. And, I'm twenty; I don't know if you consider me an adult, but if you want me to, I can try to just let you be whenever you don't really need help. Would you want to do that?"

I couldn't stop myself. I squealed. Could she really do that? Would Camp Lakewood be okay with it?

Before I had time to thank her, Carly burst through the door and ran back to us, grinning from ear to ear.

"Oh my God, guys! Guess what!"

"What?" Christine smiled, as if she knew what Carly was about to say.

"We were talking for this whole time! And he wants to go down to the lake as soon as we get more free time."

"Cool!"

Randi didn't share the excitement. "He probably just wants to push you in, because he probably thinks you are annoying."

"Randi," Carly turned serious, "you're my best friend. Why can't you at least pretend to be excited for me?"

"I am. I just think you need to be aware of the possibility he might want to throw you in the lake." Randi shrugged and leaned back on the bed next to Christine.

Christine jumped in before it went any further, though. "Hey, do either of you have a goal for camp?"

"I do!" Carly waved her daisy. "My goal is to get Gabe to go out with me."

"You would make that your goal," Randi rolled her eyes. "You're going to go real far in life. And," she turned to Christine, "what the hell is up with this DAISY thing? We never had to do anything like this before."

"You heard JT," Christine said. "He's new and just wants to try something new."

"He's old and just doesn't know what he's doing," Carly argued. "What does it stand for again?"

"DAISY? Discovering and Accepting Individuality in Society and Yourself," Christine said. She was clearly well-versed in DAISY speak. I imagined all the counselors understood what JT was trying to do, even if the campers didn't.

"That's not lame at all," Randi said, rolling her eyes. "Brynn, what's your goal?"

I shrugged. I hadn't thought anymore about it. What was my goal going to be?

Christine pulled my daisy out of her pocket and placed it on my nightstand beside my bed. "That's okay. Like JT said, you can take a few days to decide. I will keep your daisy right here, and when you know what your goal is, you can just tell us. Cool?"

I smiled.

"Alright, why don't we get ready for bed? Brynn, do you have to go to the bathroom?"

I nodded. I hadn't gone since my mom showed Christine how to help me and realized I really did have to go.

"Kay. Do you want to take your pajamas down so you can change?"

I nodded again. *Did anyone change in here?* I wondered.

"Do you care what you wear to bed?"

I shook my head and shrugged.

"My kind of girl!" She stood up and pulled out an old t-shirt and blue boxers. "Is this okay?"

I gave her a nod.

"Do you want to take a shower tonight?"

I paused for a second. I didn't like to go a night without showering, but I decided to let Christine just get the basics down first. That adventure could be for the next night. And besides, it was camp. Wasn't it acceptable to be sweaty and gross once in a while?

Randi and Carly went over to their bunk to gather their stuff just as Evelyn entered the cabin. She said hi to the others and then strolled toward Christine and me.

"Hey, Brynn," she said. "I'm sorry I haven't gotten the chance to really talk to you yet; things have been crazy. Is Christine being good to you?"

I smiled and nodded.

"What are you talking about?" Christine protested. "I'm always good to everyone."

"Sure you are," Evelyn said sarcastically, but hit Christine in the shoulder playfully. "Hey, did you tell Brynn what we were thinking about doing?"

"No, we haven't gotten that far."

My ears perked up. I was immediately curious.

"Okay. So, right before lights out, we are just going to chat and catch up, and I was wondering if you and Christine would tell the other girls in our cabin—" She paused and looked around, eyes furrowed at the otherwise empty cabin. "Huh. Guess every-one else will be here soon . . . Anyway, I was thinking you could show the others how your TechnoTalk works. I'm sure the other girls have never seen anything like it, and I really want them to understand how to communicate with you from the beginning. Would that be okay?"

I slowly nodded. I didn't realize my counselor and I would be explaining how I talked to everyone I met at camp.

"Are you sure this would be okay? You could tell me if you really don't want to do it," Evelyn said. She seemed sincere; she really wouldn't make me do it.

I nodded again.

"Alright. Cool. Thanks, Brynn. I really think this will help everyone, and it will be good for DAISY."

My smile faded a bit as Evelyn walked away. *It will be good for DAISY?*

"You know," Christine started, sensing my sudden discomfort, "I think this is a good thing. You said people your age don't really talk to you. They are probably just unsure of the process, and I think by doing this, you will help them be not so unsure of how to approach you."

I slowly agreed. Maybe nobody talked to me at school because nobody realized I was able to actually have conversations and I had just been automatically assuming all these years that they did.

"Ready to go down?"

Christine and I met Randi and Carly at the door to the cabin and we headed down to the bathrooms. The sun had set and the stars were out, though they were a bit hidden by the wisps of clouds scattered across the open sky. The temperature had dropped quite a bit, but the humidity was still intense.

Luckily, there were only a few other girls in the bathroom. Christine and I made our way over to the last stall. As she wheeled the lift over to me, I felt my body tense up. I was getting nervous. *Oh, no. No. No.* I took a deep breath, trying to keep control. *Please, not now.*

She knows what she's doing. She did it perfectly fine when Mom was here. You have nothing to be nervous about. Damn it. You're only going to make the situation worse if you don't calm down.

One thing with having cerebral palsy and not having muscle control was . . . I didn't have muscle control. This meant that my body wouldn't listen if I wanted to raise my hand. This also meant if my arm wanted to fly up in the air, I couldn't tell it not to. I had what I liked to call "CP moments," where my body just took on a mind of its own. CP moments usually came whenever I was really excited, or really nervous, or really cold.

"So," Christine reviewed the steps, "I take your TechnoTalk off, undo your seatbelt and everything, strap your feet and arms into the lift, and wheel you to the toilet? Is that right?"

I hit my typing switch. I had to warn her, but I didn't know how. I motioned for her to read my screen so I wouldn't have to say it aloud. "I'm . . . sorry . . . I'm . . . really . . . nervous . . . if . . . I . . . hit . . . you . . . I . . . don't . . . mean . . . to."

"Oh, it's all good. You don't have to be sorry. Or nervous. I totally understand," she smiled. "Are you ready?"

I nodded even though I didn't trust myself. I figured I wasn't going to get any more relaxed. Why did this have to happen on our first time? Why didn't my mom and I tell her more about my CP moments?

Christine wheeled the lift in front of me. She took my TechnoTalk off and laid it on the floor. As soon as she unstrapped my feet, my right leg jerked forward, sending the lift crashing into the wall. I felt a surge of heat spread across my face. *Crap.*

"Are you okay?" Christine asked with a little confusion.

I barely nodded. I wanted to dig a ten-foot hole, crawl in it, and die.

"Just nervous?"

I frowned.

"It's cool, I promise."

"Do you guys need help over here?" Randi came from behind me.

"Ummmmm," Christine hesitated, "yes. Could you hold the lift in place? Brynn, is that okay?"

I forced myself to nod. I didn't want Christine to have to have Randi help. I didn't want Randi to have to help. Why couldn't my body cooperate just this once? Would they not like me after this? Would Randi not want to hang out anymore? Would Christine tell the camp she couldn't help me and that I needed to go home?

Christine wheeled the lift in front of me again and Randi put both of her hands on it. Somehow (I would never know how) I managed to calm down enough for Christine to get both of my legs strapped into the lift. Alright. Alright! Maybe I would be able to do this. She then unbuckled my seatbelt and pulled my arms out of my armbands, bringing them to the straps. My right arm went in without a problem. Unfortunately, my left arm not so much. It decided it wanted to go on a flying adventure, hitting Christine in the mouth on the way. I felt my stomach drop. *Shit!*

Chapter Six

Rise and shine and give God your glory, glory . . .

What was going on? Was that singing? Who was singing? Why were they clapping? It was the middle of the night, wasn't it? I forced my eyes to open. My bed was right next to a wooden wall. My house was not made out of wood. I blinked. Where was I?

Children of the Lord!

I slowly, very slowly turned my head. Christine was walking toward me. I blinked again. Everything was coming back to me. I was not at my house. I was in a little wood cabin . . . at camp . . . where I made an idiot out of myself the night before. I closed my eyes tight. I wanted to go back to sleep and forget everything again.

"Good morning, Brynn." Christine bent down and gently pulled my covers off. "How's it going?"

I opened my eyes and tried to smile.

"Still tired?"

I attempted a head nod, but it was more of an eye nod.

"Yeah, this whole 7:30-mornings-in-the-summer doesn't work for me, either. But hey, Randi said she would help us in the bathroom again, so is it cool if I put you in your chair now and we go down?"

I wasn't thrilled with possibly repeating last night's episode, but I agreed to go. What else was I going to do?

Christine rolled me over onto my back and, just like my mom had explained, she scooped me up like she would carry a baby and lifted me to my chair. She buckled my seatbelt, slid my arms in the bands, and strapped my feet down. She then turned my TechnoTalk on and put it on my chair.

"That was smooth. I have to say, you're very light."

Still half asleep, I gave her my thank-you smile.

"What do you want to wear?" Christine reached for my clothes. "Your mom mentioned that you like to wear a lot of tank tops. Is that okay?"

I nodded.

"It looks like you have every color of the rainbow, and then some. Do you have a preference?"

I shrugged.

"How about pink? Pink is my favorite color."

Pink it was.

"Shorts? All I see are jean shorts."

Right.

"Do you have a favorite pair?"

I shook my head. I liked all the clothes I brought, so I really didn't care what I wore when. I'd chosen my clothes carefully while my mom was packing, so I was pretty sure that whatever Christine pulled out would make me look cute.

"Shoes. Your blue ones, which I want to steal. Socks. Bra. Brush. Toothbrush. Toothpaste. Deodorant. Anything else?"

I shook my head. That was everything.

"Okay." Christine put everything in the bag on the back of my chair and smiled at something over my shoulder. "Here comes Randi."

"Hi," Randi said, rubbing her eyes awake.

I jumped at the opportunity and started typing. "Hey . . . I'm . . . sorry . . . again . . ." They waited patiently in front of me. "For . . . last . . . night . . . I . . . was . . . nervous." SPEAK.

"We know," Christine assured me. "It's really okay."

"I'm . . . just . . . embarrassed. I . . . don't . . . want . . . you . . . to . . . think . . . I'm . . . that . . . hard . . . to . . . help . . . all . . . of . . . the . . . time . . . because . . . I'm . . . not." SPEAK.

"We don't think that. And, even if that's how your body was all of the time, it would be okay. You have to do what you have to do, ya know?" Christine said. She turned to Randi, who nodded in agreement.

I nodded, too. "Are . . . you . . . still . . . cool . . . with . . . helping . . . me?" SPEAK.

"What? Of course I am. Brynn, last night you just startled me a little, because I wasn't expecting it. That's all. I'm not mad or anything. I actually really like being your counselor. So far." She smiled. "Randi is just going to help until you and I get the hang of this. Is that okay?"

"Are . . . you . . . okay . . . with . . . doing . . . this? I . . . never . . . meant . . . to . . . make . . . you . . . help . . . me." I hit SPEAK and looked at Randi so she knew I was directing the question at her.

"It's cool," Randi shrugged. "I don't care."

I couldn't help but frown. "I . . . bet . . . you . . . never . . . thought . . . you . . . would . . . be . . . helping . . . somebody . . . go . . . to . . . the . . . bathroom . . . this . . . summer . . . did . . . you?" SPEAK.

"No," Randi admitted with a small smile. "But that's why I love camp! You never know what adventures you're going to have." I briefly wondered if any of Randi's camp "adventures" came anywhere close to strapping someone to a refrigerator dolly . . . in the bathroom . . .

"Brynn," Christine started, "you really don't need to worry. I'm cool, Randi's cool, everything is cool. We promise. Sometime we need to tell you about Jamie."

Randi made a face. "Aw, yeah, Jamie blew chunks all over the cabin. That was so gross. Holding your lift is seriously not a problem, but if you puke on me or anywhere near me, it's all over, dude."

Despite how embarrassed I was, I chuckled.

"Oh, just stop freaking out about it," Randi insisted. "Everything's fine. Let's go down. I'm starving. And camp breakfast isn't as bad as you'd expect!"

I cleared my TechnoTalk screen and turned my chair on. Even though half of my hair wasn't in the ponytail anymore, I went outside with Christine and Randi. It wasn't even eight o'clock yet, but the air oozed into my body.

Unlike the night before, the bathroom was more crowded with girls getting ready. I sighed to myself as we made our way back to the accessible stall. Christine pulled the lift in front of my wheelchair and took my TechnoTalk off. She then unstrapped my feet. Randi wheeled the lift up to my chair. I felt my body starting to tense. *Here we go again. I should really look into purchasing a pair of boxing gloves for the sake of everyone around me.*

As Christine reached for my right foot, I suddenly remembered what I did the last time I had a CP moment with my mom. Why didn't I think of doing this the night before? Maybe because I was an idiot. Christine put my foot down on the footrest of the lift and I focused on my left foot. I may not have had enough control of my body to hold statue-like for five seconds, but while my right foot was being strapped down, I knew I could make my left leg push against my wheelchair so it diverted all of my energy for that one moment.

Since my right foot was already secured in the lift, I switched my focus to that leg and pulled it towards me, even though it couldn't really move that much. It was almost like (although I obviously never experienced this myself) when someone broke their ankle and they had to put all of their weight on the other foot to stand and walk and climb stairs. I smiled to myself. Be smarter than the CP. That was all I had to do. *Be smarter than the CP.*

Christine stood up and assured me that everything was going well this time. As she unbuckled my seatbelt, I pushed down with both of my legs so that my arms wouldn't give us any problems . . .

or punch Christine in the face again. I was in the lift. It didn't go flying across the room. I didn't give Christine a black eye. Randi didn't seem annoyed. We were good to go!

Because we didn't encounter any problems after I was actually in the lift the night before, Randi went on to do her thing and get ready for the day. Christine wheeled me to the toilet. I peed. She wheeled me back to my chair. I sat back down. She undid the straps and simply fastened my seatbelt since I was about to get dressed. I felt my body relax. Mission accomplished—without injury. *Success!*

Christine opened the door of the stall and I drove inside. She closed the door behind her.

"See? That wasn't so bad, was it?" She grabbed my clothes out of my bag. "We'll probably keep getting better and better at it."

"Hey, guys," Randi's voice came from up above. "I just talked to Jenn."

Christine bent me over to take my shirt off. "And?"

"She wants us to try to stay away from Tommy," Randi said from outside the stall. I could picture her rolling her eyes, understanding how stupid the request was.

"Okay?" Christine leaned me back and started to put my bra on while she talked to Randi through the door. "So, what do you want me to do about it? I'm a counselor. You know I can't do something like that. And Brynn is new. I don't think it's fair for you, or Jenn, to ask her to do that without even knowing him." She looked down at me. "Do you put your deodorant on after your tank top?"

I nodded.

Randi sighed loudly. "I know . . . I'm just telling you what she said, okay? Don't shoot the messenger."

Christine rolled her eyes. "Okay."

"Okay. I'm going to head to breakfast. I'll save you guys seats."

"Cool, see you in there." Christine pulled my tank top down. "Now deodorant?"

I nodded.

She lifted my arm and chuckled. "Whenever you have this many teenagers in one place, the drama is pretty much unavoidable. What did you think of Tommy the little that you met him? Did you like him?"

I shrugged and nodded. He was okay from what I could tell. It wasn't like we spent a ton of time together.

"He was in my group last year, and I think he's a pretty cool kid. I think you two would get along," she said, folding the t-shirt I wore to bed and setting it on the side. "It sucks that Jenn is going all crazy and asking everyone not to talk to him, but I think because you're new, you don't have to listen to what she's saying. But that's just my opinion. You do whatever you want."

I smiled and nodded.

Christine bent down and put my ankles straps on. I pushed myself up in my chair so she could pull my boxers down. I sat back down and she unstrapped my ankles. She replaced my boxers with the jean shorts, put my socks and shoes on, and strapped my feet in for good. I stood up in my chair again and she pulled my shorts up and buttoned them.

After she buckled my seatbelt and slid my arms in the armbands, I turned to face the mirror. Since it was already hot out, I nodded when Christine asked, "Ponytail?" I figured I would have more opportunities to let my hair down when it wouldn't increase the sweat factor. Christine helped me brush my teeth and then stuffed everything back in my bag. We stepped out of the stall and put my TechnoTalk on.

"Good morning, girls!" Evelyn was coming into the bathroom as we were going out. "How did you sleep?"

I nodded as my answer.

"That's good. Hey, I'm sorry if I made you feel like you had to talk about your computer last night. I could tell that you didn't really want to. I just thought it would be good for everybody, but I wasn't, by any means, trying to push you into it."

I shook my head, suddenly realizing how miserable I must've looked while I was exchanging introductions with the girls in my cabin—gathered in the cabin together for the first time, I was finally able to meet my other cabin mates, Heather, Maggie, and Sheila—and showing them how my chair and TechnoTalk worked the night before. In reality, I was feeling guilty and horrible for hitting Christine, but no one else knew that was why I was upset. They must've thought I was angry or annoyed. This wasn't the impression I wanted to give my cabin mates—or anyone at camp for that matter. *Crap.* I looked at Christine for help.

"Were you okay with it? Were you just preoccupied with what happened in the bathroom?" Christine asked.

I nodded a little more enthusiastically for this conversation; I hoped Evelyn would then understand that talking to the girls about my CP, and communication device, and wheelchair really wasn't why I was so upset.

"Yeah," Christine explained. "We had a bit of a mishap in the bathroom last night, and Brynn was really embarrassed about it, so that's why she seemed not really into it."

"Oh, okay. I just didn't want you to feel like I was making you do something you didn't want to do. Glad you were okay with it, after all! Sorry about the bathroom incident." Evelyn flung her tie-dyed bag over her shoulder. "I'm gonna go get dressed. I'll check ya later, Brynn."

Christine and I continued to walk through the dining hall, which had rows and rows of picnic tables and four big heavy-duty ceiling fans that probably required everyone to speak louder than they would've preferred. In the front of the dining hall was a buffet with all different kinds of breakfast foods.

"What will it be?" Christine asked.

I motioned to my choice.

"Rice Krispies?"

I nodded.

"Kay. What'd you want to drink? Milk or apple juice?"

I shook my head.

Christine paused for a second and then realized how to make the conversation a bit easier for both of us. "Wait, my bad. Do you want milk?"

I shook my head again.

"No. Do you want apple juice?"

I nodded.

"Yes. Okay. Sorry about that. I promise I'll get better."

I smiled. I was used to people not knowing what I was saying, so this wasn't a big deal at all.

"Why don't you find Randi and I'll grab everything?" Christine motioned to the tables with her head.

I followed her direction. Randi was at a table in the back of the dining hall where Carly was sitting with a boy whose head was shaved. Oh, he was *the* boy. I smiled to myself as I pulled up to the table, leaving room for Christine to sit next to me. A moment later, Jonah came and greeted Randi with an obnoxious kiss. Randi shoved his chest, but seemed to enjoy the attention nonetheless. Christine finally made it over with our food and sat down.

"Hi, Gabe! Long time no talk."

"Hey," Carly's crush replied, his voice deep.

"How are you?"

"Good."

Personality: nonexistent . . . . The guys at Camp Lakewood . . . Interesting . . .

"That's good," Christine said and then turned to me. "Ready to eat?"

I suddenly felt nervous. I really didn't want to eat in front of these people, even though I did it the night before with no problem. Maybe it was because I was so focused on Christine helping me eat for the first time? Or maybe because last night we were more spread out so I didn't feel like they were watching me? Maybe today I felt as though Jonah may not like me, and if he really had to see me eat, he really wouldn't get me?

I took the first bite, hoping nobody was watching. Because I was so nervous, my body tensed up and my tongue danced around my mouth like a Mexican jumping bean. Half of my cereal fell out of my mouth and milk dripped down my chin. I quickly looked around to see if anyone noticed. My eyes met Jonah's and he glanced away without a word. Christine cleaned the cereal up as if it was the most natural thing. She then held another spoonful to my mouth. I shook my head no.

"Am I doing something wrong?"

I shook my head again.

"Are you just not hungry?"

I hesitated; I was even embarrassed to tell her.

"Here," Christine leaned closer to me so she wouldn't have to shout over the chatter and the whirr of the industrial-strength fans. "Why don't you tell me what's up with your TechnoTalk, and I will look at your screen so you don't have to actually say it aloud?"

I started clicking my talking switch. "I . . . know . . . this . . . is . . . dumb . . . but . . . I . . . don't . . . like . . . to . . . eat . . . in . . . front . . . of . . . people . . . I . . . don't . . . know."

"Oh," Christine whispered. "But, you did it last night?"

"I . . . know . . . but . . . I . . . think . . . I'm . . . embarrassed . . . now . . . because . . . everybody . . . can . . . see . . . me . . . more."

Christine sat back and finished chewing her pancakes. "You know nobody here really cares how you eat, right?"

I hesitated before nodding.

"And if they did, I would say something to them. And, Randi would probably try to beat them up," she added.

I smiled. All of a sudden, a loud blow horn sounded, making me jump fifty feet out of my wheelchair. The noisy dining hall quickly went silent. JT stood in front with a megaphone.

"Good morning, campers! How was your first night?"

Everybody cheered.

"Good. As I was saying last night, we are going to do something a little different this year. I know on the first day you don't really do much until after dinner, so you have time to relax and catch up with your friends. Well, this year, when you are done eating and cleaning up your cabin, you are going to go to the group that you signed up for last night. You'll spend about twenty minutes together, then the rest of the day is yours. Now, the groups are in the same places they have always been. If you don't remember or don't know where something is, ask your fellow campers. I will see you in your groups!" He went off to the side and everybody started talking again.

"Wonder what this is about," Randi remarked as she stood up to throw her stuff away.

"Hey," Christine said to me, "I have an idea. While everyone goes to clean, we could stay here and you could eat. Do you want to do that?"

I started typing. "Are . . . you . . . sure . . . that—"

"Would be okay?" she finished my sentence.

I nodded.

"We have six other people to clean our cabin. They will be just fine without us," she assured me. "But I do have a question. If I think I know what you're going to say before you're done typing, do you want me to guess, or do you want to type everything out?"

I nodded and motioned toward her.

"You want me to guess?"

I nodded again.

"Okay. I didn't know."

Randi came back. "Ya comin'?"

"No," Christine answered for the both of us. "I think we're going to finish eating."

"Sweet. You wanna hang out later, Brynn?"

I smiled and pushed up in my wheelchair, similar to how someone would jump up and down when they were excited.

"Now, don't have a heart attack. I just asked you to hang out; not if you wanted a million dollars," she laughed. "But I'm off to go sit on my bed and watch everybody else clean."

Christine chuckled. "Bye, Randi."

Randi was one of the last people to leave the dining hall. Christine asked if I was ready to try eating again. This time I was much more relaxed, so my tongue actually cooperated. Within five minutes, my cereal was being converted to body energy. I finished my apple juice, Christine threw everything away, and we were good to go.

The arts and crafts building was right across from the dining hall. I was surprised to see some people had finished cabin cleaning and were already walking to join their groups. Christine opened the door and I wheeled in. It definitely looked like an arts and crafts building: The walls were splattered with all different colors of paint. It was as though one day all the paint cans had a severe case of the hiccups. To my right, I could see any art supply any aspiring artist would ever need. To my left was a mural of the campus. The ceiling was even covered in multi-colored handprints. Simply being in the building ignited a spark within me. I suddenly really wanted to be creative. I wanted to paint.

"Come here," Christine motioned for me to follow her. "I want you to meet somebody."

I followed. She led me to a woman who looked to be in her mid-forties. Her shirt, jeans, and bandanna all matched the walls.

"Brynn, this is Bonnie. She is the art coordinator. Bonnie, this is my camper, Brynn. She will be doing Stage Stuff. We need to come up with a way for her to paint."

"Nice to meet you, Brynn," she smiled warmly at me. Her short, dark hair was graying, but I could tell she had a young heart. "I'm sure we can come up with something. That's what arts and crafts is all about."

I smiled.

Just then, JT walked in so Christine and I had to go join the twenty other kids. JT stepped in front of us, clipboard in hand.

"Hi. You're all probably wondering what's going on. Usually you get to pick your group for the talent show. Well, like I said last night, you are *not* going to do that this year. To help with DAISY, I have randomly assigned you to a group. You are going to do the talent show, as well as missions, with your group. This will help you get to know people you otherwise might not talk to. Now," he glanced at his clipboard. "Let me tell you the groups. Group one! We have Becca, Kara, Richie, and Robbie."

JT kept calling names. I wondered who I would be with and started to get excited. These were the people I was going to get to know. These were the people who were hopefully going to become my friends. A thought suddenly made my excitement dissolve into nervousness. *Friends?* Meg and Dave were supposedly my "friends." What if I had to live through that nightmare again? I didn't know if I could handle another situation like that.

"And finally," JT continued, "in the last group, we have Amanda, Tommy, Brynn, and Jonah."

My eyes rapidly searched the room and locked with Jonah's. It was the second time we made direct eye contact that morning. And, for the second time, he looked away without saying a single word.

Chapter Seven

onah and me in the same group? Seriously? *Seriously?* Just great.

Awesome.

This was going to be *so much fun.*

Ugh!

"Okay, campers," JT began, "I suggest you stay here and start to get to know your group members. There will not be any reassignments no matter how much you may dislike that person, or how bad you want to be with your friends, so don't even ask. I want this summer to be a learning experience for all of you. Nobody has ever died from talking to someone who they don't know. . . . Well, you could say some people have, but that doesn't apply here. Now, I'm off to tell the other group what's up. Have fun, be safe, and don't kill each other."

JT stepped out of arts and crafts. Maybe that would be my goal: to not kill Jonah. Would I get a prize at the end of camp if he was still alive?

Christine sighed. "It looks like the drama got turned up a notch. We can't exactly 'stay away' from Tommy now, huh?"

Oh, that was right. I didn't even think about Tommy. Jenn wanted everybody not to talk to him. But I was new. And I hadn't even had a conversation with Jenn, so this situation didn't really include me, did it? I flashed back to elementary school when Meg was mad at a girl named Molly. I didn't know Molly, but Meg made me promise to ignore her and not speak to her if she spoke to me first. Molly never bothered with me, so I never got the chance to ignore her on Meg's behalf, but I was mad at her anyway because I was loyal to Meg.

Ha. Loyal . . . Meg . . . That'd be the last time I used those two words in the same sentence.

"Ah, well, Jenn will just have to get over it," Christine said with a firm nod of her head.

I nodded in agreement just as Tommy walked up to us. "Hey, guys. What's up?"

"Not much, Tommy," Christine answered. "I'm so glad you're in our group. I'm looking forward to working with you again."

"I'm not," Jonah said, coming up behind Tommy and resting his arm on his shoulder.

I fought the urge to roll my eyes and wondered if Christine was feeling the same.

"Well, apparently, you have no choice," Tommy said, shrugging off Jonah's hulking arm. "I'm not for this DAISY thing, either, so we might as well get over it."

Jonah took a sip from the same water bottle he had last night, which now had some kind of orange drink in it. "She's telling everyone not to talk to you."

"Thanks. I've figured that out."

"Tell me, man. Why'd you want to break up with her? She's really hot."

Tommy's face turned pink; it was obvious he didn't want to talk about whatever led to his fairly recent breakup. I sensed that it wasn't so much that he didn't want to talk about *what* happened as much as he didn't want to talk to Jonah, of all people, about it.

"Yeah, Jenn is really hot." A new voice made all four of our heads turn. I recognized her as the girl who had been with Jenn when we ran into the other girls the night before near the lake. She could almost pass as Jenn's twin; they wore the same excessive amount of makeup and were dressed similarly in extremely short shorts and tight tops that stretched across their chests. Unlike Jenn, this girl's hair was dark brown instead of bleached blonde. "I don't know what your problem is," she said to Tommy.

"I don't know why you don't mind your own business," Tommy said, turning to her. The pink splashed across his face was no longer from embarrassment. He was angry. Anyone with the tiniest bit of sense could see that.

"Okay, okay," Jonah held up his hands, defensively. "Why don't we go do that? Amanda, wanna go for a walk?"

"That would be just lovely," Amanda said in a tone that passed sarcasm.

"Guys!" Christine called after them. "Not to be the annoying counselor, but didn't you hear JT?"

"What?" Jonah remarked. "Oh, about getting to know everyone? Right. About that. Don't we already know everyone? I already know everyone. We have been coming to this camp since we were eight, remember? Tommy, Christine, and Brynn. Amanda, do you know everyone?"

"Tommy, Christine, and Brynn?" she repeated.

"I think we're ready to go."

Not waiting for anyone to say anything else, Amanda and Jonah spun around and walked out of the door. I watched as Jonah passed his drink to Amanda before they disappeared.

"Well," Christine started, "that went . . . well."

Tommy sat down next to Christine. "I'm screwed."

"Hey, you can't be like that. You have to think positive."

"I'm screwed!" he repeated with forced enthusiasm.

"That's more like it," Christine said and then shook her head. "This really sucks. I'm sorry. You know I'm here if you need to talk."

"Thanks."

"If it helps, I don't think Brynn really wants to be in a group with Jonah. Do you, Brynn?"

I slowly shook my head, hesitant to tell them that I didn't want to be with my friend's boyfriend. He may do it for Randi, but I really didn't think he'd do it for me.

"That makes two of us," Tommy said.

Christine crossed her legs and took the opportunity to change the subject. "So, we have to come up with a way for Brynn to paint."

"Oh, yeah? Hm . . ." Apparently eager for a break from his misery, Tommy examined my wheelchair and my straps.

Christine turned to me. "Do you have any control of your hands at all?"

I hit my switch and started typing words on my screen. "I . . . can . . . hold . . . the . . . brush . . . there's . . . just . . ."

"Can I tell Tommy what you're doing?" Christine asked. I nodded and she explained how my TechnoTalk worked while I kept typing.

"A . . . good . . . chance . . . you . . . will . . . end . . . up . . . either . . . getting . . . a . . . paint . . . make . . . over . . . or . . ."

Tommy was suddenly behind me, watching intently, as Christine continued the speech. She was getting good at it, I noticed.

"Missing . . . an . . . eye." I hit SPEAK and my TechnoTalk read the whole sentence.

"So we should have Jonah help you that day?"

A laugh escaped my mouth before I could stop it. I nodded a big nod at Tommy.

"Sounds good to me."

Christine shook her head, smiling. "See? I knew you two would get along. Knowing you both, I could see you having Jonah hanging upside down from a tree by the end of camp."

"That's actually a good idea."

"I'm . . . in." SPEAK.

"Can we string Amanda up with him?" Tommy asked me, his tone serious. "I mean, we don't want him to be alone up there, do we?"

I pretended to think for a second. "Sure . . . they . . . would . . . go . . . very . . . well . . . upside . . . down . . . together." SPEAK.

"Alright," Christine held up her hands, "I know I'm supposed to be helping you with what you need this summer, Brynn, but I do not do people's dirty work, so don't even ask."

"Oh, I think we can handle this one ourselves," Tommy assured her.

Not thinking about what I was doing, I squealed. Whenever I would get really, really, really excited, it just happened. I figured that just came along with everything else. If I didn't have enough control to formulate words, why would I have enough control to keep random noises from coming out? This didn't mean I wasn't embarrassed by them, though. I glanced around arts and crafts. Thankfully everyone had left by now. *So much for getting to know your group.* I glanced at Christine and Tommy. They didn't seem to notice . . . or they at least didn't seem to care.

"God," Christine laughed to herself, probably imagining Jonah and Amanda stuck in a tree and at our mercy, "my two favorite campers are going to get kicked out of camp."

"All because of your idea," Tommy teased her.

"Hey! Again. I will not have anything to do with this."

I started typing again, a thought suddenly occurring to me. "Will . . . you . . . not . . . tell . . . Randi . . . that . . . I . . . didn't . . . want . . . to . . . be . . . with . . . Jonah?" SPEAK.

"Sure, but she probably wouldn't care anyway. She knows he was a jerk to you last night at the campfire. She even said so herself," Christine reminded me.

"I . . . know . . . I . . . just . . . don't . . . want . . . her . . . to . . . be . . . mad . . . at . . . me." SPEAK.

"She probably wouldn't be mad at you, but okay. I won't say anything."

I looked at Tommy.

"Oh, I don't think she's talking to me now because of Jenn, but I wouldn't anyway," Tommy said, picking up a paintbrush and playing with the soft tip. "Speaking of Randi, here she and Carly come."

The two girls came through the paint splattered door and walked towards us.

"Hey, Brynn and Christine," Carly stood with her back facing Tommy, "how's it going?"

"It's going well," Christine answered. "Tom is in our group, too."

Carly tucked a strand behind her ear and turned to Randi.

Randi shrugged. "Cool," she said, meeting Tommy's eyes and then mine. I could tell she didn't want to do this and that she thought the entire idea of ignoring Tommy was stupid.

"Alright," Tommy stepped in front of me. "I think I get the hint. I'm going to go."

Meeting his eyes, a frown slipped out of my lips. I felt bad he was being forced to go away. What was he going to go do now? Didn't JT say we could just hang out today?

"It's cool. I think we're doing a DAISY activity tonight, so I'll see ya later."

Tommy didn't even bother saying goodbye to the other girls on his way out.

"What was up with that?" Carly asked as soon as he was outside.

"What was up with *that*?" Christine repeated. "What was up with *you*? Tommy didn't break up with you. He broke up with Jenn."

"Exactly. I wouldn't want my friends talking to someone who broke up with me," Carly said, her tone indicating that she was completely serious.

"Do you guys even know why they broke up?"

"I tried to ask her again this morning," Randi said, "and she still thinks he's going to ask her back out."

"So you still think it's okay for you to not talk to your friend, even if this situation doesn't have anything to do with you? Maybe Tommy had a good reason for breaking up with her. Maybe Jenn went crazy and stalked his house or hacked into his Facebook." Christine tried to reason with Carly, but all her logical ideas were simply met with a shrug. She turned to Randi.

"Don't look at me. I will talk to him if he talks to me," she said. She tucked a piece of pink hair behind her ear. She was uncomfortable and I couldn't blame her.

"Whatever," Carly waved it off. "How's your group? Who else is in it?"

"Jonah and Amanda."

"Oh, good. At least you're with some cool people," Carly said.

I had to look away to keep myself from laughing. Really? Was she really this oblivious? These were the people she thought were cool? These were her friends?

"Yeah," Christine played along with her, "it's cool. We have to come up with a way for Brynn to paint."

The subject of me painting again broke through the tension in the room. Randi instantly perked up. "You work all your things with your head, right?" Randi asked. "Your computer and your wheelchair?"

I nodded.

"What about a hat or something? We can tape a brush to it and you can move it around with your head."

"Randi!" Christine exclaimed. "You're a genius! Brynn, do you think that will work?"

"Yeeaaahh!" I said without my TechnoTalk. She really was a genius. Her boyfriend might have been one of the biggest jerks I had ever met, but she was a pure genius.

Randi and Christine started opening drawers around arts and crafts, looking for something I could use. Twenty drawers later, Randi held up a neon green plastic visor that sometimes came in little kids' beach sets. Christine handed her the duct tape and she went to work attaching the brush. I couldn't help but chuckle. If Jonah already had doubts about me, this was really going to win him over.

"There!" Randi put the last piece of tape over the brush. "Perfect!"

Christine came over and slid it on. I moved my head back and forth.

"What do you think?" Christine clasped her hands. "Do you think it will work?"

"I . . . look . . . like . . . a . . . fricking . . . unicorn." SPEAK.

Carly pointed at my TechnoTalk. "She can say 'fricking'!"

Of course I could say "fricking." And a lot worse, if I so chose . . . .

"The important thing here is that you will be able to paint," Christine said, pretending Carly hadn't said a single word.

Another thought popped into my head and I immediately typed it out. "Do . . . you . . . think . . . this . . . will . . . help . . . people . . . know . . . that . . . they . . . can . . . talk . . . to . . . me?" SPEAK.

"Oh, screw people," Randi said, her words once again filled with the confidence I so admired. She walked toward me. "Do you want to paint?"

I nodded.

"Do you have any other ideas of how you could paint?"

I sheepishly shook my head.

"Then you are wearing the visor, ya fricking unicorn."

Minutes after the lunch bell rang, the girls and I walked into the dining hall. I instantly had a flashback to eating breakfast and I felt a surge of embarrassment flood my cheeks. I caught Christine's eye, signaling to her a reminder that I wanted to sit by myself. Message received.

"Okay, Brynn, do you want to sit at that back table?" Christine pointed to one in the corner where nobody was sitting. "And, do you girls want to go sit with Jonah and Gabe?"

"Carly doesn't smell that bad, does she?" Randi asked.

"Hey!" Carly squealed defensively.

"Just do it for me," Christine pleaded.

"Is there something you're not telling us?" Randi turned her head sideways.

"Yes. Now, go."

"Alright then. Love you, too."

Randi and Carly marched off to their boys. After I told Christine I would have macaroni and cheese and water, I found my way to the back table and parked facing the wooden wall. I already felt a lot more comfortable than I did at breakfast. I thought that I might have been okay sitting with Randi and even Carly. They really seemed to be cool with everything. And Gabe was pretty much nonexistent in my world right then. It was just Jonah who really made me nervous, I realized. There was something about the way he looked at me . . . It wasn't that he was ignoring me; I could handle that if it was that simple. Instead, he looked right at me and knew I could talk to him and was becoming one of Randi's friends, but he still chose to not acknowledge me.

Christine came and sat on the picnic bench next to me. Unlike my plate, she just had a salad and an apple. I was about to take a bite when everybody started chanting. Christine put my fork down and joined in.

"Announcements! Announcements! Announcements!"

Christine repeated, "Announcements! Announcements! Announcements!"

Soon everybody was doing it. I felt a little dumb just sitting there, but I didn't know what the hell was going on. After the fifth round of "Announcements! Announcements! Announcements!" everybody came to a startling silence again. A girl stood up from her table.

"I'm so excited to be at Camp Lakewood!" she exclaimed.

Everybody cheered and banged on the table. As soon as the girl sat down, another one stood up.

"This is going to be the best year at camp!"

About twenty other people, including campers and counselors, took turns standing and shouting stuff.

"I love camp!"

"Come to the dock for free time!"

"I love my campers!"

"My cabin smells!"

"Camp Lakewood rocks!"

"I missed camp, but didn't miss this food!"

"I want to go swimming!"

"We have bugs in our cabin!"

"I love my camp people!"

After the last person went, everybody cheered again and then returned to normal. Christine held the fork to my mouth as though nothing had happened. I figured that whole thing was just part of the lunch routine. I finally took a bite and immediately forced myself not to gag. The macaroni and cheese tasted like burned rubber. Christine held out another bite. I couldn't keep the disgust from showing on my face.

"Do you want something else? I could make you a PBJ."

I shook my head.

"You're going to try to choke this stuff down?"

I nodded.

"Good luck."

The next bite wasn't any better. I understand now why her plate was so simple.

"Hey, do you like to take naps?"

I shook my head and took another bite, thinking that the question was really random.

"Oh, because later in the afternoon we have Siesta. It's a time when you can either lie down or go somewhere to chill. We will probably have Siesta all afternoon today, because it's the first day and we aren't really doing anything. I didn't know if you would want to take a nap. Lots of the girls—and most of the guys—end up napping. The sun can really tire you out."

All I needed to hear was "go somewhere to chill." I hit my talking switch and gave Christine some time to take a few bites of her salad. "Is . . . there . . . somewhere . . . I . . . can . . . go . . . by . . . myself?" SPEAK.

"You mean away from the cabin? Sure. You can find a place outside. A lot of campers do that, too. What about the basketball court? Next to the lake? Nobody ever uses it. You saw why."

I excitedly nodded. That would be perfect! "Will . . . you . . . put . . . my . . . iPod . . . on?" SPEAK.

"Yeah! That's not a problem. Do you have it in your book bag?"

I nodded.

"Okay. We can go right after you're done eating."

I smiled. Christine tried to give me another bite, but I frowned and shook my head.

"Are you finally giving up?"

I nodded.

"I don't blame you. It looks disgusting."

By the time Christine stood up to throw our plates away, there were only a few people left in the dining hall. I turned around and followed her outside. I had to smile. I was going to get to dance! I was going to get to chill out, forget reality, and dance! Not that there was anything bad about camp. My brain just needed to zone out for a little.

Once we arrived at what was going to be my new dance floor, Christine reached in my bag and pulled out my baby blue iPod. It was on one of my favorite playlists.

"Is this one okay?"

I squealed.

"Great. Looks like you have some awesome songs on here. Do you want me to come back in an hour or so?"

I nodded.

"Kay. See you in a little."

Christine put my earphones in and put my iPod under my leg so it wouldn't fall. As she walked back to the cabin, a faster song came on. I put my wheelchair on the next speed and started doing figure eights, spinning to the left, spinning to the right. The court was completely surrounded by trees. It was like I was dancing in a pool of sunlight.

Just as I was about to start playing the guitar to a screaming crowd in my mind, I saw someone walking toward me out of the corner of my eye. It only took a second for me to figure out who it was. My stomach did a little jump.

Chapter Eight

With my music playing in my ears, I started on my way over to meet my only normal group member. Remembering the conversation we had a few hours earlier and the fact that he talked to me like he would have talked to anyone else made me smile. He had even joked with me. Granted, Randi and Christine did those things, too, but . . . there was something about having a guy on my team that made me feel pretty good, especially since this team was one where I sometimes felt like only me and my parents knew how to play the game we were in.

I was also glad that Christine and the other girls weren't around right then. Even though I knew the whole breakup thing didn't involve me, and even though Christine told me it was my choice whether I wanted to talk to Tommy, I didn't exactly like going against what everyone else was doing. That whole sense of loyalty I'd felt toward Meg was still a major part of me; I didn't want to upset the girls, especially since I wanted them to be my friends. It was true that I thought Carly was a little annoying, and I thought Jonah should go take a hike in the woods and never come back, but I really liked Randi. I didn't want to go against her. But . . . they weren't on the basketball court with me right then, so what they didn't know wouldn't hurt them (or me), right?

My excitement about seeing him immediately turned into panic as soon as I realized that I could see his lips moving, but couldn't hear what he was saying. My iPod. I couldn't exactly pick it up, turn it off, and take my earphones out. I hit my talking switch, but then remembered I was outside. *Great. Wonderful. Awesome.* How was I going to tell him I couldn't hear a word he was saying? I gave him a nervous smile. He said something again that I couldn't make out.

Some people automatically assumed that just because I was in a wheelchair (or used a communication device; I would never really know which it was) that I needed them to speak louder to me because I was deaf. Thank God they were wrong—I couldn't read lips for the life of me.

What was I going to do now? I could keep driving to my cabin and ask Christine to explain it to him, but that would involve me driving right past him without saying anything at all. People were already ignoring him; I didn't want him to think that was the reason I wasn't speaking to him. I had to do something to make him understand. I was a pro at not being able to talk. I could do this.

Since my iPod was underneath my leg, I pressed both of my legs together. I hoped it didn't look like I was going to pee any second. Just then, I caught Tommy's eyes and looked down to where the iPod was, hoping his eyes would follow mine. They didn't. All he did was give me a confused look. *Damn it.* Here the one guy who wasn't afraid to talk to me wanted to have a conversation, and he probably thought I was tweaking out.

I didn't know what it was, but something made me try again. Meg would always ask me about it. She didn't understand how I could stand to repeat actions and expressions over and over again when she didn't quite understand what I was trying to tell her. She once said that if she was me, she would just get frustrated and give up until she could use the TechnoTalk. For me, it was almost like an instinct. I think. *Was instinct the right word?* I didn't think that I had to keep going, and not give up, and whatever other motivational crap people thought I probably told myself. I simply felt the need to communicate something, so I would do whatever it took to do that.

Meeting Tommy's eyes again, I tried to get him to see that I couldn't hear him because of what was under my leg. He took a step closer to me, but still didn't get it. *So much for having a normal conversation with him.* At the rate we were going, he would probably never want to talk to me again. I repeated the motion for the third time. This time, I was able to get him to look in at my leg. I squeezed my thighs together again, lifted myself off my seat an inch or so, and looked at my iPod intensely, as though I had magic powers to turn it off myself. As soon as Tommy saw it, his confusion faded away. *Score.*

To my surprise, Tommy grabbed the iPod from under my leg and pressed the pause button. Why was I so surprised about that? What did I think he was going to do after he figured it out? Walk away and leave me to my music? He pulled out my earphones, and tucked a strand of hair behind my ear. I exhaled.

"Sorry about that, Brynn. I didn't know you were having a jam session. I just saw that you were by yourself, and I figured I would come see what you were up to. You can go back to your . . ." he glanced at my iPod, "Abbie Bonza, if you want to."

I shrugged and gave him a nervous smile. I didn't want him to have to put my earphones back in after taking them out.

"Are you sure? Because I could go find someone else to talk to . . ." he paused. "Oh wait, no I can't. That's right." He rolled his eyes.

I chuckled as I hit my talking switch again and remembered again that we were outside directly beneath the sun.

Tommy looked over my shoulder to watch what I was going to type. "Oh, yeah, you can't see your computer because there's a glare, right?"

I nodded, extremely relieved he caught on by himself without me having to tell him via a game of 20 Questions.

"Would shade help? There's a bench over there by the trees with some shade we could go sit at if you want."

I nodded again and we started over to the cement bench, which looked as if it had been at Camp Lakewood since the first rainfall. I fought back the urge to squeal. Not only wasn't Tommy treating me like an alien from the planet Freaksville, he was actually smart about talking to me.

As soon as we were in the shade and I could see my TechnoTalk, I started typing. Tommy stood next to me so he could see my screen instead of sitting on the bench.

"I . . . am . . . so . . . sorry . . . about . . . that . . . you . . . probably . . . thought . . . I . . . was . . . dumb."

"No," Tommy replied before I could hit SPEAK, "not at all. I was the one being dumb. If I would've really looked, I would've seen the white wires coming out of your ears. Where do you want me to put this, by the way?"

"In . . . my . . . bag. I . . . just . . . feel . . . bad . . . I . . . couldn't . . . tell—"

"Brynn," he slipped the iPod in the black book bag on the back of my chair, "were you able to tell me that you couldn't hear?"

I felt my cheeks turning pink. He had a point.

"Then you don't have anything to feel bad about. Trust me, with the whole camp acting like I'm a horrible person, our little miscommunication for a second was really nothing."

I smiled despite my embarrassment. Fair enough.

"You know what I really hate, Brynn?" Tommy clasped his hands together and pointed up at the sky. "I could be going to Myrtle Beach with my cousin next week. And do you know what I told my cousin when he asked me if I wanted to go? I said I couldn't go because I couldn't bail on everyone here these two weeks. I didn't want to bail on my friends who aren't talking to me, and they won't even listen to my side of the story. That's what I really hate."

I nodded, not sure of what to say.

"I'm sorry. I'm sorry, I'm sure you didn't really want to know that. But I just don't get it." He ran his hands through his hair and let out a frustrated sigh.

"No . . . it's . . . okay. I . . . know . . . how . . . you . . . feel. Nobody . . . talks . . . to . . . me . . . at . . . school . . . and . . . " I deleted the word "and" and hit SPEAK.

"And what?"

I shook my head, shrugging it off. I was going to tell them about Meg and Dave and how they didn't really even try to talk to me after what happened, but this situation was a little different. Plus, I felt like it was already taking me forever to type to him. Telling that story would just take me more time.

"What 'and'? You definitely were going to say something else."

"And . . . I . . . just . . . know . . . not . . . having . . . anyone . . . to . . . talk . . . to . . . can . . . make . . . you . . . go . . . crazy."

"You're saying I'm crazy now? Thanks. You're the only other camper I had a normal conversation with so far, and you're calling me crazy? I'm just going to call my mom right now and tell her to book me a plane ticket."

I flinched at those two words. Normal conversation. He was thinking what I was thinking. "Oh . . . you . . . know . . . what . . . I . . . m—"

"You can say I'm crazy, it's cool. I know I at least have better taste in music."

"Do . . . not . . . diss . . . Abbie . . ." Even though Tommy read my screen, I hit SPEAK just to let him know I was *not* kidding.

"Ooh, yeah, see? I think I already did."

I pretended to be offended. "What's . . . your . . . problem . . . with . . . her . . . anyway?"

"Most of her music is just about guys, guys, and guys. Oh, yeah, and how much they all suck. Now why don't you answer my question? Why do you like it?"

"You . . . know . . . I'm . . . starting . . . to . . . see . . . why
. . . nobody . . . is . . . talking . . . to . . . you."

"Because I don't like your music?"

I dramatically rolled my eyes and tried not to smile. "I . . . can
. . . relate . . . to . . . most . . . songs . . . and . . . I . . . think
. . . it's . . . cool . . . she . . . writes . . . them . . . all . . . herself."

"You know a lot of singers do that? Write their songs themselves. Not just Miss Bonza."

"You . . . really . . . don't . . . like . . . her . . . do . . . you?"

"I'm just into other stuff. Dylan. The Beatles. Zeppelin. The
Clash."

I nodded and went along with him.

"And I'm getting a blank stare. Okay. Have you even heard a
song from any of them?"

I looked away, smiling.

"Are you serious? Brynn, no! Are you serious? Can you tell
me a song by Led Zeppelin? Or Bob Dylan? Or The Beatles? You
have to know The Beatles? Everyone knows The Beatles!"

I turned back to him, still smiling.

"Okay, here's what we're gonna do. The next time I see you
rocking out, I'm going to go get my guitar, and I'm going to play
you some real music. By the end of camp, you'll be like 'Abbie
who?'"

"You . . . play . . . the . . . guitar?"

He nodded proudly. "Six years and counting."

"I . . . wish . . . I . . . could . . . play . . . the . . ."

I didn't finish the sentence. I wanted to smack myself on the
forehead. What was I thinking? Seriously, why was I going to tell
him that? Actually, he already saw it, so I did tell him. *Why?* I
couldn't exactly tell myself it just kind of slipped out, because I
had a good minute or so to stop what I was typing.

I cleared my screen. "I . . . sorry." I hit SPEAK.

Tommy squinted. "Why?"

"I . . . shouldn't . . . have . . . told . . . you."

"Why?"

He waited patiently while I typed. I could feel his presence behind me and I had to admit that it was comforting, even though I was too embarrassed and flustered at that moment to enjoy it. "Because . . . I'm . . . afraid . . . it . . . makes . . . people . . . feel . . . awkward. I . . . mean . . . I . . . totally . . . know . . . I . . . won't . . . ever . . . be . . . able . . . to. I . . . don't . . . want . . . you . . . to . . . think . . . I'm—"

Tommy stopped me. "Do you wish you could play the guitar?"

I slowly nodded.

"Then I see nothing wrong with saying you do. I would like to play a show for thousands and thousands of people in New York City. Do I think it's going to happen? More than likely that's a *hell no*. But that doesn't mean I can't want to do it."

I thought about what he said for a second before I started typing again. "So . . . I . . . didn't . . . make . . . you . . . feel . . . awkward?"

"I really don't see how you could have just by telling me what you would like to do."

"Thank . . . you." I smiled at him.

"I don't know what I did, but no problem." He smiled back at me.

"My two favorite campers, together again." We both turned our heads to see Christine walking towards us.

Tommy nodded at her. "What's up?"

"Nothing. Brynn, I have been told to come get you. The girls are at the cabin and want to hang out with you. Tommy, I would tell you to come, but—"

He held up his hands in mock defense. "I have the plague, I know."

"Sorry, Tom."

"I . . . wish . . . you . . . could . . . come." SPEAK.

"Yeah, me too. Maybe this whole thing will blow over in a few days and we can hang out. Probably won't, but hey—we can wish, can't we?"

We both smiled, somehow knowing exactly what the other was thinking in that moment.

"Alright, I'm gonna go. See ya tonight."

Christine frowned. "Bye, Tom."

He gave me a little wave and then made his way up the path. I motioned for Christine to take Tommy's place and read my screen.

"You . . . are . . . right. He . . . is . . . awesome."

"Told you! I knew you would like him."

"Can . . . you . . . not . . . tell . . . the . . . girls . . . I . . . was . . . talking . . . to . . . him?"

"Sure. Can I ask why?" Another frown.

"I . . . just . . . don't . . . want . . . to . . . create . . . more . . . drama."

Christine rolled her head. "Okay, you know what? After knowing you for the past twenty-four hours, I think I have the perfect goal for you. Follow me."

She marched off in the direction of my cabin. I had no choice but to follow her. What did I do? Was she mad at me? I honestly didn't want to create any more drama, but did I without meaning to? When we got to our cabin, she held the door opened with her foot. I tried to give her my confused look to ask what was going on. She just pointed to the back of the cabin. *Holy crap.* I did do something.

Once we were inside, she grabbed a black magic marker from her drawer and sat on my bed. I watched as she snatched my daisy off her desk. I quickly smiled as I passed the rest of the girls, but didn't stop to say hi. I didn't want to piss Christine off even more. I waited as Christine finished writing on my daisy, unsure of what to think.

"Here," Christine stood to hold my daisy where I could see it, "I helped you pick your goal. I think you really need to work on this, and I will help you as much as I can."

I nodded in acceptance as I read what was printed in capital letters on the little construction paper daisy.

SCREW WHAT OTHER PEOPLE THINK!

Chapter Nine

*L*ater that night, I could feel my dinner sloshing around in my stomach as I drove onto the huge patch of grass conveniently located in the middle of all the cabins. JT referred to it as the quad and told everyone to meet there when we were done eating. We were going to do our first DAISY activity, which meant I was going to get to be with Tommy again. It, unfortunately, also meant I was going to get to be with Amanda and Jonah. I couldn't tell if my stomach felt this way because of these reasons or if the camp just needed to find a new cook.

Wheeling from the pavement to the grass made me feel as though I was driving my chair through an earthquake. Christine and I started over towards Tommy, who was sitting by himself off to the side of the growing group of campers. I instantly flashed back to a time at school; the big blowout had just happened and I had stopped talking to Meg and Dave, which meant I would sit by myself in the cafeteria. Well, okay, I did have my aide with me, but I might as well have been by myself. A thought came to me just then: Was that the reason I didn't feel comfortable eating with anyone here? Did I let myself get used to sitting alone?

I shook the thought away. I wasn't going to think about it right now.

Just then, Tommy noticed Christine and I coming toward him and stood up to greet us. "What's up?"

"Not much, Tommy," Christine replied for the both of us, "how's it going with you?"

"Oh, you know, everything's awesome. I love being treated like I have four heads. It's really why I came to camp this year."

"I'm really sorry, Tom. Have you tried talking to any of them?"

"Nah . . ." His eyes lingered on mine for a second, but then he addressed Christine again. "At first I figured it would just blow over, but now everything is just getting more ridiculous."

"Maybe you should try talking to them."

"I really don't think it would help," he said, and shoved his hands in the pockets of his khaki cargo pants. "And besides, it's really only Jonah and Amanda who are saying stuff and being obnoxious, even though this has nothing to do with them. Everyone else is just not talking to me, which I can deal with."

"Yeah, but you shouldn't have to deal with it."

Christine was right; we both knew it. But Tommy shrugged. "What are you going to do?"

"Where are Jonah and Amanda, anyway?" Christine glanced around as JT walked in front of the group.

"You ask that like it's a bad thing they aren't here," Tommy whispered since everyone had quieted down.

"Hey," Christine whispered back, "I'm a counselor. It's my job to care for all campers, equally, without judgment."

"Lamest. Job. Ever."

"Probably why I have it, and you don't."

"Ooh, buuurn."

"Alright, campers!" JT's voice boomed through the megaphone. "You are hopefully in the groups that I assigned you earlier. I am going to start calling these your DAISY groups. Like I was saying last night, you are going to be doing activities with your DAISY groups. In the previous years, I have noticed teens have had a bit of a problem with cliques. I have created the DAISY theme to help with that."

Tommy met my eyes again. "Genius," he mouthed.

I suppressed a laugh as a little electric current passed through my body.

Meanwhile, JT rambled on. "I wanted your first DAISY activity to be an ice breaker, so that you can get a feel for your group members. There are counselors who will be coming around to give you parts of a daisy made of construction paper. I want everyone to take two petals, write a fact about yourself on each of the petals, and glue it all together. When we are done, we'll go down to the amphitheater and you'll present your daisies to the camp. Got it? Good. Go for it."

The chatter quickly built back up as Tommy knelt beside me. "Is he serious? Does he really think everyone is going to take this seriously? Hasn't someone informed him that we've all been coming here since we were little?"

Suddenly, I became more aware of his presence—specifically his scent. It wasn't the typical good-boy-smelling cologne that I loved. It was a light, sweet scent that was barely there. Maybe his deodorant? Shampoo? Maybe I was just crazy and should have really stopped trying to analyze the smell of the guy next to me, a guy I'd met only twenty-four hours earlier.

"Come on, now," Christine looked at Tommy. "How many years have you been coming to camp? You should know by now that they like to have you guys do cheesy activities."

"I think he out-cheesed himself this time."

I chuckled and nodded a big nod.

"You guys just aren't in the Camp Lakewood spirit," Christine said sarcastically.

"Oh, I won't speak for Brynn, but I can assure you that I'm not."

"Well, why don't you work on that and you two think of your facts? I'm going to go find the other half of your group."

"Do you really have to? I mean, I think me and Brynn can manage just fine."

In response, Christine turned around and started walking away. "Be thinking of your facts!" she called over her shoulder.

Tommy rested his arm on my armrest. "She really thinks she's going to get them to do this? Those two wouldn't be caught dead doing shit like this. I shouldn't be caught dead doing shit like this."

"It . . . is . . . pretty . . . lame." I didn't hit SPEAK.

"Hey, you can see your screen. I guess it is getting kind of dark."

I nodded and kept typing. "Why . . . did . . . JT . . . come . . . up . . . with . . . this? He . . . should . . . know . . . we . . . are . . . 16 . . . and . . . 17."

"Yeah, I'm going to say about 95 percent of the people here does not come to Camp Lakewood just for JT's little I'm-gonna-help-you-be-better-people activities. The 5 percent who did probably are sad, strange individuals who call home crying every night because they miss their mommies. But anyway . . ." He took a deep breath and let it out with a sigh. "Why did you come to camp?"

I hesitated. I really had to come up with an appropriate answer to that frequently asked question. I really wanted the response *not* to include that I was on the verge of a nervous breakdown because the guy who I had once imagined to be my future hus-band turned out to be dating my best friend. That wasn't exactly information I wanted to share with the entire camp. Definitely wouldn't be programming that one into my automatic list of TechnoTalk responses anytime soon.

Thankfully, another counselor came around and handed Tommy all the materials we needed to make a daisy. Mike, the counselor, quickly explained what to do (like we couldn't fig-ure it out ourselves) and asked where the rest of our group was. Tommy told him Christine went off to find them. That was a good enough answer for Mike, who moved on to the next group of kids sitting on the lawn.

"So," Tommy spread all the daisy parts on my armrest, "how do you think we should do this?"

I gave him a questioning look. *Didn't Mike just tell us how to put it together?* And, why was he working on my armrest? Not that I minded, but my armrest was, like, an inch wide. I would have thought he would do it on the ground just to have more room.

"Oh, if we have to do this . . . DAISY . . . daisy . . . thing, we are doing it together." He adjusted the materials on my armrest before asking, "Now, how do you think we should do it?"

I found it ridiculously difficult to wipe the smile off my face at that point, so I simply laughed before starting to type. "Didn't . . . you . . . pay . . . attention . . . to . . . anything . . . he . . . was . . . saying? He . . . basically . . . told . . . you . . . how . . . to . . . do—"

"I definitely paid attention to him. I just wanted to see if you were any more creative than him. Which, apparently you aren't." He shrugged and feigned innocence.

I opened my mouth to make him think I was totally shocked that he had said that. "No . . . offense . . . but . . . aren't . . . you . . . in . . . the . . . arts . . . and . . . crafts . . . group?"

Tommy started putting glue on the back of the petals. "Uh, no offense, either, but aren't you in the arts and crafts group, too?"

I turned away, still smiling. *Okay, I totally had that coming.*

"If you are going to insult people," he said, twisting the cap on the glue stick, "or attempt to insult people, I highly suggest you make sure it can't be turned back on you."

"Thanks . . . for . . . the . . . advice." I waited for him to look at me and then rolled my eyes.

He carefully stuck each petal onto the yellow circle. "Just wanted to help ya. By the way, you didn't answer my question, again. Is this going to be happening often?" He looked up from his colored papers and right into my eyes. "You not answering me, I mean."

What question?

"Why did you come to camp?" He pressed the last petal into place.

Oh, *that* question. I hit my typing switch. I decided to tell him half of the truth. "To . . . make . . . new . . . friends."

I rethought my answer. To make new friends? That was pretty lame, wasn't it?

Tommy read my screen and gave me a nod. "Glad you're not in the 5 percent."

I smiled, totally relieved. I was really starting to like being around Tommy and I definitely didn't want him thinking I was one of the lame campers he'd been referring to. Although, I probably scored a lame point or two when he found out about my obsession of Abbie Bonza's music. But . . . He would just have to get over it.

Just as he attached the skinny green paper stem, Christine came back. "Hey, you guys okay?"

"Yeah," Tommy held up what he had been working on, "see our magnificent fantastic awesome daisy?"

"Good job, guys," Christine said, a little distracted. Her eyes searched the surrounding area.

"Thanks. Any luck?"

"No, I checked the dining hall and around here. If you guys are good, I'm going to go look some more."

"I think we're cool. You cool, Brynn?"

I nodded.

"Do you need a drink or anything?" Christine asked me.

I shook my head.

"Okay. I'm going to go. Tommy, you can come get me if you need anything before I get back."

"Will do."

Christine started off in the opposite direction she came from. A part of me hoped she couldn't find them. Okay, I had to admit it was a *big* part of me, but it wasn't just because they were ridiculous morons. I was actually having fun doing this by myself with Tommy, even though this activity seemed like it was more for eight-year-olds. Since the guys from my school acted like I was the one with four heads, I wasn't in a situation like this very often. I didn't want it to end.

"Think we need these leaf things?" Tommy asked. "Or do you think we can go without them?"

I shrugged. "Do . . . you?"

"I asked you first. You're a girl. Aren't you supposed to be really into flowers, or something? Don't you know if daisies have leaves on the stems?"

I paused for a second. "I . . . don't . . . think . . . they . . . do."

"I don't think they do, either," Tommy ripped up the green cutouts and picked up the black Sharpie. "What are your facts?"

"I'm . . . not . . . sure . . . what . . . to . . . put. What . . . were—"

"C'mon! You have to have something. I really think you seem like a very unique girl. I would like to get to know you."

Did he just . . . No. Heat slowly crept up on my face. I panicked. I was not blushing. Seriously? He was right next to me. I didn't want him to see the way I was reacting. I swallowed. It was just a stupid little compliment. No need to blush over it. *Stop!* I commanded my body to cool down and my heart to slow back to its normal rhythm.

I focused all my attention on my TechnoTalk. Just answer the question and move on. Answer the question . . . and move on. I stared into the screen, thinking. "I . . . have . . . 816 . . . songs . . . on . . . my . . . iPod."

Could I be any more of a dork? Who said that?

"Okay," Tommy tried not to laugh, "that could be unique . . . if you were my grandpa. I have over a thousand songs on my iPod, and so do most of my friends. Try again."

Showoff.

"I . . . really . . . don't . . . know . . . what . . . to . . . put." How pathetic was I? I couldn't even come up with two facts about myself. "I . . . guess . . . we . . . could . . . say . . . I . . . talk . . . with . . . the . . . TechnoTalk."

Tommy didn't answer right away. I couldn't tell if he was just thinking, or if what I said made him feel awkward. I probably made him feel awkward. *Crap.*

"Do you really want that to be your unique fact?" he asked, his question emotionless.

Yes. No. Yes? No . . . Ugh!

I could feel the rush of blush taking over again. "No. I . . . don't. Actually . . . I . . ." I deleted the last two words.

They, however, didn't delete from Tommy's head. "Actually you what?"

"I . . . was . . . just . . . going . . . to . . . say . . . something . . ."

"Obviously."

I laughed nervously. "But . . . I . . . feel . . . like . . . it . . . would . . . take . . . me . . . a . . . long . . . time . . . to . . . type . . . and . . . we . . . have . . . to . . . do . . . the . . . daisy."

"Half of our group is M.I.A. The daisy is not going to get done anytime soon. But . . ." He looked around, scanning the thinning crowd of campers. "Yeah, I guess everyone is going down to the amphitheater. We should probably come up with our facts. Here, one of mine is going to be that I have four guitars."

I hit my switch. "That's . . . so . . . awesome. I . . . really . . . want . . . to . . . hear . . . y—"

"I know. You will." He printed his fact on a petal. "In the meantime, you have to come up with a fact about yourself. Actually, you have to come up with *two* facts about yourself. What do you like to do, other than listen to crappy music?"

I gave him the dirtiest, evilest look I could. It lasted for about two seconds, then I burst out laughing.

"Nice," he noted my failed attempt to act mad. "Solid. Now, are you going to tell me your damn facts? You were the one who was saying we needed to get this done."

"You . . . were . . . the . . . one . . . who . . . didn't . . . like . . . either . . . of . . . my . . . facts."

He pointed to me with the tip of the marker. "This is true."

"I . . . guess . . . you . . . could . . . say . . . this . . . is . . . my. . ." A new thought hit me and I cleared my sentence. I started with a new sentence before Tommy could yell at me. "I . . . passed . . . on . . . vacation . . . to . . . come . . . to . . . camp."

"Wow," Tommy looked impressed. "So, I'm not the only one."

It was only then that I realized Tommy and I were in the same boat. Well, kind of. He didn't go down to Myrtle Beach because he wanted to come be with his friends. I didn't go on vacation with my mom and dad because I wanted to make new friends. Granted, he probably didn't need to get out of the town where his heart was broken, and I wasn't dealing with people who refused to talk to me, but still.

Just as Tommy finished writing my fact down, someone squealed so loud that I thought the nerve endings in my ears had been lit on fire. Tommy and I both snapped our heads up at the same time. Jonah and Amanda were walking towards us, giggling, as though they didn't have a care in the world. It was clear they didn't feel guilty for missing the activity. Actually, as they got closer, we could see that Amanda was the one giggling—manically, I might add. Jonah just grinned along with her in that sly way guys sometimes did. Christine followed behind them, looking frustrated.

"Hi." Amanda's giggles stopped as soon as she saw Tommy.

"Found them," Christine walked in between them, "in the woods."

The giggles started up again as Jonah drank the last of what looked to be blue juice. What was up with this kid? I suppose he could have had an obsession with sports drinks, but as I watched him pop a few sticks of gum in his mouth and begin chewing obnoxiously, I realized why he was always sporting his own beverages. I also realized in that moment that he was spending a lot of time alone with Amanda. I wondered what Randi thought about that . . . .

"Alright, Tom," Christine turned, "do you want to tell them what you guys are doing?"

"Why can't you tell us, Christine?" Jonah quickly shot back.

"Because I haven't had a single thing to do with it; I've been running around looking for you. And I am not your group member. I am your counselor. And I really do *not* appreciate your attitude. So I suggest you drop it, and I suggest you listen to Tom." She crossed her arms at her chest and nodded to Tommy. "Go ahead, Tom."

Tommy shrugged, nonchalantly deciding to ignore the tension that surrounded the five of us. "We just had to make this daisy and put something unique about ourselves on it. We're going to go down to the amphitheater to present it in front of everyone."

Without hesitation, Amanda grabbed the paper flower out of Tommy's hand. "I can tell everyone about it. I took a public speaking class this year, and I got an A."

Tommy paused. "Okay. That's fine. But—"

"Ready, Jonah?"

"Guys, wait," Christine chimed in, "you need to finish the daisy first."

"What's there to finish?" Jonah asked.

Tommy and I exchanged quick glances. We could see that Christine was becoming impatient. "JT wanted you to write facts about yourself on the daisy. You have eight petals and only two facts."

"We don't need to write down no more facts, because, see, Amanda here said she's great at speaking to everyone. Isn't that right, Amanda?" He draped his large arm around her tiny shoulders.

"That's right," she said, slinging her arm around his waist in return. "Ready to go down?"

Jonah bobbed his head up and down. "Ready."

Christine started to say something, but our other two group members walked off before the words could leave her mouth. I looked at Tommy in disbelief and saw that he was giving Christine the very same look.

"Should I go try to stop them, or—"

"Let them figure it out by making complete asses out of themselves in front of the whole camp?" Tommy stood up and brushed his pants off. "Sounds like a plan to me."

"I'm not saying that to be a jerk."

"I know, but I am."

Christine smiled and shook the stress out of her shoulders and arms before sighing, defeated. "I just feel bad you guys put the daisy together."

"I could really care less about the damn daisy."

I nodded in agreement.

"Alright," Christine sighed again, "we better go down."

I turned on my wheelchair. We were the last people to leave the quad. So not only did everyone act like Tommy was the spawn of Satan, but he was also going to be made to look like even more of an ass by his fellow group members. This was just what he needed. I glanced over at him. He seemed pretty calm, but I wondered if the same thought was running through his mind.

Not surprisingly, Jonah and Amanda were sitting down in the front row—one I obviously couldn't reach in my chair. After debating on whether to make them come up to the last row with us, Christine decided it would be a lost cause. It would also show JT how out of control they really were. It was like they were in their own little world. Christine did decide to sit a row or two behind them, though, just in case things became too crazy.

"Okay, here's the plan," Tommy whispered in my ear. "If shit hits the fan, we run."

"If . . . shit . . . hits . . . the . . . fan . . . you . . . run. I . . . am . . . putting . . . my . . . chair . . . on . . . full . . . speed . . . and

. . . I . . . am . . . going. You . . . can . . . keep . . . up . . . with . . . me . . . or . . . you . . . can . . . not."

"Thanks. I thought we were in this together."

We smiled at each other as JT took the stage.

"Campers," JT said, his megaphone put a definite end to the conversation. "Now that you put your daisies together, we want to hear about them. I'm really looking forward to seeing what you came up with, so let's get right down to it. First up, why don't we have," he scanned his clipboard, "Amanda, Brynn, Jonah, and Tommy."

Chapter Ten

"*L*ook at those guys," Christine leaned towards Tommy and me and gestured toward our miserable-looking team-mates, sitting at a table across the room. "They look like they were hit by a Mack truck."

"I have no sympathy," Tommy shrugged. "They were jackasses in front of everyone last night and made me and Brynn look like jackasses, too."

"JT must've really gave it to them."

"That's what they get," Tommy said, absent-mindedly picking up a green marker and scribbling on the piece of paper in front of him.

Bonnie, the woman in charge of arts and crafts, came up to us. "Hello. How are you doing?"

"We're good," Christine replied, smiling at her brightly. "What do you have for us today?"

"Well, as you know," Bonnie excitingly looked each one of us in the eye, "this is Stage Stuff. You will be putting together props and backgrounds and everything else campers are going to use the night of the talent show. Since this is not a DAISY activity, you don't have to be in your group."

Tommy put the marker back. "Always a good thing," he muttered.

"I saw what happened last night," Bonnie put her hand on his shoulder, "and I'm sorry. In my opinion, I think JT needed to give them a breathalyzer test."

He raised his eyebrow and glanced at me. "No kidding."

We'd had a brief conversation about that last night—about how JT and anyone else at camp had to be blind to not figure out what Jonah, Amanda, and plenty of other campers were up to when they snuck off to the woods. Tommy had told me that the directors before JT were pretty lax with the rules so no one was ever confronted about it. Many counselors had looked the other way, but Tommy didn't suspect that Christine would be one of them. Not wanting to get anyone in trouble, though, we'd changed the subject when Christine had come by to walk me back to our cabin.

"Anyway, do you three want to work together? People have already told me what they are going to need, and you guys could choose what you want to work on before anyone else claims their projects," Bonnie said.

"They already know what they're doing for their skits?" Tommy asked, surprise evident in his voice. We hadn't even discussed ours yet. Although, not having half the group around made that difficult, I suppose.

"Some people are just that competitive, I guess," Bonnie said with a shrug.

Tommy and I agreed we wanted to work together. I fought back the urge to smile, which would have possibly led to a moderately loud squeal. I was so relieved we didn't have to be with Jonah and Amanda, who had climbed up onto the stage and then couldn't stop themselves from laughing their asses off in front of the entire camp the night before. After a few minutes of unexplainable hysterics, JT had to walk them off to the side.

Bonnie rattled off the few things campers had already told her they needed. We decided to work on the outside scenery that had been requested. Who could screw up some grass, a few clouds, and a tree or two? Tommy and Christine went to the giant rolls of paper and ripped off a blue piece that was about six feet long. I watched as they struggled to tape the large sheet to the wall. Out of the corner of my eye, I saw Randi walk into the room and walk straight up to Jonah and Amanda. With her hands on her hips, she kept her voice low, but it was clear by the looks on their faces that she wasn't holding back. If Tommy and I had been embarrassed just because they were our group members, I couldn't imagine what Randi had felt seeing her boyfriend on stage with another girl, falling over and laughing at absolutely nothing.

When I turned back to Christine and Tommy, they had successfully hung the paper and we were ready for business.

"So, how do you think we should do this?" Christine asked me, pulling my attention entirely away from the reaming Jonah and Amanda were receiving.

Staring at the large paper, I realized that I did have an idea for Christine, but I wasn't quite sure how it would work out.

When I was about four years old, my parents enrolled me in a school that a physical therapist told my parents about. It was called the Miracle Way. Although Miracle Way was a private school, it had nothing to do with religion. It was a school for kids with disabilities, ranging in age from two to twenty-one. I would never understand this, but any time I would come across a program for people who had disabilities, some type of variation of the words "amazing" or "miracle" would either be in the title or the description. Personally, I found it severely annoying. And slightly ironic.

I attended Miracle Way until I was ten years old when the administrators told my parents that I maxed out on the curriculum and that they couldn't teach me anymore. Now that I was a little older, I understood that this was almost a compliment. After all, they were basically saying I was too smart to be there. My ten-year-old brain, however, didn't see it that way. Miracle Way was my school. It was where I learned how to drive my wheelchair. It was where all my friends who had the same disabilities were. It was where my teachers knew if they called on me, they had to wait until I typed my answer. Why would I want to leave all of that behind and start over?

Along with the typical academic classes, such as math and science, Miracle Way also had classes like music and art. One of my favorite memories of going to school there was getting to go to art class. Even though the school had kids with all types of disabilities, I was the only one in my class who didn't have that much control of her hands. Once my teacher would explain the week's assignment to everyone, she would come over and help me complete it.

Miss Beth would put the crayon or the marker in my hand and hold my hand closed with her own hand. She then guided my hand to the paper. I wasn't able to draw any kind of picture or do the project for the day, but I was able to make a few marks with whatever drawing utensil I had in my hand. I always had to concentrate on keeping my arms in control as much as I could. Drawing with Miss Beth gave me the chance to actually use my arms for once. My artwork always looked like it was done by a three-year-old, but I really enjoyed the process.

I debated on telling Christine and Tommy that they could actually help me draw with my hands, but it was 9:30 in the morning, dreadfully hot in arts and crafts, and I didn't feel like typing it all out. Plus, whatever we were going to make was going to be scenery for the talent show. I didn't think any group would want the background for their skit to look like it was done by a preschooler.

"What do you think, Brynn?" Christine asked again. "Any ideas?"

"Tried that last night," Tommy said before I could type anything, "and we didn't get far. It turns out Brynn is lacking in the creativity department."

I stared at him. Then, without really thinking what I was doing, I deliberately stuck my tongue out at him.

"What? Is that your equivalent of giving me the finger?"

I gave him a very big matter-of-fact nod.

"Oh, well, in that case," he stuck his tongue right back at me. I laughed and he did, too.

"We are never going to get any work done, are we?" Christine said, smiling at both of us.

"She started it," Tommy pointed at me.

Oh, no he didn't! I furiously—pretend furiously, of course—started typing. "Don't . . . you . . . even . . . say . . ."

Tommy and Christine, trying not to smile, moved behind me so they could read my screen.

"This . . . is . . . my . . . fault. You . . . were . . . the . . . one . . . who—"

"Yeah yeah yeah. You don't have to waste your time typing excuses."

Christine walked back in front of me, shaking her head. "I was actually asking her about whether we should work with the contraption Randi made for her yesterday. She took a visor and taped a brush to it. I don't think Brynn likes it. She says it makes her feel like a unicorn."

"Oh, this will be fun to see, then." Tommy looked interested, his eyes filled with amusement.

I shot him a you-better-shut-the-hell-up look. After thinking for a second, I hit my talking switch. If I was going to paint, I wanted to paint like how I did with Miss Beth. I didn't want to use the visor, although I was more than grateful that Randi was willing to get creative to figure something out. It wasn't so much that I didn't want to look like a unicorn. I just hadn't painted like that in years. I didn't know what to do about the fact that I couldn't draw a straight line, though.

"Do . . . you . . . remember . . . when . . . you . . ."

Christine and Tommy took their places reading my screen again.

"Asked . . . me . . . if . . . I . . . could . . . paint . . . and . . . when . . . you . . . asked . . . me . . . if . . . I . . . could . . . hold . . . something?"

"Sure," Christine answered.

"I . . . know . . . I . . . told . . . you . . . I . . . could . . . not . . . but . . . I . . . can."

"Oh. Okay?" Without looking at Christine, I knew her brow was furrowed, not in frustrating or confusion, but in thought. She was trying to figure this out before I had to explain it. It'd only been three days and already I felt like we knew each other well.

"I . . . need . . . your . . . help." I could feel my own forehead crease as I thought about how to describe the process. "My . . . drawings . . . are . . . not . . . really . . . pretty. Do . . . you . . . know . . . how . . . you . . . could . . . help . . . me . . . with . . . that?"

"Ummm," Christine paused. "So, you are able to hold a brush in your hand?"

I shook my head, realizing I completely forgot to explain the thing I actually needed help with. "I . . . would . . . need . . . you . . . to . . . help . . . me . . . hold . . . my . . . hand . . . closed . . . and . . . you . . . would . . . have . . . to . . . hold . . . my . . . arm . . . to . . . the . . . paper . . . so . . . I—"

"Don't poke our eye out with a flying brush?" Tommy finished my sentence.

I nodded in a serious way, even though I knew Tommy meant it as a joke. "Do . . . you . . . think . . . this . . . will . . . work? I'm . . . just . . . afraid . . . whatever . . . I . . . do . . . will . . . look . . . like . . . crap."

"Whatever I draw always looks like crap," Tommy said, "so it'll be a contest to see who can paint the least crappiest thing."

"But . . . it's . . . for . . . the . . . talent . . . show. I . . . just . . . don't . . . want . . . anyone's . . . scenery . . . to . . . look—"

"It's camp," Christine shrugged. "Nobody expects the talent show to be a Broadway play."

"If . . . we . . . do . . . it . . . like . . . this . . . do . . . you . . . have . . . any . . . ideas . . . of . . . how . . . it . . . can . . . not . . . look . . . like . . . something . . . a . . . kindergartener . . . painted?"

"Well, I could always just direct your hand in specific directions. Would that work?"

I frowned. "I . . . would . . . be . . . okay . . . with . . . doing . . . that . . . because . . . I . . . always . . . liked . . . being . . . able . . . to . . . use . . . my . . . hands . . . but . . . it . . . will . . . seem . . . like . . . you . . . are . . . doing . . . all . . . the . . . work . . . and . . . I . . . don't . . . want . . . you . . . to . . . feel . . . like—"

"Brynn," Christine cut me off. "Remember your daisy goal? I'm not going to care. If you really want to paint like this, I'm cool with this. I would be cool with just about anything you would want to do, except throwing Jonah in the lake, or whatever you two wanted to do to him."

"Hang him upside down from a tree," Tommy corrected her.

"Oh, yes, that was it."

"What . . . do . . . you . . . think?" I looked at Tommy.

"I think that you want to do this, so you should do this. You say you did this before?"

I nodded. "At . . . my . . . old . . . school . . . where . . . I . . . wasn't . . . the . . . only . . . one . . . with . . . a . . . disability."

"I see," he paused. "So you don't want to do it here because you're the only one who has to paint this way? Do you think we would think you were weird? Because I definitely would *not* think that."

I shook my head. "It's . . . not . . . that . . . I . . . think . . . everyone . . . will . . . be . . . freaked . . . out. . . I . . . just . . . don't . . . want . . . to . . . need—"

The sound of Bonnie's voice startled me. "Okay, Stage Stuff campers! Time to go to your next activity. Clean 'em up, and move 'em out!"

In a panic, I immediately cleared my screen. "I'm . . . sorry. We . . . didn't . . . get . . . any . . . work . . . done . . . because . . . I . . . was . . . talking."

Tommy chuckled. "We have about ten days until the show, so I'm gonna say it's probably okay that we didn't do anything."

"You worry too much," Christine chimed in. "What did I say about remembering your goal? I didn't suggest you have it for nothing."

I nodded. I wanted to say "I know, I suck at this," but I didn't want to take more time to type it.

We decided to leave the paper taped to the wall where it was since we would be coming back to Stage Stuff every day until the talent show. I still wasn't sure if I wanted to paint the scene with my hands or my head. For one thing, I really didn't like needing that much help from Christine. Having my art teacher help me paint when I was seven years old was totally different from having my camp counselor help me paint when I was seventeen. Then again, would my paintbrush on the visor reach the paper? I would probably have to get so close to the wall I would look like I was making out with it.

Since my cabin happened to have arts and crafts next, Christine and I stayed put. I watched as Tommy made his way up the hill in the morning sunlight by himself. I frowned to myself. What were Carly and Jonah and everyone thinking when they saw him walking by himself? Eating by himself? Did it give them a sense of satisfaction when they caught him sitting alone? What kind of "friends" were they?

These questions startled me. I knew for a fact that at school Meg and Dave saw me in the cafeteria by myself; I was the only one who sat at a table with just a teacher's aide right beside me, so I was pretty sure that I stuck out like a sore thumb. And, more than once I caught Meg's eye when I was walking to class with only Mrs. B. I always told her how much I thought having a pet adult with me all day everyday fended off all of the other students. She knew how much I hated not having a lot of friends. So why wouldn't she even want to attempt to make up? If she'd made an effort and apologized for everything that she had done behind my back and just sat down and talked to me about it, maybe I would have forgiven her. Maybe I wouldn't have lost my best friends. I always wondered, though, if maybe she liked seeing me having to deal with the one thing I hated? Did one negative situation really turn an entire friendship into a battlefield?

I couldn't think about this anymore; I was clearly not over everything that had happened in school last year. I had a feeling it would take me a little while longer to get there. But camp had been a good distraction so far. Other campers had enough drama going on in their lives to keep me from thinking about my own.

My stomach had been twisting and turning when I'd been thinking about Meg and Dave, but when Randi and Carly walked into arts and crafts, it calmed down. I waited for the excitement to kick in like it usually did from seeing them, from seeing Randi. But it never came. All I could picture was Tommy walking up the hill, and Randi and Carly walking down, and them not saying hi to each other. I bet they didn't even make eye contact.

I forced myself to smile as Randi put her hand on my wheelchair handle. "What's up, my friend?"

I nodded my greeting to Randi as I turned my wheelchair on, the image of her not looking her old friend in the eye stuck in my head. I realized that I didn't really know too much about the relationships between these campers. How long had they known each other? Who were friends outside of camp? Which ones of them had dated in the past and who broke whose heart? How good of friends were they really? Maybe they were more of acquaintances rather than BFFs. But still, Carly seemed so excited when she saw Tommy before she knew what happened with him and Jenn. There had to be some kind of connection with all of them, right? Having recently gone through this, I wasn't okay with anyone who was throwing away any kind of relationship, especially for a reason that didn't have anything to do with them.

Bonnie told everyone to come sit around the table. Just about my entire cabin was there, including Evelyn. Another realization hit me just then: I didn't really know anybody other than Randi and Carly. These were the people who I was living with for the past three days, and I didn't even know where they were from. I needed to change this, and it wasn't just because Randi and Carly were starting to annoy me with the Tommy thing. I was here to make more than one or two friends; I wanted to get to know everyone and I wanted to hear their stories. That was what I should be doing.

I looked for a new place to sit, an open space next to someone new. Unfortunately, Randi and Carly sat down by Christine, leaving a space in-between them for me. I guess I could have just pulled up to someone else and struck up a conversation with them, but that would be awkward for a number of reasons, one being that I would have to explain why I didn't sit by Randi and Carly when they specifically made room for me. Christine would also have to get up and move when she already had a seat. Not to mention, it would be a little weird to go sit by a group of girls who I didn't know for no immediately apparent reason.

I started to inch my way to the spot without a folding chair beside Christine, trying to get as close to the table as I could. This wasn't really easy, considering that frustration with my lack of new friends and disappointment in my current friends was taking over my body, like any emotion did. I should have stopped when my mount for the TechnoTalk was about two inches away from the table. I really was close enough to feel like a part of the group. However, I found myself wanting to be right up against the table. I knew it would bother me if my TechnoTalk bar didn't touch the edge of where the group was going to be working. I figured just a tap to my forward switch would do it. I soon found out, under my current circumstances, just a tap to my forward switch wasn't going to be possible at that moment.

Instead of hitting my forward switch for just a split second, my neck jerked. My head slammed against my headrest, making my wheelchair jolt forward more than the two inches I had intended. It rammed into the table and everyone jumped—a few girls even screamed out in surprise. I managed to put my head down to release the switch, but it was too late. The entire table had skidded across the floor, tapping some girls seated on the other side in the chests or stomachs. It was obvious that no one was hurt, but I could feel my face exploding with red as every set of eyes around the table turned my way. I certainly hadn't won any friends with *that* maneuver.

"Are you okay, Brynn?" Christine jumped up from her seat.

I barely nodded. I focused on hitting my knee switch. *Reverse! Reverse! Reverse!*

"Good job," Randi joked as I backed up in my spot. "Were you drinking this morning?"

She was clearly attempting to lighten the moment and I tried to laugh, but the sound I made was more comparable to a nervous guinea pig giving birth than a cute giggle.

"That's what I thought."

"Oh, you guys," Christine said, pulling the table back toward her with the help of a few girls on our side. "Be nice to Brynn. She probably wants to die right now."

I gave a huge nod. She had *no* idea.

"Hey," Randi helped pull the table as everyone pushed it toward us, "what did I tell you? As long as you don't puke on me, we're good."

Once the table was back in place (the TechnoTalk bar was touching the edge; no need to obsess about that now), and once everyone seemed to forget about my bulldozing moment, I went to hit my talking switch. I wanted to apologize for my CP moment—and almost taking out a few people. It was only then I noticed it: the blank screen. It was dead. I tapped my talking switch a few more times. Nothing. *Oh, no! Please?* When I hit the table, it must have jarred something inside the TechnoTalk. Damn it! This was not happening!

I looked at Christine. Whenever I looked at someone to try to tell them something, I felt like it was different from when I looked at someone when I was saying hi, or when I was having a conversation with them, although I could never pinpoint why this look was different than others. Maybe I looked at people with more intensity? Maybe it was my facial expression? Nevertheless, I caught Christine's eye. I pointed at my TechnoTalk with my eyes, and then looked back at her.

"You okay?" she whispered while Bonnie explained something about collages. "You don't have anything to worry about. Everyone knows that you didn't mean to run into the table. They probably won't even remember it by tonight."

I shook my head. *We have a much bigger problem than me running into the table.* I looked at my very dead communication device again and then back at Christine. She looked at my screen and I knew the exact moment when she saw the dark screen and understood what had happened. She tried to hide her reaction, but I recognized it because it was the same one I was having: *Oh shit.*

Chapter Eleven

"Oh, that's not good. . . ." Christine said, getting out of her chair and beginning to inspect my TechnoTalk. "Did it happen when you hit the table?"

I lowered my head.

"It's okay. I'm sure we'll get it working. How about if I try hitting the power button?"

I nodded eagerly. *Please work!*

Christine pressed the button above the screen. I waited for the little green light to flash inside the button like it always did when it powered up. It didn't. She then held the button down for a few seconds and let it go. Nothing. *Really?*

"What if I unplug your switch and plug it in again? Will that work?"

Unplugging and plugging my switch would be like unplugging and plugging a mouse to a computer. It didn't have anything to do with the power. But, of course, I couldn't tell Christine this, so I let her do it. If I didn't, she would have probably wanted to know why she couldn't, and I couldn't have answered that, either. Just like I thought, the TechnoTalk didn't turn on despite the many times Christine unplugged and plugged in the wire.

"Hmmm," she paused. "What do you think we should do?"

I consciously pressed my lips together. "Maaah."

"What was that?"

By now, Bonnie had finished explaining the project and everyone was busy getting to work, so I didn't have to worry about sounding like an idiot. I tried to make more of a O sound. "Maaooh." I sounded like Dory from fricking *Finding Nemo*.

"Something with a M?" she asked.

I could tell Christine was really trying to understand me and it somehow made me want to cry.

I nodded, tears pricking the corners of my eyes.

"Okay. It's okay," she reassured me. "M. Can you say the next letter?"

I concentrated. It wasn't that I couldn't talk; I could say a few words. I just really had to work to be able to. "Ohhh."

"O? Is it an O?"

I nodded again.

"Okay! M. O. What about the next letter?"

"Maaahh." I didn't know why, but M's were always the easier letter for me to say.

"M? So it's M—"

"Mom," Randi said, suddenly on my other side. "It's M-O-M, Christine. Mom. Call her mom. I figured that out, like, two minutes ago," she said, shaking her head as though she was disappointed with my counselor. Randi was clearly trying to lighten the situation a bit and I was grateful.

"Is it mom?" Christine asked, just to confirm.

I enthusiastically nodded.

"You want to call your mom?"

Yes! I did. I knew my mom was about two hours away and couldn't really do anything, but she knew the TechnoTalk better than Christine. She was able to talk more than I could at this point, and I figured having her on the phone was the best option I was going to get right then.

"Okay," Christine agreed, "why don't we go to the office? They have your mom's number, and I think they have a speaker phone we could use."

Christine caught Evelyn's eye and motioned to the door. I locked eyes with Randi and smiled at her, silently sending a thank-you. She smiled back and took her seat next to Carly.

"Where ya guys going?" Carly asked loud enough for everyone to turn our way.

"Brynn's TechnoTalk turned off when she hit the table," Christine explained, "and it won't turn back on, so we're going to go call her mom."

Great. Not only was I the girl who ran into the table with her wheelchair and gave everyone a heart attack, but now I was the girl who ran into the table with her wheelchair and gave everyone a heart attack who broke her communication device while doing it who now had to go call her mom to fix it. I was really going to win them over now. *Go, me!*

The Camp Lakewood office was just down the hill from arts and crafts, and unlike any other building at camp, it was air-conditioned. It'd only been three days, but I'd almost forgotten what being cool felt like. The artificial arctic air hugged my sticky body, giving me goosebumps all over. I sat by the phone in the empty conference room while Christine went to find the card with all of my phone numbers on it.

"Okay, here we go," Christine said, walking back into the room. "Which number do you think we should try first? Your house?"

I nodded. I realized it was the first time that I didn't know if my mom was working or not. It wasn't like I was a mama's girl or anything; I just always knew where she was in case a situation like this occurred when I was at school or with anybody else. I suddenly was struck by a strong sense of independence, even though I happened to be calling my mom for help at that moment.

Christine picked up the receiver, dialed the number to my house, and put it on speaker. My dad answered after two rings. "Hello?"

"Hi, Mr. Evason, this is Brynn and her counselor, Christine, from Camp Lakewood. How's it going?"

"Good, Christine. Is everything okay?"

"Well, we had a little bit of an accident. Brynn ran into a table in arts and crafts. She's okay, but her computer won't turn on. Do you have any ideas of what we could do to get it working again?"

"Oh, Brynn! What did you do that for?"

I looked at the phone, my brows furrowed. *Like I really wanted to hit the table, have my TechnoTalk go off, and call you for help.*

"Oh, it was just an accident." Christine waved it off.

"You know what? I'm not the best person to ask. You can call Sherry at work. Do you have her number?"

"We do. Thank you, Mr. Evason."

"No problem. Are you having any fun there, Brynn?"

"Yeaaahh," I replied.

"That's good. Alright, Brynnie. I love you. And, please be more careful. Don't run into anything else. You really have to watch."

I rolled my eyes at Christine.

"She will," Christine smiled. "Thanks, again."

"Okay. Take care."

My dad hung up the phone just as Christine hit the speaker button. I knew my dad wouldn't be much help. For being the man of the house, he was never really into anything society typically dubbed as "male" tasks—anything to do with technology or wiring or wood work. Even if something little broke on my chair, my mom was usually the one to fix it. Christine dialed my mom at work; I hoped she would have better advice.

"Pittsburgh Dental. This is Sherry speaking. How can I help you?"

"Hey, Mrs. Evason! This is Christine. I'm with Brynn at Camp Lakewood."

"Hi . . . is everything okay? What's wrong?" I could sense the panic in my mom's tone. Of course she would think something was really wrong or that there had been a serious emergency.

Christine explained what happened again.

"Is she there with you?"

"Yeah. You're on speaker, so she can hear you."

"Brynn!" I looked up when my mom addressed me, all worry gone from her voice. "Why did you hit the table? Were you drunk or something? You know better than that."

I smiled and put my head down. If I did something wrong, CP moment or no CP moment, I still did something wrong.

"Oh, it was just one of those things," Christine said, trying to make light of it, just as she had done with my dad. "Everything will be okay, but do you have any idea how we can get it to turn back on. We tried hitting the power button a few times."

"Hm . . . I don't know. Did you try charging it?"

"No, but we can do that."

"Yeah, try charging it. Other than that, I don't know what to tell you. I'm working the next three days, so I can't come up there. Brynn, you really shouldn't have run into anything."

Really? Did not know that. Thank you for pointing that out, Mom.

Christine grinned at me. "Okay. I think we're going to go try charging it."

"If that doesn't work, you could always call the TechnoTalk tech support."

"Oh, okay. Glad to know that's an option."

"Do you want Paul to come get her and bring her home?" Mom asked.

"Nah, I'm sure we'll get it working."

"'Kay, thank you. Call me if you don't get it working."

"Will do."

"I love you, Brynn. I miss you. Home is not the same without you."

I nodded at Christine so she knew to answer for me. "She misses you, too."

"Be careful. Pay more attention!"

"She will."

"Good. See you later."

Christine hung up the phone and put my card back in the file. We headed up the hill. It was lunchtime now. Before I went into the dining hall, Christine took my TechnoTalk off to take it back to the cabin. I went in without it and headed for the table where we'd been sitting by ourselves, only it wasn't empty, as I figured it would be. Tommy was sitting next to my spot, already eating a sandwich.

It took my brain a few seconds to switch from my thoughts from my-TechnoTalk-just-died-and-we-couldn't-get-it-to-turn-back-on (ignoring the fact that I obnoxiously ran into the table and made a moron out of myself) to I-was-still-at-Camp-Lakewood-and-Tommy-was-sitting-at-the-table-where-I-usually-sat-by-myself. The two gears slowly collided and the wheels started to churn once again as I realized I wasn't going to be able to explain to him that I didn't like to eat with anyone else because I didn't want to gross them out.

I could just drive to (not *into!*) another empty table, but just like when he came up to me on the basketball court, I didn't want to drive away from him without any kind of explanation. That and there wasn't another empty table around that I could drive up to . . . which was probably why he was there in the first place.

"You don't have your computer?" he asked when he saw me approach. Relief washed over me; the fact that he immediately noticed meant that I had one less thing to explain to him.

Tommy took a bite of his sandwich, which looked like it was made up of every food I hated. I was never a fan of lunchmeat or anything that went with it.

I frowned.

"Probably a good thing," he said.

I gave him a drastic what-the-hell look.

"Just sayin'. Did Christine get sick of you making excuses?"

I glared at him. Giving him a dirty look was just about the only thing I could do to him at this point, even though I wasn't the least bit offended.

"No? Did you get sick of yourself making excuses?"

I nodded a big nod. *Yep. That was it.*

"Oh, okay. Well as long as we're on the same page," he said, taking another bite. "Oh, hey, Christine," he said through a mouthful of gross sandwich.

I turned to find my counselor next to me. "Hey, Tom. You're joining us, I see."

"That was the plan. Is that okay with you?"

"Fine by me. Are you cool with it, Brynn?"

I shook my head, more of a joke than an actual answer.

"But it's Tom. He won't care how you eat." She turned to him. "Brynn doesn't like to eat in front of anyone, because she doesn't—"

I shook my head, interrupting her.

"That's not it?"

For lack of any other way of telling her, I stuck my tongue out in Tommy's direction.

"I think it's because I wasn't exactly being the nicest person a few minutes ago," Tommy said, "so she feels the need to be not the nicest person back to me?"

I nodded. Glad he understood.

"You two have fun with that," Christine said. "I'm going to go get our food. It looks like they're having sandwiches. Do you like turkey? Bologna? Ham?"

Ew.

"PB&J? Again?"

Again. For the third time this week.

"Do you want me to see if they have strawberry jelly or something, so you can have a little variety?"

I hesitantly nodded. I wasn't really a fan of strawberry jelly, but then again, I was never really a fan of peanut butter and jelly sandwiches in general. They were the type of food that was just there. And they just happened to be here at camp. So why not?

"'Kay, I'll be back."

Tommy took a sip of his water. "So what makes you want to sit over here with only Christine instead of with the clan? Not that I'm for anybody sitting with them right now; they're all a bunch of bastards. You just seemed like you were getting cool with Randi."

I glanced to where they were sitting. They were on the other side of the dining hall. Randi with her boy, Carly with hers. Jenn and her friend Amanda. Jonah seemed like he was telling a story and everyone was laughing. For the first time, I felt like I didn't want to eat with them for more reasons than being worried about sometimes making a mess while I was eating. I realized that maybe I didn't really fit into that group as much as I wished I had. I turned back to Tommy and shrugged.

"It's better this way." He finished the last bite of his sandwich. "I wouldn't have been able to sit with you if you were sitting with them."

Chapter Twelve

I made it through lunch with having few tongue spasms. Whenever food did come out of my mouth, Christine did a pretty good job cleaning it up as fast as she could, and it didn't seem to faze Tommy at all. If I was sitting by someone and they had a stream of jelly drooling down their chin, I had to admit I wouldn't be able to eat anymore. That was part of why I thought people, especially people like Jonah who appeared to be close-minded, would be grossed out. It was because I knew I would get grossed out. And if I didn't think I could handle it myself, how could I expect everyone else to handle it?

When we were done eating, Christine and I went into the bathroom. By now, I was comfortable enough with Christine for my body to relax so we didn't need Randi to help with the lift anymore. When we came out, everybody had left the dining hall—everyone except Tommy.

"Have any plans for Siesta?" Tommy's brown eyes met mine, shocking me the tiniest bit.

I glanced away for Christine's help with an answer.

"Were you just going to listen to your music on the basketball court again?" she asked me.

I shrugged, nodded, and looked back at Tommy.

"You're not going to listen to that crap again, are you?"

"Are you talking about Abbie Bonza?" Christine jumped in. "She's not crap. She's awesome. Even I like her."

I blew her a kiss. *Thank you!*

"Oh, I see how it is. I get the f-you tongue and she gets the you're-awesome kiss."

"Well, I'm not the one bashing her favorite singer," Christine said in my defense, "so it would make sense I would get the you're-awesome kiss."

"Whatever," Tommy replied with a mock eye roll. "I was going to go hang out in arts and crafts. Do you want to come with me? Bonnie usually has some decent music playing, so you will be able to expand your music knowledge."

I turned to Christine.

"Don't look at me!" she said, throwing her hands up. "I'm probably going to go back to the cabin and catch up with the other campers, unless you guys want me to come, so do whatever you want to do."

I turned back to Tommy. Giving him my questioning look, I craned my neck to look at my talking switch.

"Uhhhh." He blinked, not catching my drift. "What?"

I repeated my maneuver.

"Your TechnoTalk?" Christine guessed. "You want to go see if it's working now?"

That wasn't exactly what I was asking, but close enough.

For the obvious reason of not wanting to get his head chopped off by the girls inside, Tommy and I chose to wait outside the cabin when we got there while Christine went in and checked on my device. Something told me it wasn't going to turn on. The battery was full this morning and it always lasted throughout the day.

I am so screwed! I thought, tilting my head up toward the sun and trying to enjoy the warmth on my face. *No worries, Mom. I'll come home with the tan you wanted . . . and maybe an expensive piece of broken equipment.*

I tried to remember what I did before I had my TechnoTalk. I received my first communication device when I was about eight years old. Before that, my old school, Miracle Way, had rigged up this poster board with pictures on it, such as a picture of a bathroom and a picture of a stick figure eating. Because I couldn't use my hands, someone had to go through the pictures one by one, which kind of defeated the purpose of the board. I didn't know why they couldn't just ask me if I had to go to the bathroom or if I was hungry instead of wasting the time pointing at the pictures.

By the time I was eight, the school decided I was old enough for a communication device, only what they provided me wasn't a communication device. It was actually a regular laptop computer. It worked like my TechnoTalk—I would hit a switch by my head to select letters on the screen. It just didn't have word prediction or the ability to program messages I would want to say over and over. Being that I was eight years old, I didn't want to use it very much. It took a lot of work and my complete concentration to use that big computer in front of me. And, really, how many words can an eight-year-old spell?

When I was ten, I got my first TechnoTalk and it didn't exactly take me much time to get used to; I had already been typing with my head for two years (when I would actually use my stupid laptop), so it just came naturally to me. I still didn't like the fact that I had to use such a big thing or that it was attached to my chair in front of me. I felt that my friends, teachers, and my parents knew what I was saying without it. I was irritated with how slow it was, but I knew that everyone else was happier when I was successfully able to get my point across. Now, at seventeen, I wondered when and how my feelings about using my device had ended up on the opposite side of the pole. I couldn't imagine—and didn't want to imagine—spending more than a few hours without it.

Just as I expected, the TechnoTalk didn't turn on for Christine. She said the light didn't even come on to show it was charging. I sighed. *Why did this have to happen now? Why did I have to be a total idiot and drive into the table?* She asked me if I still wanted to go with Tommy or if I wanted to try calling the company. I looked at Tommy with my question.

"What do I think you should do?" he asked.

It was more like *Are you okay hanging out with a girl who can't talk all afternoon?*

"I say screw your computer. Come hang out with me."

I could feel that familiar flush inching up my neck as my mouth dropped open.

"What? If you spend all that time on hold and then they can't tell you how to fix it, then you would've wasted all that time when we should've been hanging out."

I looked at Christine. She smiled back, slyly. *She knew!*

"You don't need to check with me every time you want to do something," she said, her smile stretching across her face. "If you want to go down with Tom, go. We can call the company some other time."

I hesitated before smirking at Tommy.

"Have fun," Christine said in a sing-song voice before heading back inside. I watched her until the door closed behind her, willing her to keep my secret. If the other girls found out that I was starting to develop a serious crush on Tommy . . .

Tommy and I started down the hill to arts and crafts. I wondered again how this was going to go. Meg and Dave could always manage without my TechnoTalk. Granted, I couldn't exactly tell them about the dumbass that cut me off in the hall that day, but I always seemed to find a way to be a part of the conversation. I hoped it would be the same with Tommy.

Wait a minute. What was I thinking? Of course it was going to be okay with Tommy. Not only did he know my TechnoTalk wasn't working and still wanted me to come with him, but within twenty-four hours of meeting him, I had already communicated something to him without being able to hear *and* without using my device. If that didn't make him run away from me, I was sure we would be good to go. As we entered into the most creative building at Camp Lakewood, I felt myself relax.

Tommy went over to the giant piece of blue paper that we hung on the wall just a few hours earlier. I followed. Luckily, there were only three other campers in the building, being that it was an off time for activities. None of them seemed like they wanted to crucify Tommy, so we were in good shape.

"Notice the music we're listening to," Tommy motioned in the direction of the stereo. "Can you name this tune?"

I chuckled.

"Can you name this artist?"

I smiled and shrugged.

"Of course you can't," he said and rubbed his eyes. "He was before the . . . girl . . . singer . . . era. Nick, do you know what this song is?"

The uber tall guy who was walking by turned around, confused. "One Love?"

"And who is the artist?"

"Bob Marley?"

"Thank you, Nick . . . and Nick, could you tell Brynn here what Bob Marley songs are usually about?"

The tall guy shrugged. "Weed?"

Tommy collapsed on the table, burying his head in his arms. "Thanks, Nick," he muttered.

The guy shrugged again and walked off.

"What is wrong with our generation?" Tommy exclaimed, keeping his face tucked tightly away. "You don't know what good music is, and when somebody does recognize it, they don't even know what it's about."

I chuckled.

"Oh, glad you think this is funny," he said and lifted his head. "Marley is probably rolling in his grave right now. Yeah, he did a lot of drugs, but his songs were about so much more. He's a fricking legacy. He would write about political and social issues that were going on in Jamaica at the time. He had great, great,

great songs that actually meant something more than 'I want to be with you. Let's hold hands and smile at each other.'"

I smiled and tried to look interested.

"And you don't care. Alright then," he stood and looked around the room. "Anyway, how were you saying you used to paint?" He grabbed a paper bowl and filled it with green goo.

I stared at him. *Nobody said anything about having to paint if I joined you.*

Tommy reached for a brush left behind on the table. "You just need help holding your hand closed and putting it to the paper, right?"

I slowly nodded. I suddenly knew where this was going.

"Seems easy enough. Let's do it, then."

Are you serious? I didn't need a device to communicate this thought; my face said it all for me.

"What?" He put the paint and brush on the table. "Do you think I'm going to let the brush slip and you're going to get paint everywhere? Which, actually, could very well happen, I'm going to be honest, but it could also be pretty hilarious."

He was serious.

"What if I told you if paint gets on you, you can get paint on me?"

I could feel my cheeks getting warm . . . again! I wondered briefly if he knew the effect he was having on me. The sly smile on his face told me he had some clue.

"Look, Brynn." Tommy suddenly stopped with the jokes. "I don't care that I have to help you. I'm not going to think I'm doing all the work, if that's what you are worried about. I could tell by your face this morning that you really wanted to paint. I just want you to be able to do whatever you want to do, and I really want to help you if you'll let me."

It was times like these when I was actually thankful I didn't have my TechnoTalk, because I would have been staring at my screen not knowing what to say. Tommy caught me off guard.

He wanted to help me paint, because he knew I wanted to paint. Realizing he was not going to let me say no, I carefully drove up in front of the paper so I was facing the wall.

Tommy set the paint on the floor. "Do you want me to take your arm out of the arm strap?"

I nodded, silently willing myself not to sock this guy in the face. Although, even with a black eye, he'd still be pretty cute.

He gently held my wrist as he pulled the armband off. Usually whenever someone I didn't know reached for me, my body would tense up, like it did with Christine the first time she helped me in the bathroom. I waited for my body to tense up even more because a guy, a cute guy for that matter, was holding my arm. To my ultimate surprise, my body did the exact opposite.

Somehow—and I had *no* idea how or why—for a brief instant, Tommy's hand ended up in my hand. My fingers wrapped around his warm fingers. What the hell was going on? My body? My hand? It was as calm as could be. I was almost just as amazed at that as I was at the fact that I was practically holding Tommy's hand. Why wasn't I pulling away? I always imagined, in a situation like this, my hand would jerk away or I'd have a major CP moment. I wasn't doing any of those things. I was completely wonderstruck.

"The brush," Tommy stuttered. "You need the brush. The brush."

Holy crap. Was he flustered, too? Did he mean to grab my hand, or did it just happen and he was embarrassed? Needing to think about something else, anything else, I looked down and concentrated on the brush. *The brush . . . the brush . . . the brush.* My heartbeat, which I hadn't even realized was accelerated, slowly returned to normal.

Tommy picked it up and dipped it in the paint. "So, do I just hold your hand when you close it around the brush?"

I barely nodded. He put the brush to the palm of my hand. My arm was still calm from his touch, and all five of my fingers closed around the brush similar to how a two-year-old would grab a crayon. This was a first. I couldn't manage to nod my head at that moment, but . . . I had total cooperation from my arm? Tommy gently put his hand over my fist, and I thought my entire arm was going to melt away.

"Ready?" he said, almost in a whisper.

Concentrate on painting. Concentrate on painting. Concentrate on painting.

Tommy guided my hand up to the paper. Because the brush was angled at the ground, it was perfect for painting vertical lines. We painted four lines before we had to dip the brush again. I let go, still amazed at how calm my body was. It made me want to run off and tell somebody about this new discovery.

"Hey!" Tommy suddenly exclaimed.

I turned toward him—and felt a glob of cool goo press against my cheek.

Chapter Thirteen

"What the crap happened to you?" Randi asked as I entered the cabin. "You look like you were attacked by the Wicked Witch."

I pulled up to Carly's bunk, where Randi was sitting, as usual. I had green paint all over my face and my arms, which probably did make me look like I got into a fight with the green witch herself. I wondered what Tommy's cabin mates would make of the big green splotch on his arm. Did guys notice stuff like that?

"She was just down at arts and crafts," Christine came up beside me.

"The Wicked Witch is down at arts and crafts?" Randi mused. "Is she going to go swimming in the pool again this year?"

"I have no idea. Why don't you go ask her?"

"I just might," Randi said, an evil grin slowly crossing her face.

Relieved that Christine didn't mention Tommy, I chuckled.

"So like I was telling you on the way up here," Christine started, "the cabin is going to go play soccer with one of the boys' cabins. I'm not entirely sure how you could play, but I'm open to any ideas you might have."

I actually could play soccer (Well, okay, I actually could kick a soccer ball if my feet were unstrapped and if my footrests were out of the way; I never played the actual sport before.), but I thought it would be awkward to play with fifteen other kids who were able to run much faster than my wheelchair could go.

"Sit on the sidelines with Car and cheer me on while I kick my boyfriend's ass. It will be a good time," Randi said, hopping off the bed and opening the trunk at the foot of it. She rummaged through her clothes and pulled out a new set of clothes—t-shirt, cute mesh shorts, and knee-high socks. I couldn't imagine wearing that much cotton on a day like today, but I also knew, from my few experiences playing soccer, that the socks took some of the sting out of being smacked in the shins with the ball, so I understood why she picked them out.

Carly, however, scrunched up her nose as Randi pulled the purple and white striped socks up her legs. That expression reminded me why I wasn't exactly eager to hang out with Carly on the sidelines, but I went along with it.

"By the way, that sucks about your computer not working," Randi said. "Want me to throw the thing in the lake? Because I'll do it."

"What good would that do?" Christine exclaimed. "Instead of not having it for a day or so, she wouldn't have it permanently. And besides, that computer probably costs more than I made in the three summers I worked here. I don't want to be responsible for it when her mom comes and we have to tell her it's now a permanent part of Camp Lakewood."

Randi shrugged. "I just thought I would offer."

Carly stood up from the bed and straightened her dress. "I'm ready to go down."

"You really look like it, too."

"Hey! You know I'm not playing. I am going to watch you play."

"You are going to watch me play while you wait for Gabe to look at you in between plays being the only one on the field wearing a dress," Randi corrected her. "I'm your best friend. I know you."

"Shut up. I'm awesome," Carly huffed.

"Well, I'm not ready yet," Randy said, gesturing toward the clothes on the bed she'd yet to change into.

"But the boys are probably already down there," Carly whined.

Christine sighed loudly and gave me a look. I smiled and shrugged at her. "Brynn, how 'bout you wait for Randi and I'll head down to the field with Carly now? It's clearly important for her to be punctual today. That okay?"

I nodded and Carly skipped out of the cabin, eagerly following Christine and chattering about how cute Gabe was.

"It'll all be over in like, twelve days, you know," Randi was saying as she changed from one pair of shorts to the other. "Carly and Gabe, I mean. Carly's camp relationships truly are *camp* relationships. She never carries them past the front gate. But I guess whatever makes her happy."

I couldn't respond without my TechnoTalk, and Randi knew that, but she didn't seem to mind. I was grateful that she was so comfortable with me already; I hoped that our friendship wouldn't be like Carly's camp relationships.

"Carly and I have been friends since sixth grade, when she transferred to my middle school. We go to the same high school now. Have I told you that?" She waited for me to shake my head and then she resumed looking for her brush, which I could see was peeking out from beneath the bed. I knew if I could catch her eye, I would be able to motion with my head to its location, but she was too busy searching.

"People are really surprised we're friends," she continued. "Sometimes I'm even surprised we're friends. But I think she like . . . adds something to my life, you know? She provides all the drama I need without me having to go out and find my own. She's a really sweet, caring girl. She doesn't always show it, and sometimes I question her judgment on stuff, but she really is pretty cool. I think you'd like her more if you got to know her better. Aha!" She waved the brush in the air and yanked out her ponytail holder.

She filled me in on how her friendship with Carly worked (a whole lot of advice not taken, occasional fighting and tears, and tons of movies, trips to the mall, and nights spent driving around their city simply listening to music and gossiping), but it was another one of Randi's relationships that I was most interested in. If I'd had my TechnoTalk, I would have asked her about Jonah—how they met, how long they'd been together, why they were together when they were clearly two different types of people. But . . . that conversation would have to come later. I felt comfort in knowing that Randi felt she could talk to me about her personal life, and I had a feeling that the conversation I wanted to have—and many others (I was *dying* to tell someone about Tommy!)—would eventually take place.

After Randi pulled her pink hair back nice and tight, she shoved her feet in her shoes and turned to look me up and down. "Want to stop at the bathrooms and wash all that paint off?" she asked.

Although I appreciated the feeling of acceptance from Randi's offer to help me, I shook my head. I'd wear my green like a gold medal. I liked looking down at my arm. It reminded me of how much fun Tommy and I had in the arts and crafts building. No drama, no worrying about what other people were thinking. It'd been just us—and it'd been *awesome*.

"Okay, suit yourself!" Randi said and headed toward the door. We joined the others at the field where our cabin would be taking on Cabin 8, which was Jonah and Gabe's cabin. Christine and Carly were already seated on the grass, so I pulled up beside them as Randi ran up to the cabin huddle. The sun beat down on my shoulders and legs, sending chills throughout my body. If nothing else, this would be the perfect time to work on that tan my mom had mentioned.

"Did you ever end up trying out for cheerleading last year, Carly?" Christine asked.

"Yeah, I did. I didn't make it. I think it was because I screwed up my split."

"I'm sorry to hear that. I know how much you wanted to cheer. But don't they have different cheerleaders do certain things? I'm sure not all cheerleaders are able to do everything in their routines."

Carly blocked the sun with her hand. "Yeah, but you know how they are. If you aren't perfect, they don't want you."

"Are you going to try out again this year?"

"I don't think so. Once a cheer reject, always a cheer reject."

"I think you should try. Ya never know."

By now, the two teams took the field. Jonah and Randi were both on defense for their cabins. A boy counselor blew a whistle and the guys kicked off.

"Heyyyy!" Carly shouted. "What's up?"

I glanced in the direction where she was calling. *Oh, no.* Jenn and Amanda took a seat on the grass next to Carly. I was surprised again with how much they looked like each other. Not so much with the physical features, but they both had way too much makeup on. (I was surprised it wasn't melting under the summer sun and dripping off their chins.) They both had jeans and a tank top on and they were wearing their extremely long hair down. It was almost like they actually wanted to be carbon copies of each other.

I sighed to myself. This was going to be interesting. Shouldn't they be with their cabin? Why were they here?

"Hey, guys. How's it going?" I was so surprised with how neutral Christine could be. Even when I knew she didn't really agree with what someone was doing, she always treated them with respect. I guess it was just part of the job.

"Good," Jenn said flatly.

"I'm so glad you came to visit us," Carly squealed. Where did she get all that energy?

"Yeah. Our cabin was playing baseball, the boringest sport ever, so we decided to come find you. Where's Randi?"

"Playing."

"She would." Jenn turned her attention to the field and immediately spotted Randi, standing with her arms on her hips, clearly irritated that it was taking so long for her team to wrestle the ball off the guys.

Jenn was still talking. "So, our cabin is playing Tom's cabin right now, but he's not playing either, and he kept, like, staring at us."

I shifted in my chair. *Here we go.*

"That sucks," Carly commented. "Did you say anything to him?"

"No, because, he's just weird. That's when we decided to come find you. We like you."

"And," Amanda chimed in, "he, like, had this big blotch of paint on his arm. He's so weird. Like, why would you not wash that off? He's just walking around, looking all dirty. I have no idea why you were ever with him."

Carly paused for a second, and then pointed to me. "Wait, Brynn has paint on her face."

I sucked in my breath. I knew this had to come out sooner or later.

Christine nodded. "They were hanging out in arts and crafts, and I guess they got into a paint fight."

"Tom and her were hanging out together?" Carly repeated, making sure she heard Christine right.

"Yep."

She then asked the question all three girls were so obviously wondering. "Why?"

I jolted and forced myself to look away. *They are just being like this because Tommy broke up with her. It has nothing to do with you. They are just mad and they don't want anyone, including you, to be talking to him.*

148

"What do you mean 'why'?" Christine asked. "Jenn, I am so sorry you and Tom aren't together anymore. I really am. And, if you don't want to talk to him anymore, that's cool. I'm not going to tell you what to do. However, I know for a fact that he would never do anything to intentionally hurt you or anyone else, and I don't think it's fair to have the whole camp shun him, especially the campers who don't really know him. Like Brynn."

Jenn didn't say anything. Amanda didn't say anything. Carly didn't say anything. I wouldn't know what I would say if I could say something. In my mind, however, I was cheering, *Go, Christine!* Was she being a little too harsh? No, not at all. She was being honest and straightforward; she was saying what other people (including me!) had wanted to say ever since Jenn arrived at camp. This was necessary. Was it fair that Tommy was being treated like crap just because he didn't want to be in a relationship anymore? Absolutely not. Should someone have tried to make Jenn see that she was kind of ridiculous? Absolutely. And Christine seemed perfectly happy to take on that role.

"I'm sorry," Christine continued. "I'm really not trying to be the bad guy here. I just think what's going on is a little unfair to Tom. Like I was saying, if you don't want to talk to him anymore, that's your choice. I wouldn't have a problem with that. I just don't think the whole camp needs to be brought into this. Am I making any sense at all?"

"Yeah," Jenn shrugged like it was no big deal, "I guess we know now whose ass Tommy has been kissing."

Christine just shook her head and turned her attention back to the soccer game. I respected her so much in that moment that I could've squealed. But I didn't. I just watched Randi kick ass until the other girls got up and walked off, taking all the tension with them.

I waited outside of my cabin for Christine to get my TechnoTalk. After her attempt at mending the Tommy versus

Camp Lakewood battle backfired and the girls left, we had lost track of who was winning the soccer game and decided to go try and call the TechnoTalk company.

I had very little hope they would be able to tell Christine what to do to make it turn back on—especially since charging it wasn't working. I only had to call the company twice before, and both times I had to send the device into the TechnoTalk office, which was in Kentucky. I hoped, I *prayed*, that was not the case this time. I didn't know what I would do. What would be the point of being at camp if I couldn't have in-depth conversations with anyone? Yes, I could communicate a little without my device, but that would get old after a day or two. Wouldn't it?

"Where are you ladies off to?" Tommy's voice came from behind me, making me jump.

"Hey, Tom," Christine and I both turned around. "We were just going down to see if we can get the TechnoTalk fixed. I hear you still don't like baseball very much."

"The world would probably be a better place without sports, but that's just my opinion."

I nodded in agreement. The big blob of green that I managed to slop on his arm was still there. I smiled to myself. He didn't wash it off. I didn't wash my face off, either, but I probably looked like more of a goof than he did.

"Have you thought more about talking to Jenn?" Christine asked.

"Nah." Tommy kicked around a pebble. "I figure there's no point, really."

"Brynn and I were just chatting with her. She still doesn't want anyone to talk to you or hang out with you, not even Brynn, who has nothing to do with any of this. I just think that's unfair to you."

"If people are dumb enough to listen to her without hearing what I have to say, I don't really want to have anything to do with them," he said. Our eyes met and my breath caught in my throat a bit. His eyes were so big, and so brown, and so deep. I could probably stare into them all day. *Stop being such a cheese ball. Get a hold of yourself.*

"Okay. It's your choice. I just feel bad for you. But, we should probably go down to the office before the dinner bell rings. Cross your fingers we get this to work."

"Can I come with you?"

Christine threw this question to me.

Suppressing what probably would have been a huge cheesy grin to reflect all the cheesy feelings and thoughts floating around inside, I simply nodded.

The cool office air met my body again, only this time it had a little sting to it. My legs and shoulders were becoming pinker and pinker every minute, just like they always did when I was out in the sun, even if it was for no more than a half hour. Christine bent and wrote down the phone number from the back of my device. She dialed it and pressed the speaker button.

"Thank you for calling TechnoTalk Communications," a computerized voice much like my own said. "Your call is very important to us. Please stay on the line and a representative will be with you shortly."

Elevator music filled the room twice the volume of the voice.

"What did you do to it again?" Tommy leaned against the wall.

"Can I tell him?" Christine asked.

I closed my eyes and nodded. *No use saying she can't.*

"She ran into the table at arts and crafts."

"Smooth."

I sarcastically nodded as if I was proud of my gracefulness.

Tommy studied my device. "Is it just like a laptop?"

I nodded.

"Can I try something?"

I gave him a questioning look.

"I just want to try something. I probably won't screw it up any more than you did. And if I do, we have the company on the phone."

Sure. Why not?

Tommy knelt down in front of me. He pushed down on the bottom of the device. There was a snap. What did he do? Was that the battery? He stood and pressed the power button. The obnoxious elevator music still blared through the phone. Not only did the TechnoTalk green light flash, but the screen came back to life a few seconds later.

Chapter Fourteen

"Tonight, we will be doing another DAISY activity. I'm more than aware that this one may be a bit more appropriate for the younger groups, but keep your snarky comments to yourself and just humor me, okay? I received positive feedback from a lot of the counselors when I explained it to them and I think it'll really help with breaking the ice for everyone, regardless of age. Because DAISY is all about getting to know people you normally wouldn't, I have decided to do it with all of you in this session, too. I am now going to ask everyone to get in a big circle."

All sixty or so of us arranged ourselves in a gigantic oval around JT. I was beside Tommy. Christine was beside me, separating us from our other group members. It may have just been my imagination, but Amanda and Jonah seemed more standoffish than last night. It's not like I was planning on having a heart to heart with either of them, but tonight they wouldn't even look in my direction. The fact that Tommy was standing next to me probably didn't help matters, either.

"Okay. Now that we're together in the circle, I am going to call out some things that might be relevant to your lives. For example, I might ask if anyone has blue eyes. If you do have blue eyes, you are going to come forward . . . and then step back."

JT demonstrated by taking a large step forward, looking around the circle, and then stepping back into his original position. Around me, a few campers shifted their weight from leg to leg, others crossed and uncrossed their arms, and I was able to catch Randi's eye just before she tipped her head back to gaze up at the sky, which had switched from orange to a gray-ish purple since we'd been in the field.

"The main goal of this activity is to see that we all have more in common than we think. After I finish going through the list, I want you to take your most important, or most interesting, identifier and find someone who you don't know very well who has the same identifier. Strike up a conversation with them. Like I've been saying, it's not going to kill you if you talk to someone different for a bit. Got it? Good. Now, let's go for it."

"Someone really needs to tell him to cut this crap," Tommy whispered. "I mean, really? Knowing that someone might have six toes isn't going to make these people want to talk to each other. They already decided way before he came around who they want to be friends with—and who they don't."

I agreed, watching his eyes flick in Jenn's direction across the circle and back to me.

"Okay," JT held up his trusty megaphone, "let's start with an easy one. Who here is from Pennsylvania?"

I wheeled up about two feet, along with most of the camp, except Tommy and a few other campers. After a few seconds, we all returned to our places.

I gave Tommy a look.

"Right across the border of New Jersey."

Oh.

"Great. You all got the hang of it. Next question. Who here has been out of the country?"

Only a handful of counselors, including Evelyn, stepped forward. That was cool. I wondered where she went and made a mental note to ask if I got the chance.

"Who here has ever dyed their hair?"

Practically all of the girls went forward, including me. I chuckled to myself. What was so bad about having our natural hair color? Did we really think one color looked better on us, or did we just get bored with ourselves?

"Who here has ever received straight A's on their report card?"

I was kind of glad JT asked that question. This was my chance to show the whole camp I wasn't cognitively disabled. I rolled up and felt Christine come with me. To my surprise, only a few campers joined us. We backed up.

"I see we have a brain with us," Tommy said, his hands in his pockets and a smirk on his face.

I flashed him my you-better-believe-it grin.

"That's great," JT went on. "Now the questions are going to get a little more challenging. I want you to know I am not here to judge anyone, and I hope in turn that you will not judge anyone. If any of the questions are too personal, and you don't feel like sharing with everyone, you don't have to. I don't want anyone to feel uncomfortable. However, I encourage you to show us who you really are so that we can love you for you."

There were snickers coming from all around. Counselors shot campers looks to make them shut up. (I particularly loved the icy glare Christine gave Jonah, whose jaw immediately snapped shut while his eyes dropped to the ground.) I wasn't so sure JT was going to get as much "positive feedback" this time around.

"Are all of you ready?" JT was either totally oblivious to everyone thinking he was completely lame or he was simply able to ignore them.

The most unenthusiastic cheer (I didn't know if it could even classify as a cheer) came from the group.

Mike cupped his hands together. "Hey!" he yelled at the top of his lungs. "JT asked if you guys are ready!"

We all seemed to put ten times more effort in the cheer, although it wasn't because we were any more excited about the activity. From what I had seen and heard the past couple of days,

Mike had a way of making people excited about mundane tasks. He was able to turn everything into a silly competition, which many of the campers seemed to enjoy.

"Wonderful!" JT took over again. "Thank you, Mike. Okay, let's continue with the questions. Does anyone here have parents who are divorced?"

Jonah's voice startled me. "Does it count if they are both remarried?"

My mouth fell open a bit. That was the first time I saw him willingly participate in something.

"Yes," JT turned to him, "it could. If you want it to."

Jonah took three steps forward. Along with Randi. And half of the group. Then they all retreated back.

"Has anyone here ever made fun of someone?"

He considered that an identifier? What kind of person would choose that as a conversation starter? I then remembered who was standing in the circle.

One by one, people began to step toward the middle of the circle. Evelyn. Girls from my cabin. Tommy. Randi. Jonah. Gabe. Amanda. Jenn. Did finding satisfaction that I wasn't like the kids at my school who went to a special classroom all day constitute as making fun of them? I sighed to myself and hit my forward switch. This was not one of my prouder moments. Eventually, the entire camp was in a much tighter circle. It seemed to me that if we had to choose one thing that we *all* had in common, it was that we all felt so bad about ourselves sometimes that we had to make other seem less worthy so that we could feel better.

Disappointed in everyone—myself included—I reversed back to my original spot.

"Who here has ever felt like they were stabbed in the back by a good friend?"

I was the first one to move forward. Immediately, I wished I waited; I didn't want this kind of attention. Blending in was supposed to be my goal; not throwing myself out in the middle of everyone. I guess it was kind of hard not to stare at the girl in the wheelchair who couldn't talk and who happened to be the first person saying she had been hurt by a good friend. My arms became like iron rods against my bands. *What was I doing? What was I thinking? This was not the kind of attention I wanted.* Looking like a victim was not going to earn me friends! I could feel new beads of sweat making their way down my back.

The whole group was silent. I closed my eyes. I tried to hit my reverse switch. My leg would not move. This was not happening. How many times did I have to make an idiot out of myself today? Once was apparently not enough. I opened my eyes. Christine was standing next to me. I made myself smile at her. I felt a hand on my other shoulder and quickly turned my head.

Tommy.

His warm palm on my bare shoulder made me relax. He was with me. Christine was with me. I was not alone anymore. I glanced to my right. Randi had come up. Carly had come up. Guys from Jonah's cabin had stepped up, too. Soon, most of the camp was back in that tight-knit circle, just as we had been only moments before. I was not alone anymore.

Within a few seconds, it was over. My leg regained movement. Everyone was back in their places. JT switched back to asking questions about our favorite sports or who truly liked vegetables. He probably figured we all needed a break from what just happened. I definitely needed a break from what just happened. Here was an opportunity to forget the whole incident and put it behind us. I knew I was going to attempt to take the offer, but was anyone else?

I turned my head and looked at Tommy. He didn't notice me watching him, and I didn't want him to. I could still feel the exact spot on my shoulder where he'd placed his hand. My mind was racing. I hadn't known Tommy more than a few days. I had known Meg and Dave for years. How did he know (when he probably couldn't even see my face) that I wanted to die in that instant? What made him think that even though he didn't really know me, putting his hand on my shoulder would help me relax? How could have Meg and Dave not known when I needed them? Did I do such a good job with pretending that I was okay that they truly didn't know I wasn't, or did they actually know and simply decided it wasn't their place or responsibility to do anything about it?

"And, finally," I stopped spacing out and turned back into JT, "the last question. Who here loves Camp Lakewood?"

For once, no eyes were rolled. No laughs. No timidity from anyone. I could almost feel all our guards drop at the exact same moment. The tension, once so thick and prominent, evaporated. Everyone charged at JT, a swarm of screaming campers and counselors huddled around him. They really did love this place, despite the fact they sometimes acted like they thought the activities were right from a preschool teacher's lesson plan. Although all I wanted to do was find somewhere I could go be alone, I rolled up to the crowd. I tried to absorb the powerful energy. They seemed to completely forget my embarrassing moment a few minutes earlier, so why couldn't I? After all, this was exactly what I wanted to begin with.

"Alright," JT started as everyone finished attacking him, "I hope you know Camp Lakewood loves you, too. Now—"

Another cheer erupted from the group. What? How could they think what he said was any less lame from what he was saying ten minutes before? I expected that by this time tomorrow, everyone would be back to mocking JT behind his back and making comments about DAISY, but tonight JT had brought us all together—and we were all feeling the love. I imagined this is what camp was supposed to feel like all the time, and I was a little sad that so much drama deterred us from this feeling.

He chuckled into the megaphone. "Okay. As I was saying, now is your chance to go up and talk to someone who you didn't know had something in common with you. I really would prefer if you didn't really know the person, however, if one of your friends surprised you tonight by admitting something that you didn't know about them, I suppose I can make an exception and let you talk to them about it . . . ."

JT's voice faded into the distance as a lump formed in my throat. I was still a bit embarrassed that I'd rolled myself out in the middle of the circle, only to admit my own heartache and defeat, but at the center of my sudden upset was the pain I still felt when I thought of Meg and Dave. I had been trying so hard the last few weeks—and especially the last couple of days—to forget about the way they betrayed me. But calling attention to those issues in the circle just brought it all back. I knew I was pretty much over the idea of ever dating Dave, but knowing they'd hid their relationship from me and lied to me about it . . . knowing that Meg was fully aware of how I felt about Dave and she went after him anyway . . . I honestly wasn't even hurt anymore. I was angry and I was disappointed. Unfortunately for me, I expressed those emotions the same way I expressed sadness, fear, and occasionally happiness. Tears welled in my eyes.

"That was intense," Tommy was saying, as the crowd around us broke into smaller groups, having been dismissed by JT.

I knew he was referencing the awkwardly silent moments I spent in front of the entire group, alone, having admitted to my recent heartache at home. I didn't know if it was hearing him recognize the frustration and embarrassment of it, or if it was simply the knowledge that he was going to try to talk to me about it, but either way it was enough to force my tears to finally spill over. I felt my throat tighten as I tried to stop what I knew was coming. *No!* I didn't want to cry with everyone around. I didn't want to make more of a scene. I didn't want to cry in front of Tommy. I ducked my head and tried to hide my face.

Luckily, Christine turned to Tommy and asked him to help her gather a few spare water bottles that some of the campers had left in the grass. While they talked and gathered the empty bottles, I slowly and quietly spun my chair around and then kept my head on the forward switch. I was sure they'd eventually notice I was gone, but right then, I just needed to be alone with my thoughts so I could calm down.

As I moved through the grass, my chair bumped like a school bus over potholes and I let myself cry. I kind of felt like an idiot, running away from everyone, crying. But I knew in a few moments, Tommy and Christine would be calling out my name and when they found me, I wanted to have my shit together. I kept going toward two trees I had spotted off to the side of the quad. When I reached them, I let go of the switch and put my head down, giving into the real, angry sobs I'd been holding back.

When I heard myself crying, I suddenly achieved some sort of clarity. This was ridiculous. Why was I *still* letting Dave—and Meg, specifically—control the way I felt about myself and everyone around me? I had to find a way to shake their influence. I had to find a way to put them in my past, for good. So at that moment, I resolved to do just that. I'd make the most of my time here at Camp Lakewood, and when it came time to go home . . .

I sniffled and took a deep breath.

I'll think about that later.

I heard Christine call my name, her voice growing louder as she approached me. I took another deep breath and scooted out from behind the tree.

"Brynn!" Christine ran up to me and then stopped, her hands on her knees, gasping for breath. "Are you okay?"

Before I knew what was going on, I felt Tommy grab my upper body. He pulled it to the side of my chair where he was kneeling. I leaned my head on his shoulder, a few final tears dampening his black shirt. He didn't seem to mind, though. He just wrapped his arms tighter around me.

"If you guys are okay for a minute," Christine whispered, "I'm going to go get some toilet paper from the bathroom."

Tommy didn't turn around, but I felt him nod his head.

Christine ran off without saying anything else.

I lifted my head up. There were more seconds between sobs now, and the stream falling from my eyes seemed to be coming to an end.

"Do you want to talk about it?" Tommy wiped my one eye with his thumb.

I slowly shook my head.

"That's okay. For now, at least. I mean, I'm just a little curious as to—"

"Well, would you look at this . . ."

We both turned. It was Jonah, twisting an empty water bottle in his hand. What the hell was he doing here? I didn't want him to see me like this.

"I just don't get it, Tom. Jenn's suddenly not hot enough or cool enough for you, but you're out here in the dark trying to make a retard who talks with a Gameboy feel better? What you gonna do next? Make out with her? You gonna—"

I didn't have time to process what Jonah was saying, nor did I have time to try to stop Tommy before he leapt up and tackled Jonah to the ground.

Chapter Fifteen

Since that night you came into my life
    I swing my hair back, letting it fan out into the air.
    Nothing has been the same
    I stand at the microphone. I don't have a band with me. Just me, and the microphone, and the guitar . . . and the lyrics.
    When your light came down from above, it took away my pain
    My arm pumps up and down in a steady rhythm as I near the end of the song. Meg and Dave are in the crowd off to the side, but there are other faces I know. They are people from camp. Randi, Christine, Evelyn. They are all in the back row, bobbing their heads like this is their favorite song. In the front row, however, is Jonah. Amanda. Carly. Gabe. Jenn. They are staring up at me in wonderment. They never heard this song before.
    And now that I have felt your love
    I know you'll always stay with me
    I'm sure you'll always stay with me
    My eyes scan the crowd and I find what I'm looking for, positioned right in the middle of Jonah and Amanda. Those familiar brown eyes catch mine. I smile into the microphone, keeping my eyes locked on his.
    I know you'll always stay with me.

    I spun my wheelchair around. Something out of the corner of my eye startled me. Christine and Randi stood at the end of the basketball court. *Shit!* How much did they see? At the rate I was going, the whole camp was going to think I really was "retarded." With the music still blasting in my ear, I pulled up to the girls.

Christine grabbed my iPod and took my earphones out. "You were really going out there. Now I see why you like to come out here. I wish I had time in my day to go somewhere by myself and just let loose."

I blushed.

"Not that I don't like helping you or anything. I wish I could do that even when I'm not at camp."

"What was she listening to, anyway?" Randi leaned towards my iPod.

"Abbie Bonza," Christine told her, wrapping my headphones around the iPod.

"Oh, God. You and Carly. And every other girl our age. Ridiculous! But," Randi paused, quickly changing tunes, "at least we now know you'll be good to go for tomorrow."

I raised my eyebrow. *Tomorrow?*

"Oh yeah, you're the new girl. I keep forgetting that! The first Friday night, we have a dance. It's kind of a tradition. JT better have kept it up with this session."

"He did," Christine reassured her. "It's on the schedule."

"Good. I don't have to kick his ass, then."

"That's not really funny to be joking about, especially after last night." Christine turned to me. "That's why we came to get you. JT wants to know what exactly you saw since you were the only other one there when Tommy and Jonah started fighting. Would you be willing to go talk to him?"

Hesitantly, I drove over to the bench in the shade so I could see my TechnoTalk to type. This was where Tommy and I sat and talked every day, only today we couldn't. It was why I was dancing alone on the court instead. Tommy, along with Jonah, was in "isolation" down at the camp office. They even had to sleep there last night. Although it was nice to have time to listen to music and let my mind wander, I wanted Tommy to be there. I wanted to be able to talk to him. I didn't want him to be stuck in a room by himself just because he tried to defend me. That was the last thing he needed.

Rather than sitting on the bench in front of me, Christine and Randi stood beside me so they could read my screen.

"I . . . will . . . talk . . . to . . . him . . . " I took a deep breath, "but . . . I . . . have . . . to . . . be . . . honest . . . Randi. I . . . don't . . . think . . . you . . . would . . . want . . . to . . . be . . . in . . . there . . . with—"

She interrupted me. "I'm probably not going to be. I didn't see anything that went down, so JT probably won't allow it. But, why don't I want to go to the office with you?"

"I . . . don't . . . want . . . to . . . get . . . in . . . between . . . you . . . and . . . Jonah."

"I'm so confused right now." She folded her tanned arms across her chest and I could tell she was frustrated, but I knew I had to continue to be honest with her.

"He . . . said . . . something . . . " I paused.

"Okay? Is that why Tom attacked him?"

I slowly nodded.

"It is? Holy shit!" Randi almost laughed, in disbelief rather than amusement. "What did he say?"

I looked up at Christine for help. How could I tell Randi her boyfriend called me a retard? In some way or another, I knew it would put a wedge between the three of us. I liked hanging out with Randi, and I didn't want to force her to choose sides. She'd been dating Jonah for a while, and she'd known me five days.

"Did Jonah say something about Tom?" Christine asked, trying to help me.

I shook my head.

"No. Did Jonah say something about Randi?"

Another head shake.

"No. Did Jonah say something about you?"

I could feel the heat creep up my neck as I nodded.

"What did he say?" Randi asked again. "I will go kick his ass right now."

"Hey, now! Enough with the ass kicking!" Christine grabbed her shoulder. "Apparently Tom already did that, and we really don't need a repeat of it."

"What did he say to you?" Randi demanded. There was no mistaking the force behind her words, but I just couldn't gather the courage to tell her.

I hit my talking switch once and let the TechnoTalk scan through the letters. I really didn't know what to say. I didn't know, and I really didn't want to be the one to tell Randi her boyfriend was a complete asshole. I tried hitting my talking switch again, but the same thing happened.

Christine seemed to pick up on this. "You really don't want to tell us, do you?"

I hit my switch for a third time, finally able to spell out some words. "I . . . just . . . don't . . . want . . . to . . . get . . . in . . . the . . . middle . . . of . . . everything."

"Well, you kinda already did," Randi blurted out. For a second, her comment stunned me, but when she knelt down in front of my chair and fought me for eye contact, I knew she really didn't mean any offense. "But Brynn, I really would need to know if my boyfriend was being a dick to anyone. To you or to someone else. Randi don't do that shit."

"If you really don't want to tell us what Jonah said," Christine started before I could type anything, "you don't have to. But will you please go down and tell JT that Jonah did indeed say something to egg Tommy on so that he doesn't think he really is absolutely insane? Right now, he doesn't know who, or what, to believe."

I turned my wheelchair around and slowly nodded.

"Cool. Thank you, Brynn. I'm sorry you got dragged into this."

Randi crossed her arms again and narrowed her eyebrows. "I still want to know what Jonah said. Seriously, I'm gonna kill him."

"Randi! Why don't you go down to the lake with the cabin? I'm sure they're waiting for you."

"Sure. But Brynn, don't be afraid to tell on Jonah. You have my permission to tell JT everything he did or said. If he really was an ass to you, you have nothing to feel bad about. You don't have to cover for my boyfriend. Why would you want to do that when he didn't think about you first?"

I nodded at her and she walked up the path and turned to the lake. Randi had a point. Why was I trying to protect their relationship when he didn't give a crap about me? That kind of person didn't really deserve to have their relationship spared. But was that really what I was trying to do?

Had it been just Randi and me standing there, I was positive she could've pulled the truth out of me, but Christine's influence was strong and I didn't think having this conversation in front of her was super appropriate. I vowed then to make some time to talk to Randi, one-on-one. Maybe we could talk about Jonah, maybe we could talk about Tommy, or maybe we could just talk about us. Either way, it had to happen.

"The cabin is going canoeing," Christine explained as I drove beside her. "I figured this was a little more important than getting into a boat right now. However, if you really want to try canoeing, we can go sometime when we have free time. Maybe we can get Tom to come with us."

I smiled faintly.

"Ya know, I think Tom really likes you. The way he was with you last night when you were crying . . . as embarrassing as it might have been for you, I never saw him like that with anyone else. Not even Jenn when they were together. And if he really punched Jonah because he said something about you? I know Tommy. He would never hurt a fly. Which is why I just don't understand how everybody can deliberately be avoiding him. There must be something more to the breakup than we know."

I pulled off into some shade right by the office. "I . . . need . . . help."

"Are you okay?"

"I'm . . . afraid . . . to . . . tell . . . JT . . . what . . . happened. You . . . know . . . how . . . Jonah . . . feels . . . about . . . me . . . already. You . . . can . . . tell . . . me . . . it's . . . not . . . going . . . to . . . matter . . . but . . . it . . . is . . . going . . . to . . . matter . . . with . . . him . . . because . . . he's . . . like . . . that."

Christine sighed. "I know. You are absolutely right. I'm not going to tell you it's going to be okay, because it might not be. Jonah will probably be angry if you tell JT what you said, but that's only because he's a seventeen year old man-child who thinks he can do no wrong, so exposing his wrongdoing isn't exactly going to win you his friendship, but it's the right thing to do," Christine said, giving my shoulder a gentle jab. She sighed. "That's the hardest thing about working with teenagers; you're all so stubborn! That, and things that are so irrelevant in the world matter so much to you guys. I really can't stand to see you so upset about something that you will probably forget about in a week. Am I making any sense at all?"

I nodded.

"I didn't mean to ask you to tattle on Jonah. I'm sorry that he said something to upset you, I would never want him to, but I'm so relieved to hear what Tommy did was attempting to stick up for you. I asked you to do this for Tommy. Yes, it wasn't right for Tommy to take him down, but I think it would help so much if JT knew the reason why he did what he did. I don't know if Tommy's already tried to explain himself, but knowing those two guys the way I do, I fully expect that they were both tight-lipped during JT's interrogation, not wanting to own up to anything they may have done wrong."

I nodded again.

"If it makes you feel any less guilty, you're not doing this because you want to get back at Jonah. You're doing this because you want to help Tommy. I think he will be so, so, so thankful that you are trying to help him. And besides, it seems that you like to hang out with him the most out of everyone at camp."

Another nod.

"So, don't worry about what Jonah is going to do afterward. Think about helping Tom get out of some trouble. Now, do you want me to be with you when you talk to JT, or do you want to do it yourself?"

I nodded.

Christine smacked her forehead. "I'm sorry I keep doing that. Asking you two questions instead of one and waiting for your response. Do you want me to be with you?"

I nodded again.

"You don't want to go by yourself?"

I shook my head. Having Christine there would help me feel like I wasn't going to puke everywhere. I don't know why I was so nervous about talking to JT. Christine was right; I wasn't going in there to tell the world how horrible Jonah was. I was just trying to clear Tommy's name.

"Okay. Just making sure. Let's go."

I took a deep breath and went through the door she held open for me. We stepped into the office where JT was seated at his desk, writing. He looked up when Christine closed the door.

"Hi, girls," JT said and put his pencil down. "Glad you could make it. Are you having any fun, Brynn?"

Moving towards him, I nodded.

"I told Brynn you wanted to know what happened last night," Christine said. "She agreed to talk to you."

"That's great. What do I need to do?"

Christine gave him an unsure look. "What do you mean?"

169

"I would like to ask her some questions. Do I just ask you and you relay them to her, or does her computer type what I am saying?"

What? He didn't get that I had only a physical disability, either? What the hell! Why did people always assume I was deaf? Or dumb? Or both? My nervousness about the whole 'ratting out Jonah" thing quickly changed into annoyance. In that instant, I officially decided, for more reasons than one, that JT should not be running this camp.

"No," Christine laughed it off. "Brynn can hear you just fine. She just uses this computer to type what she wants to say. It's called a TechnoTalk. Actually, Brynn, would you mind if JT comes around and takes a look so he can better understand how it works?"

Without waiting for me to answer, he stood and walked to my side. "Yes, I would really like to see."

I couldn't believe it. I came down here to have a serious conversation, actually terrified of how things were going to go, of making Jonah more upset, of messing things up for him and Randi, and the camp director was more interested in how I talked than who took out who the night before. He seemed much more professional when he was in front of everyone.

"She does it with her head," Christine pointed to my talking switch. "She just types out word by word until she has what she wants to say."

"Amazing," JT whispered under his breath.

There was an awkward pause. I stared at my screen because I didn't know what I was supposed to say. JT stared at my screen as if he hadn't ever seen anything like it. And he probably *hadn't* seen anything like it. It wasn't his fault if he was intrigued by something he had never seen before, was it?

"So," Christine broke the silence, "you wanted to ask Brynn some questions?"

"Yes. Is that okay with her?"

Alright. This was not going anywhere. I tapped my talking switch. *Major chaos: here we come!*

"Christine . . . told . . . me . . . you . . . wanted . . . to . . . know . . . what . . . happened . . . last . . . night . . ."

"This is amazing," he whispered to Christine again. Then, without warning, his voice level raised about ten notches, like he was talking into his megaphone. "Yes, I did, Brynn. Can you tell me what happened on your computer?"

No, actually, I will not. I just said that for the hell of it. Can we go to lunch now?

"You really don't have to talk to her that loud," Christine said coolly. "Like I said, she doesn't have any trouble hearing."

"Right."

"I . . . don't . . . feel . . . comfortable . . ."

"She doesn't feel comfortable with telling me what happened?"

"No, she's not done typing."

I wanted to hug Christine. She was trying so hard, and he just wasn't getting it.

"With . . . telling . . . you . . . what . . . Jonah . . . said . . . but . . . that . . . was . . . why . . . Tommy—"

"Is that what started it? Jonah said something to Tommy?"

I nodded, this time less irritated that he had interrupted me. If he was understanding what I was trying to say, then I could deal.

"What did he say?"

I looked at Christine.

"That was what she was saying she didn't feel comfortable with. Telling you what Jonah said."

"Do you know what he said?"

"I don't. She doesn't want to tell anyone."

"Why not?"

Enter aggravation, again. Talking to whoever was with me— my mom, dad, Meg, Mrs. B, Christine—as though I wasn't sitting *right there,* was always a sure sign that people didn't get that I was 100 percent cognitively "there."

"I'm not sure, JT," Christine said, exasperated. "I think he might have said something about Brynn?"

"Jonah said something about her?"

Christine shrugged. "That's what I've gathered."

"We're going to find out right now." JT opened the door to the conference room. "Guys, would you please come out here?"

He was going to ask Jonah what he said . . . in front of me! This was *not* in the deal when I agreed to come down here!

"He really put them in a room together?" Christine mouthed. "Is he nuts?"

Tommy and Jonah stepped out of the room, wearing the same clothes as the night before. Was the conference room "isolation"? I met Tommy's eyes, frowning as I noticed the huge scratch below the left one. He looked tired, worn out, and slightly defeated. All night in isolation was probably uncomfortable, especially with Jonah right by his side.

"I asked Brynn to come and tell me what happened last night since she was the only one with you," JT said, walking in front of the boys and crossing his arms. "And she did with her computer. That thing is just so amazing. Have you guys had a chance to watch her in action?"

I let my head drop down. *And once again, my equipment trumps everything that's going on around me.*

"She indicated that you, Jonah, might have said something that led to the fight. Christine also thinks you might have said something about Brynn. Whether you did or did not, you know what to do. If you did, I expect you apologize to her."

Jonah's bloodshot eyes met mine. He looked as tired as Tommy, but he also looked irritable. His right hand, clenched in a fist, shook a bit, but I knew it wasn't from anger. I imagined his head hurt quite a bit, and I wondered if JT had gotten close enough to him last night to smell the alcohol on him.

"Nevertheless, I am going to let you go from isolation. Consider this a warning. If I hear of anymore funny business from either of you, I am going to have to ask you to leave camp. Did I make myself clear?"

Both Tommy and Jonah muttered their responses and then we all turned for the door. Tommy fell into place beside me and reached out to run his hand gently on my shoulder. I looked up at him and hoped that my smile indicated how much I wanted to spend some time alone with him and talk about everything we'd both been putting off. I wanted to tell him about Meg and Dave, and I wanted him to tell me the truth about Jenn and why everyone hated him right now. I wanted us to put all that drama out in front of us so we could then successfully put it behind us.

Just as we were stepping out into the sunlight, JT reappeared in the door to his office and called out to Jonah. "One more thing!" he said. "I want you to spend the rest of the day with Brynn. Eat lunch with her. Sit at the activity with her. Try getting to know her before dinner. I think you'll think her and her computer are neat."

Everyone was silent as JT said goodbye and then went back into his air-conditioned haven to continue being oblivious to the real world and very real teenagers running rampant across camp grounds.

"Well, this sucks," Tommy said, clearly speaking for everyone.

Chapter Sixteen

*L*uckily, when JT had given Jonah his assignment, he'd forgotten that most of our afternoon would consist of sitting in the amphitheater, listening to a panel speak about how important JT's DAISY initiative really was. It was another activity that would've worked best on a younger crowd, but I would've sat through it three more times before having to spend another hour one-on-one with Jonah.

The time between leaving JT's office and arriving at the amphitheater for the panel discussion wasn't as unbearable as I thought it'd be—mostly because Christine had been there to facilitate conversation, as little of it as we had. We walked around the lake, mostly in silence because I couldn't see my screen (and Jonah wouldn't have wanted to hear what I really wanted to say to him, anyway) and then we went to the dining hall.

Even though we were supposed to spend the entire day together, Jonah asked Christine if he could sit with Randi, Carly, and Amanda during lunch. She looked to me for the answer, and I had no objections to it. I wasn't a fan of eating in front of people in general, but sitting at a table with only Jonah and Christine would be a nightmare for me.

JT's assignment was completely lost on Jonah and me; we were different people with different values. We couldn't be forced to get along, no matter how hard JT tried. And maybe that's where the DAISY initiative failed.

I was contemplating this while the people on stage spoke about their disabilities, their struggles with alcohol and drugs, and how hard it was to tell their parents they were gay. I felt . . . guilty. I hadn't even *tried* to talk to Jonah all afternoon. Here I was, at a camp where this summer's theme was understanding and acceptance, and I had been just as big of a jerk as Jonah had. Yeah, he was the one who had been difficult and rude and obnoxious to begin with. But now I was being stubborn. I wasn't supposed to become best friends with him this afternoon, but I could've at least tried to take our relationship into some sort of civil realm where we could both coexist peacefully. A small smile here, a nod of recognition there, no tension in the room.

But then again, did it really matter, anyway? We probably aren't going to see each other after camp, I was thinking while the four panelists wrapped up their discussion of a question JT had asked them.

JT said he knew all of the people on the panel, but I couldn't help but wonder what their reactions were when he approached them about doing this. Maybe they were like him and just wanted to help more teenagers like us understand. Maybe they were sick of being the victims of judgment. It still seemed like the opposite of being politically correct to ask these people to come talk to us based on their race, sexual orientation, religion (or, in this case, lack of religion), and, yes, disability.

"Well, I think it's so important for anyone to keep the saying 'don't judge a book by its cover' in mind," an older woman with glasses said into the mic. "As I was saying with my answer earlier, while I was doing graduate studies years ago, if I walked into a library to work on my research, I felt like most people would do a double take. They didn't expect a black woman to be elbow high in medical journals. And I can't say I blame them. There weren't any other black people in my program, but it was still frustrating to have someone's eyes on you just a second longer. Point being;

yes, stereotypes didn't come out of nowhere. They exist because most of them are true to a certain extent. However, I would like all of you to keep in mind that every once and a while, someone will come along who doesn't fit the mold."

"Thank you, Dr. Codeman," JT said without his megaphone but loud enough so we could hear in the back row. "I think that is excellent advice. What about you, Adam? Do you have any closing remarks you'd like to share?"

I perked up on hearing his name, eager to hear him speak. Adam was the most gorgeous guy I had ever seen with his tan skin and a smile that would make any girl go insane. However, making any girl go insane was not what he was going for.

"I came here today hoping I would change some of your minds about people who are gay. If I helped just one of you think differently about someone like me, I consider the day a success. With that being said, the biggest thing that you can do right now is just accept everybody as they are. I know, you're probably thinking 'how much gayer can this guy get?'"

Campers politely chuckled all around me.

"But do you really think calling someone a dyke is going to make them say 'You know what? You are so right. I should like guys, not girls. My bad'? Did my dad really think if he kicked me out of the house, it would make me want to break up with my boyfriend? I don't know. So, my suggestion for you guys is rather than possibly making an ass out of yourselves and offending somebody, just accept that we are different and go on with your life."

"Thank you, Adam," JT said and put his hands in his pockets. "That's exactly what we're working on at camp, and that's exactly what the DAISY theme is all about."

I glanced down at Jonah, who was seated in front of me. I could only see the back of his head, but if I was trying not to roll *my* eyes, what was he doing?

"When I heard about the DAISY theme, I thought it was just an awesome idea. I hope it's helping you guys a lot," Adam said, flashing a killer smile.

This guy had to be in his twenties. How could he think it was an awesome idea? Maybe JT didn't tell them about the activities we were doing—the ones designed for middle schoolers who possibly still ate paste. Maybe he just told them about the DAISY theme, which, I can admit, did sound like an awesome idea. I just didn't think it was being executed correctly. I'd come up with other ideas the past few days that would have put JT's activities to shame, especially with this age group, but it's not like I was running the camp, so . . .

JT then turned to Professor Mullen.

"I agree that there should be more acceptance and more tolerance. I think tolerance is a very important part of getting along with others who might have different views from you. I didn't come here to talk religion with you. I came here because I thought my story of being discriminated against by my students because I was suggesting there was no God would be one that you all needed to hear. Among other things, I found it highly unacceptable, and I hope you found it highly unacceptable as well."

From what he told us, "unacceptable" was not the word. The professor may have crossed a line by calling for God—if there was a God—to show himself via a sign in the classroom, but that was in no way an excuse for the kid to get up and slug the professor, claiming God told him to do it. If I was Professor Mullen, I would have called security on that kid based on hitting an authoritative figure, not on anything related to religion.

"I hope your story has helped everyone understand how being tolerant and accepting is so important, too," JT said and nodded. "Thank you, Professor Mullen. Last, but certainly not least, we have Kendra. Kendra, do you have anything else that you would like to tell the camp?"

"Yes, I do. You guys are all in high school. When I was in high school, nobody would talk to me. Even now when I am out of college, people will ask my husband questions when they should be asking me. Like the guy I was telling you about from the bar; he asked my husband what I would like to drink. Hello! I'm right here! Just because I walk like a duck doesn't mean I am one!"

Everyone laughed while I tried to suppress a squeal. Although she didn't have CP like me and could do a lot more than I could, it still felt good to know that I wasn't the only one people treated like an alien. Or a duck.

"Anyway, you guys shouldn't be afraid to talk to anyone who might be different from you. It doesn't matter if they are gay, straight, bi, black, white, purple, Chinese, Japanese, disabled, not disabled, or whatever. We are all people. Why not talk to each other?"

Her words hit home and the guilt I felt in the pit of my stomach grew a bit bigger. I wondered—but doubted—if Jonah was thinking the same thing.

"You have a very good point, Kendra," JT said and stepped toward the campers. "I hope now that some campers won't be afraid anymore to talk to anyone here. We had a little bit of a problem with that today, so I hope hearing Kendra talk about how it made her feel will change how those people think about the situation."

Maybe in your world, it would. Probably not in the world of Camp Lakewood, though. Assigning Jonah to be with me still hadn't made Jonah and I want to have a normal conversation with each other. All it did was make "the situation" more awkward. And kept Tommy at a far distance during the day, when all I really wanted to do was hang out with him.

JT turned to us. "Do any of you have questions for our guests tonight?"

Not surprisingly, not a single hand went up.

"That's okay. If you have a question for one of them and you don't feel comfortable asking it in front of everyone, they're going to be hanging out here for a little, so feel free to come up and chat with them. If you don't have a question for them, you can enjoy some free time before dinner. Let's give our guests a big round of applause for coming out today."

We erupted in a cheer as we started to become individual people again rather than one big group. If there was one thing we were good at, it was acting like someone hit a homerun at a baseball game even if we weren't feeling the least bit enthused about what was going on around us.

"Can I go now?" Jonah was on his feet, holding a full bottle of red juice. I hadn't even seen him fill it and briefly wondered when he had the time to make himself a drink and, more importantly, where all the alcohol was coming from. *And why wasn't anyone doing anything about it?*

"Yes, Jonah," Christine said, sighing and standing up. "You can go."

Jonah raced off without saying another word to me or Christine.

"I'm not entirely sure what all that was about."

Before I could figure out if she was talking about the Jonah thing or the panel thing, Randi plopped down beside me.

"Hey," she greeted us, a bit more tired-sounding than usual. "That was kind of lame, huh?"

"It wasn't too bad," Christine said, exchanging glances with me. "They made some good points. And we all know why JT asked them to come."

"Yeah . . ." Randi replied and reached down to tug at her shoelaces.

I couldn't see my screen, but I wanted to ask her if she was okay. I looked up at Christine, who shrugged her shoulders.

"Something wrong, Randi?"

Randi was silent for a second before looking up at Christine and then at me. "Wanna hang out for a little, Brynn? I kind of want to talk to you. We could go back to the cabin. I'm sure everyone's out in the sun or on the lake."

I nodded, already nervous about what she wanted to talk about, and she stood. And then, of course, Tommy appeared.

"And now you show up," Christine joked.

"Hey, I was in a room with that kid since last night and I sucked it up. I think that's enough." He looked at Randi for a second and quickly added, "Sorry."

She shrugged it off and placed her hands in her back pockets.

"Are you okay?" Christine asked Tommy.

"Yeah, I'm fine. Brynn, are you okay? You were the one who I was worried about. How was it?"

I shrugged, trying to show him that it was okay and that I was fine. Christine's presence really helped. And it hadn't been so bad that I'd suffered another meltdown in the middle of the quad like I had last night.

"You wanna go hang out at the basketball court for a while?"

I didn't try to hide my smile. I wanted that more than anything. But I'd already made plans. I looked at Randi, but she wasn't paying attention to the conversation, her eyes were angled up at the bright, brilliant blue sky. So I turned to Christine.

"You're a few minutes too late," she told him. "Randi and Brynn are going to hang out for a little while. But you're welcome to come sit by the lake with me for a bit. I'd love to hear about your plans for the rest of the summer and senior year."

"Oh, okay. Yeah, sure," he said, though he did seem a little disappointed. I should've felt bad, but seeing his smile falter a little gave me butterflies and assured me that he really did want to spend time with me. That he really did seem to like me. "Later tonight, then? After dinner?"

I gave him a big nod to let him know I definitely wanted to. He reached out to squeeze my shoulder before walking away with Christine. I turned my chair on and Randi and I headed in the opposite direction toward the cabins. We walked in silence.

When we got to the cabin, Randi closed the door behind us and then walked to her bed, where she collapsed and shoved her face in her pillow.

I immediately went to work.

"What's . . . wrong?" SPEAK.

She sighed and rolled onto her side, facing me. She looked so tired, like she'd barely slept last night. I hadn't noticed this morning because she'd been so angry when she heard about Jonah being in trouble.

"Is . . . it . . . Jonah . . . or . . . me?" SPEAK.

"It's not you, Brynn. I promise," she said. "I just don't know what to do about him sometimes."

I didn't know enough about her relationship with Jonah to feel like I could offer her advice. He seemed to be somewhat of a jerk, and she was so sweet and energetic and fun to be around. On the outside, they didn't seem to work. But I knew things had to be different when they were alone.

"Have . . . you . . . talked . . . to . . . Carly . . . about . . . it?" SPEAK.

Randi smirked. "Carly thinks that as long as she has a boyfriend, all is right in the world. She moves from guy to guy, a new interest every summer, every school year. Life can't be all that bad if you have a boyfriend, right? Every girl wants one, so if you have one, things are perfect. Except . . . not . . ."

I blinked. I really didn't know what to say.

"Listen, Brynn," she said, sitting up and pulling her pillow onto her lap. "I asked you to talk with me because I wanted to apologize, again, for Jonah's behavior. I know you don't want to tell me what he said, but I know him well enough to think that I know exactly what he did and I'm so embarrassed. For him and myself. He can be such a jerk sometimes. And I'm truly ashamed for him. He shouldn't have done what he did and I hope you don't hold that against me. Because I think you're pretty fricking cool and I want to make sure we leave here as friends next week."

She waited patiently while I typed my response, deleted it, and then typed a new one. I wasn't sure how honest I should be. We were friends, and we should've been completely honest with each other, but I didn't want to hurt her feelings. She'd already had a rough day.

"I . . . just . . . don't . . . think . . . Jonah . . . understands . . . me. And . . . he . . . doesn't . . . want . . . to. And . . . that . . . makes . . . things . . . hard." SPEAK.

Randi nodded. "You're right. He doesn't get it, and he's not trying to. I don't know what the big deal is. When we started dating freshman year, he was so . . . sweet. And considerate. And the politest guy I ever met. When I first met him, I thought this was it; we'd be one of those high school couples that made it."

Well, that wasn't the Jonah I knew . . .

"But then he made the varsity baseball team as a freshman. And those guys were older and they'd invite him to parties and he wanted them to think he fit in, I guess. I don't know. We never really talked about it. I was fifteen, was finally dating a guy I *really* liked, and I didn't want to question him or fight with him and have him break up with me. So I just let it happen . . . and now I feel like sometimes, he can't stop himself."

"The . . . drinking?" SPEAK.

She nodded again and pulled her attention from the pillow in her lap to meet my eyes. "I just don't know when it got to be this way. He's okay during the first half of the school year, almost like his old self, except sometimes moody, but then baseball season starts and the late nights with the team and the weekend parties and . . . he just loses himself in them. And he's such a jerk when he's drunk. I really thought when he agreed to go to camp with me the summer between freshman year and sophomore year, we'd be able to get away from all that nonsense. But it's just the same thing here. And has been every year so far."

I hadn't noticed many of the other campers with bottles of their mixed drinks, but then again, I didn't really know many of them, so maybe I'd been blind to other people's behaviors. Maybe this was a type of camp culture I didn't know about?

Or maybe camp supervision had been so poor the past few years that now everyone knew what they could and couldn't get away with. JT may talk a big game, but we all were figuring out that he didn't really know what the hell he was doing. Maybe he'd be better with the younger crowd, but he just didn't have control over us. No one did.

I wanted to ask her if she'd ever thought about breaking up with Jonah. She didn't seem happy; she seemed stressed and irritated and embarrassed and hurt. But I didn't feel like it was my place to ask. They'd clearly been together for a few years, so she knew him better than I did. Randi was an intelligent girl. I had to believe that she would know when enough was enough.

"Do . . . you . . . drink?" SPEAK.

"Yeah, sometimes. After school dances or big games or whatever. But not as much as Jonah and his friends. And not nearly as often. I'm too afraid I'm going to get caught. But I want him to stop drinking *every day*. He's not himself when he's drunk." She spoke the last of her words so quietly, I had to lean forward to make sure I could hear her.

"Have . . . you . . . ever . . . talked . . . to . . . him . . . about . . . his . . . drinking?" SPEAK.

"A few times, but he promises he'll stop and then he starts again. . . ." She climbed off the bed and went to the mirror that hung on the wall of our cabin. She raked her fingers through her hair and then started to pull it back in a ponytail. "Hey, has Tommy ever told you about why he and Jenn broke up?"

I shook my head and she watched me in the mirror.

"Well, I think I know. And I'll just say that . . . I think I understand. And I think I'm about ready to put my foot down and try to stop all this petty bullshit of not speaking to one another."

I smiled. I knew she'd be the first one to come around completely. She'd stopped ignoring Tommy already, but it sounded like she was ready to break her loyalties to Jenn. I wondered how the other girls would react. Which made me think of Amanda . . .

SPEAK. "Does it bother you that Jonah and Amanda spend so much time alone together?"

In the mirror, I could see her purse her lips. I'd hit a nerve.

I was actually surprised at myself for asking at all. This wasn't my business, and it wasn't something I'd planned on bringing up.

"Sometimes," Randi finally answered. She checked herself in the mirror one last time before turning to me. "But Amanda's supposed to be my friend. And Jonah's supposed to be in a relationship with me. So, I have to trust them." She paused. "Right?"

Before I could even come up with an answer that I felt was honest, but wouldn't hurt her feelings, the door burst open and the other girls from the cabin piled in, wrapped in towels, their bathing suits dripped as they crossed the room. They all seemed to get along so well and I wondered if Randi and I were the outcasts of our cabin. Or, maybe, we just happened to naturally fall into two groups. As long as we were friendly with each other and respected each other, it didn't really matter, I guess.

Which was exactly how I should have been looking at my relationship with Jonah. Randi, however, had a bit more thinking to do about her relationship with him. And we both knew she couldn't do that with a room full of half-naked, chatty girls. She nodded toward the door and I followed.

"Let's just go get dinner, okay?" she asked.

I nodded, but pulled over into the shade of a cabin to type quickly. She leaned over to read. "I'm . . . here . . . if . . . you . . . want . . . to . . . talk."

"Yeah, I know," she said with a sad smile and started walking again.

Chapter Seventeen

*A*fter dinner, Randi went down to the lake with Carly and Amanda, but not without thanking me for spending time with her earlier.

"Still want to go to the basketball court? There's a couple hours of daylight left we can enjoy," Tommy said. I nodded, eager to spend time with him, and we headed down the path to the bench on the sidelines of the court. Christine waved at us before we left and I couldn't help but smile.

I loved Camp Lakewood. Scratch that—I *really* loved Camp Lakewood. If I were with Dave or even Meg and if we were at school, I would never be allowed to do this. Mrs. B would always be required to tag along behind me. I didn't know why Christine was so cool with letting me go off by myself—outdoors, for one, and near a huge body of water at that—while the school acted like I was going to have a heart attack just moving through the halls.

"Glad to see that your TechnoTalk is still working and that I didn't do more damage to it," Tommy said and took a seat on the bench.

I pulled up to him. And maybe I was just a *tad* closer than usual.

"So, you want to talk about last night?"

I sighed and hit my talking switch. "Not . . . really . . . but . . . I . . . don't . . . have . . . a . . . choice."

"This is true," he said, quite matter-of-fact. "Before we start, though, I'm sorry, again, about how I behaved. I guess I could've yelled at him instead of lunged at him, but . . . I was in the moment. And he was being a serious ass."

"I . . . know. Thank . . . you . . . for . . . defending . . . me . . . though. . . . I . . . needed . . . that . . . last . . . night . . . of . . . all . . . nights."

I had spent all night thinking about it, and though I had struggled to fall asleep because I was worried Tommy's actions would get him kicked out of camp, part of me was also happy that he did it. I'd never had anyone defend my honor before.

"No problem. I'd do it again if I had to," he said, his mouth turning up in a half-smile.

"I . . . guess . . . you . . . want . . . to . . . know . . . why . . . I . . . started . . . bawling . . . last . . . night."

Tommy casually placed his arm on my armrest and leaned closer to me. "Well, yeah, I do. I want to know what happened to make you so upset."

He was talking about the question JT asked the night before. Who had been hurt by a friend or . . . something. I couldn't remember the exact wording of it. I had been too caught up in my own head to really pay attention to everything going on around me.

I took a deep breath.

"Basically . . . I . . . really . . . liked . . . this . . . guy . . . and . . . my . . . best . . . friend . . . knew . . . how . . . I . . . felt . . . and . . . she . . . went . . . after . . . him . . . anyway . . . and . . . tried . . . to . . . hide . . . it . . . from . . . me. And . . . then . . . when . . . I . . . did . . . find . . . out . . . she . . . acted . . . like . . . it . . . wasn't . . . a . . . big . . . deal."

"Assholes," he breathed.

I strongly agreed with him.

"Did you, like . . ." Tommy paused. "Were you actually together, or did you just like him?"

I shook my head. "We . . . never . . . dated . . . but . . . he . . . said . . . we . . . were . . . best . . . friends."

"But you wanted more?"

I nodded.

"That's shitty. I'm sorry."

"I . . . just . . . don't . . . get . . . why . . . they . . . didn't . . . tell . . . me. Meg . . . knew . . . how . . . much . . . I . . . liked . . . him . . . and . . . she . . . had . . . to . . . have . . . told . . . Dave. Wouldn't . . . you . . . think . . . that . . . they . . . would . . . want . . . to . . . tell . . . me . . . so . . . I . . . could . . . get . . . over . . . him?"

"Yeah. Maybe they really knew how much you were into him, so they didn't want to upset you."

I shrugged.

"I have a question. This might be a really stupid question. I apologize for that."

I nodded for him to go on.

"Was Dave in a wheelchair?"

I slowly shook my head and furrowed my eye brows, showing my confusion. *Why would he be?*

"He wasn't?"

"He . . . didn't . . . have . . . a . . . disability."

"So you're not opposed to dating someone who could walk?"

I told myself this was a perfectly okay question. Actually, it was better that he asked rather than just assumed. He probably never knew someone with a disability on a personal level, so how could he know who we dated, or if we dated at all? Still, there was a tiny pang inside of me that wished he didn't need to ask that question.

"One . . . of . . . my . . . aides . . . at . . . school . . . thought . . . I . . . needed . . . to . . . be . . . with . . . somebody . . . in . . . a . . . wheelchair. She . . . even . . . wanted . . . to . . . set . . . me . . . up . . . with . . . this . . . kid . . . who . . . was . . . severely . . .

cognitively . . . disabled . . . and . . . I . . . cried . . . for . . . two . . . days. "

Panic came across Tommy's face. "Oh, God. That's not what I was getting at. I told you this might be a stupid question. I'm sorry."

"No . . ." I thought for a second. How did I want to say what I was thinking? "It's . . . good . . . for . . . me . . . to . . . know . . . that . . . even . . . people . . . like . . . you . . . wonder . . . those . . . things. Sometimes . . . I . . . forget . . . I . . . have . . . a . . . disability . . . and . . . I . . . see . . . guys . . . going . . . for . . . girls . . . like . . . Meg . . . and . . . not . . . me. I'm . . . not . . . saying . . . I'm . . . jealous . . . of . . . them . . . but—"

"You don't have to justify yourself, Brynn," Tommy said, reaching out and rubbing the tension from my shoulder. "I definitely understand."

I tried to ignore his soft hand warming my skin. "I'm . . . just . . . saying . . . I . . . forget . . . I'm . . . a . . . little . . . more . . . involved . . . than . . . the . . . typical . . . girl . . . and . . . guys . . . probably . . . don't . . . know . . . what . . . to . . . do . . . with . . . me."

He nodded. "Hate to agree, but that's probably true."

"Anyway . . . please . . . don't . . . be . . . afraid . . . to . . . ask . . . me . . . anything. I . . . would . . . rather . . . you . . . ask . . . me . . . the . . . question . . . than . . . assume . . . the . . . wrong . . . answer."

He nodded again. "Will do."

I kept going, realizing I had nothing to lose. Tommy seemed so open to me as a person; I didn't feel at all like I was being judged. It felt good to be open and honest, too.

"And . . . in . . . my . . . mind . . . my . . . future . . . boyfriend . . . is . . . not . . . in . . . a . . . wheelchair. He . . . doesn't . . . have . . . a . . . disability. I . . . don't . . . really . . . have . . . a . . . reason . . . for . . . that. I . . . just . . . see . . . myself . . . with . . . somebody . . . who . . . can . . . walk. Don't . . . you . . . have . . . an . . . ideal . . . girlfriend . . . in . . . your . . . head?"

I braced myself for his answer, unsure if I really wanted to hear it.

"I never thought about it like that, but I suppose I do."

Time for a new subject.

"Okay . . . since . . . you . . . asked . . . me . . . your . . . question . . . I . . . get . . . to . . . ask . . . you . . . my . . . question."

"Who made this rule?"

"I . . . did."

"Oh. Of course," he teased.

"What . . . happened . . . with . . . Jenn?"

I'd been thinking about his breakup with Jenn since Randi asked me about it in the cabin earlier. It was time to get this all out in the open. We were getting closer every day and I wanted to learn all his secrets.

Tommy stretched out his arms and rolled his neck from shoulder to shoulder. "Ah, I knew it was only time until that one came up. Can I take a rain check?"

"I . . . just . . . told . . . you . . . a . . . whole . . . lot . . . more . . . than—"

"I know," Tommy grinned. "I have to warn you, though. This might make you not like me anymore."

"So . . . the . . . camp . . . has . . . an . . . actual . . . reason . . . for . . . not . . . talking . . . to . . . you?"

"Nah." He waved off that idea. "I highly doubt anyone knows what really happened. Are you sure you want to know this?"

I slowly nodded. What could be so bad?

"Well, I . . . used to drink, Brynn. Not a lot or anything; just when I was hanging out with my buddies. We also would drink here at camp. Someone would be in charge of bringing the alcohol, and we all would go out in the woods one night and get wasted. It was usually after the dance. I think a bunch of them are still doing it tomorrow night. I don't know."

He took a breath in and continued.

"Anyway, my dad died in October of liver problems. . . ." He drifted off for a second and my chest tightened. I had no idea he'd gone through something so horrible so recently. "We all knew he had a drinking problem, but he wouldn't admit it. And no matter how many times my mom pushed him to get help, he wouldn't. And then it just got to be too much for his body. And then he was gone."

"I'm . . . so . . . sorry . . . to . . . hear . . . about . . . your . . . dad."

"Thanks," he said, smiling sadly.

I wondered what his dad looked like and if they were close. I wondered why he wouldn't admit that he had a problem, even when confronted by his family.

"What my dad went through . . . It scared me, so I stopped. I wasn't drinking a lot to begin with, but I know alcoholism could be hereditary, and I didn't want to risk it. I told Jenn this and said that we could stop together. We didn't drink that much, anyway, so it shouldn't have been a challenge. I said I would be there for her if she would be there for me. She got pissed and said I was ruining her fun. And somehow that turned into the whole camp hating my guts."

I tapped my switch. "I . . . don't . . . not . . . like . . . you . . . anymore."

He smirked. "I'm glad."

"I'm . . . sorry . . . she . . . didn't . . . understand . . . what . . . you . . . wanted."

"Eh, it is what it is. I'm just glad I—"

"Hey!" A voice broke through the quietness of the woods. Although it was nearly dark, we didn't need to see to know who it was. "Hey, losers!"

"Seriously?" Tommy whispered. "Again?"

I typed as quickly as I could. "Don't . . . punch . . . him . . . again."

He laughed bitterly. "I'll try my best."

Jonah came down the path, fueled with energy and possibly rage. Randi ran up behind him. She threw her arms around him and flung him to the side. "Jonah! No!"

He lost his balance for a few steps and his orange juice splashed everywhere. Orange juice? Didn't he have red juice at the activity? How many drinks did he have each day? Was camp really that bad that he couldn't get through an entire night sober?

"Look at what you made me do to my drink!" Jonah shouted at her.

In one quick move, Randi yanked the old water bottle out of his hand. Turning it upside down, she took off in a sprint with orange juice trailing behind her. Jonah tried to keep up with her, but stumbled every few feet.

That night, thoughts of Tommy kept me up again. However, these didn't bring fear and anxiety. Instead, butterflies flew around my stomach and a smile played on my lips. I still wanted to be careful, because I'd so recently been hurt by my feelings for Dave, but I felt like Tommy might be different. He wanted to get to know me, and he wasn't afraid to try to do just that. Even if it meant having to throw a punch or two along the way.

Chapter Eighteen

*C*hristine poured the last cup of warm water over my head, chasing any soap that had been left in my hair down the drain. She twisted the knob and the water came to a stop. Since we were without a handheld showerhead like I had at home, Christine used a giant plastic cup she found in the camp kitchen. And since the shower stall wasn't made for anyone who might need a shower chair and somebody in there helping them, it was a little cramped—to say the least. Because Christine needed to be in the stall with me, she had to wear her bathing suit.

This was how I had been taking my showers for the past five days.

Christine wrapped me in my purple towel and made sure nothing was showing. She then wheeled my dripping wet shower chair out of the stall and parked it next to my wheelchair. When I was home, my dad usually carried me right from my shower to my bed without even moving my shower chair, but obviously I couldn't do that here. Still in my towel, Christine lifted me from my shower chair to my wheelchair and put my seatbelt on. She was becoming a pro at this. Then again, after five days, did she really have a choice?

She moved my shower chair out of the way and went to grab my clothes from my backpack. Tonight was the dance. It was why I was taking my shower in the middle of the day when I would usually be hanging out with Tommy. It was also why I agreed to borrow a dress from Carly, even though I wasn't crazy about the idea since Carly and I never really talked—about the dress or much of anything else. Randi said I had to look cute and that I could borrow something of hers, but I was closer to Carly's size.

"Ahhh," Christine groaned, "I think I left all of your stuff on your bed. Will you be okay if I run back to the cabin? You can go back in the shower stall so you're not sitting out here in your towel. You can drive without your feet being strapped in, right?"

I turned my chair on and spun around to back in.

Christine held the shower curtain open. "I'm sorry I'm such an idiot. I promise I'll run as fast as I can."

I smiled at her as she let the curtain fall.

The main door to the shower room opened and closed. I laughed to myself. I was reminded again of how totally opposite school and camp were. What would the administrators do if they knew I was left in a shower stall . . . by myself . . . completely naked . . . and still alive to tell the story?

I heard the main door open and close again, but knew it was too soon to be Christine returning; the cabin wasn't that close. I recognized the voice right away. Carly.

"So you really think I should wear this dress?"

"Yeah. I mean, it's cute." That had to be Jenn. It definitely wasn't Randi. "But don't you have that, like, blue one?"

"I let Brynn borrow it. She didn't have anything."

"She doesn't even have dresses?"

My leg shot out. Luckily, I was far enough away from the curtain, so it didn't hit it or make any sounds.

"No, I think she said she didn't know to bring one because she was thinking it was camp. She didn't expect there to be an occasion to dress up for," Carly said.

I could hear someone rummaging through a bag and I imagined she was sorting through various hair products, soaps, sprays, and God knows what else. If I learned nothing else about Carly so far, it was that she was a high-maintenance type of girl—even in the middle of the woods.

"So she actually can talk?"

"Yeah, with that computer thing in front of her. I think she does it with her head, or something?"

"Does it, like, read her mind?"

My other leg flew out. I decided this was why I had feet straps: for when stupid people made stupid comments.

"I don't think so," Carly replied, "but who knows?"

How could she not know? Randi explained it to her, and she was there when we explained it to everyone in the cabin. Had she not cared enough to pay attention? Or was she just acting dumb?

"Tom would want to hang out with her," Jenn said. Her words were followed by a muffled thud; she must have dropped her shower stuff on the floor. "He did always like to do nice shit like that for people."

Nice, Jenn.

"Same with Randi. I think they just feel bad for her."

"I know. Because there's no way they can really be friends with someone who needs a robot to talk for them."

Carly had to start talking over the water. "We have such good friends."

"I know, right!" It sounded like Jenn turned her water on, too. "We should try to be more like them."

At this remark, both girls erupted into giggles.

What was left of the warm air from my shower felt like it was sucked out of the stall. I was freezing now, and this was not going to make getting dressed any easier. I focused on not shivering to death and on not having a CP attack. I needed Christine to come back; I needed her to come back so that we could get out of here before they were done with their showers.

Water from my hair dripped down my back while Jenn and Carly's words tugged at my mind. I highly doubted that what they said was true, but I learned quite a bit about people's intentions through my "friendship" with Meg, and I didn't want to get burned again. Were Tommy and Randi only talking to me because they felt bad for the only girl in a wheelchair at camp? Did they think this girl who wasn't able to talk had the ability to be their actual friend?

Tommy opened up to me and told me some pretty personal stuff. I didn't think he would waste his time doing that if he was talking to me just because he felt bad for me. And after our conversation in the cabin about her insecurities and Jonah yesterday, I didn't think what Carly had said about Randi made much sense, either. Carly was her best friend. She should have known her better. I suddenly felt disappointed; Randi deserved better people in her life.

Christine stepped inside of the shower stall, startling me and chasing my thoughts away. "So sorry about that, Brynn. I don't know what I was thinking. Are you okay?"

I nodded.

"Are you sure? You don't look okay. You can tell me if you're mad at me."

I shook my head and forced a smile. This was one thing I hated about needing help all the time. If I was mad, someone would figure it out right away and make me tell them what was wrong. The same thing happened when I was really excited or upset. I couldn't exactly say I needed to take five minutes for myself. My aide one year at school even took it so far that if I didn't come off of the bus smiling from ear to ear (and this was at 7:15 in the morning), she would tell everybody I was "miserable" that day. Thank God she wasn't around for the Meg/Dave saga. She would've probably told people I'd been possessed by the devil himself and to steer clear if they didn't want to die a horrible, painful, spiteful death.

I didn't miss her one bit.

"Are you just freezing?" Christine asked me.

That wasn't the case anymore, but I nodded again. She'd given me an out, and I gladly took advantage of it.

Christine reached for another towel and rubbed my legs with it. "I'm sorry. I probably should have dried you off more before I went. I'm just not thinking today."

To my surprise, my legs were as loose as Jell-O, probably because my anger had dissipated while thinking about how little Carly seemed to really know about her "best friend," which made it easier to put my underwear and blue Converse on. Christine strapped my feet down and I did my usual and pushed myself up so she could pull up my underwear.

Christine went for the dress. The blue dress. I had originally been so excited because it had a V neck so I was going to get to show off my cleavage at the dance. Now I didn't want to have anything to do with that dress. The pity dress. I didn't think I could stand to have it on me, but what was I going to do? I didn't have any other clothes down here, and I couldn't go across camp in a towel. I could put my old clothes back on, go back to the cabin, and change, but I didn't have my TechnoTalk down at the shower room. It would take forever to explain to Christine what I wanted.

I closed my eyes as Christine rolled up the dress and slid it over my head. She slipped both of my arms in. I then pushed myself up again so she could pull it down. It came down right to the middle of my shins. I plopped back down and she adjusted the spaghetti straps on my shoulders.

"It looks so cute on you! Really, it does."

I didn't feel cute at all. I wanted to rip the dress off me, throw it into the lake, and go put my own clothes on. But, alright. It did match perfectly with the baby blue color of my shoes. And it did show just the right amount of cleavage; not too much that I looked like a slut, but not so little that I looked like a twelve-year-old.

"You want to go do your hair and makeup now?" Christine opened the shower curtain.

I drove out of the stall and motioned to the door.

Christine gave me a confused look. "You want to go do your hair and makeup back at the cabin?"

I want to get the hell out of here before Jenn and Carly got out of the shower.

"Do you want to do something specific with your hair and want to go back to the cabin so you can tell me with your TechnoTalk?"

I thought about that for a moment. *Yes, yes I did.*

We didn't even have to open the screen door of the cabin to know there were a bunch of girls getting ready for a dance. The air smelled like Bath and Body Works decided to take up shop in what I had been considering my temporary home. The mixture of aromas became ten times stronger once we were actually inside.

I drove past girls with straighteners, sprays, curling irons, and lotions right to my bed, absolutely relieved that I made it out of the shower room without seeing Carly and Jenn, although I had no idea what I was going to do when Carly came back to the cabin. I positioned myself in front of the little square mirror on the wall that I could only see my head in. Christine put my TechnoTalk on. I started typing.

"Okay . . . I . . . want . . . to . . . have . . . my . . . hair . . . down . . . but . . . whenever . . . I . . . do . . . it . . . falls . . . in . . . my . . . face . . . and . . . gets . . . in . . . my . . . mouth."

If everybody thought I was just some girl in a wheelchair they needed to feel bad for, I was going to look as hot, and sexy, and cute as I could. Or attempt to, anyway. No one would be feeling bad for *me* by the night's end.

"Do . . . you . . . know . . . how . . . I . . . could . . . have . . . it . . . down . . . but . . . not . . . have . . . it . . . go . . . in . . . my . . . face? Because . . . I . . . can't . . . use . . . my . . . hands . . . to . . . tuck . . . it . . . behind . . . my . . . ears."

"Right. I get what you're saying," Christine paused. "Ummm. I am more than willing to help you keep it out of your face, but you probably don't want me with you all night."

I fought back a smile. I just loved her.

"I don't know. It's down right now and is staying back, but that's probably because it's sopping wet. I take it you want it dried?"

"Yeah . . . but . . . I . . . don't . . . have . . . a . . . hair . . . dryer."

"Randi!" Christine turned around. "Do you have a hair dryer?"

"Maggie!" Randi called. "Can I have your hair dryer?"

Two seconds later, Randi showed up with a pink hair dryer. "Now I do. That dress looks so much better on you than it does on Carly."

I hoped she couldn't tell I was cringing.

"Thanks, Maggie!" Christine yelled across the cabin. "Randi, you're creative. How can Brynn have her hair down and keep it out of her mouth?"

"Do you want to have it all down?"

I nodded.

"What about bobby pins?"

"I . . . tried . . . that . . . and—"

"They don't work?"

I nodded again.

"Ah, but you've never tried it the way *I* do it," Randi proclaimed, positioning herself so that I could see her reflection in my mirror. She grinned at me. "Mind if I give it a shot?"

I smiled back at her and nodded for her to go ahead. "Work . . . your . . . magic."

"Don't mind if I do," she said, pulling some spare bobby pins out of the pocket of her bright pink—though not obnoxiously pink—dress and sticking them in her mouth for easy access.

Christine bent down to unplug my TechnoTalk charger and plug in the hair dryer for Randi. As the hot air dried my hair and warmed my upper body, I stared at my suitcase. Would it be too much to have Christine change me again? Did I have time before dinner? But a lot of people had already seen me. They would notice that I didn't have the dress on and ask me why I changed, and I really didn't want to explain it to them. Plus, I would be back to my original problem of not having any "dance clothes."

Once my hair was dry, I watched her work in the mirror, pulling back the front pieces of my hair, which always fell in front of my eyes, and pinning them into place. She asked Christine, who had been standing idly by for the first time all day, to fetch her products like hair spray and defrizzer. Randi knew what she was doing, and she seemed happier doing it. If we were alone, I might have asked her if she'd gotten a chance to talk to Jonah about his behavior—and also about what happened after she ran off with his drink the night before.

"I . . . like . . . your . . . dress." *More than mine.*

"Thanks," she said, her teeth still clenched around a few pins. "They kept telling me I couldn't wear normal clothes to this dance, like I've done the past few years. I don't get it, but whatever."

"If . . . you . . . want . . . to . . . wear . . . your . . . clothes . . . you . . . should." If Randi changed back into her everyday clothes, then I'd have a reason to change into mine, too.

"Eh, it's easier this way. Fewer lectures and less whining and pleading to deal with. 'You're the worst girl, ever,'" Randi said, imitating Carly's high-pitched voice. I giggled. "Plus, sometimes it just feels good to dress up, ya know? Though I did take it down a few notches with these rad tights, right?"

I eyed her tights: black with lime green, yellow, orange, and pink polka dots. On her feet was a pair of Converse similar to mine, but orange and way more beat up than my own. She looked like she was ready to have fun.

202

I understood where she was coming from, wanting to dress up now and then, but I really did wish she would change her mind.

Christine suddenly squealed as if she were Carly. "I think Randi is on to something! This looks awesome!"

I looked in the mirror at myself and smiled. It really seemed like all my hair was down past my shoulders, except for the pieces that made up the front layer of my hair. Randi had put them at the top of my head in a delicate type of poof. I'd always hated when girls walked around with high, obnoxious poofs that fought for attention with their orange skin and cakefaces. But on me—with a little bit of pink on my cheeks from the sun and a natural look—it worked!

"You love it. C'mon. Tell me you love it," Randi teased, clearly proud of her work.

I nodded enthusiastically and felt even better about it when none of my hair fell into my eyes or found its way into my mouth.

"We . . . need . . . to . . . take . . . a . . . picture . . . so . . . I . . . can . . . show . . . my . . . mom. We've . . . never . . . tried . . . this."

Christine hustled to the night table beside my desk and pulled my camera out of the tiny drawer. We hadn't taken nearly enough photos at camp so far. A few of us on the basketball court and at arts and crafts. But I wanted more. And I especially wanted one of me and Tommy before camp was over.

"Okay, Randi get in there with her," Christine demanded. Randi bent down so that our faces were level and we both grinned at the camera. Christine took two more and then set the camera down.

"Makeup time!" she announced and held up her makeup bag. "I have to be honest, I'm really looking forward to putting—"

"Someone's at the door for Brynn!" Evelyn shouted.

"Or not," Christine tossed the makeup bag on my bed. "Someone is at the door for you! You don't need makeup, anyway.

You look really great. Do you want any jewelry or anything? Do you have a necklace or something?"

I shook my head. Carly had been right about one thing: I hadn't come prepared for anything remotely formal at all.

"That's okay. Like I said, you really look awesome. Why don't you go see who's at the door and meet me at the dining hall? I need to go change out of my bathing suit."

She shoved the camera in my bag and I headed to the door.

"Looking hot, Brynn!" Evelyn said and opened the door for me.

I smiled at her to say thank you as I drove outside. Not to my surprise, Tommy was waiting for me.

He wasn't wearing anything special; just a black T shirt and khaki pants. It was what he was wearing the first time I met him if I remembered correctly. His hair was still in a curly mess of a fro and he still had that awful scratch below his eye from his fight with Jonah. All the frustration I'd felt in the shower earlier simply melted away when I saw him.

"So your hair is not permanently stuck on top of your head," Tommy observed, coming forward and leaning his arm on my chair.

I jokingly stuck my tongue out at him.

"Oh, I try to give you a compliment and you give me the tongue again."

I nodded to confirm that was how it was going to be.

"Thanks. You do look very nice, by the way."

I looked down and smiled.

"And I was thinking. We could have dinner with just the two of us before the dance, if you want."

I looked up at him. We couldn't really have dinner by ourselves. The whole camp was always in the dining hall, and there was nowhere else for us to go. Was he crazy?

"I could help you eat."

Tommy's face was a carbon copy of the confused one I wore as I started over to the patch of shade next to my cabin. My brain raced through thoughts almost too fast for me to keep up. Carly. Jenn. My suggested "pity" friends. My very real "pity" dress. My awesome hair. Me telling Tommy that I didn't understand why guys didn't go for me. My stomach twisted at the next thought.

But Tommy had proven himself to be different so far, right?

"Why . . . do . . . you . . . want . . . to . . . help . . . me . . . eat?" Tommy was standing beside me reading my screen, so I didn't have to hit SPEAK.

"Do I really need a reason for offering to help you eat? Can't I want to just because I think it would be fun for us to not have your counselor around?"

I frowned at him. He did have a point.

"Look, you either do want me to help you eat, or you don't. Whatever you want to do. I was just offering. I thought you and Christine might need a break from each other."

I turned to start typing only to smack my head off of Tommy's hand.

I faked being in pain to lighten the mood a little and he laughed.

"Stop," he whined, chuckling a bit simultaneously. "I'm not saying Christine is getting sick of you, so don't you even take it that way. I'm just saying I would be willing to help you if you want."

Looking into his eyes, I began to see that he was growing a bit irritated. I knew then that he definitely wasn't doing this out of pity. If he really didn't want to help me eat, he wouldn't have offered.

A smile broke out of me. Screw Carly. Screw Jenn. A cute guy who has witnessed me eat over the past few days and who didn't get grossed out when a piece of bread occasionally fell out of my mouth wanted to help me eat, not because he felt bad for me, but because he genuinely wanted to spend time with me. Alone.

"So, are you done with your little freak-out-slash-self-doubt session? Can we go to the dining hall now?"

I rolled my eyes and hit my switch to turn around.

"Rolling your eyes at me. Right. Great way to start a date."

Date?!

Chapter Nineteen

The dining hall seemed to have been turned into a garden of daisies. A string of daisies (paper daisies . . . this was Camp Lakewood, after all) bordered the door. Daisies had been placed on every table as a centerpiece, probably made by Bonnie or another group in arts and crafts. Even vases of real daisies were scattered throughout the buffet in front of the dining hall. I wondered how JT came up with this DAISY theme. Did he have a secret obsession with flowers and wanted to do something with that, or was he really just on a mission to change American society and the word DAISY just happened to be the acronym he came up with?

"For some reason," Tommy explained as I followed him to the back of the line, "they decided that the dinner before the dance should be like Thanksgiving. I'm not entirely sure why, but this is one out of two nights where we don't have crap for food. Do you like turkey?"

Turkey wasn't exactly my favorite, but it was okay. It could be chewy at times, and if I was going to have Tommy help me eat, I wanted something fairly easy. I nodded at the mashed potatoes. Now *those* were my favorite.

"Mashed potatoes, okay. What else do you want?"

I shrugged. I didn't really want anything else.

"Alright." Tommy scooped a big helping of potatoes on each of the plates he was balancing on his arm. "After sitting with you for the past couple of days, I couldn't help but notice that you kinda eat like a bird. I say you're trying something new tonight."

Really? This wasn't typically part of what people did when they helped me eat.

"Oh, come on. I'm not saying you have to like it. Just that you should try something out of the realm of peanut butter and jelly and, apparently, mashed potatoes. I haven't seen you eat one vegetable. They have green beans. Wanna try some?"

I squinted up my face as if he was trying to force bleach down my throat. Long story short—when I was at my old school, I once saw a kid squashing a green bean in his hand that had fell onto his wheelchair. The kid wasn't aware of what he was doing, but soon his hand was covered in a green gooey mush. Since then, a green bean had never been able to make it even a foot away from my mouth.

Tommy grabbed some turkey and a roll for his plate. "Ya know, people have been eating green beans for centuries now, I believe, and I don't think I've heard of anyone dying from it. Just try one. If you don't like it, you can spit it out at me."

You're going to bug the hell out of me until I taste the damn green bean.

"Please? I'll even have the napkin ready to go."

I sighed. *Here goes my attempt at being hot and sexy tonight.* Thank God we weren't sitting with anyone else.

"You will?" Tommy looked surprised. "You're actually going to do it? Here, I'll only put one on your plate. If you like it, I'll come back and get you more. And if you keel over and die, I'll call your parents myself and take full responsibility for making you eat a deadly vegetable."

I gave him the screw-you tongue and headed off to our table.

Tommy unloaded the plates of food from his arms and then went back to get the drinks and the apple pie we decided to have. Somehow, even though this was the way Christine and I had been doing every meal, and even though this was the way we did it whenever my family and I were at picnics and get-togethers, I couldn't help but feel a pang of sadness.

Here was a guy (although I wasn't ready to admit it aloud, especially to anyone here) I definitely liked. Tommy shouldn't be carrying my food and getting my drink for me. I didn't want him to have to do that. Only snobby girls had their boyfriends wait on them hand and foot. Not that I was saying Tommy was definitely going to be my boyfriend, but whether I was with Tommy or another guy, this was probably how it had to be if we ever wanted to be alone.

Maybe this was the reason guys didn't ask me out, let alone try to have a conversation with me. A girl like Meg or Carly or Jenn didn't need them to get their food, help them eat, or even wait for them to speak when they were having a discussion.

"Hey," Christine's voice pushed away my thoughts, "did Tom help you get your dinner?"

I nodded and smiled at her outfit. She had on white capris and a blue flowery sleeveless top.

"Oh, you like my shirt? Thank you. Randi was right; if you don't get dressed up for the dance, everyone will get on your back about it. Anyway, I'm going to get myself something to eat. I'll be right back."

I started to shake my head.

"No?"

"Brynn decided that she doesn't need you tonight," Tommy said and slid into the seat next to me with two non-Camp Lakewood looking pieces of pie. (They were huge!) "She's being brave and letting me attempt to help her."

"So I've been replaced?" Christine translated. "I see how it is. Thanks, Brynn. I feel the love."

I blew her a kiss and she winked at me.

"Well, you guys have fun. I'm going to go sit with Randi and the others. Come get me if you need me."

"Will do." Tommy popped a piece of turkey into his mouth.

By now, the dining hall was pretty much full. As soon as Christine was gone, I hit my switch. "She's . . . going . . . to . . . go . . . sit . . . with . . . everybody—"

"Do you want butter on your mashed potatoes? I got some. I just had this feeling that you don't like gravy."

I nodded. "I . . . mean . . . I . . . love . . . Christine . . . but . . . wouldn't . . . she . . . know . . . this . . . will . . . probably . . . create—"

He continued to talk while he put some butter on our potatoes and then his roll. "The mashed potatoes are usually homemade on the night of the dance and the last night of camp. I have no idea why they don't cook like this for every meal. They probably think it's too much work or something."

I stared at him. Couldn't he see that I was typing?

"Brynn, I'm fully aware that shit will probably hit the fan when they see Christine without you. I'm choosing not to think about it. I'm with someone much more fun and interesting than they will ever be."

I blushed. "I'm . . . sorry."

"How about you tell me how to help you eat rather than worrying about everyone else?" Tommy scooped up a small spoonful of potatoes. "Do I just put it in your mouth and pull it out?"

We both paused and I couldn't keep myself from laughing. He chuckled, too, and then cleared his throat.

"Yeah, yeah. Dirty mind. Seriously now, is that how you do it?"

"You . . . have . . . to . . . wait . . . until . . . I . . . bite . . . down."

"Okay. Put it in your mouth and wait till you bite to pull out."

I laughed again.

"Got it. Do you want me to hold a napkin to your chin like Christine sometimes does?"

I nodded a definite nod.

"What? You don't trust me?"

"This . . . is . . . not . . . my . . . dress."

"Good," he said, holding the napkin to my chin. "Then we don't have to worry as much about getting anything on it."

I smiled. I should leave Carly a little surprise for later. That would teach her. Then again, with my luck, it would probably make matters worse.

I opened my mouth for the spoonful of potatoes. Tommy did what I told him to do; I bit down when the spoon was in my mouth, scraping the food off with my front teeth. I mashed the potatoes before swallowing. They didn't taste like the instant crap from a box like I had expected. They tasted like my mom drove up here for the day and was back in the kitchen cooking for everyone.

"Told you." Tommy scooped up another bite. "It's, like, a transformation."

I ate another bite, and another, until all of the potatoes were gone. My tongue only spazzed out once, kicking the white mouthful of mush onto the towel in his hand. My cheeks grew warm, but he didn't even bat an eye. He just shook the gross goo off to the side of my plate. Although part of me wanted to hug him for not acting like it was something straight from my intestine, another part of me couldn't help but wonder what he would have done last summer if Jenn was the one who spit up into his hand.

"Okay." Tommy picked up a fork and stabbed the one lone green bean. "It's time."

"You ... need ... to ... eat." I typed out. He hadn't touched his food since Christine left us.

"Oh my God. You are completely stalling!"

"No ... really ... I ... don't ... want ... you ... to ... not ... eat ... because ... of ... me. It's ... probably ... getting ... cold."

Tommy sighed. "You're doing it again. The worrying thing. I can eat whenever I want to eat. I know this. Okay?"

I frowned, but nodded.

He held up the fork and grinned. "Ready?"

"I . . . have . . . to . . . be . . . honest . . ."

"Yes?"

"I . . . might . . . gag."

Tommy chuckled. "This is hilarious. You're really scared of the green bean? What? Did the big bad green bean monster come after you when you were little or something?"

I thought about that. *Kinda.*

"Like I said, I'll have the towel ready to go. You can spit if you need to."

I closed my eyes. I tried to imagine I was about to take a bite of a big peanut butter cup. I felt the fork go in my mouth. I bit down. The green bean squished between my teeth. Immediately, the picture of the green gooey hand flooded my mind. The green bean flew out of my mouth, along with a gag so loud that I was sure everybody inside and outside of the dining hall had heard.

"Okay," Tommy chuckled again. "I see what you mean."

I excitedly went for my talking switch. I knew I looked like a total lunatic. "Tommy . . . I . . . tried!"

"I know you did. You had the gag to prove it. Good job!"

"No . . . you . . . don't . . . understand! This . . . is . . . very . . . big . . . for . . . me! I . . . know . . . it . . . probably . . . seems . . . like—"

"Is everything okay? Where's Christine?"

A panicked voice startled both of us and made us look up and away from my screen.

"Yeah," Tommy explained, "everything's fine. I was just being a mean friend and made Brynn try a green bean. Apparently, it doesn't work too well."

"Where's Christine?" JT asked again. "Is there a reason why you're feeding her?"

Tommy shrugged. "We just thought it would be fun to have dinner by ourselves. Christine is right over there with everyone else. She said we could go get her if we need her, and if we need her, I definitely will."

"I don't think this is such a good idea," JT crossed his arms. "She could choke, and if she does when you're feeding her, and not a counselor, it could be a big liability on the camp."

I had to try to explain it to him. He obviously wasn't listening to Tommy. "I . . . wasn't . . . choking."

"Is she writing something?"

Tommy didn't say anything. He just nodded and watched my screen. JT moved so he could see what I was typing too.

"I . . . just . . . have . . . a . . . thing . . . where . . . I . . . don't . . . like . . . the . . . texture . . . of . . . vegetables . . . and . . . I . . . tried . . . one . . . and—"

"Why did you make her eat something she didn't want to?"

I kept typing before Tommy had time to answer. "He . . . just . . . wanted . . . to . . . get . . . me . . . to . . . try . . . something . . . new. It . . . was . . . actually . . . a—"

"You need to be eating with your counselor," JT said to me. I knew it was directed to me. His voice went from a normal level to a booming level. "I am going to go get her. We'll be right back."

I slammed back against my chair with more force than I intended.

"Hey," Tommy rubbed my shoulder, "it's cool."

"No . . . it's . . . not . . . cool . . . I . . . really . . . want . . . to . . . keep . . . going . . . with . . . just . . . us."

"I know, babe. Believe me, I really, really want to, too. But I wasn't going to fight JT. I already got crapped on because of Jonah, so I don't think I'm his favorite person right now."

"I . . . tried . . . to . . . tell . . . him . . . I . . . was . . . okay. It . . . was . . . like . . . he . . . didn't . . . want . . . to . . . listen . . . to—"

Christine came bolting over. "Are you okay? You started to choke?"

People have told me whenever I got really angry, they couldn't believe I didn't give myself a concussion with how hard I banged my head off my switch to type. "I . . . was . . . not . . . choking. I . . . tried . . . to . . . tell . . . him . . . that . . . and . . . he . . . would . . . not . . . listen."

"Oh? Okay." Christine nodded. "You look like you're really peeved right now. What happened?"

Tommy filled her in. I was pretty sure I hated green beans even more now, if that was even possible. Instead of seeing that gross, green goo when I thought of green beans, now I'd also think of JT and how hypocritical he was. "Everyone should be respected despite their disabilities! Everybody should be treated as equals!" If only he practiced what he preached . . .

"So you really didn't choke?"

I shook my head harder than I usually did to emphasize my point.

Christine let out a breath. "Okay, I see where you're coming from, and I get that you weren't choking. I'm sorry that JT didn't really listen to you. That was wrong of him. If you want, we can go talk to him later, and I will try again to explain to him that you don't have a cognitive disability."

"I . . . don't . . . think . . . he . . . is . . . ever . . . going . . . to . . . get . . . it . . ." I paused. "You . . . already . . . were . . . doing . . . everything . . . you . . . could . . . to . . . make . . . him . . . understand . . . yesterday . . . and . . . he . . . just . . . was . . . still . . . talking . . . to . . . me . . . like . . . I . . . didn't . . . know . . . that . . . the . . . sky . . . was . . . blue."

Christine put her hand around the back of my chair. "I can't even imagine how you're feeling right now. To be mentally all there, and to have someone like JT or Jonah come along . . . and to not only have them think that you *don't* know what they're saying, but have them be disrespectful about it. I'm really sorry, Brynn. I want you to know that even though JT is my boss, I don't agree with how he handled yesterday or today."

"I . . . just . . . want . . . to . . . know . . . why . . . they . . . do . . . it. Why . . . do . . . some . . . people . . . think . . . I . . . have . . . a . . . cognitive . . . disability?"

Tommy leaned forward, resting his elbows on his knees. When he spoke, his voice was gentle, but not condescending. "Maybe they don't realize they're being offensive. Maybe they knew someone like you, or saw someone like you, and they really had a cognitive disability. So they just assume that everyone like you has a cognitive disability. I'm not saying they're right to do so, and I'm definitely not supporting what Jonah did the other night, but maybe they just don't know any better. You know how people can be; we get one little tidbit of information about something, and we think we know how everything is. Look at what Jenn did to this camp. She only told them God knows what, and now nobody wants to talk to me."

I nodded.

He continued, leaning in a bit closer. "Do you remember when I asked you if you would consider dating someone who could walk? I wasn't trying to be mean or offensive. I really didn't know if you did, and I really didn't know that was kind of offensive to you. And you said it was good for you to know even people like me have questions like that. Maybe this is like that. Maybe they just need you to explain to them that you don't have a cognitive disability. They need to hear it from *you*."

I considered this for a second. Why did I need to prove myself to them? Although, if I didn't, I knew they would never believe I was aware and more than able to converse with them and understand them. I guess they were the type of people who needed to see it to believe it. But even then . . . neither had given me a chance to show them. And that wasn't my fault.

"Will you at least think about talking to JT?" Christine asked, combing a strand of hair behind my ear. "I know you say I already did, but maybe it really would help if he hears it from you. You could even explain how what he's doing makes you feel."

I reluctantly nodded. A part of me knew they were right. If people like JT and Jonah didn't understand I actually had a brain inside my head, I probably needed to tell them. How else were they going to know? But how did you tell someone that you really weren't as clueless as they thought you were? Seriously, was there anything I could say to make him really understand, or was he just going to go along with whatever I said, but still think I wasn't totally with it?

"I know this might be a stupid question, but do you want to finish eating?" Christine held up the plate with the pie on it. "The pie is really good tonight. It might make you feel better."

I slowly shook my head.

"Okay," Tommy started, "if you don't want to eat anything else, you don't want to eat anything else. I get that. I personally lost my appetite, as well."

"But . . . you . . . hardly—"

"Dahhh!" he held up his hand. "Stop. Just stop. Let me finish what I'm saying. We are not going to let JT and his parade of stupidity ruin our night. It's dance night, for God sakes. Now, Brynn, will you be my awesome date to the dance?"

I couldn't help but laugh at his very cheesy, over exaggeration about the whole thing, even if it was just to make me feel better.

"Hey!" Christine exclaimed. "This boy just asked you a very, very important question! You should not be laughing at him! You should be answering him! Now, you heard him! Are you going to be his hot date to the dance tonight?"

Giving into the ridiculousness, I smiled and nodded.

My now-date to the dance let out an exaggerated sigh of relief. "Okay, good. I was getting a little nervous that I was going to have to go by myself. Do you want Christine to help you drink so that we don't get into any more trouble?"

Christine reached for my cup and napkin. The cool water helped the heat of my frustration dissolve. Although dinner was—apparently—supposed to be a date, it'd been wrecked by JT. But now I'd been given a second chance. I was going to the dance with the boy I liked. Granted, he might have just asked me to distract me from the JT situation, and never mind the fact the entire camp was going to the dance anyway, with or without dates. In the end, I still managed to have a date with the boy I liked.

My first date.

Chapter Twenty

Tommy placed his hand on my shoulder and we made our way down the hill. All of the counselors had moved their cars for the night. I couldn't help but chuckle to myself. My first dance was going to be in a borrowed dress from someone I didn't particularly like . . . with a guy that was just yelled at for trying to help me eat . . . who didn't necessarily have a choice in going to this dance . . . which was in the camp parking lot.

And I couldn't stop smiling.

Two giant speakers had been placed at the far end of the parking lot and when we arrived they were already blaring a popular hip hop song. A lot of people were still coming down the hill from dinner, but the campers who had already arrived were standing off to the side, talking in groups.

"Do you like this song?" Tommy looked down at me.

I shook my head. I was never really into hip hop.

"Glad to know your crappy taste stops at Abbie."

I leaned over and punched him in the chest.

"Did you just head butt me?"

I matter-of-factly nodded.

"Oh. Okay. I can deal with that." Tommy smiled. "So, this is how the dance usually is. We all stand off to the side, acting like we're much too cool to dance until there's a song everybody likes, and then we all go out and go for it, and then when the song is over, we all come back and think we're hot shit again."

The sun was just starting to set, which allowed me to type. "You . . . don't . . . seem . . . like . . . you . . . would . . . like . . . to . . . dance."

"Is it that obvious?"

"Did . . . Jenn . . . ever . . . get . . . you . . . to . . . dance?"

Tommy shrugged. "Maybe. I know *you* like to dance. Did you ever go to dances at your school?"

I frowned. "Do . . . you . . . really . . . want . . . to . . . know . . . my . . . dance . . . stor—"

"Yes! I do," he interrupted me. "I . . . want to know everything I can."

I met his eyes just in time to see a slight blush creep onto his face. I felt that mine was doing the same.

I continued with my story. . "I . . . always . . . wanted . . . to . . . go . . . to . . . Homecoming . . . even . . . when . . . I . . . was . . . in . . . middle . . . school . . . "

The song changed as more people flowed into the parking lot. More hip hop.

"And . . . one . . . day . . . I . . . even . . . asked . . . Dave . . . to . . . go . . . with . . . me . . . but . . . he . . . had . . . been . . . to . . . two . . . other . . . homecomings . . . that . . . year . . . with . . . his . . . other . . . friends . . . and . . . he . . . told . . . me . . . he . . . was . . . danced . . . out."

Tommy's brow furrowed. "This dude really sounds like a Grade-A asshole."

Before I could say anything else, Evelyn came up to us. She handed Tommy two little paper daisies that had a number on each of them.

Tommy groaned. "Don't tell me he's going to try to make even the dance a change-the-world activity."

Evelyn simply smiled and moved on to pass out the rest of her daisies.

"He's . . . really . . . getting . . . into . . . it."

I waited for him to lean over and read my screen, and when he didn't, I looked up to see that he was staring off into the distance, a frustrated look on his face.

I followed his line of sight and my jaw dropped opened in amazement. Carly, Jonah, Gabe, Jenn, and Amanda all were coming down the hill with water bottles in hand. Disappointment filled me when I saw Randi emerge from behind Jonah's large shadow. I knew she said she drank with Jonah occasionally, but I thought after our heart-to-heart the day before, she may have decided to stop doing so.

I quickly hit my switch. "All . . . of . . . them . . . are . . . doing . . . it . . . now?"

"Well," Tommy hesitated, "all of us normally would. Me, Jenn, Carly, everybody."

Why didn't Randi mention this to me?

"How . . . do . . . the . . . counselors . . . not . . . know?"

"I have been wondering why we never seemed to get caught, though," Tommy admitted. "Ever since the first time we all drank together a few years ago. This year, though, it just seems so obvious, but I'm not sure if that's because we *know* what's going on or not. It only takes two seconds to figure out that Jonah is drinking something that's not from the camp kitchen, and it's even more obvious he has been smashed ever since he got here, so I have no idea how it slipped by the counselors; maybe I just know him so I could tell right away. Or maybe they just don't care?"

"Isn't . . . it . . . their . . . jobs . . . to . . . care?"

"Yeah, but . . . If everyone's happy and no one's causing a ton of problems, sometimes people tend to forget they see or know things," Tommy reasoned.

"But . . . he . . . attacked . . . you."

"I hit him first. And I was completely sober." He sighed. "Whenever we would do it the past few years, though, we would do it in the woods where nobody was around. I think they're dumb as shit for doing it at the dance."

I paused, debating if I should ask this question, and decided to go ahead with it. "What . . . made . . . you . . . want . . . to . . . drink?"

Randi and I hadn't been able to talk about my own experiences with drinking or what I thought about it. At a few parties or get-togethers during our last year of friendship, Meg and Dave had offered to help me drink a beer. Although Dave had always accepted my refusal to do so, Meg had given me more of a problem. She'd offer multiple times throughout the night and I could never figure out why it was so important to her that I give it a try. In fact, her pushing made me want to drink even less. Now that I looked back at it, she probably just wanted to hear how awesome she was for getting her disabled best friend drunk. Even though I wanted to be at these parties, surrounded by my best friends, I didn't have any interest in drinking. I simply had no desire to chug something that probably tasted horrible, no matter what it was combined with, only to sit there all night laughing at nothing. Not to mention, how could I possibly get around the whole parents-putting-me-to-bed thing?

Tommy sighed. "I don't know. It was just something to do, something to break up the monotony that sometimes comes with camp . . . or life in general. I was dumb. But, old friends. Old me."

Having shimmied her way onto the dance floor, Carly reached for Gabe and dragged him to her. Despite what Tommy had said about everyone being much too cool for this dance, I watched as Gabe danced right up against her like he owned the song that was playing. Jonah and Randi joined her. And then Jenn and Amanda. Soon other people clustered with them.

Tommy shook his head in disbelief. "So this is why they call it dancing juice."

"Really . . . good . . . job . . . describing . . . how . . . the . . . dance . . . usually—"

"Ohhh, zip it!" He poked my shoulder.

"Do . . . you . . . wish . . . you . . . could . . . be . . . with . . . them?"

"Dancing like I'm on crack? No, thank you."

"Dancing . . . but . . . having . . . something . . . make . . . you . . . not . . . care . . . that . . . you . . . look . . . like . . . you're . . . on . . . crack."

Tommy shrugged. "I don't need to drink to not care what everyone is thinking of me." He broke into a smile and then motioned to the dancing campers. "Come on! Let's go."

I gave him a look that clearly said, *Are you actually on crack?*

"Oh, don't give me that. I saw your crazy dance moves before I even knew you. And besides, you said you always wanted to go to Homecoming. What the hell did you think you were going to do there?"

Have an excuse to wear a very pretty dress.

"What are you guys up to?" Christine asked, wandering up to us.

"Getting rejected by my own date," Tommy pouted.

"Oh, don't you think he got enough of that this week?" She nodded to the parking lot. "Go dance with this boy. You're making him feel bad!"

I smiled and rolled my eyes.

"Of all people, I would have thought you would be into this! You love to dance! You asked me the first day if there was anywhere you could go to dance."

"Alright," Tommy walked back over beside me, "is this thing on?"

What?

He turned to my counselor. "How do you turn her chair on?"

"With the button by her hand."

Finding the small black switch on the side of my armrest, he smacked it. It was a knowing smack—like he had done it for years.

"You drive it with your head, right?"

Did I tell him I drove with my head?

Before I could answer, Tommy slipped his hand right behind my head. I held in a squeal and tried to act as if I didn't have a clue what was going on. I didn't think I told him how I drove. No, we definitely hadn't had a conversation about my chair, or my TechnoTalk, or my CP for that matter. The way this fact, in addition to the idea that he felt comfortable enough to start driving my wheelchair without me saying it was okay, made me feel as if he'd given me ten bouquets of roses.

Tommy pushed my switch once, making my wheelchair jump forward.

"I think you need to hold it down for it to keep going," Christine explained.

She wasn't trying to stop him! She was encouraging him!

Any other girl here or at my school probably wouldn't understand how I was feeling right then. In fact, some people, like JT, would think it was absolutely unacceptable to push a disabled girl's head out of the way and take over driving her wheelchair, just like he did with Tommy and the green bean. But it made me feel accepted, and the feelings that came from that were too big to put into words.

Tommy pressed my switch again. This time he was able to make me go to the edge of the parking lot. He gave Christine a thumbs-up behind him.

"Okay . . . genius . . ."

"I like where you're going with this."

"If . . . you . . . are . . . so . . . smart . . . to . . . drive . . . me . . . out . . . here . . ."

"Or I'm getting told off. That's awesome, too."

"How . . . are . . . we . . . going . . . to . . . dance?"

"It's . . . dancing? Do we . . . really need a set strategy?"

"I . . . mean . . . I . . . just . . ."

Yes, I loved to dance. I needed to dance. But in my bedroom, or on the basketball court. By myself. I had never done it with anyone or in front of anyone.

He found the plug to my talking switch and ripped it out. "Did I hurt anything?"

I laughed in shock. *Too late now.*

"This thing comes off, right?" He grabbed the TechnoTalk mount. "Of course it comes off; you were without it when you had your little . . . girl . . . driver moment."

I pretended to be offended by that statement.

"I'm going to go lay this somewhere. Don't worry, I'll put it somewhere nobody will trample it."

I watched as he carried my communication device out of the way of the dance and then left it with Christine, who was seated at a table with a few other counselors and campers. Was this really happening to me? Did this guy not care at all about how he was going to look to his old friends? And did he really care so much that I liked to dance that he wanted to dance with me? Did he really feel comfortable enough to take my TechnoTalk off so I could dance with him? I felt like I had stepped inside my own fairy tale.

"Okay," Tommy walked in front of me, "computer is being protected by Christine and a tree. Did you figure out how we're going to do this?"

I shrugged.

"Good, 'cause I did. Can I take your arms out?"

I half nodded, half ducked my head, trying to hide my smile. *I will not be a cheesy girl!*

Just as he reached for my armband, the music stopped, startling us both.

"Okay, campers!"

Really? The megaphone? Tonight?

225

"We are going to do something a little different this year, instead of just having a regular old dance. You all should have received a daisy with a number on it when you came down. I want you to find the person who has the same number as you. Dance one dance with them. Yes, some boys may be with boys, and some girls may be with girls. It's just one dance, people. Got it? Good! Go for it!"

The music started again and Tommy threw his arms up, exasperated.

"I'm not going to put up with this crap anymore! I didn't come to camp to learn a magical lesson of how to get along with everyone! Especially these people! This is just ridiculous!"

I frowned and nodded.

"Tommy, my man!"

We both turned. "What do you want, Jonah?"

"I'm pretty sure Jenn has the same number as you." He took a swig of whatever the hell he was drinking. "You should go dance with her!"

Tommy laughed out loud. "Is that so? I'm pretty sure you have absolutely no idea what my number is, and I'm pretty sure you should not be telling me what to do right now."

Please don't get into a fight right now! I just want to be with you tonight! I don't want you to get in more trouble!

Randi was at Jonah's side in an instant. "What are you doing? Why can't you just let them be? You've been such an asshole to both of them and they never did anything to you!"

Jonah nodded. "Yeah. You are *so* right. Tackling me to the ground was nothing!"

"Because you called Brynn a retard, you retard!" Randi exclaimed.

My eyes darted from Tommy to Randi to Jonah and then back to Tommy. I didn't know what to do. I felt like an idiot just sitting there, but I didn't have my TechnoTalk. I didn't even know what I would say if I had my TechnoTalk.

"Don't compare me to her!" Jonah shouted, jabbing a finger in my direction.

I'm not sure if Randi's next move was because she was drunk, angry, or a mixture of both, but when she slapped her boyfriend across the face, I swear everyone in the general vicinity heard and felt it. And after she'd done it, she looked just as shocked as Tommy and me.

"You, bitch!" Jonah's hand rose and Tommy tensed as my mind went into a panic, but he simply pressed his giant hand to his already reddening cheek.

Tommy and I exchanged brief looks and I knew we'd both expected the same thing to happen. I briefly had time to wonder if Jonah had ever hit Randi during one of his drunken tirades.

While Jonah was nursing his face and his pride, Randi turned him around so his back was to us. "Go!" she mouthed. "Both of you! Get out of here!"

Tommy did a double-take. "You sure? You okay?"

"Yes! You guys need to go! If he can't see you, he will forget about it," she whispered. She put a hand on Jonah's back and pushed him in the opposite direction and then turned to meet my eye. "I'm so sorry."

I watched her walk him away, tossing her own drink in a trash can at the edge of the parking lot, and then glanced at Tommy.

He ran his fingers through his curly hair and then looked down at me. "You head to the basketball court. I'll go get your TechnoTalk and catch up with you."

Suddenly feeling like I was dropped into an action movie, I sped up the hill as fast as I could. I hoped Christine would know where I was. I hoped Jonah really was so drunk that Randi could distract him from what happened. Thankfully, we were at the back of the parking lot, so nobody seemed to notice. Or if they had, they hadn't reacted or informed any of the counselors or JT.

"You want your voice back?"

I turned around and let Tommy slip my TechnoTalk on my chair.

"That was interesting," he said and plugged my switch in. "Are you okay?"

I nodded.

"I'm sorry we didn't get to dance."

"You . . . don't . . . like . . . to . . . dance . . . anyway . . . and . . . maybe . . . I'm . . . just . . . not . . . meant . . . to . . . go . . . to—"

"I actually wanted to dance this time, because it was going to be with you."

He started rubbing my shoulder with his thumb. I had to battle the heat that was rising up my neck and focus on typing. His thumb made my entire body turn to Jell-O. My anxiety subsided.

When Dave and I hung out alone, I always got the urge to tell him how I felt about him. Sometimes I would even want to subtly hint for him to ask me out. The closest I had gotten to telling him that I liked him, before that devastating day when I found out about him and Meg, was asking him to go to Homecoming. My gut had always told me to lock my thoughts inside my head, throw away the key, and let whatever happened happen. But . . .

Now my gut was telling me that it was time to stop acting so afraid. I pressed my head against his forearm as he continued to rub my shoulder, his thumb coaxing away knots that had formed from the tension of the past few days—and possibly from the last few months, from all the drama at home.

"I'm sorry tonight didn't exactly turn out how I think we both imagined it," he said, his voice soft.

I inhaled. I . . . just . . . want . . . to . . . be . . . with . . . you . . . tonight."

His thumb moved from my shoulder to the back of my neck. "Okay. I think we have some time before I have to go to the stupid cabin campout. I don't know why they are even having one tonight. Stay here at the court. I'm going to go get something from my cabin. I'll be right back."

"You . . . don't . . . have . . . to . . . get . . . anything . . . for—"

"You will like what I'm getting. I promise. Just head to our bench and I'll be there in a sec."

When he jogged away, I found our bench—o*ur bench*—in the dark and parked my chair beside it. My body still felt as loose as it had ever been. Every day of my life I was touched; getting dressed in the morning, each time I went to the bathroom, getting a shower at night. I didn't have a choice to have people's hands all over me. Likewise, those people did not have a choice *not* to touch me. But Tommy did. Tommy chose to touch me, and I could still feel every spot where he made his decision.

I could still hear the music from the dance. I could have easily had my own dance party, but I didn't feel like it. I could have easily thought about the Jonah Situation and made myself upset, but I didn't want to do that, either. I just wanted to enjoy this moment and simply be.

The sun was almost completely down when Tommy appeared on the path to the basketball court. In his hand was a black guitar case.

Chapter Twenty-One

otally giving up all resistance, I let my completely ridiculous, ultra cheesy girl side out. I squealed.

"And you said that I didn't have to get anything for you," Tommy smirked. He placed the guitar case on the bench. He paused, scratching his head. "Although . . . I underestimated how loud the music would still be up here," he said, almost to himself. Then he shrugged—again to himself more than to me—and asked, "So how about that dance?"

"You . . . really . . . want . . ."

He resumed his now natural place beside me to read my screen. His thumb also resumed its place on my shoulder, rubbing circles into my muscles and sending little chills up and down my spine.

"To . . . dance . . . here?"

"Do you have any reason why we shouldn't?"

I smiled.

"Alright, you say you love to dance. Tell me how you do it at home."

"You . . . saw . . . how . . . I . . . do . . . it . . . when . . . you . . . probably . . . thought . . . I . . . was . . . absolutely . . . insane."

His thumb. My shoulder. The connection I felt, both physical and emotional. It was all making me feel like I could tell him anything. The words just seemed to come across my screen.

"Whenever . . . I'm . . . at . . . home . . . I . . . either . . . listen . . . to . . . music . . . in . . . my . . . wheelchair . . . or . . . I . . . actually . . . get . . . on . . . my . . . bed . . . and . . . I—"

"So you like to dance out of your chair?"

I paused. "I . . . don't . . . know . . . if . . . you . . . can . . . call . . . what . . . I . . . do . . . dancing. I . . . just . . . put . . . music . . . on . . . and . . . get . . . on . . . my . . . bed . . . and . . . move . . . around. "

"Sounds like dancing to me. Do you want to do that now? I could get you out of your wheelchair and we can dance."

My heart sped up. He wanted to get me out of my chair? I tried to play it cool.

"I . . . just . . . meant . . . I . . . usually . . . lay . . . on . . . my . . . bed . . . and—"

"Right, but we don't have a bed here. But I could still get you out of your chair. I could hold you up and we could move around to the music, as you like to call it."

I never had a guy want to get me out of my chair before. Dave had done it in the past, but I had always requested that he help me out and sit with me on the couch. Or lay with me on the bed . . . . I forced that memory out of my head and brought myself back to the present. I had never had a guy *want* to take me out of my chair. And up until that night, I had never had a guy ask me to a dance, or offer to help me eat, or do any of the things Tommy and I had done.

"I say we're doing it," Tommy said, making a move for my TechnoTalk plug. "You game?"

"Are . . . you . . . really . . . sure . . . you . . . " I couldn't let myself go in an all-out cheesy girl-fest just yet, even though I knew the moment he picked me up, I was going to melt inside his arms.

"Here we go again," Tommy groaned, rolling his head back and forth on his shoulders, stretching his neck. When he stopped, he knelt in front of my chair so we were eye-to-eye. "Yes, I really want to get you out of your chair. Yes, I really want to dance with you. No, I don't care that I have to get you out of your chair to dance with you. Here's the funny thing: I actually *want* to get you out of your chair, because I actually *want* to dance with you."

I continued typing what I had planned on saying before he interrupted me. "Can . . . do . . . it . . . without . . . dropping . . . me . . . and . . . cracking . . . my . . . head . . . open?"

"Oh." Tommy nodded. "I can see how that could be a concern of yours, too. You want to tell me how so I can make sure I don't?"

I laughed. "Were . . . you . . . really . . . going . . . to . . . get . . . me . . . out . . . without . . . me . . . telling—"

"You girls like to plan out every little detail, don't you? Can't you be more spontaneous?"

After I once again gave him my F-you tongue, I gave him the run down: I told him I could bare my weight and that he just had to make sure that I didn't fall. I also warned him about my occasionally flying arms and that if I hit him, it was all the CP's fault.

"Ask . . . Christine," I said, jokingly, though I did still feel a pang of guilt for clocking her in the face.

Tommy's eyes crinkled when he laughed. "I'm almost positive you can't even come close to what me and Jonah did to each other. I didn't see a single bruise on Christine, so I'm sure you won't do too much damage even if you do manage to catch me off guard. But have a little faith in me, Brynn, okay? I want to drop you on your head just as much as you want to go to the hospital."

I met his eyes and for the first time all night, what he had been saying began to slowly register. He *wanted* to do all this. To him, helping me eat and getting me out of my wheelchair wasn't just a job like it was to Christine or Mrs. B. He wanted to do this just as much as I wanted him to do this. Was it like when he had wanted to kiss Jenn, or if he had wanted her to give him a hug? Maybe. Maybe not. I wasn't going to have that answer. All I knew was that Tommy had made it perfectly clear that he genuinely wanted to be here with me.

My heart skipped a beat and my stomach tightened—but it all felt just right.

"Are you ready?"

I nodded as he pulled my TechnoTalk off and laid it on the ground by my chair. I could not believe this was happening.

"Okay. I want to tell you something. I know this might be a little rude to do without your computer on," Tommy started, "but I didn't want you to stop me and ask me if I was sure over and over and over again."

I nodded, making a mental note to try not to do that anymore.

"Brynn, I think you are awesome as hell. I'm pretty damn sure Christine, and Randi, and even Carly think so, too."

Oh, no! He didn't get it. And how would he get it? He had no contact with Carly. He didn't have a clue what she was saying about me.

"I just want you to know that helping you is not a big deal. I like you, you know? I want to get to know you more, and if I have to help you to be able to do that, then I have to help you. Helping you with the physical stuff is nothing compared to what we will get to do." He took my hand. "I just don't want you to feel bad every time you need help, because you are awesome anyway."

My fingers curled perfectly around his two fingers. I so wanted to be in his arms right that second, but he had to know what I was thinking and why I felt the way I did. I didn't want him to think I was that unsure of myself.

I motioned down at my TechnoTalk.

Tommy tilted his head. "You want your computer?"

I nodded, hoping he didn't think I wanted to question him again.

"Sure, but you know you don't have to feel like you have to say anything back to me. I just wanted you to know. Do you still want it?"

I nodded again. Letting go of my hand, Tommy bent down and grabbed my TechnoTalk. I cringed at what was possibly running through his mind.

"I . . . have . . . to . . . tell . . . you . . . something . . . and . . . I'm . . . not . . . questioning . . . you."

"You better not be questioning yourself, either." His thumb was back on my shoulder, but this time I couldn't let it take me over.

"I . . . have . . . to . . . tell . . . you . . . why . . . I . . . am . . . unsure . . . of . . . how . . . you . . . feel . . . about . . . helping . . . me."

"I was serious about what I said, babe. I really like you, and I want to be able to hang out by ourselves, and I want to do the things that you want to do, so if that means I need to help you with whatever, I will."

Trying to ignore the fact that he called me babe (for the second time!), I kept typing. "I . . . overheard . . . Carly . . . and . . . Jenn . . . talking . . . in . . . the . . . shower . . . room . . ."

"Ah. I'm sure they had some wonderful things to say." I couldn't see him right then, but I knew he rolled his eyes.

"They . . . didn't . . . know . . . how . . . you . . . could . . . be . . . friends . . . with . . . me."

Tommy let out a laugh. "You gotta be kidding me! What the hell did they mean by *how*? How is anyone friends with anyone?"

I shrugged, actually realizing how dumb that question really was.

"So what do you want to do about it?"

I looked at him, stunned.

"You heard me. We could sit here and mope about how they don't get it. We could go tell off the people who think they are just *so cool* because they are getting smashed right now. Or we could forget about it and have a little fun ourselves. Which do you want to do?"

A smile crept onto my face.

"That's what I thought," he said and unplugged my TechnoTalk again. "Dance with me!"

I shook my head, wondering how the crap I ended up at this camp with this awesome guy.

Once Tommy set my device on the ground like he did before, he gently took my arms out of my armbands and undid my feet straps. I didn't feel like I was going to hit him or kick him at all. My body seemed to have turned into Jell-O again. The effect was still absolutely amazing to me. Maybe my mom was right; maybe I was just a brain inside of a bowl of Jell-O.

He unbuckled my seatbelt. "Trust me?"

I nodded, relaxing even more when I realized that yes, I did trust him.

He then took hold of my arms and slid them around his neck. To my surprise, I managed to keep hugging him, so he could gently pull me out of my wheelchair into a standing position.

"Well," he whispered, "what'd ya know? You're way taller than the chair let on."

I only came up to his shoulder, but if he wanted to think I was tall, that was perfectly okay with me.

"Walk with me?" he took one step backwards.

With both his hands supporting my back and my arms still clinging to his neck, I took one shaky step forward. When I was in physical therapy when I was little, my legs never had a CP attack if I was baring weight on them. My therapist would stand behind me and hold me when we walked. Having Tommy in front of me and leaning my chest against his chest almost made me feel like I was the closest I had been with anybody, and not just in a physical way.

We slowly took another step, and another. In the light of the solo lamp post in the front of the basketball court, my feet seemed to follow his feet. It was definitely not as graceful as if we were partners in a ballet, but I was walking with Tommy.

I was walking with Tommy!

"So what are the chances they will play a slow song after this hip hop crap?"

The last *boom boom boom*s of the current song faded away.

This is it! I am about to have my first dance! And it was going to be with Tommy!

Both of us looked in the direction where the music was coming, as though our thoughts were going to make the song come on that much faster.

Possibly.

"And the next song is going to be?" Tommy repeated, this time calling out to the DJ positioned an acre or two away from us.

A ruffling sound came from off within the woods. But no music.

I started to laugh.

Still, there was nothing.

We knew then that the dance had ended.

"Really?" Tommy joined in. "This really is happening?"

It was in that moment I decided that I was not supposed to dance with any guy. At all. Ever.

"Alright. Plan B. Trust me?"

Before I had time to answer, Tommy flung me backward. An uncontrollable laugh slipped out of me. With one scoop, he was holding me the same way Christine often picked me up. He then, by whatever crazy powers that possessed his mind, started twirling around the basketball court.

"Dum dum dum da da dum dum dum," he sang out in no recognizable melody.

I could not stop giggling as the night sky spun in lazy circles before my eyes. I could feel the breeze fanning out my hair. Once we both were out of breath, he carried me back to my chair. To my surprise, he didn't put me back in.

Still holding me like a baby, I could feel Tommy carefully kneel to the ground. He positioned himself and leaned against the bench. He then positioned me so that I could sit between his legs and lean against his chest.

"How was that for a first dance?" he asked, running his fingers through my hair.

I looked up at him, attempting to give him a smile. I could only hold his eyes. As calm as my body was, it didn't seem to want to do anything else.

"I think I have an idea." He reached behind him.

The guitar case landed with a thud. He was going to play while holding me? How was he going to do that?

With one hand, he opened the case, got the guitar out, and set it across my lap.

"Play with me?"

I glanced up at him, making sure I heard him right.

"I can do the chords, and you can strum. You turn your chair on and off with your hand, so you have a little control. I can hold your arm close to the strings like we do when we're painting, and you can just go for it."

He thought this out!

"Here, wanna give it a shot?" He guided my left wrist in front of the guitar. "Let's do a G first."

Overly careful so I didn't grab all of the strings and crunch them in my hand, I ran my thumb over them. It was slow, and it was a noise that a three-year-old would make with a toy guitar, but I did it! I played a G note!

"Nice!" Tommy adjusted his fingers on the frets. "Give me a D!"

Again, I very consciously repeated the movement, making sure I didn't accidentally smash his guitar. Again, a not-so-perfect D note rang out, but I didn't care. I was sitting on the ground wrapped in Tommy's arms playing his guitar under the stars.

"And how about an E?"

I did the movement one more time before my arm shot up in the air and I squealed. I was aware that I looked like a complete idiot, but I just couldn't keep my body calm anymore.

"I assume you enjoyed that?" Tommy chuckled, setting the guitar to the side. "I believe your buddy Abbie has some competition now."

Meeting his eyes again, my arm came right back down.

I always pictured how my first kiss would be. It was with Dave, and it was the version of me whenever I was dancing. We would be on my bed, or in his car, and I would run my finger behind his ear, and we would then have a full-out make out session. I didn't know why, but I always left my CP out of the equation.

It wasn't until Tommy ran his finger gently over my lips that I knew my body wouldn't know it had CP; that I wouldn't have to worry about smacking him across the face; that I would want it more than anything at the moment.

Tommy leaned down and my eyes seem to know they were supposed to close. I felt his lips on my eyelids. I let myself feel every time he kissed them. He made his way down my cheek, gently pressing his lips to my warm skin. Goosebumps took over my entire body. Finally, he came to my lips. His soft lips upon my lips sent an automatic signal to my brain and I kissed him back without a moment's hesitation.

Chapter Twenty-Two

It took me forever to fall asleep that night. My brain wouldn't rest; my heart wouldn't stop fluttering inside my chest; my lips wouldn't stop smiling. Every time I closed my eyes, I replayed either our "dance"—which I already knew would be unlike any other slow dance I experienced in the future and which I would always remember—or our first kiss. And second. And third.

I had to calm myself down a few times to keep from squealing out of sheer happiness and waking my cabin mates. Heather and Maggie had been standing outside of the cabin, taking photos of the full moon, when Tommy and I returned. He bid me goodnight, kissed my cheek gently, and squeezed my shoulder before heading back to his own. The other two girls looked at each other and then at me and both broke out into huge smiles. I felt that they understood me, perhaps for the first time since I'd arrived. I was certain they'd all had camp crushes and perhaps even carried relationships outside camp and into their everyday lives. And now, I felt like I had finally become one of them.

The entire time Christine helped me get ready for bed, a smile resided on my face. She asked me where I'd ended up after the dance, and I simply told her I was with Tommy. That seemed to answer all her questions.

When Randi and Carly finally showed up, it was just past curfew and they looked beyond exhausted. I figured they were both *too* drunk to function, as neither of them said a word to anyone else before climbing into their beds. They hadn't even bothered to undress. And their headaches and attitudes the next morning more than gave away what they'd been up to the night before. But no one—campers or counselors—said anything.

The next morning, Tommy helped me with breakfast and Christine sat and sipped her coffee, chattering about . . . Actually, I wasn't even paying attention. Tommy captured all of my attention throughout breakfast and later on our walk to meet our group.

"Alright, Brynn and I think we have a pretty good idea of what we should do for the show," Tommy told Jonah and Amanda.

Even though his statement was simple and had no meaning behind it at all, I couldn't stop smiling at the sound of his voice.

"I'm sure you do," Jonah mumbled.

Amanda pressed her finger and thumb to her eyes. "My head hurts! And this sun is not helping."

"I'm sure it isn't," Tommy said. "Look, Brynn and I don't want to be working with you just as much as you don't want to be working with us, so let's just suck it up, get camp over with, and never have to see each other again."

My arm jerked in my armband.

"Only the ones we don't want to." He reached out quickly and stroked my leg from where he was sitting on the grass, but unfortunately, he wasn't quick enough.

"Oh my God!" Amanda exclaimed. "It *is* true!"

"It is true," Jonah slyly confirmed.

I could tell Tommy was losing his patience. His brows furrowed. "What?"

"Nothing." Jonah glanced to Christine, who was walking toward the patch of shade we were sitting in. We were supposed to be coming up with our skit for the talent show. "Nothing at all."

"Hey, guys," Christine began, "Bonnie sent me down here. Apparently, we're doing something different for the closing ceremony at the end of the week. I don't know what it is, but she needs to know what color daisy you would like. Don't ask me anymore questions, I'm just the messenger."

"Blue?" Tommy shrugged. "Don't you think they're taking this DAISY crap a little too far? We never had to do anything like this at our regular camp."

"I can't comment on that. Just give JT a break, okay? Jonah, your color?"

"Green. Green is the shit."

"Amanda?"

"Pink, I guess."

Christine must have had a good memory. She wasn't writing any of this down. "Blue, green, and pink. Got it. Brynn, what about you? Can you see your screen?"

I motioned to Tommy.

"You want blue, too?"

I suddenly remembered who I was in front of. Jonah and Amanda. I sheepishly nodded.

"Okay. Sounds good. Hey, Tommy, Brynn, I need to talk to you. You guys want to come with me?"

"Ohhhh!" Jonah and Amanda said at the same time, as though they were back in seventh grade and someone got called down to the principal's office.

"Real mature, guys." Christine headed to another shady spot.

Tommy stood up and we followed. I could feel Jonah and Amanda's eyes on us. What now? Were we in trouble?

Christine took a deep breath. "Okay, I'm not entirely sure how to say this, so I just am going to. Someone saw you guys on the basketball court last night. They saw you out of your chair, Brynn, and they panicked and reported it to JT."

My mouth dropped open. I must have not been hearing her correctly.

"You have got to be shitting me!" Tommy rubbed his eyes. "Now I can't even kiss a girl? This is getting fucking out of control."

"I know. I know." Christine had never looked this uncomfortable in front of me. "Brynn, I know you were really trying to hide it when you came into the cabin, so I didn't want to say anything to embarrass you. That was the happiest I have seen you all week, so I know it wasn't—"

"They think I forced myself on her?" Tommy shouted so loudly I was sure Jonah and Amanda were smiling from ear to ear. I wanted to go smack them. "Fucking ridiculous!"

"I don't know who said what, Tom, but JT wanted you to go talk to him. Maybe you can explain to him what—"

"Oh, I will go explain myself alright! Are you coming with me, babe?"

"That's the other thing," Christine cringed. "He wants to call Brynn's mom, because . . . he thinks she should know."

An uncontrollable scream leapt out of my throat. I immediately smacked my power switch to my chair, threw it on the fastest speed, and slammed my head against my headrest. If anyone was going to tell my mom I was making out with a guy I really liked, it was going to be me! Not this jackass camp director. And definitely not this jackass camp director who thought I was so out of it that I could be "taken advantage of" that easily.

Tommy and Christine followed me as I powered forward to JT's office. When we got there, Tommy flung the door open and we both raced inside, startling JT at his computer. At that moment, I realized I didn't know what the hell I was going to say. He didn't know I was coming down. He only asked to see Tommy. The anger rose in my throat with that thought. JT didn't ask to hear my side of the story. He probably didn't think I had a side to the story.

"You brought Brynn down here with you?" JT turned in his chair.

Christine quietly shut the door behind her and stepped beside me. "I informed her of what's going on. I thought she had the right to know."

"I want to know who told you what!" Tommy demanded. He was not himself, and why should he be?

"I'm not at liberty to discuss that with you right now," JT said and folded his hands. "I wanted to talk to you because they said they witnessed inappropriate behavior with Brynn, and that's my—"

"Inappropriate behavior? Define inappropriate behavior!" Tommy didn't wait for an answer. "You want some inappropriate behavior? Take a walk around camp after a dance, or at free time. I guarantee you will find much more inappropriate behavior than what Brynn and I were doing."

"I really don't appreciate your attitude. Right now, my main concern is Brynn, and what happened to her last night, and whether or not I should call her mom."

I didn't know what was coming over me. I started to feel like I didn't have control over what I was doing, and not in a CP kind of way. I looked directly at JT and gave him a big drastic nod.

"Is she typing something?" JT asked.

I was. And so the awkward silence began.

A minute had gone by. JT shifted in his chair about fifty times. I kept typing. Two minutes had gone by. Tommy had not said anything. I kept typing. Three minutes had gone by. Christine had not said anything. I kept typing. Four minutes. I was ready to talk.

I wanted to do this just as much as I wanted JT to know what happened last night. But I knew my mom. I knew exactly how she would react to this situation. And maybe, just maybe, she would get it through his small, little brain that I was a normal teenager who could make her own decisions and not some special little girl who needed to be babysat and worried over.

I tapped my talking switch, not believing I was the one who typed the words that were about to come out of my TechnoTalk.

SPEAK. "If you think you need to call my mom and be the one who tells her I just had my first kiss, go right ahead. I was going to tell her all about this awesome guy I met when I got home, but if you really think she needs to know now, you can call her. And you can be sure to tell her that I like the boy who kissed me. A lot. And that I have chosen to spend time with him these past few days and that I also chose to kiss him back last night. But, since you dragged Tommy and Christine into this, they need to be here if you do call her. They are my friends, and if you get to tell my mom my good news, they get to be here when she hears my good news."

There was a fire burning inside of my stomach. My arms and legs were so stiff, they felt as though they were going to break right through the straps that were supposed to be keeping me calm. I had never done that before. I had always made it a point to go along with whatever was going on around me, because I needed so much help with everything. I felt like I should be as easy going with everything as I could be, because I wanted to do everyone else this one favor for always being there to help me. But not this time. Not when my personal life was becoming a possible sexual assault case. And especially not when JT had done absolutely nothing to help me; in fact, he'd done the complete opposite. He refused to accept me for who I was, and he constantly made my life more difficult than it needed to be.

"So . . . I . . ." JT was at a loss for words. "So she *does* think I should call her mom?"

I let my head fall. He completely missed the point of what I was saying. All that, and he didn't even get the gist of it.

"No, she doesn't want you to call her mom to tell her we were making out," Tommy spelled it out for him. "She was being sarcastic, 'cause, ya know, she *can be* sarcastic."

I lifted my head up and started hitting my switch again, but this time it wasn't really my anger that was driving me.

A minute had gone by.

"Is she typing something again?"

"Whenever Brynn is hitting the blue button on her headrest," Tommy started, trying to be as calm as he could be, "you can probably assume she's typing something."

"Uh huh," was JT's only response.

Two minutes had gone by. I kept typing.

JT could call my mom if he wanted. I knew her reaction would be something along the lines of: "She is seventeen and is doing what all your other campers are probably doing and if you call me about something like this again . . ."

Three minutes. I kept typing.

Or I could try to make him understand myself. Maybe Tommy and Christine were right. Maybe JT really had no idea what I could and could not understand. Maybe he didn't even know that I went to a public school, and was in all regular ed classes, and typed all of my papers by myself.

Four minutes. I kept typing.

And as much as I didn't want to face it, JT wasn't—and wasn't going to be—the only person I encountered in life who would act like this. Jonah, Carly, Amanda, and Jenn, for instance, all didn't seem to understand that I was just like them. I knew that I couldn't go crying to my mom every time someone didn't understand. I had to learn how to explain myself so that people like JT and his misinformed and hard-headed campers would understand, and I had to start somewhere.

Five minutes. I typed the last word.

SPEAK. "JT, there is something you need to understand about me. I only have a physical disability. Not a cognitive disability. You have been talking to Christine when you should be talking to me. I can understand everything you say. I can make my own choices. I chose to get out of my wheelchair with Tommy because I like him. You can call my mom if you really think what we were doing is considered inappropriate behavior, but she is just going to tell you the same thing I just did."

247

JT looked at Christine before he looked at me. His face was emotionless. It was impossible to tell if I'd gotten through to him. And if I did, what was he feeling? Did he feel dumb? Embarrassed?

Without giving his feelings away, he leaned forward at his desk, folded his hands, and finally spoke. "Okay. I apologize, Brynn. If you don't think there's a reason to call your mom, I won't."

I nodded. My entire body was shaking.

"Okay, if we don't have anything else to discuss, then I think we're done here," Christine said, trying to usher us out the door and away from all the tension. "Let's go get some lunch."

Christine opened the door and I sped out of there as fast as I could. Tommy ran up behind me and put his arms around me. He kissed the top of my head almost aggressively.

"Brynn!" Christine raced over, too. "That was so awesome. I'm *so* proud of you!"

I looked up at her, and then I burst into tears.

Chapter Twenty-Three

After Tommy and Christine calmed me down from the initial shock of what I had done, and after I forced down some lunch I had no desire eating, it was time to get back to work. Apparently, we weren't the only group behind on what we were doing for the talent show, so JT cancelled all of the day activities so we could figure it out. Tommy and I groaned simultaneously when Christine told us we should call a group meeting. She knew how much we didn't want to do it, but she also knew it had to be done.

On our way out of the dining hall in search of Jonah and Amanda, one of the girls from my cabin, Heather, rushed past us, but then skidded to a quick stop in the doorway.

"Oh! Brynn!" she called.

I stopped and turned my chair to face her.

"We're making cupcakes for Randi's birthday in the kitchen of the dining hall. Carly wanted it to be a surprise, so we're doing it today instead of next week on her real birthday. Do you want to come?"

I chose to focus on the fact that Heather was inviting me to join her instead of the fact that Carly had planned this and hadn't said a word to me about it. I was kind of hurt, but . . . what did I expect from Carly at this point? Oh, right. *This.*

"Is it a girl thing?" Tommy asked, shading his face with his hand, his forehead accumulating beads of sweat. The sun beating down on us was brutal. I could feel it making its mark on the top of my shoulders, and I knew then that I would make the most of just about any opportunity that included either being indoors or in the shade.

"I think so. I'm sure you can eat the cupcakes later because we're making a ton of them, but I think Carly just invited Randi's girlfriends." Heather mimicked Tommy, holding her own hand up to block out the sun.

"Ah, okay. Well . . . Brynn, if you want to go, that's cool. If there's an extra cupcake, bring it back?"

I nodded and smiled at him.

"Okay, great! Let's go!" Heather rushed to the doors and held one open. She turned, waiting for me to follow.

"Have fun; don't let *them* bother you," Tommy said quietly before he leaned in to kiss my cheek. I could smell his cologne, and I wondered for a few seconds if I should maybe spend my time with him instead. But then I remembered why I came to camp in the first place: I wanted to make friends. Randi was my friend. Carly was . . . not really my friend, but she was Randi's. And, hey, Heather seemed to like me, too. This thought put a small smile on my face as I moved past Heather and into the cooler dining hall.

We walked to the kitchen located at the back of the long hall, passing a few campers and counselors still finishing their lunches.

"So, you and Tommy, eh?" Heather asked, her voice quiet as one of the counselors brushed past us on his way to the garbage can.

I shrugged, unsure of exactly how to respond. I wanted to talk about everything that had happened with Tommy, but I wasn't sure that Heather should be the first person I told. After all, she'd only recently started talking to me. She seemed like a nice enough girl, but I wasn't sure if she was genuinely interested in getting to know me, or if she was just looking for juicy camp gossip. I hated to doubt her, but I'd been duped before. Of course, a few months ago, I would've run to Meg with this news, but now . . . her spot as my best friend was empty. And I was still searching for someone to replace her.

"I always thought he could do better than Jenn," Heather whispered as we neared the kitchen. I could hear giggles and shrieks and the whir of stand mixers inside, but I didn't let those noises distract me as I met Heather's eyes. She was serious; I was glad.

I smiled at her and she smiled back. Maybe I'd try to spend some more time with her the next few days, too. And maybe we could also talk after camp. Only time would tell. For now, I felt like I really did have her support.

Carly and Amanda stood at the counter, their arms and faces spotted with baking flour. Jenn sat on a stool a few feet from them, flipping through a cookbook with little interest in what she was reading. Maggie, also from our cabin, and two girls I had been introduced to before—Joanie and Tia—stood in another section of the kitchen, spooning batter into cupcake tins.

"Hey guys, we're here! What can we do to help?" Heather asked, looking from one girl to the other.

"We?" Amanda asked, turning around to find Heather and me standing at the entrance to the kitchen. "Oh, hi, Brynn."

I nodded my greeting to Amanda and the other girls while Jenn snickered, never looking up from the cookbook. I watched her lick her finger and forcefully turn the page. I was surprised by the paper's strength; I was certain she wanted to tear it to shreds right then and there.

"We're kind of already close to finished," Carly said, sticking her finger in the bowl of the stand mixer. When she removed it, it was covered in bright blue icing. She popped it into her mouth, sucked off the icing, and then nodded her approval. "Sorry," she added, turning back to the icing. I saw her meet Amanda's eye before she completed her turn, her brows high on her head.

I wasn't blind, and I wasn't stupid. But I was self-conscious, despite all the work I'd been doing to try to modify this. I didn't want to start any problems with these girls, especially because we were gathered with the purpose of doing something nice for Randi, whom everyone loved. Maybe I'd gather the courage to speak my mind before camp ended, but I wasn't going to bring more drama into what was supposed to be a sweet gesture—with sugar and spice and everything nice. Everything that girls are *supposed* to be made of.

"There's a batch of cupcakes cooling on the racks over there," Maggie told us, pointing across the room. "If Carly and Amanda are done with the blue frosting, you guys can probably do that while they start on the pink. Then we'll ice this batch in pink when it's finished."

"We can do that!" Heather exclaimed, just as Amanda opened her mouth to interject. She promptly closed it. I gave her my sweetest smile and followed Heather across the room.

As Heather iced the first batch of cupcakes, working quietly at first, I tried not to listen to the whispering and muttering going on near the stand mixer. Even over the sound of its motor, I was able to hear bits and pieces of Amanda and Carly's conversation. Jenn never said a word, but she also hadn't looked up from the cookbook since Heather and I showed up. She was now faking being completely engrossed in its glossy pages.

"How's she going to *help* us?" Amanda asked Carly, literally behind my back.

"Moral support?" Carly replied. I imagined her shrugging and trying another finger-full of icing. "Who cares? Let's just finish this so we can surprise Randi! I told her our group was meeting under the tree by the lake at three."

"Ugh, whatever," was Amanda's only response.

"Forget them," a small voice whispered in my left ear.

I turned to find that Tia, Maggie, and Joanie had joined us. They each grabbed a cupcake and a butter knife and began covering the cupcakes Heather hadn't finished yet.

While the girls finished the blue cupcakes and waited for the next batch to cool, they told me about their high schools and hometowns—Tia was from upstate New York, Maggie and Heather were friends from Delaware, and Joanie hailed from Jersey—and I answered any questions they had for me. No one asked about Tommy, though I'm sure Jenn's presence in the room kept them from even thinking his name.

At 2:45, Christine showed up to help us carry the trays of cupcakes to the meeting place. We all huddled under the shade of the trees, Carly chatting happily about how great her idea was. No one disagreed with her. Gabe, who had showed up along with some of the other guys from various cabins, patted her on the back for a job well done. A quick glance at the group told me that two very important people had not yet arrived: Tommy and Jonah. If this celebration was for Randi, Jonah should've been there. And I knew Tommy had been laying low due to all the drama, but I also thought that if he was really Randi's friend, he'd come out of hiding.

Two seconds after this thought crossed my mind, Tommy appeared beside me. He squeezed my shoulder and I felt my entire body relax. I shouldn't have doubted him.

"How was it?"

"I'll . . . tell . . . you . . . later," I typed. He read it over my shoulder and sucked a bit of air in.

"That bad, huh?"

I shrugged. It wasn't horrible; I could tell him that part, at least.

"I . . . spent . . . a . . . lot . . . of . . . time . . . with . . . Heather . . . and . . . Tia . . . and . . . Maggie . . . and . . . Joanie. They're . . . all . . . really . . . cool."

The smile that crossed his face was one I couldn't quite fig-ure out. I think he was proud of me for making new friends and walking into an environment—and coming out alive—that I knew would be uncomfortable. I think he was also really happy that the other girls weren't taking after Amanda, Jenn, and Carly.

"Glad some people around here can think for themselves," he muttered under his breath.

Amen!

Just then, Randi appeared at the top of the hill that led to the lake. When she saw such a large group of people, she paused. She was still far away, so I couldn't read her facial expression, but I'd guess it was one of confusion.

Carly emerged from the group, carrying a single cupcake with a candle on top. The flame burned without any trouble; a cool breeze was nowhere to be found.

"Happy birthday, Randi!" she shrieked.

Despite the heat, Randi sprinted toward us and was envel-oped by the entire group, everyone wishing her well and laugh-ing at the expression on her face.

At a loss for words, all she could manage was, "Guys!" And then moved in for more hugs.

When everyone had settled down and eaten a cupcake—or three, *Tommy*—Randi collapsed on the grass beside me.

"Notice anyone missing?" she asked.

I nodded. *Yes.*

"He totally wins Boyfriend of the Year," she said, her tone flat. I looked down at her in time to see her eyes well with tears before she covered them with a pair of large sunglasses. When I looked away, Christine locked eyes with me from across the grass. I shook my head, disappointed and disgusted.

How could he?

Later that day, I had decided that I would rather eat a plate full of vegetables than be with Jonah and actually work on a project with him. JT never came right out and said who tattled on us, but I had a pretty damn good idea.

Heading back to the spot under the tree with Tommy (Christine was awesome at only being around when I needed help with something), all I really wanted was to turn and go to the basketball court. I *so* wanted to be back sitting in his arms, my head resting on his shoulder, having nothing—nothing—else matter.

I literally had to make myself keep driving forward into the grass; the basketball court beckoned me as I drove.

"I still can't believe he didn't even show for her birthday thing," Tommy was saying, having fallen into step beside me. "Like, we all know he's a jerk, right? But for whatever reason, Randi gives him one chance after the next, and he just keeps blowing it. And it's not even like he'd snuck away with Amanda, because she was there the whole time!"

I remained quiet as we approached the tree. He needed to vent, so I let him.

Just then, a head poked out from around the trunk.

"You're *still* here? Really?" Jonah raised an eyebrow. "I thought your 'inappropriate behavior' with the Mrs. here would've landed you on your ass outside the gate."

Tommy clenched his fists, but kept them at his sides.

"You know what, Jonah?" he said. "I want to know what the *fuck* your problem is! Tell me! Explain to me how *my* breakup with Jenn has suddenly become so much of *your* problem. What did I ever do to you to make you work so hard at making my life a living hell?"

Jonah jumped up from the ground and came within two feet of us. I glanced around, slightly panicked, afraid of what would happen if they started to fight again and no one was around to see who threw the first punch. My relationship with Tommy compromised my testimony; no one would believe me now.

"I want to know what the fuck *your* problem is!" Jonah yelled back. "Jenn told us why you ended it. You didn't want to drink anymore? You suddenly too cool to have fun with your friends? Too 'above the influence'? Fuck that, man. Too fuckin' good for us, that's what you think you are!"

"I knew she didn't tell you why I decided to stop! My dad died in October, you moron. You wanna know why he died? His liver! He was an alcoholic. You wanna know when he started drinking? Our age. Sixteen, seventeen. So if you think that's real cool, keep drinking! Drink every night until you pass out. I don't care! I don't want any part of that anymore."

Amanda suddenly emerged from behind the tree, having been listening and hiding the entire time. "I just want to know why you won't give Jenn another chance! She's in love with you and was going to talk to you when we got to camp, but you wouldn't even give her the time of day! She was thinking about not drinking anymore if it meant getting you back."

A dark laugh escaped Tommy. "Right. That's exactly what it seemed like last night, when you were all parading around the dance, drunk as hell. And see? Here's the thing that I feel like you girls don't understand. If you are only doing something that you think will please guys, it will only make him want you *less*. Or at least, that's how it is for me."

Amanda tried to respond, but Tommy talked over her. He'd been waiting a long time to tell people the truth, and now that they'd attacked him, he was finally able to.

"For example, *I* wanted to stop drinking. I encouraged Jenn to stop drinking because I cared about her. I didn't want her to become dependent on it, and I didn't want her to get into any stupid shit because of it. Now she's saying she would stop drinking to *get me back*? See? That's a turn off to me! What if I tell her to go jump off a bridge? Would she do it just because she thought it would make me want her? I wanted her to stop drinking because *she* wanted to stop drinking, not because I wanted her to. What I wanted was for her to think for herself and to make her own decisions, regardless of anyone else's opinions and beliefs. That's why *I* broke up with *her*. It wasn't the drinking; it was the idea that she doesn't know who she is or what *she* wants. She isn't her own person."

Jonah shook his head. "You are such a wuss," he spat. "Mand, you want to go?"

"I have one more question!" She stood her ground, her chin held high.

My stomach twisted into a tight little knot.

"And I am done with this conversation!" Tommy threw his hands up.

"You say Jenn wanting you is a turn off?" Amanda continued.

"What part of 'I am done with this conversation' don't you understand?"

She took a step closer to him, lowered her voice, and narrowed her eyes.

"What is it about Brynn that turns you on, huh? Do you think her wheelchair is sexy? Or is it her Gameboy that does it for you?"

My body was too exhausted to feel the sting of her words. I shut my eyes.

Please don't punch her. Please don't punch her.

I felt like I knew him well, but I was still afraid he was going to hit her. That he was going to punch her just like he had punched Jonah for calling me retarded. He was going to hit her and get kicked out of camp for good this time. He was out of second chances, according to JT.

A few seconds of silence passed and I forced one eye open. Instead of winding up for a swing, he simply shrugged.

"I don't know. Get to know her. You tell me."

He picked up his guitar case, which he'd carried all the way to the tree so we could tell them about our idea for the talent show, and headed to the basketball court. I followed, not wanting to be alone with them even for a second.

The talent show was the farthest thing from my mind right then. They could figure out what they were going to do—without us. The four of us didn't want to work with each other and that was going to be clear as day to anybody in the audience. The group had officially disbanded as far as we were concerned.

The last morning of camp was the morning of the talent show. Camp would, essentially, be over by then. What was JT going to do if we didn't have an act ready?

Throw us out?

Chapter Twenty-Four

After he calmed down, Tommy sat down on the bench and pulled out his guitar. He slowly started to strum, like nothing had happened. "So are you still down for writing a song together? You writing the lyrics and me writing the music?"

I shook my head.

"No? Oh, babe, we don't need them. They probably would be no help to us, anyway. And we could ask JT if we could go on ourselves. Granted, I know we aren't his favorite people right now, but if you tell him this is what's up like you did earlier, I'm sure he will make an exception."

"Why . . . do . . . you . . . like . . . me?" SPEAK.

"We're really going through this again?" Tommy stopped strumming. "Really? I don't know. Because you're . . . you . . ."

"With . . . what . . . you . . . said . . . to . . . Amanda . . ."

He didn't get up to see what I was typing. Good. I didn't want him to. I didn't want him to have the chance to assume what I was going to say next.

"You . . . know . . . damn . . . well . . . I . . . care . . . about . . . what . . . everyone . . . thinks . . . about . . . me. I . . . go . . . out . . . of . . . my . . . way . . . to . . . make . . . people . . . happy. I . . . won't . . . say . . . what . . . I . . . am . . . thinking . . . just . . . to . . . avoid . . . conflict. I . . . worry . . . that . . . I . . . am . . . being . . . too . . . much . . . trouble . . . for . . . everybody . . . by . . . needing . . . help . . . with . . . everything. I . . . feel . . . like . . . I . . . need . . . to . . . go . . . along . . . with . . . whatever . . . just . . . so . . . people

259

. . . won't . . . think . . . I'm . . . hard . . . to . . . be . . . around. Why . . . do . . . you . . . want . . . somebody . . . like . . . that? What . . . makes . . . me . . . different . . . from . . . Jenn?" SPEAK.

Tommy stared down at the cement for a long moment before looking me directly in the eye.

"Because you *are* different. And I don't mean that in a dumb cliché kinda way. I get why you feel like more of a bother to people rather than the awesome person that you are. At first I didn't. I didn't understand why you were so reluctant to have help. In my perspective of being your friend, I was just like, 'Okay. She needs a little more help than everybody else. This is just what I have to do, and this is what I will do. No big deal.' But after I got you out of your chair—and please don't take this the wrong way—Do you promise you won't take this the wrong way?"

I slowly nodded, creeping towards him.

"Well, once I got you out of your chair last night, I thought to myself 'This must suck.' To have to rely on everybody to do everything for you? No wonder why you're so unsure of . . . I don't want to say yourself . . . but I definitely get why you could be unsure of what people would think of you. You just don't want everybody to burn out by helping you so much, right?"

I nodded and urged my body not to cry.

"Yeah, I definitely understand how you could feel that way. I'm not saying it's right and I actually think you need to work on that, and I'm willing to help you in any way I can, but I definitely understand where you're coming from."

He grabbed my hand and I clenched his thumb.

"I just want you to know this. You never have to feel that way with me. Whenever you're with me, I want you to think of the adventures we're having, or how much I smell because I didn't shower for two days, or the oh-so-disgusting foods I'm making you try. You never have to worry about how much help you need. I'll tell you if it's getting too much for me. I'm nothing if not honest."

" . . . Promise?" SPEAK.

"Such a girl." Tommy rolled his eyes. "I promise."

He leaned forward and kissed my forehead and then settled back onto the bench.

"Now, about Jenn. First, she's just a bitch. So how are you different from Jenn? Let's see. Oh, right, you're *not* a bitch. Then there's the fact that she is being completely unsympathetic that my dad is dead right now. She totally missed the point of me wanting her to stop drinking, and because of that, she turned all my friends against me. They all apparently think that I broke up with her because I'm too good for her and for them. You heard what Jonah said. And then there's the whole idea of her not knowing who she is or what she likes and doesn't like and what she thinks versus what others think. That was getting on my nerves for a really long time. It didn't just happen right when my dad died; I'd been thinking about breaking it off for a while."

He let go of my hand and ran his fingers through his hair. He wasn't frustrated, but I could tell there was more he wanted to say.

"I can give you one very simple example of when I knew you weren't like Jenn, or any of the other girls here. The first day we hung out on this court, when I caught you jamming out to Abbie Bonza. I straight up told you that you had shitty taste in music, and you refused to believe it. You weren't embarrassed by it, you didn't try to say, 'Oh, it's a guilty pleasure.' You didn't make an excuse. You fought me on it. Her music is something you like, and that's all that matters. The fact that you were willing to make this point to someone you barely knew showed me that you were different. You had your own mind, and you weren't afraid to use it. Is that an okay answer?"

I shyly nodded. Point received. I blew him a kiss.

"Finally! I got the you're-awesome kiss instead of the screw-you tongue! I did it!" Tommy stood and walked over to me. "And here's a little something to let you know you're awesome."

This time when he kissed me, my brain only got a signal to smile. The rest of my body took on that Jell-O feel again. When he pulled away, I could do nothing but stare at him.

He smiled and sat back down, pulling his guitar onto his lap.

"Come on. I really think I have a good idea for a song. Even if we don't do it for the show, I still think we should write one together. Will you give it a shot with me?"

After that kiss, I was all ears to any ideas he had.

"So we have been brainwashed with all this DAISY crap for the last week, right? And I can't help but think about the damn flower. So I have a question for you. What's the most important part of the daisy?"

I blinked at him. Seriously?

"Oh, just go with me here! What's the strongest part of the daisy? How does it get its water, and food, and nutrients, and whatever else daisies need to grow and be strong?"

JT is having too strong of an influence on you.

"Would you say it's the stem? I say it's the stem, so you should say it's the stem."

I chuckled. Where on earth was he going with this?

"So, we both agree that the strongest part of the daisy is the stem. Without the stem, the daisy would shrivel up and die. I'm guessing. I'm not a flower expert or anything."

Obviously.

"Now, what would you say the prettiest part of the daisy is?"

Okay, I really like you, but do you know how ridiculously lame you sound right now?

"The petals? Right. Exactly what I was thinking. So, like I was saying before, if the petals don't have a good strong stem to get water and crap, the petals would just eventually be ugly and die. But, if they have a stem then they can get all the vitamins and nutrients they need, and the daisy will just keep being beautiful." Tommy smiled. "Are you following the metaphor here? Kinda like an Abbie song, eh?"

No. Not so much like an Abbie song. But okay.

Tommy sat back down with his guitar. "I think this would be a perfect song to write together. Especially if we do end up doing it for the show, but I doubt those idiots will actually get the message. Are you down for trying it with me?"

At the rate we were going, if we did a song about how daisies grow, and be strong, and blossom, and whatever the hell else he was going on about, it would be social suicide. Guaranteed. And I was not being self-conscious this time. I was being realistic.

"So, what do you think would be a good . . ." Tommy trailed off. I watch his brow furrow as something behind me caught his attention. "What the hell?"

I turned to see what he was so confused about. Christine, JT, and Tommy's counselor, Mike, were all coming down the path. Tommy and I exchanged a look as we went to go meet them. What could it possibly be now?

Had Jonah run to JT and tattled that Tommy was being mean to him? And he had the nerve to call Tommy a "wuss." Ha!

Or maybe somebody saw us kissing again? Oh! If that was the case . . . If somebody really thought it was "inappropriate" for me to get a kiss from the boy I liked . . .

JT stepped forward. "Tommy, I am going to have to ask you to leave Camp Lakewood."

Chapter Twenty-Five

"*E*xcuse me?"

"You heard me," JT said, his tone firm. "You need to leave."

Exasperated, Tommy asked, "What the hell did they tell you now?"

JT crossed his arms and lifted his chin. "Nobody told me anything. Mike found empty vodka bottles in your duffel bag. Now if you will come with me, please. I've already called your mom. She's on her way."

"What?!" Tommy exclaimed. "I don't even get to explain myself? If you want to see where the empty bottles came from, why don't you check out Jonah's stuff? Amanda's stuff. Jenn. Carly. Even Randi! Go look in the girls' cabin! I wasn't going to stoop to their level, but I guess I have to now. I was *not* drinking at this session! They were! They were all week. Are you so blind that you couldn't see that?"

"We did check everybody in the cabin—all of the cabins," Mike said and stepped to JT's side. "We didn't find anything, and your duffel bag was out in the open. I'm sorry, Tom, but you know the rules. If we find any alcohol on you, it's an—"

"But you didn't find it *on me*! You found it *in my bag*! When I wasn't even in the cabin! Did you ever think someone might have planted it on me? You've seen the way I've been treated this week. And you know who would've done it." Tommy shook his head and didn't wait for a reply. "You know what? This is bullshit!

Everything! All the people! All your stupid activities! Bullshit! Bullshit! Bullshit! I don't even want to be here anymore! I'm out!"

He stormed off before anybody could say anything else.

I watched his back as he retreated, my chin quivering and my cheeks warm.

"Mike," JT started, "go see that he packs up and take him to the office. Christine, you should probably take Brynn to—"

I didn't let him finish. I raced off without waiting for Christine. I didn't want anything to do with them. I didn't want to hear what any of them had to say. They didn't listen to what Tommy had to say, so why should I listen to them?

I sped along the path to the cabins, not seeing Tommy anywhere. I wouldn't have the chance to say goodbye to him. After everything we had been through; after all the crap we put up with, I wouldn't have the chance to say goodbye to the one guy who wasn't afraid of me and who thought of me as the girl I was and not a creature of my own kind.

I couldn't open the door to my cabin. I slammed my back against my chair while my body had a full-blown CP attack. Why didn't Christine say anything? She just stood there with her hands folded. She knew Tommy! She knew me! She knew Tommy and I would not be drinking at camp. And why didn't JT ask me about it? He had to know that I was pretty much with Tommy all the time. Hadn't I just told him this morning that he could—and should—talk to me?

"Brynn, is that you?" Evelyn came to the screen door. "Do you want to come inside?"

She opened the door and, without giving her an answer, I zoomed in straight to my bed. Thankfully, there was nobody in the cabin. Of course there was nobody in the cabin. They were all out busy working on their skits for the talent show like normal people. People who didn't hate each other so much, they successfully got each other kicked out of camp.

"Are you okay?" Evelyn walked over to me.

No! I am not okay!

"Do you want me to go get Christine?"

No!

"Okay. Do you want to talk about it?"

Even though I said no, something made me hit my talking switch anyway. "They . . . are . . . making . . ." Somehow, actually typing the words made the tears come.

"Awww, hun." Evelyn rushed over and hugged me. "You don't have to cry. Do you want me to read your screen like Christine does?"

I nodded. "Tommy . . . leave . . . camp."

"What? What happened?"

"They . . . found . . . alcohol . . . in . . . his . . . bag . . . and . . ."

"Here," she ran to her bunk, "let me get you a tissue."

Tears were running. Snot was flying. Drool was drooling. "They . . . didn't . . . let . . . him . . . explain . . . himself. I . . . was . . . with . . . him . . . all . . . the . . . time . . . and . . . he . . . was . . . not . . . drinking! He . . . quit . . . drinking . . . when . . . his . . . dad . . . died."

Evelyn stopped drying my mess. "Tommy's dad died? Does Christine know this?"

I shrugged. She wasn't around when he told me. And she never acted sympathetic when she was around him, so probably not. I shook my head.

"I see," she said and started wiping the other side of my face. "Anyway, yeah, we always had a no-tolerance policy. If you are caught drinking, or have alcohol in your possession, it's a no question, automatic see-you-later."

By now, I was beating my head against my switch. "Then . . . why . . . hasn't . . . Jonah . . . or . . . Amanda . . . or . . . Jenn . . . been . . . kicked . . . out . . . of . . . camp . . . yet? Can't . . . you . . . tell . . . they . . . have . . . been . . . drinking . . . all . . . week! They . . . were . . . the . . . ones . . . who . . . put . . . the . . . alcohol . . . bottles . . . in . . . his . . . bag!"

She put her hand on my shoulder. "Okay. I understand that you are extremely pissed off right now, and you have every right to be. But I think you need to take a minute and calm yourself down or you are going to make yourself more upset."

Calm myself down? The best friend I had made at this camp was just told he has to leave for something that he didn't do, and you want me to calm myself down?

"I . . . just . . . want . . . to . . . know . . . why . . . they . . . did . . . it! Why . . . did . . . they . . . get . . . so . . . pissed . . . off . . . that . . . he . . . was . . . with . . . somebody . . . who . . . was . . . so . . . different . . . from . . . them . . . they . . . wanted . . . him . . . to . . . leave?"

Evelyn bent down, but it wasn't a condescending move. It was comforting; it said *I'm here for you.*

"I know I'm not as different as you think I might be, but I *am* different. A different kind of different. And I know sometimes it sucks. People do things that you don't understand. They do it just because they think you are so different. But you have to know yourself, and when there is nobody to stick up for you, you have to stick up for yourself."

"Tommy . . . tried . . . to . . . do . . . that . . . and . . . they . . . would . . . not . . . even . . . consider . . . what . . . he . . . was . . . saying."

The screen door opened. It was Christine. The tears, and snot, and drool all started again.

"I am so sorry, Brynn." Christine took a seat on my bed; the last place I wanted her to be. "I know you and Tommy were getting close."

"Then . . . why . . . didn't . . . you . . . try . . . to . . . stop . . . JT?"

If I continued with this conversation, I was pretty sure my switch was going to break. But I kept going anyway.

"You . . . know . . . Tommy . . . was . . . not . . . drinking. I . . . was . . . with . . . him! He . . . stopped . . . drinking . . . when . . . his . . . dad . . . died. Jonah . . . and . . . Amanda

... or ... somebody ... put ... the ... alcohol ... in ... the ... bag. They ... have ... been ... drinking ... all ... week. Why ... didn't ... you ... try ... to ... stop ... JT?" I hit SPEAK.

Christine's face went from understanding, to shock, and back to understanding. What? Were these counselors specifically trained to keep calm when a camper was going off on them?

"You're mad. You're crying. You're furious. You just lost the guy you like. And you know what? You are allowed to be mad, and furious, and cry. This is perfectly okay. But JT is my boss. I'm just a counselor; I'm not even Tommy's counselor. I don't have much of a say in anything, especially the camp rules. And we do have a strict no-alcohol rule. And we did find alcohol in Tommy's bag. So we didn't really have a choice."

"That's what I told her," Evelyn nodded. "Did you know about Tom's dad?"

"No, I didn't. I wish I would have; I would've talked to him about it if he wanted to. But Brynn, rest assured, now that you and Tom say that there were other people drinking, we will be watching them like hawks. I think JT is talking to Jonah and Amanda now."

"Yeah," Evelyn wiped my face a second time, "and I'm going to tell all the other counselors to be on the lookout. I know this doesn't make up that Tommy is gone, but if we see anything else from anybody, you better believe their asses are going straight home, too."

I guess I should've been happy they were finally deciding to enforce a few rules, but this really wasn't making me feel any better. They should've sprinted out of the room, found JT, and told him what they now knew. They should've fought for Tommy to stay, regardless of whether they were "his" counselors. They should've done *something*. But all they did was sit there.

Christine sighed. "Why don't you go to the bathroom and cool off, and then we can go find your group and try to—"

I uncontrollably screamed, which caught them both off guard. Then I started typing again.

"I . . . am . . . not . . . working . . . with . . . them . . . anymore! I . . . don't . . . care . . . if . . . I . . . don't . . . do . . . anything . . . for . . . the . . . talent . . . show! I . . . can't . . . work . . . with . . . them . . . anymore!" SPEAK.

"Remember how we were talking about being different and sometimes people do ridiculous crap?" Evelyn knelt down beside me. "I found out that the worst thing you can do is let it get to you. Now, I can't say Jonah and Amanda put the alcohol in Tom's bag, but Christine did tell me they haven't been very accepting of you. I know that you don't want to, but please keep working with them. If you stop, they'll win."

"Evelyn is right," Christine said. "I think you absolutely need to keep working with them. Show them the awesomeness Tom saw in you. If you want me to, I will stay with you from now on. Would that make you feel more comfortable?"

I reluctantly nodded. "Okay. I will do that. Do you want to go to the bathroom now? Even if you don't have to go, I think it would be good for you to splash off with cool water and maybe get a drink."

I wasn't like a running faucet anymore, but it felt like somebody took a jackhammer to my head. It was pounding. Even with the whole Meg and Dave thing, I had never cried this much in one day.

On the way to the dining hall, Christine and I stopped in our tracks when we heard shouting.

"I can't believe you would do this to me!" a woman was yelling. "This is absurd! Absolutely absurd! I have never been so embarrassed! And alcohol?! After everything happened with your father?"

"Mom, I—"

We rounded the corner as she continued to yell at him. Again, Tommy wasn't allowed to speak, to voice his mind, to tell the truth.

I pressed my forward switch as hard as I could. I was going to get to say goodbye to him! Maybe I could talk to his mom. Maybe she would listen to us and maybe she would put the smack down on JT! My mom would. Maybe she was like that, too.

Tommy must have seen me out of the corner of his eye. He dropped all of his stuff and ran to me.

"I am so sorry, baby," he whispered, wrapping me in his arms. "I am so sorry that I have to leave you."

I shook my head no. I motioned to my TechnoTalk and then to his mom who was now standing in front of me.

"She wants to tell you something."

Damn it! I couldn't see my scream.

"Oh, like she was the one you were behaving inappropriately with?" She scoffed and then yanked on his shirt. "Let's go!"

He shook her off and then shoved something in my hand. A piece of paper. He kissed my cheek and wiped away a tear I hadn't even known was falling.

Chapter Twenty-Six

I sit on the stool in the middle of the basketball court, my legs tucked closed together. I am strumming the guitar. Tommy's guitar.

There is a book inside the room
It's laying on the bed
There is a book inside the room
No longer being read

Jonah is there. And Amanda. And Jenn. And Randi. And Carly. And Christine. And JT. They are all huddled around me. Tommy told them I had written a song and they all wanted to hear it. They all begged me to play it for them.

Although it may have fooled the reader
With a cover bright and new
It turns out that the tale inside was nothing but untrue

More and more campers and counselors trickle onto the basketball court.

So just because a book may seem that on the surface it's quite a read
The other book instead may be the one you really need

I look directly at Jonah.

Open the book
Just take a chance

Tommy is suddenly by my side. He places his hand on my knee, which is bouncing to keep time with the notes I'm playing, and sings the rest with me. Our voices are perfect together.

And you may find
Love and romance
Open the book
And what you'll see
Is a true friend
Who is just aching to be free

I literally jumped back into reality when I noticed Christine was at my bed. She reached for my earphones.

"I'm sorry, Brynn, I didn't mean to startle you," she said and turned off my iPod. "Did Abbie make you feel any better? It sure seemed like she did. Even when you're out of your chair, you still love to dance."

I gave her a half smile, kicking myself for forgetting I was in the cabin.

"Ready to get up? It's time for dinner."

I shook my head.

"No? Aw, Brynn, I know you're upset, but you can't stay in here forever. Remember your goal?" She pointed to my daisy. "Screw what everybody thinks. Just come have fun with me!"

Oh, I didn't care what they thought of me anymore. I just didn't want to be around those bastards. I didn't even want to look at them.

"Come on," Christine pulled my body to the side of the bed. "It's not going to be as bad as you think. I promise. I will be there with you."

I realized that she didn't have a clue as to why I was so upset, which made me think it was going to be worse than I thought.

I let Christine scoop me up. When I got in my chair, I felt my body go limp as a noodle, even though I was just dancing around on my bed a few minutes earlier. There were people in the cabin. How many of them saw me flopping around like a total idiot? With how my luck was going today—probably all of them. Christine slipped my TechnoTalk on. Whether I wanted to be or not, I was ready to go to dinner.

Christine and I walked into the dining hall. I didn't want to look for them or at them, but my eyes found them anyway. Yep. There they were. Jonah, Amanda, everybody. Sitting at their usual table, eating, talking, laughing as though they were sweet, innocent angels. I could feel my mouth automatically forming my I-want-to-kill-you face.

"It looks like we are having hoagies. Do you do hoagies?"

I shook my head.

"I didn't think so. Do you want another PBJ?"

Another head shake.

"Okay, I know you're really, really upset right now, and you don't want anything to do with anybody, but you do have to eat something. You can't go without dinner, and I won't let you. Will you at least try a half of a peanut butter and jelly?"

She'd made it clear that she was not going to give up. I gave in. I rolled over to my regular table and for the first time since we started talking, Tommy wasn't there waiting for me. I let my head fall. Did seeing me sit by myself satisfy Jonah, Amanda, and Jenn? Did seeing Tommy not sitting with me make them feel like they finally were able to win this battle? Did Tommy's mom even believe what really happened, or was he eating alone tonight, too?

"Hey! Can I join you?" Evelyn's voice made my head pop up. "Christine told me that you don't really like to eat in front of people, but you don't have to be nervous with me. I've seen many different people eat, so it's all good."

She sat down without me answering. In Tommy's spot.

"Christine told me you really like Abbie Bonza, and from what I saw from when you were in your bunk, I could tell you really do. I'm not into her, but that's cool."

I attempted to give her my best fake smile.

"Are you into any other bands, or just Abbie?"

I shrugged and slowly shook my head. If she didn't like Abbie, she probably didn't like anything else that was on my iPod.

"Ya know," Evelyn took a bite of her hoagie, "we've been living together for the past week, and I feel like I barely even know you. Tell me something that you think I wouldn't guess about you."

Really? I went from having every meal with Tommy, who was just . . . Tommy . . . to small talking to a counselor a week into camp who I probably wouldn't even see again. Granted, this was why I came to camp—to get the chance to talk to new people, and if she would have done this a few days ago, I probably would have been really happy—but why was she doing this now?

I shrugged. "What . . . would . . . you . . . like . . . to . . . know?" SPEAK.

"What about your favorite subject in school? Or, I guess, people ask that all the time. You could tell me your least favorite subject in school, if you want to."

This was what she thought people wouldn't guess about me?

"I . . . like . . . English . . . and . . . don't . . . like . . . Math." SPEAK.

"That's cool. I hate doing math, too. Do you like to read? What are some of your favorite books?"

"I saw you have the Sisterhood series on your iPod," Christine said, taking her regular seat beside me with all of our food. "They were a few of my favorite books, too. If you ever want to listen to one, just tell me. I'll find the place where you were."

Christine poured the water into my cup and stood up to give me a drink. I drank it all in three quick swigs. I didn't feel like eating, but I felt like maybe if I drank five gallons of water, it would make my head stop pounding.

Sitting back down, Christine held up the half of the peanut butter and jelly sandwich. I managed to take a tiny bite. Out of the corner of my eye, I could see them. Talking, laughing, eating, as though they didn't make, not one, but two people's summers miserable just a few hours ago.

"You want another bite?" Christine asked.

The sandwich being pushed into my face was not going to distract me. "Do . . . you . . . think . . . Randi . . . and . . . Carly . . . had . . . anything . . . to . . . do . . . with . . . it . . . or . . . do . . . you . . . think . . . it . . . was . . . Jonah . . . and . . . Amanda . . . and . . . Jenn?" SPEAK.

"Aw, hun," Evelyn started, "this is still really bothering you, isn't it?"

No shit it's still bothering me. Tommy didn't do anything wrong. And it just happened this afternoon!

"Look," Christine said in a calm voice. "Mike, JT, and I searched Tommy and Jonah's cabin, and we searched our cabin, and we didn't find anything else. JT took Jonah and Amanda down to the office, and they're still here, so he must not have found a reason to send them home. However, I'm a firm believer in what goes around, comes around, so if they did do anything, it will come out. And like Evelyn said, if it does, we will do something about it. I promise you that."

I nodded, giving into the realization there was nothing else I could do.

"You aren't going to eat anymore, are you?"

I shook my head.

"Do you want more to drink?"

"Can . . . I . . . have . . . two . . . more—"

"Cups of water? Sure! Of course!"

As Christine went to the drink station, JT called everyone's attention to the front of the room. I wanted to take his megaphone and shove it . . .

"How was dinner, campers?"

There was the usual "wooooooo." I was too exhausted, annoyed, and however else I was feeling to try to have any emotion come across my face.

"That's great! When I was walking around Camp Lakewood today, I saw some fantastic things that we might see at the talent show Friday, and because you were working so hard and were with your group members all day, I am going to give you a choice of what you would like to do tonight. Would you like to either do an activity with your cabin, or do—"

Immediately, there was another "wooooooo."

"Alright. I think I get the hint. The activity options are taking a hike, going canoeing, playing basketball or soccer, arts and crafts, or just hanging out by the campfire. Decide what you want to do with everybody in your cabin. When you're done, as always, you can have free time. Got it? Good. Go for it!"

"Hey!" Christine came back with my water. "You don't have to work with Jonah or Amanda tonight. That has to make you feel a little better."

Yeah, but I have to be with Randi and Carly who may or may not have been accomplices to their heinous crime.

She poured the first cup of water into my cup. I drank. She poured the second cup. I drank. She asked me if I wanted more, and although tempting, I said I was okay. Soon, Evelyn, Christine, and I went outside to meet our cabin, but to our surprise, Randi was the only one standing there.

"Where did everyone go?" Christine looked around, confused.

"Yeah, about that," Randi started. "Problem. Everyone decided they wanted to go out on the lake. I know, Brynn, that you and canoes are probably not friends, so I thought I would hang back, and maybe you and me could go to the campfire? I feel like we haven't talked in forever. You've been so busy with your new guy. Who are you? Carly?"

I didn't even smile at her small joke. Seriously? The *one* time I was actually going to participate in a cabin activity, they decided to go canoeing? Of course they did. Nothing else was working with me today. It seemed only appropriate that this would be the way it was going to end.

"Well, wait a minute," Christine began, "Evelyn and I were going to try to get you in a canoe the other day, but JT needed to talk to you. I'm sure we could do it now, and I'm sure Randi would help if we needed her to. Do you want to try to go canoeing?"

Evelyn raised her hand. "I vote we try to go canoeing!"

The last thing I wanted to do right then was attempt to get in a fricking boat. Although I was going to be lifted in and didn't have to do much, my head still felt as if it was going to explode if I had to try to sit anywhere but my wheelchair. But I really didn't want to miss another cabin activity. Who knew what they already thought of me? And how many of them knew about Tommy and expected me to sulk in the cabin for the rest of camp? Like Christine had said, I couldn't let them win. So, with my pounding head and exhausted body, I hit my forward switch, and the four of us walked towards the lake.

Chapter Twenty-Seven

When we got to the water, all the girls from our cabin—and a few from a neighboring one—were already in canoes and on the lake. When Heather spotted us on the shore, she enthusiastically waved at us, accidentally rocking the boat and causing the other girls in the canoe to shriek.

"Okay, it looks like it's going to be the four of us." Christine clasped her hands together. "Here's what I'm thinking. You can put your life preserver on in your chair. You're light enough so I think I can carry you from here to the dock with no problem, but I don't think your chair is light enough for the dock. Evelyn, Randi, could you steady the canoe while I step in and sit down? Brynn, once we're in, you can sit between my legs and lean against me. How does that sound?"

It was late enough in the day that I was able to see my screen. "Since . . . it . . . is . . . only . . . going . . . to . . . just . . . be . . . us . . ."

All of them crowded around me.

"We . . . can . . . just . . . go . . . to . . . the . . . campfire. I . . . don't . . . really—"

Christine jumped in. "I don't care that I have to carry you, and Evelyn already said she was more than willing to help, and I'm sure Randi doesn't care about helping. And besides, you seemed like you wanted to go when I mentioned about trying it with Tommy."

Yeah, but that was when Tommy was here, and my head wasn't throbbing, and my body didn't feel like it was run over by a truck.

Although, my exhausted body could very well work to my advantage. I wouldn't be all CPish in a boat on the water. Our boat would probably even be steadier than Heather's.

"I say you're trying something new!" Evelyn said, grabbing an orange life preserver and waving it in front of me. I guess I didn't have a choice.

"And," Randi added, "we're *here* now. You are not going to make me walk all the way back to the campfire. Unless you really want to go canoeing with Tom. I know everyone hates him right now, but if you really want me to, I'll secretly go find him and make him come with us. He probably would rather be with you than his cabin, and Carly and whoever else is here can just get over it."

I blinked at her.

She blinked back. "What?"

Christine put her hands behind her back and pursed her lips before speaking. "Tom had to go home today."

"What?" Randi's tone went from what-are-you-looking-at-me-for to are-you-serious?

"JT called his mom to come get him this afternoon. He won't be with us anymore."

"What? Why? What happened?"

For a brief second, I was hopeful that someone at the camp would believe Tommy wasn't responsible for the alcohol on the premises. Maybe she didn't know what Jonah did. Maybe she didn't have anything to do with it. I flashbacked to the previous night: Randi had told us to run before Jonah could attack us. And she just offered to go get Tommy so I could go canoeing with him. She seemed to be on our side—and completely oblivious to anything that had happened earlier in the day.

But . . . Jonah was her boyfriend. She had to know what he did, or at least how much he hated Tommy this summer. Maybe she was playing dumb to remain on my good side. Maybe she knew she and Tommy were my only close friends here, and maybe she didn't want me to be by myself. But if she knew something was starting between me and Tommy, why would she help Jonah get him kicked out? I looked at her, amazed, not knowing if she was good at faking it, or if she really had no idea what her boyfriend had done.

"Oh, nothing you need to worry about." Evelyn handed us our life preservers. "Brynn! You ready?"

I caught a glimpse of Randi's concerned, furrowed brow and tried to give Evelyn a smile, knowing her words couldn't be farther from the truth.

Christine pulled my TechnoTalk off and put it beside my chair. After taking my arms out, she bent my upper body forward just a little and slipped the life preserver around my neck. She wrapped the buckle around my chest. I tried to lean back, but the orange foam was getting in my way.

"Could one of you help her stay up while I put mine on?"

Dodging my arms, which had made my body turn into a T-shape, Evelyn and Randi grabbed each of my shoulders. I laughed to myself. Why couldn't we just go to the campfire and hang out? Oh, that was right. They thought this would be fun for me after my completely horrible day.

Once Christine was ready to go, she undid my feet straps and unbuckled my seatbelt. She scooped me up like she always did, the life preserver not giving her much of a problem. I found myself looking up at the sky as she carried me across the dock. I made myself keep looking at the sky until they got us into the boat. I was now beyond caring that I was going to go canoeing. I just didn't particularly like being in front of everyone having Christine hold me like an infant. But, like my DAISY goal, eff it. *Eff everything!*

Randi and Evelyn did a pretty good job with keeping the canoe steady. Christine placed me between her legs (I had to actually sit on the bottom of the canoe because the bench wasn't big enough for both of us which, of course, got my shorts all gross) and I leaned against her. The girls grabbed some paddles, gave the canoe a push, and jumped in.

"You gonna help us row?" Randi tried to hand me a paddle. "Or do you expect me and Evelyn to do all the work?"

"Yo!" Christine shouted. "I think we pushed our luck with just getting her in the boat. Maybe next time we can work on rowing."

"You guys were the ones who were all about going canoeing," Randi muttered, turning around. She and Evelyn started to move the little green boat. "If you remember correctly, I was the one who suggested we go hang out down at the campfire."

I did an amen *ahhhhhh.*

"Okay, Brynn," Christine looked down at me, "what would you be doing if you were up at the campfire? You would probably be sitting there, moping. You might be still sitting here moping, but at least you're out here doing something you have never done before."

"Without her computer so she can't complain to you about whatever she's upset about. Really nice, guys!"

"Randi! You are *not* helping! Brynn, that was not our intention. I promise. We just know you had a bad day and wanted to help you forget about it."

Forget about it? A dumb little boat ride was supposed to help me forget about Tommy and how unfairly we'd both been treated the past few days?

As we were passing another canoe, the sound of Carly's voice made my feet begin twitching. "Raaaaaandi! I waited for you! What took you so long?"

Amanda saw me staring her down. Her eyes darted away.

More twitching.

"I told you I probably wouldn't be down!"

Every time Amanda glanced at me, she saw that I was still staring at her.

"Why aren't you in this boat with me?" Carly whined.

Amanda started twisting her hair. She glanced down at her feet, smiled at the other girls in the canoe, did anything she could not to look at me.

Good. Let me make her so uncomfortable that she doesn't know what to do with herself.

"Because I'm in this boat with Brynn," Randi called back as we floated farther and farther away. Randi never stopped paddling. "And it looks like you're doing fine without me."

Christine chuckled. "You guys are inseparable."

"No, she's just obsessive. God forbid I'm friends with anyone but her, but she can run around all day with her nose up Amanda and Jenn's asses," Randi said. She blew a strand of pink hair out of her face and turned her attention back to us. "But what happened with Tom? Is everything okay?"

"Yeah," Evelyn reassured her. "He's okay. Like I said, you don't really need to worry about it. Do you guys just want to make a U-turn here?"

"Sure. But something obviously happened to him, and I'm going to find out sooner or later, so you might as well just tell me now."

There was a pause while we switched directions. Why did she care about him so much now? Granted, she had always wanted her boyfriend to stop being a jackass to him, but she never made an effort to have a conversation with him while everyone else ignored him. Was this all to make me believe she didn't have anything to do with it?

"We found empty alcohol bottles in his bag," Christine finally said.

That's right. You only found them in his bag. You didn't actually find them on him. And, you probably weren't the one who found it, because you aren't even his cabin counselor. Mike was probably the one who found it, and he probably came to tell you, because he probably knew Tommy was with me a lot, and Mike probably thought that the

*wheelchair girl shouldn't be around anyone who was drinking because
he, like so many other people at this camp, hadn't taken the time to get
to know me.*

I shook my head at myself. I needed to get into a better mood;
I needed to adjust my attitude—at least toward Christine, anyway. Like she said, she was just a counselor. She couldn't really
have done anything to save him unless she saw Jonah physically
putting the alcohol in Tommy's bag. But still . . . I was so pissed
about the entire situation. I just wished someone, anyone, would
consider our side for more than two seconds.

"Oh," was Randi's response.

I waited for her to say more—for any clues if she was or wasn't
a part of this. She didn't say anything.

"Do you guys want to keep going to the other side of the
lake," Evelyn stopped rowing, "or do you want to get off here?"

I did another *ahhhh.*

"I think Brynn's had enough," Christine translated.

"Okay." Evelyn looked at me directly. "I'm so proud of you for
trying something new. You did a really good job!"

What? How could she be proud of me? She and Christine,
and eventually Randi, all forced me to go. I didn't really have a
choice in the matter.

As we approached the dock, I looked up at Christine, and
then up the hill, and then back to Christine.

"Do you want to go back to the cabin?"

I shook my head.

"Bathroom?"

I mixed a head nod and a shake.

"What?"

I looked up the hill again.

"Oh, do you want to get a shower?"

I smiled. *Finally.*

"Gotcha! Let's go!"

Even though I would much rather be at home taking a shower with a hand-held showerhead, each cup of warm water made my head stop hurting slightly. It felt so good. Indescribably good. I closed my eyes and tried not to think about the events of the day. No matter how many times I replayed everything in my mind, it wasn't going to bring Tommy back. I had to accept that. I had to just be.

I knew I could make it to the end of the next week without him. I had to. What other choice did I have? If I called my mom and asked her to take me home because the boy I liked had to leave, she'd probably tell me to suck it up. It wasn't the end of the world, and I knew that, but that didn't make me feel any less awful that Tommy had become a scapegoat and it didn't make me miss him any less.

Christine turned the water off and proceeded to do the usual; dried my body, dried my feet, dried my hair as best as she could. Since everyone was out enjoying free time, she transferred me into my chair out in the open. She put my pajamas on, brushed my hair, and put it in its regular ponytail.

"Did the shower help?"

I slowly nodded.

"That's great! I know showers always help me when I'm having a crappy day. Do you want to go get your TechnoTalk? I think everyone is at the campfire if you want to join."

Now they decide to go down to the campfire.

Hesitating, I shook my head.

"Do you just want to go to bed?"

I shyly nodded.

"Okay. That's fine. But promise me this? I know you are really, really upset with what happened today, and I don't blame you. I know you really like Tom, and I think he really liked you. But promise me this little mishap will not ruin your time here. Me, and Evelyn, and Randi all want you to have fun here. So promise me tomorrow is another, new, better day?"

I gave her a half a smile as I nodded.

"Good! Ready to go?"

She gathered up my things and we went to the cabin. I parked in my usual spot against the back wall. She plugged my wheelchair in to charge and undid my seatbelt. She scooped me up, laid me down on my bed, rolled me over onto my stomach, and pulled the covers over me.

"Will you be okay if I go down to the campfire for a little bit? I will only be a half an hour at the most."

I gave her my permission. As soon as I heard the screen door shut, I reached for my monkey that I was so thankful my mom made me bring. I grabbed him by his leg and awkwardly managed to put him under my head.

I stared at the nightstand next to my bed and pictured the inside of it. My brush, my camera, and the charger for my iPod were in there along with the note that Tommy had given me before he left. I had clutched it in my hand long after he ran after his mother, and I refused to let Christine remove it until after I was on my bunk and ready to nap earlier. She'd asked me if I wanted her to read it to me, and I'd shook my head and eyed the nightstand. She nodded, understanding, and placed it inside.

Now, lying alone in the dark cabin, I imagined what it said. He hadn't had much time to pack his things before his mother came, so I'm not sure what he would've been able to convey in the message, but I hoped for a lot of different things. A completely unnecessary apology for having to leave, a promise to stay in touch, a declaration of "like" . . . (I wasn't naïve enough to think he already loved me; I knew that came in time.) I'd ask for it and read it myself when I was ready.

I closed my eyes and tried to picture Tommy's handwriting on the paper. Having never studied the shapes his letters took on paper before—only on daisy petals—I wasn't sure what it'd look like on lined notebook paper. It occurred to me that there were still many, many things I didn't know about him. That thought alone made my chest tighten and brought tears to my eyes. We should've had another whole week to get to know each other.

Christine was right; tomorrow would be another day. But . . . today was still the day in which they thought a guy was taking advantage of me and kicked him out of camp for something he didn't do. Still holding my monkey's leg, I let him catch my tears.

Chapter Twenty-Eight

The days after Tommy left passed slowly, but I managed to keep myself together. Christine had been overly enthusiastic about every activity there was at Camp Lakewood, including making me go swimming with all the girls at camp. During this activity, my boob decided to pop out right in front of Amanda and Jenn. I couldn't even imagine what they had to say about that incident in the showers later that day. I was just glad I wasn't around to hear it. Evelyn was also trying to share in Christine's enthusiasm—which I appreciated, but only up to a point. That point being when she decided during a softball game—our cabin against one of the boys'—to bat for me so I could "run" the bases. My chair barely made it to first before I was called out. I may have enjoyed the experience if I was six years old . . . .

It wasn't all bad without Tommy, though. The weather was beautiful, the independence I had gained from being away from my parents and home was still energizing, and I enjoyed spending time with most of the girls from my cabin. I'd spent the first week of camp with Tommy and rarely anyone else, and I didn't regret a single second of it, but I did feel a little guilty. Some of the girls at camp, like Heather and Maggie and Joanie and Tia, were really fun to be around.

One night, when Christine was called to an impromptu camp counselor meeting, Maggie climbed out of her bunk and rummaged through her trunk, emerging with her cell phone. Cell phones were allowed on premises, but when we registered for camp, we promised we would only use them in case of emergencies. The website for Camp Lakewood said that handheld devices would only distract campers from their environment and fellow campers, so they were, in a sense, banned. Knowing this, I hadn't even tried to connect to the Internet or send a text using my TechnoTalk. I had all the capabilities, I just hadn't thought to use them. Next time I was alone for a bit, maybe I'd see if I could connect and search for Tom's profile online. I didn't have his cell number to text him, but if I at least found him online, I could tell him how much I missed him. And if I couldn't get a connection, then I'd do it first thing when I got home later in the week.

Maggie's phone lit up her face, reflecting off the glasses she only wore at the end of the day, after she'd taken her contacts out. I watched her from my bunk, wondering why the other girls didn't do the same. Heather, on the bed above Maggie's, continued flipping through her magazine, while Randi and Carly sat on Carly's bunk, going through photos Carly had taken on her camera. At one point, Maggie glanced around the room and our eyes met. She smiled, stood, and was suddenly sitting on the floor near my bed, her back against my mattress.

"I'm addicted; I can't help it," she told me, letting me see her screen over her shoulder. Facebook.

She scrolled through her friends' status updates, liking and commenting on a few, and then responded to a text that interrupted her stalking.

"My boyfriend sends me a few texts a day, because he doesn't know when I'll actually be able to respond to them," she told me, clicking away at her touch screen. "He doesn't understand why I still go to camp when I'm sixteen years old, no matter how many times I tell him I just like being here, in the woods with my friends, pretty much on vacation. I think he's just jealous because he's had to work every summer since he was fifteen." She sighed.

"Next year, my parents told me I have to, too." Another sigh. "What about you? You'll be a senior next year, right?"

I nodded. Maggie, as well as Heather and Randi, of course, had mastered the art of talking to me without my TechnoTalk. I appreciated it; it made things easier and conversations late at night, like this one, possible and not frustrating for anyone involved.

"You'll apply for colleges soon, right?" she asked.

I nodded again.

"Will you have to work or anything before you go to college?"

I shrugged. I hadn't really thought about it—work or college. I spent my junior year just trying to survive emotionally and mentally. Meg and Dave ruined most of it for me, and before that, daily irritations with teachers, students, and aides had made the year one of my more challenging ones.

I thought about my plans for next summer briefly while she continued to scroll through her phone, updating her social media accounts. It was such a long way off, but I really did enjoy being at camp—Tommy or no Tommy, though I did have to admit that his presence made the experience better. Maybe I'd come back, if they'd have me. . . .

"I'm going to friend you, okay?" Maggie said, just as the door to the cabin opened. She quickly stuck her phone under her shirt and we both looked at Christine with wide eyes.

"I'm back, guys. We were just trying to figure out the schedule for the last few days," Christine said to no one in particular. "Really looking forward to that talent show!"

"Woo," Randi deadpanned.

Christine rolled her eyes as Maggie scurried across the room and into her bunk. She held her finger up to her lips, imitating a "shh," and I nodded. Her secret was safe with me.

Thinking about contacting Tommy reminded me of the note that sat in my nightstand drawer. I still hadn't found the courage to read it. Although I was almost certain it'd contain something sweet and reassuring, a very small part of me feared that maybe he'd used the note to break things off: "It was fun getting to know you, but I don't want another long distance relationship. Forget about me." Just the chance that the note might include words that would hurt me kept me from wanting to read it. I'd been hurt too much this year, and I had wanted to put off the potential pain as long as I could. But . . . now I felt ready.

Tomorrow, I thought, staring at the nightstand. *I'll read you tomorrow, no matter what.*

I had noticed since Tommy had left that Randi seemed to be distancing herself more and more from Jonah, and even Carly, to hang out with me. I still couldn't figure out if she knew what her boyfriend did and just felt bad for me, or if she knew what he did and wanted to get the hell away from him. Although we didn't have the openness Tommy and I had where I felt like I could talk about anything with her (she stayed far, far away from even mentioning Tommy or Jonah when we talked), it was still nice to have a hey-doesn't-this-activity-suck / I-don't-care-what-you-say-I-am-eating-with-you friendship with her.

Despite our lack of conversations pertaining to him, I decided that I wanted her to help with Tommy's note. It just wasn't something I wanted to share with Christine. Christine understood why I was upset and why I was angry about what had happened, but her hands were tied by camp rules and regulations and JT's hardheadedness. She couldn't help me, so I just didn't want to involve her. I wasn't sure what I was expecting from Randi, but I just felt like she was the right girl for the job.

After lunch, JT granted us some free time before we had to get in our groups and work on our talent show skits. Over the past few days, Randi and I had gotten into the habit of going to the lake, where she would lay back on the grass and I would listen to music. We relaxed. Sometimes we barely spoke. But we were there if either one of us wanted to talk about anything. Today, I asked her if she wanted to go back to our cabin.

"Are you sure? It's going to be kind of hot in there," she said. I nodded. "I . . . need . . . help . . . with . . . something."

She didn't question me. She just nodded and walked by my side to the cabin.

Once inside, I pulled up in front of the nightstand and shut off my chair. I gestured to it with my head. Randi examined the contents on the top—an old lamp, my brush, and a spare hair tie—and then opened the drawer.

SPEAK. "Note."

She picked up the folded piece of paper and began to open it for me. My heart beat a little faster and louder as I watched her movements. She seemed to be moving in slow motion. I'd tried to convince myself before I fell asleep last night that there was nothing to be scared of, but the fact that I really didn't know Tommy as well as I thought I did never escaped my mind. It really could all be over.

I suddenly closed my eyes, too chicken to read it for myself.

"Want me to read it?" Randi volunteered. "It's just a few lines."

I found myself nodding my response.

She cleared her throat and began:

"Brynn: First thing's first—this is not a Dear John letter. I know you well enough to know that that's probably what you've been thinking since the moment I gave this to you. So stop."

My entire body relaxed. My shoulders fell away from my ears, my lungs took in a deep breath, and I opened my eyes.

Randi continued reading:

"I just want to make sure you know how much I've liked spending time with you, and how much I look forward to spending even more time together when you're done with camp. Try to have a good time, keep trying to connect with people, and remember to think for yourself. Don't let Amanda, Jenn, or Jonah ruin your summer like they did mine."

Randi's voice lost its edge as she read the last line. I should've been ecstatic with the message, but I couldn't help but feel for her. She now had written confirmation that her boyfriend was a complete jackass.

"And then he gave you his phone number," she finished, folding the paper along its creases. Her eyes glossed over a bit. "So I guess it's true, huh? Jonah really got Tommy kicked out?"

I still had no physical evidence—like a confession on tape or anything—but I nodded. Everyone knew it was him.

It took a little while, but I told her about Tom's dad and why he told me he broke up with Jenn. Actually, I told her about all of it—what Jonah had called me that made Tommy hit him, what I overheard Carly and Amanda say in the shower about me, what Amanda had said to Tommy the day he was kicked out. She hid her face in her hands as my TechnoTalk voiced my words.

When she pulled her hands away, her cheeks were as pink as her hair and tears rolled down them. "Brynn, I am *so* sorry. Oh my God. I had no idea it was *that* bad."

It wasn't her fault. I didn't know how she'd missed it all—how everyone had missed it all—but she hadn't called me a single name, she hadn't taunted Tommy about his father, and she didn't seem to be responsible for getting him kicked out in any way. Randi was innocent, like me, and she was hurting.

"I don't think Carly had anything to do with this, and I'm sorry for what she has said and the way she's acting—she's so easily influenced by the people around her. Jenn and Amanda have really strong personalities, ya know? So she just kind of falls in line. She's always been like that. When it's just us, we might as well be twins. But when there are other girls involved, she loses herself among them. The way she dresses, the way she talks, what she cares about and what she doesn't . . . I can't explain it. I hate it, but I really don't know why it happens."

I thought of Tommy and about what he said about Jenn. It was true for Carly, too. And even Meg, come to think of it. If

Dave didn't like a certain movie or song or activity, suddenly Meg didn't like it either, even if I knew she loved it. They didn't know who they were or who they wanted to be. Instead, they settled with being reflections of everyone else.

"And Jonah . . . Oh, Jonah. I am so disgusted." She threw herself back on my bunk and covered her face with my pillow. Her voice came through, muffled. "I figured he was involved. I knew it, actually, the second Christine said what happened. But I didn't have any proof—and knowing him, no one does. I've been trying to get him to admit to it, but he just shrugs it off." She rolled on her side and pulled the pillow off. "He'll brag all about it when he gets home, but for now, he's keeping his mouth shut."

I typed the only thing I could think of. "I . . . don't . . . want . . . him . . . to . . . get . . . away . . . with . . . this." SPEAK.

"I don't either, Brynn, but I don't know what we can do. I can talk to JT, but camp's over in a few days. I doubt he'll investigate the matter again. And he'll probably just think I'm trying to get Jonah kicked out."

"Why . . . would . . . you . . . do . . . that?" SPEAK.

"Because . . ." She closed her eyes. "I think I'm going to break up with him."

I didn't know what to say.

"This summer—these two weeks at camp—have just painted him in such a negative light in my eyes. At first I thought it was just the drinking; I couldn't get over how different he is when he drinks. But then . . . the way he's treating people. And it's not just you and Tommy. I've seen him bully a few people, demanding they either move their seats or let him have the last of the dessert after dinner. And God forbid you want to play soccer instead of basketball. He's changing. And I really don't like whoever it is he's becoming."

I started typing, but quickly backspaced when she added, "And he's definitely cheating on me with Amanda. Which is why,

I think, he cares so much about what happened between Tommy and Jenn. Amanda and Jenn are best friends, and if Amanda's pissed about something, and Jonah's with her, then . . ."

I'd never been in this situation before. Was I supposed to offer my sympathies that her boyfriend is a jerk and a cheater? Or was I supposed to tell her that I thought she was doing the right thing? Did she need my support? Was my opinion even necessary at this point?

The panic in my head must've been displayed on my face, because Randi let out a small laugh and shook her head.

"It's okay, Brynn. This isn't your fault; I was going to come to this conclusion at some point, anyway. But thank you for getting me there faster. It'll give me all summer to get over him and have some fun with my friends . . . and with Carly, when she's back to normal."

She checked her watch and wiped her eyes one last time, her cheeks now back to their normal tone. "We better get to our groups or JT will hunt us down."

I simply nodded, still a bit dumbfounded. I had just watched Randi fall apart and put herself back together again in a matter of minutes. It'd taken her a little while to figure it all out, and she'd been in denial for a few days—and, honestly, who wouldn't be?—but I'd just watched her gather the courage to do what was right for *her*. Not for her relationship or her boyfriend or her friends. For her. Tommy would be proud.

As I followed her out the door, I decided to use Randi as my model from now on. I'd thought she was cool from the start, but now . . . she was beyond that. With her as an example, and my DAISY goal at the front of my mind, I would make sure to put an end to the part of Jonah's game that concerned me. He may have beat Tommy, but this time, I was going to win.

Chapter Twenty-Nine

Since Tommy left, JT designated every afternoon from 1:30 to 4 "talent show rehearsal time." While I was sure every other DAISY group was practicing their already thought of and probably awesome skits, Jonah, Amanda, and I still didn't have a clue what we were doing. We didn't even know what the concept of the act was going to be. Every time we went to work on it, one of them would "have to go to the bathroom" or "go check on something," and when they didn't come back, the other one would "go look for them," leaving Christine and I sitting under the tree where we met.

I studied Jonah as Christine and I approached him and Amanda, relaxing against the wide trunk of the tree. He didn't seem upset or depressed or anything related to a breakup. I wondered if Randi had done it yet, or it she'd wait until they were home to avoid even more drama. This summer had already had enough of it.

"I have to pee," Jonah announced about right on schedule.

"No, you don't," Christine said, surprising me.

"Who are you to tell me when I have to take a piss or not?"

"That's disrespectful, Jonah. You think I don't know what's going on here? It is Wednesday. 1:47 p.m. The talent show is a little less than forty-eight hours away. What are you going to do when JT calls your names, in front of your dad, and you don't have anything prepared? Do you really want a repeat of your first night?"

"Why do we have to have you here with us again? Oh, that's right, Tommy boy isn't here to take care of *her* for you. You're not here to tell *us* what to do."

I smacked my talking switch.

I am done. I am not going to do the talent show with them, no matter what anyone says about it. I will have my mom say we need to get home right away. I am not doing it.

Christine looked up at me from her spot on the grass and crossed her legs.

"Hello?" Jonah waved at her. "Did you hear what I just said? Aren't you gonna tell me I'm being so disrespectful again, or go get JT, or something?"

"Brynn is typing something."

"Oh, really?" he scoffed.

I kept typing.

"Yes, really."

"How does that thing even work?" Amanda blurted out. "Does it, like, know what she's thinking?"

"No," Christine laughed, "and that's probably a very good thing right now. See that switch that she's hitting by her head? Well, her screen has a lot of words and letters on it, and it scrolls through them, and whenever it gets to what word or letter she wants, she just hits her switch by her head. Do you want to see how she's doing it? Brynn, can Jonah and Amanda see what you are doing?"

I gave them a definite head shake. I didn't want them to see what I was saying until I was done. And I didn't want them that close to me, hovering over me, when all I wanted to do was punch both of them in the face.

"No? Okay. Maybe some other time."

"Why not?"

I stopped typing and stared at Jonah. *Seriously?*

"If you were Brynn right now, and if Brynn were you," Christine started, "would you want her looking over your shoulder after everything you've done to her these past two weeks?'

Amanda completely missed Christine's point. "Is it like an iPad? Why isn't she doing it with her hands?"

Where had this girl been the last few days?

"Can I at least tell them about your CP? I think this will really help them."

Doubt it.

I nodded anyway and went back to typing.

"Okay, so, Brynn has a disability called cerebral palsy. Basically, different parts of your brain control different parts of your body. For example, one part of your brain controls things like walking and talking. Another part of your brain is in charge of listening to things and understanding them. Well, in Brynn's case, the part of her brain that controls her walking, and talking, and moving was damaged when she was born. It doesn't work like yours does. But the part of the brain that controls all her listening and thinking was not damaged. She can understand anything you say. Does that make any sense?"

They both nodded, seeming to understand everything she said. Again, I wondered why they couldn't have just asked these questions earlier. Why did they want to understand me *now?* Maybe they were bored. Since they'd dumped all their alcohol to fill up Tommy's bag with empties, I couldn't even fathom what they'd been doing to keep themselves amused all week.

"Are you ready to talk, Brynn?"

I nodded, although feeling a tad bit guilty for what I was about to say. Christine just explained my CP to them and they listened. Did it help? I wasn't entirely sure. But they listened. I then shook my head to myself, remembering what they did to Tommy and how they abandoned me for the last week and a half. I needed to say this. It was what we all were thinking.

301

SPEAK. "You know what? I am done. You don't want to do the talent show with me, and guess what. I don't want to do it with you either. I am out. You guys are on your own, although I don't think you will even be able to come up with a skit by Friday. Christine, you can tell JT I am not doing it. I don't care if he kicks me out. I will just have my mom take me home early. And another thing. I know what you did to Tommy. You did not respect the fact that his dad passed away, or the fact that he wanted to be with someone who was different, so I don't respect you."

I didn't even feel like hearing their reply, or Christine's reply for that matter. I turned my chair on, spun around, and rushed off to the basketball court.

There. I did it. I was going to hold my ground. I was not going to try to come up with a stupid little skit that nobody was going to remember in five years with people who couldn't stand each other long enough to make it through a conversation. Why should we? Why should we pretend?

And, even though Christine's little talk could have changed their minds about me, I didn't feel bad about telling them off. They deserved every word of what I said. If anything, it might have helped them understand that I was a normal person who was able to get upset.

Now that . . . was an interesting concept.

I always tried to avoid conflict just so people would think I was easy to be around, but had I actually been hurting myself this whole time by doing exactly that? Did people think I was a push over or less cognitively aware because of it?

I drove over to the bench. Mine and Tommy's bench. I so desperately wanted to see him sitting there right then, and I just as desperately wanted to be in his arms, leaning against him. On the first day, Randi said the lake had magical powers. She was wrong. This bench—and maybe even the basketball court as a whole—had all the magical powers in the world. I closed my eyes, wishing I could telepathically transport him here. I opened one eye and then the other. Of course. No Tommy.

If things didn't work out with Tommy when I left camp, would there be somebody else like him? Would this new guy not care that he would have to help me eat, or that he would have to wipe food off my face? Would he care that sometimes I wouldn't be able to kiss back because I was having a bad CP attack? What about if we got serious and wanted to do more than kiss? Would he care that he would have to undress me every time we wanted to and help me get dressed when we were done?

Some people probably just assumed people with disabilities couldn't have relationships, only could have relationships with other people with disabilities, or some other variation of that. But like I told Tommy, I always pictured myself having a boyfriend, and the guy I pictured had never been disabled. My disability was never a part of my relationship expectations. If there were so many Jonahs and Amandas and Jenns in this world, there had to be more Tommys, right?

I stared at the spot where Tommy had been sitting before JT came and dropped the bomb on us, and I remembered the conversation we were having. He was going off about how daisies needed more to be beautiful. At the time, I thought everybody had got to him. I thought he completely took a dive off the deep end into a pool of DAISY-related nothingness. But now? Now, not so much. Now, I think I understood what he'd been talking about.

With possible words running through my head, I looked at my screen, and with a click of my switch, I began typing.

The sound of footsteps almost made me jump out of my chair. Christine and Randi. How didn't I notice them coming down the path? I went for the SAVE FILE button as fast as I could.

"Writing something intense?" Christine noted.

I hurried and cleared my screen.

"Wait, was that a poem you were writing?"

Damn it. I was too slow.

"I want to hear!" Randi exclaimed.

I slowly shook my head. I really, really did not want to share it with them. They wouldn't get it. They would think I was insane just like I thought Tommy had been insane.

"Is it about Jonah? If it is, all the better."

Not . . . exactly.

"I told Randi what happened. I hope you don't mind."

Of course you did. You tell everybody everything.

"Brynn knows how annoyed I am with him right now," Randi said with a shrug, giving me a look that seemed to go over Christine's head.

Not meaning to, I *ahhhh*'d.

"Aren't we all?" Christine muttered, surprising us both. We giggled quietly.

"So, do you want to go get ready for the campout?" Christine asked me. I had completely forgotten about the campout. "Have you decided if you want to sleep out tonight? If you do, I'll carry our mattresses down to the campsite now, and we can come up later so you can go to the bathroom using your lift. If you don't, we can go down now and just come up whenever everyone is going to bed. It's up to you."

Every night for the past week, each cabin had the opportunity to camp out. Tonight, the second to the last night of camp, it was our turn. No iPods, no cell phones, no anything electronic. Just the people from our cabin, sprawled out in sleeping bags, on our mattresses, or in the grass for the entire night, listening to the sounds of crickets, owls, and the wind. It sounded nice, in theory. But I'd never slept directly under the stars before, and I couldn't say I'd ever actually expressed a longing to do so.

I didn't particularly want Christine to have to bring both of our mattresses down and have her come back up to help me in the bathroom. And, even though I was really starting to understand why I shouldn't do things just because everyone else wanted me to or was doing them, I really didn't want to be the only one who wasn't. Remembering what Tommy had said time and time again—that everyone understood why I needed help and that they were okay doing it—I nodded at Christine. If she wanted to bring the mattresses down, then I wasn't going to stop her.

"So you do want to sleep out with everyone?"

I did. I wanted to spend time with some of the girls I'd become friends with, without the distraction of girls from the other cabins dropping in and stalling all conversation or making everyone feel uncomfortable.

"Okay. That's great. Why don't we get you down there first, and then I'll bring everything down? I'm going to be honest. It's not the most accessible path in the world, so I just want to make sure you can get down there."

"Do . . . you . . . think . . . I . . . can? I . . . don't . . . have . . ." I deleted the last three words.

"I'm not entirely sure, but we are going to try. Ready?"

At the end of the basketball path, Christine turned. I looked at the hill I was supposed to be going down. The pavement stopped two feet in front of me. It wasn't even gravel, which I sometimes did okay with in my chair. It was a mixture of mulch and grass with a few random tree stumps. I might be able to get down it (more like slide down and possibly tip over and crush my skull), but I was never going to get back up.

"What do you think?" Christine asked. "Do you think you can make it?"

I found a patch of shade so I could type. I had to tell them more than a yes or a no.

"Okay . . . I . . . want . . . to . . . be . . . with . . . everybody . . . because . . . I . . . haven't . . . gotten . . . the . . . chance . . . to . . . but . . . I'm . . . afraid . . . I'm . . . going . . . to . . . roll . . . right . . . down . . . the . . . hill . . . and . . . never . . . get . . . back . . . up."

"What if I get behind you and Randi gets in front of you, and we both hang on to your chair?"

"Who said I would be in front of her? I don't want to get run over if her chair decided to take off! I say we call Jonah over and make him be in front." Her eyes glistened.

I couldn't help but smirk at the idea. *Payback. Ultimate payback.*

"Do you want Randi to go ask him? I'll really make him do it if you think it will work."

"Here's . . . the . . . thing. I . . . will . . . have . . . to . . . go . . . up . . . and . . . down . . . at . . . least . . . twice . . . regardless . . . of . . . what . . . I . . . do . . . unless . . . you . . . want . . . to . . . help . . . me . . . pee . . . in . . . the—"

"I will totally help you pee in the woods!" Randi exclaimed.

"I will hold your upper body and Randi can hold your legs, and there we go! Instead of 'Singing in the Rain,' we'll have 'Peeing in the Woods.'"

I chuckled. "Do . . . you . . . think . . ." I couldn't believe I was about to ask this. "Jonah . . . is . . . strong . . . enough . . . to . . . catch . . . me . . . and . . . push . . . me . . . back . . . up? Or . . . what . . . about . . . Mike?"

"You really don't think your chair can make it?"

I frowned. "But . . . I . . . really . . . want . . . to . . . be . . . with . . . everybody."

"Can we move the campout to the basketball court?" Randi suggested. "Do we really need to be under all the trees? Is it going to rain tonight?"

"Randi! You're a genius! I don't think it is, so I don't see why we couldn't. I'm sure everyone would much rather carry their mattresses over here than down there, anyway. Brynn, what do you think of this?"

I hesitated. Initial reaction; I didn't want to be the one who changed what we were going to do. But—

"Never mind. It doesn't matter what you think. This is what we are going to do." Christine waved me anxieties away. "Randi, go tell everyone already down there what's going on. Tell them they can sleep in the grass around the court if they don't want to bring their mattresses. I'm going to go tell Evelyn and everyone still in the cabin. Brynn, you can go back to the basketball court and just wait for us."

Within forty-five minutes, all the mattresses from my cabin were spread across my dance floor to the point where I barely had enough room to drive. Girls were chatting it up as if they had no idea we were supposed to be in a different location. A portable fire pit was brought in to the middle of everything, and it was almost as large as the one in the amphitheater. And I was about to have my first mountain pie.

Once Christine and I returned from the bathroom (everyone did mention they liked that they didn't have to pop a squat by a tree), it was just about the time where my TechnoTalk began to be brighter than the daylight and Evelyn had already started making s'mores.

"My favorite part of campouts!" Christine said. "Are you going to have one?"

I shook my head.

"No? Too hard for you to eat?"

I nodded.

"Okay. I knew you would like the mountain pie, though. They are basically grilled cheese with pepperoni toasted over the campfire. But if you don't need anything else, I'm going to go help Evelyn. Cool?"

"Of course it's cool," Randi resumed kneeling beside me. "We don't always want you around."

"You and Jonah. I'm telling ya! I really feel the love, guys."

Randi put her arms on my armrest, just like Tommy did when we were doing our first activity together. Tommy. I would have done anything, anything in the world, to be able to talk to him right then.

"What . . . do . . . you . . . think . . . of . . . this . . . DAISY . . . thing?" I knew what I thought. I knew what Tommy thought. I definitely knew what Jonah thought. But I didn't really know what anybody else thought.

"Eh, it's lame, but it's camp. I don't think JT will make it another year, but we probably won't be here to know that answer. But I know how much you liked it." She smirked. "I know I've told you this a million times, but I am sorry for Jonah, and everyone else, and all the shit that went down. They don't get it, and I don't know why they don't."

I didn't know if Carly talked about me to her, and I still didn't know if she had taken care of all her business with Jonah. I could have asked, but that would have taken energy that I just didn't have.

"I . . . just . . . wish . . . we . . . all . . . could . . . have . . . hung . . . out . . . more."

"Me too."

"I . . . really . . . like . . . you . . . and . . . I . . . really . . . like . . . Tommy . . . and . . . I . . . just—"

"Okay, guys," I was interrupted by Evelyn. "I have an activity for us to do."

We all groaned in unison.

"Hey! This one is cool, I promise. We have paper and pencils for all of you. This is something we do every year, and something that I personally think is cathartic—it helps you release some of the tension you're carrying around on a daily basis that you don't even know about. We want you to write a letter to anyone you want. It can be somebody that you love, someone you hate, your mom, your sister, your best friend, somebody that hurt you, anyone. It doesn't really have to be a letter, actually. It can just be ramblings about strong feelings toward someone, or even something. Anyway, you can either keep it for yourself, or you can give it to that person, or if you're writing about something or someone that you feel extremely negative toward, you can throw it in the fire if that will help you get rid of your thoughts. Christine and I will be coming around to give you your paper, and you can start whenever."

"Do you mind if I lay on your bed?" Randi kicked off her flip flops. "I swear my feet don't smell that much."

I laughed lightly and nodded.

What was I going to write about? Who was I going to write about? It would be so easy to write a letter to Jonah, but I already told him off, so a letter probably wouldn't do anything more. I could write a letter to Carly and tell her to wise up, as my grandma would say, but again—that would take energy that I didn't want to spend on someone who I might never see again. Maybe I could write to Tommy and have Christine send it to him.

Christine handed Randi her paper and a pencil. "Brynn, would you like me to write what you type?"

I paused; I wasn't necessarily a fan of that idea. Christine would have to see every word, and not that I didn't trust her, but I didn't particularly want her to see what I would eventually have to say.

"Okay. Just let me know if you want me to. Even if you want to throw it in the fire, I would not have a problem writing for you. We could even take your arm out so you could throw it in yourself."

I watched Randi as she started to craft her letter, although I couldn't make out the name. Jonah? Carly? Someone else back home? It wasn't until then that I knew what I was going to do. I looked at my screen and took a deep breath. Yeah. This was exactly what I needed to do.

I made it through the first three sentences before (surprise, surprise) the tears ran down my cheeks.

"Hey, are you okay?" Christine hurried over and grabbed a Kleenex. "Are you sure you don't want me to write down what you're writing? I'm dead serious. I will make it so that you, yourself, can fling it in the fire. It helps a lot more than you think."

I shook my head. The tears kept coming and I kept typing. I had to do this.

"Okay. How about I'll just be here to wipe your eyes? I won't look at what you're typing."

I turned, let her wipe my face, and then went back to writing.

After a full hour, six eye wipes, and four nose wipes, I was finally done. I glanced around. Girls were still doing what I was doing. Writing and crying. Maybe this DAISY activity wasn't so lame after all. I looked back at my screen. For a long moment, I considered hitting CLEAR. That would have been my equivalent to throwing it in the fire. Instead, almost as though I was possessed by some power, I followed the scan to the SAVE FILE button. This letter, unlike some of the others written tonight, would be delivered eventually.

Chapter Thirty

*S*omehow, over the course of the night, my head ended up completely under my comforter. Even though my body was totally under the blanket, I was still having a hell of a time opening my eyes. Bright. So. Very. Bright.

"It looks like you learned the first thing about sleeping outside." I heard Christine laugh. "Cover your face so the bugs don't eat you to death."

Oh. Right. Bugs. Didn't even think about that.

"I'm going to pull your covers off and get you in your chair. Ready?"

I tried to make a yeeaaah sound, but I had a throat full of snot.

The covers came off and I thought my eyes were going to explode. Sunlight. Everywhere. Even once I was in my chair, was strapped down, and had my TechnoTalk on, I couldn't open my eyes.

"I know. The first time I slept out, I was like 'holy sun!' Do you want me to push you?"

I didn't really want her to, but there was no possible way I was going to be able to drive and not run myself off the path.

"That's cool." Christine put my chair into manual mode. "Since you didn't take a shower last night, and since we have an hour and a half before breakfast, do you want to take a shower now? You probably feel gross. I know I always do after campouts."

I nodded a big nod. I was so sticky from the humidity, I felt like somebody stuck me in a pool of glue.

"Kay. Evelyn said she would carry our mattresses up for us. We just have to go to get our clothes and my bathing suit. By the way, today everyone wears their camp shirts. I take it you want to wear jean shorts with yours?"

I nodded. I still could only keep my eyes opened for a few seconds at a time. She ran into the cabin to get everything we needed and we headed to the shower room. What was a new experience for both of us ten days ago was now a regular routine. She parked me in the same spot and threw on the same bathing suit. She positioned my chair in the same way. And within thirty minutes, I was done with my shower, my sinuses were back to normal, she was rinsed off, and we were both in our blue Camp Lakewood t-shirts.

Only a few people were starting to trickle in when we went in the dining hall. I told Christine I would have a blueberry muffin and apple juice and I wheeled over to my regular table. Randi had been eating with me and Christine recently—to avoid Jonah, I assumed (who was all too happy to chat up Amanda day in and day out)—but told me that since it was basically the last day of camp, Carly was pretty much forcing her to sit with her.

It hit me right then.

"I don't know about you," Christine put our food down, "but I am starving. That little mountain pie and s'more just didn't do it for me. . . . What's wrong? Why the sad face?"

"Camp . . . is . . . almost—"

"Oh. I know." She broke off a piece of my muffin and popped it in my mouth. "Today and tomorrow are always the hardest. But that's the good thing. We still have today and tomorrow."

"Are . . . you . . . on . . . Facebook?"

"Yes! I am! Are you?"

I nodded and took another bite.

"Sweet! We aren't really supposed to be friends with campers, but nobody really follows that rule, and you know we aren't supposed to have our cell phones, but I have my iPhone with me, so when we go back to the cabin, I will definitely add you. I bet Tommy added you first thing when he got home." Christine winked at me.

I squealed, and I didn't even care that I did.

Christine chuckled. "So that's how you feel about him? I thought so. Oh! And I was thinking. I know how much you liked painting with him that one time, and since we aren't going to do anything in Stage Stuff today, do you want to just do some painting like that? You could maybe paint a picture for Tom."

I nodded cheerfully. She could have asked me if I wanted to go to the moon, and I still would have nodded cheerfully. I didn't care. This conversation had once again reminded me that I was going to get to talk to Tommy when I got home! In fact, I might even text him from the car once we were off camp property and cell phones were allowed again.

"Okay. Why don't you finish your breakfast first?"

Christine had taped a huge piece of paper to the wall and I had pulled my chair right up to it, but five minutes into painting with the brush, we decided it wasn't necessary. We found ourselves finger painting as though we were three years old, and I didn't give a crap who saw. Camp was almost over, I'd made a handful of friends, I had experienced the beginning of what I hoped would be a promising relationship, and I'd told the people who didn't try to understand me how I felt. All that was left was my DAISY goal, which I was attaining every time I pressed my hand to the paper.

"What do you think? More blue?"

I went with that.

She carefully dipped my hand in the bin of water she was holding and then traded it for the bin of blue. She held my arm tight enough so that it wouldn't fling away and get paint everywhere, but loose enough so I could move it anywhere on the paper. I smeared the blue goo across the pink splotch. It actually started to look kind of cool.

Suddenly, Mike was at my side.

"Hey, Brynn and Christine," he said, "how's it going?"

"Good. We're just doing a little painting. What's up?"

"Can I talk to both of you when you have a second?"

"Right now?"

"Whenever you're done. No hurry."

Christine rinsed my hand off once again and dried it with a paper towel. She then put my TechnoTalk back on and we turned to face Mike.

"Is everything okay?" Christine asked.

"Everything is cool. Brynn, I have some things for you, and I just figured now would be the best time to give them to you. Contrary to all of the drama here with Tom, our cabin stayed pretty neutral to the situation with him and Jenn. We're guys. We usually stay out of each other's personal business, and if we do have a problem, we usually beat each other up, shake hands afterward, and move on."

Except for Jonah. Or anyone who is drunk half the time.

"When we were having our campout, we somehow ended up talking about you, and Tom started telling us how cool you were, and that you were just like everybody else, and that your disability didn't matter to him at all. I think him just talking about you really, really helped my cabin with this DAISY thing, and I just want to say thank you for that. Anyway, you know those letters we asked all the campers to write when we camped out?"

I nodded.

"Well, some of my campers wrote letters to you. I think there's even one in there from Tom, and I wanted to give them to you before camp was over. Again, I think just having you here, and just hearing Tom talking about you, really helped them understand disabled people can actually do stuff and should be treated like 'regular' people. I can't thank you enough for doing what you do. So here you go. Read them on your own time."

Christine grabbed the folded pieces of paper. "Thanks, Mike."

"Stay cool. See ya tonight at the closing ceremony."

After Mike left the arts and crafts building, we both went to the table. I stared at the little pile of papers that were supposedly for me.

"What are you thinking right now?"

I looked at my screen, hit my switch once, and looked back at the notes.

"How about you just see what they are? Do you want me to read them to you, or do you want to read them yourself?"

I nodded at her.

"You want me to? Okay." She unfolded the first note and began to read.

Brynn,

You have so much courage coming to camp. Keep it up! If I was in your situation, I would not have wanted to come.

Chris

My mood of painting and possibly talking to Tommy slowly started to fade as she reached for the next note.

Hey Brynn,

You don't know me, but we were just talking about you at the campfire. You are my inspiration. I know you will be good to Tom so much more than Jenn was. You are amazing!

Never give up,

J. B.

What the hell did Tommy tell these people? They were acting like I was a miraculous superwoman, not just a regular person. I decided I wanted to save Tommy's note until the end, so Christine read the last one from someone who I didn't know. It was the same as the other ones; telling me how I was just so amazing and that I had so much more "courage" than he would ever have.

"Okay," Christine laid the letter down. "I can tell this is making you uncomfortable. Let's talk about it."

I held my switch down until I found the words I wanted to say. "These . . . people . . . don't . . . know . . . me. I . . . don't . . . have . . . courage. You . . . know . . . this. Tommy . . . knew . . . this. I'm . . . always . . . afraid . . . of . . . being . . . too . . . hard . . . for . . . people. I . . . can . . . feel . . . myself . . . getting . . . better . . . because . . . of . . . you . . . and . . . Tommy . . . but . . . I . . . still . . . have . . . that . . . issue . . . very . . . much."

"I see."

"And . . . I . . . don't . . . feel . . . like . . . I . . . had . . . a . . . choice . . . about . . . coming . . . to . . . camp. I . . . had . . . to . . . get . . . away . . . from . . . my . . . hometown . . . because . . . my . . . friends . . . stabbed . . . me . . . in . . . the . . . back. I . . . didn't . . . have . . . a . . . choice . . . of . . . staying . . . home . . . because . . . I . . . would . . . be . . . sitting . . . at . . . my . . . house . . . bored . . . and . . . depressed. I . . . wanted . . . to . . . come . . . to . . . camp . . . to . . . make . . . new . . . friends. What . . . is . . . so . . . courageous . . . about . . . that?"

"Can I ask you a question?"

Surprised, I nodded.

"How much do you think about your CP?"

What? What does that have to do with anything?

"I mean, I know you don't like that you need so much help, and I know you feel bad every time you have a CP moment, but whenever you're driving to the dining hall, or if you're doing an activity, do you . . ." she paused. "Is your wheelchair and computer on your mind at all?"

I hesitated.

"I'm not trying to yell at you, but do you understand what I'm asking. Are you conscious of your disability at all times?"

"I . . . guess . . . not."

"Okay," Christine shifted in her chair, "so, to you, it's normal to be in your wheelchair. To you, it's normal to talk with a computer. It's normal for you to have your hands strapped down. I know you hate needing help, but everything else is normal to you. Is that kinda how you feel?"

I excitedly nodded. She pretty much understood.

"Right. So, you don't know what it's like to be able to walk. You don't know what it's like to be able to talk. So you don't really miss it. Is that right? You can tell me if I'm not correct and if you want me to shut up."

I shook my head and gestured for her to keep going.

"So for some of us who heavily rely on walking and talking, we probably can't even begin to imagine what we would be like if we were in your shoes. I'm not saying I can't, but for some people, especially sixteen- and seventeen-year-old guys who don't have very open minds, I think that is the case. They put themselves in your shoes without actually being you. Does that make any sense?"

I nodded. "I . . . just . . . don't . . . want . . . people . . . to . . . think . . . I'm . . . this . . . superwoman . . . when . . . I'm . . . not."

"Well, I definitely think you were Tom's superwoman. You want to read his note?" She unfolded it and held it beside my screen so I could read along.

Hey, babe,

Whoever had the idea of having my cabin camp out after the dance is a total idiot. I wish I could have spent all night sitting at the basketball court with you. You looked amazing. Anyway, I just told everybody about you, and I think these guys are starting to get it. They're definitely not like Jonah. We still need to hang him by a tree . . . . Did you bring any rope with you?

I just want you to know that you are awesome. I hope someday you will realize that. Can't wait to write a song with you! We're gonna kick Abbie's ass!! :)

Catch ya in the a.m.,
Tommy

Chapter Thirty-One

I repeated the words from Tommy's letter over and over again throughout the day. I was thinking about what he'd written, and how excited I was to get home and get to talk to him again, when I entered the dining hall to eat my last dinner at Camp Lakewood. Tommy had been right about dinner on the last day: it was as if they could only afford to hire the "good" cooks on dance night and the last night of camp. Again, I had a plate full of mashed potatoes and a giant piece of vanilla cake, the most I had eaten all week.

Now, after my stomach felt decently full, we all migrated to the amphitheater for the start of the closing ceremony. Before it could start, JT was insisting on a group photo.

"I need everybody to get as close as they can get. Come on, campers. You've been living together for the past two weeks. A little closeness won't kill you now."

Oh, I will not miss that infamous megaphone.

"If you don't all squeeze in together, we won't be able to get anybody on either side, and what's a camp picture without everyone? Now, I need everybody to move in as close to the middle as possible."

"Randi!" Carly yelled from the crowd below us. "Why don't you wanna come sit with me? It's the camp photo! It's tradition!"

"I'm not crawling over fifty thousand people just to keep up some dumb tradition! It's a camp photo! You'll live! And, you have your boyfriend with you, anyway. Make a new tradition!"

"Some best friend you are!" She sat back down with Gabe and everybody else. I guess she reached her goal.

"And some best friend you are," Randi mumbled.

"Oh, she just loves you," Christine remarked. "Brynn, do you want me to take your TechnoTalk off so we can see your face more?"

I thought about that. When I would take pictures with Meg and Dave, I would always take it off just so we could do fun poses and whatnot. But since I was in the back row now, they probably wouldn't be able to see my face anyway. And, my TechnoTalk went through camp just as much as I did (except that one day where I pulled that wonderful driving stunt) so why shouldn't I keep it on?

I shook my head.

"It looks like we're all ready." JT gave the photographer the thumbs up. I recognized the girl as an employee in the camp office, but I'd never learned her name. "Now, I've been told that Camp Lakewood tradition calls for a regular picture first, and then you do a funny picture. Is that—"

"Yesss," everyone said in the same annoyed tone.

"Alright. I want to see some big smiles! I want to see how much fun you had in the last two weeks! Make this the best picture you have ever taken! On the count of three. One . . . two . . ."

Acting as though they were sharing a brain wave, Christine and Randi leaned in and wrapped their arms around me. For a brief, brief moment, I wished they were Tommy's arms. I was with him most of my time at camp. I wanted him in this picture with me. But Tommy was not here. That was not going to be possible.

Then I remembered something. Both of these girls were the first people at camp to treat me like a "regular person." I mean, they told me secrets, brushed my hair, and even helped me pee when I was having a CP attack with no questions asked. Even without Tommy, this picture would be a picture to frame.

By the time JT announced "three!" and the flashes were flashing, I knew I was beside the right people for this picture.

"Very good, everyone! As you know, you will be getting these pictures in the mail shortly after camp is over. They will also be up on the website. Now, are you ready for the silly one? I want to see some funny faces, but make sure they are camp appropriate!"

I was in the midst of rolling my eyes when I felt Christine rip my arm out of my armband. *Seriously?* She flung it over her neck and grabbed my hand. Randi hurried and pulled my other arm out and flung it over her neck. This definitely was going to be the funny photo. Even when the flashes were going off, I could not stop laughing at how ridiculous we must have looked.

"The hell if you were getting away with not doing any lame poses," Randi said and put my arm back in.

"I know! I was like 'Brynn needs to have her arms out; go!'"

I smiled at both of them to say thank you.

The photographer climbed down her ladder and JT went back in the middle of the stage.

"Those were some very excellent photos. I can't wait to see them! Now, it's time to move on to the second part of the closing ceremony. I know you usually have a little celebration on the lake, but I thought we would do something a little different this year."

Such a surprise. I wondered briefly what camp would've been like this year if JT hadn't been in charge.

"As you can see, there is a table full of daisies in the colors you asked for late last week. Bonnie was so nice to have planted them for us this summer. When you get your daisy, I am going to ask you to go down to the lake. We have canoes waiting for you to take you to the other side. You can plant your daisy wherever you would like. Preferably, I would like you to be with your DAISY group when you do this, but you don't necessarily have to be. When you are replanting your daisy, I want you to think of something you learned from camp. Something that you hoped you gained from being here. Something you would like to do in your future. Whenever you are done, feel free to talk about it with your group, your friends, or your counselor. And one last thing: I have to say it was an absolute honor working with you at this session. I hope you always keep the spirit of DAISY within you. Your counselors will be around to give you your daisies."

Randi went off to be with Carly since she was throwing a hissy fit that her "best friend" wasn't with her. This was going to be the first time I was going to see Jonah and Amanda after I told them off. I braced myself for a whole other kind of awkwardness.

I spotted Amanda and Jonah coming up the stairs with . . . four daisies? I blinked my eyes to make sure I wasn't just seeing double.

"Oh, Jonah." Christine reached for the flowers. "You got Brynn's daisy? Thank you very much!"

"They gave me Tom's daisy, too. I don't know what you want to do with it."

"Well, we're going to plant it for him. Why not? Are you guys ready to head down?"

Once we got to the fork in the path that led to the lake on one side and the basketball court on the other, I stopped my chair. What was I doing? I didn't want to get in a canoe with these people. I didn't want to go plant flowers with these people. I had wanted so desperately to fit in my entire time here, to be treated like everyone else and acknowledged as no one special, but now I wanted nothing of the sort. My daisy didn't belong with the rest of the camp's, and I would imagine Tommy would feel the same way about his. I was going to do something different, and they were just going to have to get over it.

I started typing. "Would . . . you . . . mind . . . if . . . I . . ."

"Are you okay, Brynn?" Christine asked.

I nodded. "Didn't . . . go . . . down . . . to . . . the . . . lake . . . with . . . you?" SPEAK. I looked directly at Amanda and Jonah.

They, in turn, looked at Christine.

"I guess that would be okay? Did you still want to replant your flower? And Tom's flower?"

I nodded and glanced at the basketball court.

"Ohhhh, I think I know where you're going with this. Sure! Would you guys mind if we don't go with you?"

They sheepishly shook their heads. I realized that grabbing my daisy was their way of showing me a shred of respect, but I was so over them—over the chances I'd given them to not act moronic, over the way they treated and betrayed Tommy, over their attitudes toward other campers and their friends, like Randi—that I didn't even care. This time, I really was done.

"Okay. You guys can go down. Brynn, I'm going to go get a shovel. You head to wherever you want to go, and I'll find you."

As I went down the different path from Jonah and Amanda, I started to think about what JT said he wanted us to consider when we were planting our daisies. Cheesy as it was, I knew exactly what I wanted to take away from this experience. I came here because I wanted to avoid Meg and Dave for two weeks. And I came here because I wanted to make a few new friends. But I also came here to prove to my parents that I could be independent if given the chance. And now, thinking about all the reasons I came, I realized that I was actually getting something totally different and unexpected out of the experience.

Courage.

Not that kind of courage that those guys in Tommy's cabin thought I had, and that some people probably thought anyone with any disability had. I didn't exhibit courage when I got out of bed every day or when I showed my face in a restaurant. I didn't think that was courageous at all. To me, that was more like human nature taking its course.

I felt that Tommy, Christine, and Randi would understand the courage I had desperately needed to find when I first arrived at Camp Lakewood. These were my friends now; they didn't see the technology first instead of the girl. I had needed the courage to be myself without comparing myself to other people; the courage to tell people how I felt, whether if I loved them or if they hurt me; the courage to ask for help when I couldn't do something myself and not feel like I was inconveniencing anyone.

I already felt like I had started the process of changing, but I still felt like I had so much further to go. And I would probably be going on this journey by myself. My mom and dad were wonderful people, but they wouldn't understand. Whenever they asked me how camp was, I would probably just smile, nod, maybe even tell them about Tommy and Randi. But I felt like this lesson Camp Lakewood had given me should be kept to myself. It was for me to figure out on my own.

"Two blue daisies, coming right up!" Christine was beside me in the next minute. "Where would you like them, mam?"

I nodded towards the direction.

"By the bench? Okay. Do you want one on either side of the bench, or do you want them to be together?"

A daisy on each side of the bench would look cool, but my instincts were telling me otherwise.

"Together? Okay? Which side?"

I looked exactly where Tommy and I were sitting on the night of the dance. The right side.

I pulled up to Christine as she knelt down and started digging. "So have you thought about what you want your daisy to stand for?"

I smiled as I typed my one word answer. "Courage." SPEAK.

She stopped digging and looked up at me with a huge grin. "I'd say you've met your goal. Congratulations."

Once she had a hole big enough, she took my daisy out of the pot and put it in. She then moved the dirt back into place.

"So I know how you feel about people telling you how courageous they think you are," Christine said and started on the other hole. "And I definitely get that you want a totally different kind of courage from what they were talking about."

I knew she would understand right away.

"You have made such an improvement from when you first got here, and I can't tell you how proud I am of you. But how do you feel about people calling you an inspiration?"

I gave her a mixture of a nod and a shake. That was always a debatable topic between me and my parents, and this was why I wasn't even going to try to explain the courage thing.

"You don't really like it?"

"I . . . know . . . people . . . who . . . say . . . it . . . to . . . me . . . are . . . just . . . trying . . . to . . . be . . . nice . . . but . . . the . . . people . . . who . . . usually . . . say . . . it . . . to . . . me . . . don't . . . even . . . know . . . me. They . . . don't . . . know . . . my . . . flaws. I . . . could . . . be . . . a . . . mass . . . murderer . . . for . . . all . . . that . . . they . . . know . . ." SPEAK.

"I see." Christine spread the soil around the second blue flower. "Well, let me put it this way. I go to college at Slippery Rock. I was unsure if I wanted to major in child psychology or nursing. I knew I wanted to help people; I just didn't know who. I figured I liked kids, so I went with that. But after getting to know you and helping you, I realized that I wouldn't mind working somewhere that helps people with disabilities. Yes, I know you have some flaws, but doesn't everyone? Now, is that okay that I said that to you? I want to know if it's not."

Nobody had ever put it to me like that before. Usually, all I got from people was "You are such an inspiration," and then they'd walk away. They didn't even try to talk to me or get to know me. But Christine knew me. And I knew Christine. I knew she wasn't saying it just to say it.

I slowly nodded. Yeah. I was okay with being someone's "inspiration" this time.

"Cool." She grabbed the empty pots and stood up. "Thank you, Brynn, for everything you have taught me this summer. I would give you a hug right now, but I don't think you want me to touch you. Maybe after I wash my hands?"

I did a definitely nod.

There was another gust of wind, and out of the corner of my eye, I saw the two daisies. I turned. The daisies were swaying back and forth, getting used to their new home, in a rhythmic kind of way. It was almost like Tommy and me on our last night together, dancing to their own melody.

Chapter Thirty-Two

The last morning of camp. Chaos. Everywhere.

I didn't eat my breakfast. Within three hours, I wasn't going to be with any of the people I had spent every hour with for the last twelve days. I had no idea if I was going to see any of them again. And now that it was almost over, I was realizing how much I would actually miss some of them.

DAISY groups were scattered everywhere outside trying to get one last rehearsal in before the big show. I had absolutely no idea where Amanda and Jonah were. I didn't even care. Those two would not be part of the group I'd miss.

Suitcases and dirty clothes were being tossed around my cabin. Parents were coming to get their kids early because they had somewhere to be. Counselors were calling parents to remind them that today was pick-up day. Campers were volunteering in the dining hall to help get ready for the brunch before the talent show.

"I'm going to put your sheets in with your dirty clothes and towels," Christine said as she stripped my bed. "Is that okay? From my experience, you want to wash anything and everything you brought to camp when you get home, even if you didn't use it."

I nodded and she rolled them up and stuffed them into the garbage bag.

"Everything else; toothbrush, hairbrush, shoes, shampoo, all that good stuff is in your suitcase. I'm going to leave your shower chair and lift in the bathroom so your dad can just take it from there, and I figured you might want to pee before you go." She peeled off the daisy from my bunk. "Do you want to keep this?"

I nodded again. I wanted to keep everything I could from this camp.

"Okay. I think you need to stick it on your TechnoTalk so you can always remember this is what you need to focus on everyday. Also, I have something for you." She reached up to her bunk and grabbed a piece of construction paper. "I wanted to get you real daisies, but I didn't have time to run to the store, and I didn't want to take any of Bonnie's, so I made you this after you went to bed."

She unrolled the paper and held it out for me. Drawn in crayon, there were two blue daisies, side by side, with the stems intertwined. On the bottom of the page, it read in green crayon:

To Brynn,

Always be yourself!

Love,

Christine

Immediately, the tears started coming. For as much crap as I went through these past two weeks, and as much as I was looking forward to never seeing Jonah again, and as much as I wanted to talk to Tommy, I really, really did not want to leave. Although it might have seemed like a regular old camp, this place did have the power to change people. It had changed me.

"Aww, Brynn." Christine let the paper fall and ran to hug me. "Don't cry! I'm sure I will see you again. I don't know when, I don't know how, but I know I will. So don't cry, okay?"

I nodded.

She picked up her picture and my daisy and rolled them up. "I'm going to put this in your suitcase, cool? And I think you have some people here to see you."

"Brynnie!" My dad shouted as he burst through the door of the cabin and kissed my forehead. "How's it going? We missed you!"

Instead of giving him the same enthusiastic greeting as he gave me, I cried even harder.

My mom pulled her purse up on her shoulder. "What? Did you not stop crying from the time we left you? Christine probably thinks you're an emotional basket case!"

You have no idea.

"Brynn doesn't do very well with goodbyes," my dad said to Christine, "if you haven't figured that out."

"It's all good. It has been an emotional week. Brynn definitely has some stories to tell you."

My tears died down and my mom also gave me a kiss on the forehead. "Hi! I missed you. I really, really missed you! I'm so glad your TechnoTalk is working. It's weird without you home. I don't like it. What do we need to take to the van? Everything?"

"Yeah, you can take her suitcase and her dirty clothes to the van now, if you want, and you can even grab her shower chair. But she said she will probably need to go to the bathroom after the talent show, so you might want to leave her lift."

"Talent show? You guys are having a talent show? Are you in it?"

And with that, a switch inside me flipped. I laughed. I did a full out belly laugh. My mom was right: I was an emotional basket case.

"Well," Christine began, "she decided she didn't want to be in it, but that's a long, long story. Brynn can tell you all about it on the way home, if she wants to. Actually, Brynn, you don't have to stay for it, if you don't want to."

"You are staying," Randi commanded and appeared behind my parents. "You definitely want to see me make an idiot out of myself, and you definitely want to see Jonah make a jackass out of himself in front of everybody again, so, I say you are definitely staying!"

"Who are you?" my mom asked.

"I'm Randi. Who are you?"

I smiled to myself. If Randi and my mom were ever around each other enough, I knew they would pretty much become best friends.

"These are Brynn's parents." Christine did a proper introduction. "Mr. and Mrs. Evason, Randi was also in our cabin."

"Nice to meet you, Randi!" my dad said. "Was Brynn good?"

"Yeah, except I think she wants to push my ex-boyfriend in the lake."

"You want to push who in the lake?" my mom blurted out.

I rolled my head. If Christine and Randi didn't shut up, I would be forced to type up a novel-length explanation as soon as I was in the van.

"Why don't we all head over to the dining hall for something to eat?" Christine suggested. "Brynn and I can fill you in about everything over there."

Inside the dining hall, there were a lot more people than usual, and there was a lot more food, too. Hot dogs, hamburgers, pasta salad, fruit, cookies. It was basically a repeat of the first night of camp. Tommy forgot to tell me about this.

"You want a hot dog?" Christine asked. "Or one last Camp Lakewood PBJ?"

"Oh, I'll feed her," my mom offered.

Without even knowing what I was doing, I shook my head and frowned at Christine.

"What? You want her to feed you?"

I shyly nodded.

"Thanks. I missed you, too." My mom pretended to be hurt.

"It's cool," Christine nodded. "I'll help you eat. You want a hot dog? Water? Cookie?"

I nodded at all three.

"Okay. Go to our table, and I'll bring your parents over."

"You really got her down," my dad commented. "If you know what you're doing, Brynn is really not hard to help."

Christine shrugged. "That's what happens when you're with someone for two weeks. You get to know them inside and out."

"Sherry and I were thinking on the way here, and we wanted to ask you something. If you feel comfortable enough with Brynn, and you seem like you do, would you ever be willing to come stay with her for a weekend if we wanted to go away?"

I almost jumped out of my wheelchair and started doing cart-wheels at the thought of that idea.

"Calm down!" my mom yelled with a laugh. "You're going to break your chair!"

"Sure, I would love that!" Christine grinned at me. "See? I told you I would see you again. You wanna go to the table and we'll meet you there?"

I drove over to the table feeling like a big cheesy clown with a smile plastered on my face. I might be leaving Camp Lakewood, but Christine said she would come to my house. And I was going to get to talk to Tommy again—it was only a matter of hours! I had already memorized the phone number he'd written in his note. And I was planning on adding Randi, Heather, and the other girls from the cabin on Facebook, too. Thinking about everything I planned to do over the next few days reminded me that I had met my secret goal after all. I made friends at camp. Granted, they might not have been the I-will-message-you-every-day and we-need-to-see-each-other-every-weekend kind of friends, but what was I really expecting?

I glanced around the dining hall one last time. I could take so many memories, both good and bad, away from the time I spent here. And the best part was, what I chose to remember about my experience at Camp Lakewood was entirely up to me. If I wanted to forget the rest, I totally could.

I spotted Randi and her mom. From a distance, she looked like she was one of those cool moms, with a bandanna around her head. They sat awkwardly across the table from Jonah and a guy who looked like his older brother. I assumed Randi hadn't told her mom that she and Jonah had decided to see other people, and I began to imagine how that conversation would go when I realized that both Jonah and Older Jonah had . . . *Holy shit!*

I did a double take.

Holy shit!

Christine and my parents came and sat down. "And this is where Brynn and I have been eating all of camp."

"All right, Brynnie!" my dad said. "You got your very own table here!"

"Ready? I bet you're starving from not eating this morning."

Holy shit! Holy shit! Holy shit!

"What's wrong?"

What do I do? Do I tell on him? He's breaking camp rules again! And if I don't, I'm going to have to stomach him and Amanda being in the talent show (if they had even planned on doing anything for it at all), when it was supposed to be me and Tommy doing our song and I don't think I could handle that.

I glanced at him one more time before I typed the words. *Goodbye, Jonah.*

"I . . . think . . . you . . . need . . . to . . . go . . . check . . . on . . . Jonah."

Christine, with my cup in her hand, peaked over my head. "Oh." She set my water down on the table. "If you will excuse me, I have to go take care of something."

I watched as Christine found JT and pulled him over to the side. I moved beside my mom.

"Is everything okay? Will she be back?"

Frowning, I shook my head.

"Ha ha! You're stuck with me now! Serves you right for blowing me off!" She pulled my plate towards her. "I truly missed you. I don't like not having you home, or not having your music blasting from your room, or not making your buttered noodles for you."

I smiled. I knew my parents loved me, but I didn't know if they minded doing everything for their seventeen-year-old daughter just as much as I minded needing the help. I didn't know if they minded feeding me every meal, or giving me a shower every night, or taking me to the bathroom again twenty minutes after I had gone. I didn't know if the extremely loud music on my bad days bothered them. I was so glad to hear that they actually wanted me, all of me, home.

My mom shoved a piece of hot dog into the side of my mouth. Although I wanted to eat with Christine one last time, I had to admit it was kind of nice having someone help me eat who knew exactly where to put the food so I didn't have to work as hard.

I stopped eating for a second. Jonah and his brother were being escorted out of the dining hall by Christine. I could only imagine the words she was hearing right now. For a millisecond, I started to feel bad about what I did . . . until I remembered the image of Tommy running off, framed for a crime we knew he hadn't committed.

I finished my cup of water just as JT quieted everybody down. Christine still hadn't come back yet.

"I hope you all had a wonderful lunch. It truly has been a pleasure working with your sons and daughters this session, and I'm so glad Camp Lakewood made it possible for them to come to camp. Now, it's time for a real treat. These campers have been working on some wonderful acts for this show. So, campers, if you want to take your parents down to the amphitheater and get ready that would be wonderful. Good luck to all of you, and I really can't wait to see what you have come up with."

"Do we really need to stay for this show if you're not in it?" my mom asked.

I nodded. I really didn't give a crap whether or not I saw the show, but Christine still wasn't back. I couldn't leave camp without saying goodbye to her.

"That Randi seemed like she really wanted Brynn to see her in the talent show," my dad said. "You want to go down with her while I pack up?"

My mom sat where anybody who was with me always sat— in the top left row. The amphitheater was packed. There were even people behind us. Down in front, a clothesline had been hung between two trees so all the scenery could be put up.

The first piece of scenery? Mine and Tommy's masterpiece.

Randi walked to the middle of the stage with her blue Camp Lakewood t-shirt and khaki shorts. From behind her, she whipped out that damn megaphone.

There was an eruption of laughter.

"Okay, campers! I need you to get in your DAISY groups!"

Out popped three boys (two of whom I thought were in Tommy's cabin) with white paper petals all around their faces. A paper daisy was attached to each one of their shoulders.

Another round of laughter and a tap on my shoulder. Christine. She motioned for me to come with her. Quietly, I turned my wheelchair on and started to back up. My mom gave me a look. She didn't really understand the whole talent show to begin with; she really wasn't going to understand what the hell was going on now.

I followed Christine to a patch of shade away from everyone.

"Look, you were right. We caught Jonah with alcohol. JT talked to him and he finally admitted that he planted it in Tommy's stuff. We're going to call him and apologize to him and explain to his mom what happened. I am so sorry, Brynn. It's not that I didn't believe you. It's just that as a counselor, I have to stay neutral to campers until I know the facts."

The audience applauded. For Randi and her group, of course, but it was like they were a part of this conversation.

"Jonah was disqualified from being in the talent show, and Amanda will not go on without him. JT asked me if you would be interested in taking their spot in the talent show. I know this is very, very, very short notice, but I know you have been working on a poem. Would you be interested in reading it for everybody?"

I couldn't help but look at her as though she just asked me to take off my clothes and strike a pose in front of everyone.

"Come on, Brynn! I don't usually like to ask you to do anything that you don't want to, but please do this! You have it done, right?"

"It's. . . something. . . that. . . Tommy. . . and. . . I. . . came. . . up. . . with. . . and. . ."

More applause.

"It. . . would. . . be. . . kinda. . . lame. . . to. . . anybody. . . else."

"So? Randi's group just had daisies coming out of their heads! And this would be your chance to show everybody here that you don't have an intellectual disability! Some of them will finally see you for who you really are. Please do this for me! Do it for Tommy! Do it for Randi! Do it for yourself!"

I glanced at my mom. My dad was with her now. They looked completely out of place. They didn't have a kid who could get on stage and spit out random ridiculous jokes, so I would imagine they weren't really sure what to make of this.

I glanced back at Christine and rolled my eyes at her before I let her lead me down the side path to the front of the amphitheater.

Sara Pyszka

To be a beautiful daisy
And to be able to dance the night away
You need plenty of water
So your colors won't fade away

To be a beautiful daisy
And to be able to grow and grow
You need the strongest roots
To let your knowledge flow

To be a beautiful daisy
And to be the favorite one
You need to not hide in the shade
To be able to get some sun

Epilogue

Tommy fingered the frame hanging on my wall that held the poem I'd written and recited at camp. "Not bad. You were totally making fun of my idea, and then you stole it! I should probably take you to court for plagiarism! Although, in my opinion, you definitely outdid your buddy, Abbie!"

I chuckled and my heart fluttered a bit. I still wasn't used to seeing Tommy in my house, let alone in my bedroom looking absolutely handsome in his best suit. We'd been officially dating since the day I left camp (we'd talked through text the whole way home and then again all night) and he did his best to come see me on the weekends when he could. His mom had made him get a part-time job and the six-hour drive wasn't always do-able, so sometimes we had to cancel plans, but that just made the days he could spend with me even better.

"You look beautiful in that dress, babe," he told me before planting a kiss on my forehead.

I beamed, briefly flashing back to the last time I'd gotten really dressed up. At least this time I was wearing my own clothes and not a dress borrowed from Carly.

"Are we ready to go?"

I nodded as I drove out to the kitchen where my mom was still cleaning up the dishes from dinner.

"Thank you again for dinner, Mrs. E!"

"No problem," my mom said as she loaded the dishwasher. "Baked ziti. Brynn's favorite!"

337

"Are you sure you don't want any help?"

I rolled my eyes and shot him a look. *Now is not the time to kiss ass, Tommy! We're running late!*

He shrugged, and I sighed again. He'd recently decided to grow a little goatee and every now and then I realized how much more handsome it made him look. I was truly lucky; sure, he had great features, but before all that, he was honestly one of the nicest, most honest and genuine people I'd ever met.

"No, thank you, though," my mom said. "I wanted to ask you, do you remember how to work the van?"

"I think so. Guess it's been a while since we took any trips."

I nodded. On most of his visits, we'd just hang out in my room or in the living room. My mom made us lunch and dinner and we watched movies with my parents or by ourselves. And we talked, a lot. Tommy didn't mind having to wait for me to type my thoughts, and though it made for some lengthy conversations, he never seemed to get bored or tired of waiting. My favorite part was the cuddling, though. When I was out of my chair and we were wrapped in a blanket together in the corner of the big, comfy couch. I'd fallen asleep with my head on his chest and our hands entwined multiple times.

"Come outside and I'll show you how to work the van again," my mom instructed, so we followed.

My mom showed him the button that opened the side door and extended the ramp. After I drove in and got myself situated, she showed him how to attach the straps on the floor of the van to my wheelchair. After putting the address of my school in my GPS, she hit the button to close the door.

"Have fun," my mom called from the driveway. "Don't get into any wrecks! And don't get pregnant!"

"Your mom is absolutely insane," Tommy said, pulling out into the street, "and I absolutely love it!"

"Turn right."

"You don't have to tell me where to go, babe. I have the . . ." he paused. "Oh. I'm an idiot."

I laughed.

"Yeah, shut up! At least I didn't drive into anything and couldn't talk for a day."

I gave him the screw-you tongue in the review mirror.

"Hey, now! Your mom specifically told you not to get pregnant."

I giggled.

We pulled into the parking lot of the school and I felt my stomach tighten and twist. I still hated being at school; I'd been pretty successful making friends at camp (Randi texted me daily, Heather and Maggie talked to me online, and Carly even added me as a friend, though I think that was more out of curiosity than anything else) but school was still tough. I did my best to avoid Meg and Dave—and they really didn't try to talk to me, either—and Mrs. B was still my buffer to the rest of the world. There was one difference between this year and last, though: Amy.

Amy and I had never, ever been friends. We'd known of each other for years, but she was a cheerleader and I was not and that was pretty much all we needed to know. The day I left for camp, though, she'd added me on Facebook, and once I'd gotten back and posted all my pictures and changed my relationships status, she messaged me. And we talked as though we were just meeting each other for the first time. And the messages continued throughout the summer, and I tried not to overthink it. She'd always seemed so . . . self-absorbed and snotty, but here she was, expressing an interest in my life, so I filled her in. She asked a lot of great questions—she was definitely more familiar with my disability than I thought, and she was more open to me than Jonah and Amanda had been at camp—and I answered all of them. On the first day of senior year, she sat down at my lunch table and she had yet to move her seat. In fact, another one of her friends—not a cheerleader, but someone from the chess club (I know, I know. Cheerleaders and chess? Blows my mind, too)—recently started eating with us in the cafeteria. Amy and I hadn't hung out outside of school yet, but I felt like that was where this friendship was headed.

Now, in the school parking lot, the anxiety crept into my bones. This was our big debut. Amy and her friend, Toni, were the only people at school who knew I had a boyfriend (unless we were Facebook friends). I'd wanted to keep Tommy to myself as long as I could. But when my mom let it slip that Homecoming was coming up and Tommy remembered that I'd always wanted to go to a school dance, I couldn't get out of it. My mom took me dress shopping, Tommy brought me flowers, and here we were.

Once he was out of the van, he opened the side door. Before he undid my tie downs, he kissed me. I didn't want him to stop. For a brief moment, I felt that we didn't have to go into the dance. I would have been perfectly okay with staying in the van all night.

"You want to go dance with me?" Tommy kissed my bare shoulder. "Like, really dance this time? With real music and everything?"

I chuckled and he stood to the side to let me out. I wheeled myself out and he closed everything up. We were walking toward the gym when we saw them. Yep. They were here. Of course.

"Brynn? Is that you?"

No. It's another girl in a wheelchair that goes to this school with a communication device.

"I didn't know you were coming to Homecoming!" Meg walked right up to me. Dave sheepishly followed, but didn't say anything. Classy. "Who are you?" she asked Tommy.

"I'm Brynn's boyfriend, Tommy. Hi. You must be Meg and Dave. I've heard *so* much about you."

She blinked. "Do you go here?"

Nice.

"No. We actually met at camp. You know, the one she went to this summer? I'm sure she probably told you all about it."

I didn't think I could love Tommy anymore. Until now. I'd forgotten how sarcastic he could be.

"Oh. Well, do you want to come hang with us? I know how you just love your music, Brynn."

I stared her straight in the eye. *Are you really this dumb? Or do you just want to make yourself look good in front of my boyfriend who you never met?*

I started to hit my switch to make my chair turn in the direction of the gym, but then I turned myself back around and turned my chair off. I was actually prepared for this situation. I'd been holding onto this for months now, and since we hadn't been talking, I hadn't had the opportunity. But here it was, practically served to me on a silver platter. I couldn't pass it up. I hit my talking switch and waited for the scan to get to the OPEN FILE button, thanking Camp Lakewood, DAISY, and the night of the campout every step of the way.

SPEAK. "You know what, guys? We are not friends anymore. I don't know how you could think that we are. Meg, you knew how much I liked him! Why would you do that to me? You were my best friend, but apparently, I wasn't yours! And you know what, Meg? It took me a while to figure it out, but I realize now that all I was to you was an opportunity to make yourself look good. I have no idea why I put up with it for so long. If you haven't noticed already, I'm done. I don't want to be friends with either of you anymore."

"Oh. Okay. I wasn't your friend that whole time? Right." Meg was being so sarcastic that I was thankful my feet and arms were strapped down. "You're so ungrateful! You know, I did everything for you! I—"

Trembling, I turned my chair on and spun around. I was not going to give her the satisfactory of putting me down any more than she already had. Let them think whatever they wanted to think. If I ruined their night, fine! If they thought I was the biggest bitch in the world, fine! I did what I needed to do.

"I know it's a little late, but I think you just officially met all your DAISY goals in a matter of thirty seconds," Tommy said as he caught up to my chair and placed a hand on my shoulder. He waited until I calmed down and then he kissed the top of my head. "Now, can I finally have a dance?"

Thank you for reading!

6538494R00204

Made in the USA
San Bernardino, CA
11 December 2013